Sixteen Shades of Crazy

Also by Rachel Trezise

In and Out of the Goldfish Bowl
Fresh Apples
Dial M for Merthyr

RACHEL TREZISE

Sixteen Shades of Crazy

blue door

Blue Door
An imprint of HarperCollins*Publishers*
77–85 Fulham Palace Road,
Hammersmith, London W6 8JB

www.harpercollins.co.uk

Published by Blue Door 2010
1

A catalogue record for this book
is available from the British Library

ISBN: 978-0-00-730560-5

Typeset in Minion by Palimpsest Book Production Limited,
Grangemouth, Stirlingshire

Printed and bound in Great Britain by
Clays Ltd, St Ives plc

Mixed Sources
Product group from well-managed
forests and other controlled sources
www.fsc.org Cert no. SW-COC-001806
© 1996 Forest Stewardship Council
FSC

FSC is a non-profit international organisation established to promote the responsible
management of the world's forests. Products carrying the FSC label are independently
certified to assure consumers that they come from forests that are managed to meet the
social, economic and ecological needs of present and future generations.

Find out more about HarperCollins and the environment at
www.harpercollins.co.uk/green

For Gwyn Thomas (1913–1981)

ACKNOWLEDGEMENTS

There are many individuals to whom I will always be indebted for having helped me make this book a reality. A huge thank you to John Williams who read the very first draft, Tristan Hughes who read the second; thanks also to Rhodri Jones, Pete Hurley, Dafydd Williams and Christian Saunders. For their support and guidance I'd like to thank my editor Susan Opie, my brilliant agent Broo Doherty, my wonderful publishing editor Patrick Janson-Smith and Laura Deacon at Blue Door, along with everyone at the Dylan Thomas Prize. I also acknowledge the financial assistance of the Welsh Books Council. For continued encouragement and friendship along the way, many thanks to Des Barry, Charlotte Greig, Sabrina Merralls, Claire Leakey, Patrick Jones, Lisa Hocking, and of course my husband, Darran Frowen.

'Perhaps when we find ourselves wanting everything, it is because we are dangerously near to wanting nothing.'
Sylvia Plath

1

They looked like any other group of twenty- and thirty-somethings, living the salad days of their lives, organs plump and red and juicy like the insides of ripe tomatoes, minds crisp like iceberg lettuce, sex powerful and biting like onion. Just another Saturday night at the Pump House, laughing big belly laughs, torsos bowed against the edge of the table as they concealed their illicit activities from the bar-staff, treasure moving around as if they were playing pass-the-parcel, the smell of perfume and alcohol shrouding their bodies like vinaigrette.

Ellie held the baggie in her fingers, fiddling with the knot, the plastic slippery with perspiration. Nowadays, street dealers were only concerned with their fleeting profits. There was no time for presentation. Nobody used paper wraps any more. She pushed her fingertip into the powder, kept it there for as long as it was polite, maybe longer, then smeared it over her taste buds, absorbing the sweet, glucosic tang.

'What do they call this in America?' she said, cheeks already tingling with anticipation. The south Wales valleys had been empty of soft drugs for eighteen months, no amphetamine, no MDMA. The new police chief had declared war on the B and C classes. Zero-tolerance policies sent all of the Drug Squad's manpower to intercept shipments of party-starters in Bristol, while savvy London traffickers cruised the M4, Mercedes loaded with kilo packages of

Afghan opiates. The skeletons of mining towns were populated by zombies, kids so thin and hopeless the wind would blow them over. Smackheads congregated in the gulleys, needles poised; the way women used to meet for chapel with their leather-bound bibles, honest-to-goodness recreational users left with nothing.

Ellie felt like an adolescent again, doing drugs for the very first time, a glorious thrill in her blood. 'Is it crystal meth?' she said, 'or is that something totally different?'

Rhiannon snatched the baggie and balanced it in her lap. 'Ooh cares?' she said. She sprinkled a pinch of the powder into her wineglass. It was Rhiannon's special wineglass, an unusual, egg-cup-shaped goblet that she demanded on every visit. She reached for another thumbful of the powder, her enthusiasm forcing the bag into the dip between her bare legs, an inch away from the hem of her new miniskirt. She was closer to forty than thirty; too old to wear that skirt, a shadow of a moustache on her top lip. Her hair was black, short and spiky, her eyes a soft, bovine brown. She had a huge laugh, like a drag artist's. One of the stories about Rhiannon was that she'd been walking through Cardiff at three in the morning when some Grangetown wide-boy tried to drag her into an alley. She'd pulled a knife out of her handbag and slashed the tip of his nose clean off, left him for dead. It gave her a precarious allure that attracted weak men – men like Marc, who wanted to be neglected. There were lots of stories about Rhiannon, every one of them involving the opposite sex. Andy reckoned she'd married an octogenarian at eighteen, given him a heart attack in the bedroom; something he'd heard on a building site in Bridgend. The locals on the Dinham Estate said she'd made a pornographic video with Tommy Chippy for thirty quid, some of them swore they'd seen it; Rhiannon lying naked across the counter, eyes blacked out with tape, deep-fat fryers sizzling away in the background. All Ellie knew for sure was that she was a manipulative bitch; she hated women and women hated her.

'Billy Whizz we call it in Wales,' she said, hooting. 'That's where ewe live, El. Wales.' She never overlooked an opportunity to remind Ellie where she was, because she knew Ellie wanted to be elsewhere, beneath the skyscrapers of New York. Rhiannon had resigned herself to a monotonous existence in the Welsh gutter, and no one else was allowed to look up at the stars.

The pub door opened. Rhiannon quickly balled the plastic into her fist. Big Barry the Disco came in and heaved his amplifier towards the squat stage, sweat stains forming under his yellow trouser braces. 'The bloody prodigals' return again, is it?' he said as he shuffled past the boys.

Marc took the parcel from Rhiannon and hurriedly opened it on the table. 'Just what the doctor ordered,' he said, rubbing his hands together, a grin from ear to ear. He was wearing the same Liverpool football jersey he always wore, his chocolate-colour hair clipped close to his skull, receding quickly at the forehead. He was a genial man, the bassist and lead singer of a punk band called The Boobs. They'd been on a toilet circuit tour of Scotland, sleeping on the hard floor of their Transit van for six weeks, fighting for space amongst their beaten up guitars and drum-kit. They did this every five months or so, despite the lack of a record company, a tour agent, or even a cult fan base. They tossed every pound they made into the venture, as though their lives depended on it, and in Aberalaw their absence gave them the illusion of success. The stupid hacks at the local newspaper seemed to think they spent half of the year in their Malibu beach homes. Old women approached Ellie in the post office and asked her, 'How are your Boobs doing?'

The band had got home earlier that day to the news that John Peel had listened to a demo they'd thrown at him through a back-stage fence at last year's Glastonbury Festival. He'd invited them to record a live session for the radio. Marc was happy as hell. He scoffed a whole gram of the powder, chasing it around his mouth with his roving tongue.

'Sweetheart!' Rhiannon barked, seizing the baggie from his hand and pushing it along the table. 'Take it easy, will ewe? Ewe're tiling the downstairs toilet tomorrow, remember?'

'There's hardly any left now,' Griff said. Griff was the drummer, a fat, proud man with neon-orange hair; the bumptious disposition of a spoiled 12-year-old. His mother still made him corned-beef pie and salmon sandwiches to take-out on the road. He sullenly rubbed a small rock into his gum and then wiped his fingers on his check shirt, keeping the baggie in his hand, ensuring he had an audience for what he was about to say. Like a schoolboy carrying clecks to the dictatorial teacher, he looked sideways at Rhiannon. 'He's been a total arsehole all fucking tour,' he said. 'He stole a tray of muffins from Glasgow Services and kept them all to himself. He ate every bastard one and there were forty-eight of the fuckers. The only reason I'm staying in the band is because of this Peel session.' He was always threatening to quit, and never did. 'Should have seen the women in Scotland though,' he said. 'Lapped it up, they did.'

'What women?' Siân said. She whipped the baggie from him, turning it over in her hands. Siân was Griff's wife. She hadn't taken a narcotic since her first child was born. Three babies in as many years and she was down to a size twelve one week after each. No Caesareans, no stitches, no maternity leave. She worked at the video shop on a Tuesday and Wednesday and the Chinese takeaway on a Thursday and Friday – anything to keep the kids in shoes, since Griff wouldn't lift a finger. Her glossy black hair reached down to the small of her back, framing her almond-coloured face. She had an enormous pink mouth. In any other place she would have grown up to be a catwalk model: long, sleek legs sauntering down a runway, an impossible pair of platforms on her flawless feet. But this was Aberalaw, and life wasn't fair. She always looked like an advert for designer cosmetics, as though someone followed her around with a soft, pink light, no matter

4

what kind of dive she was drinking in, no matter how drunk she got. In Ellie she never inspired envy as much as awe, the way people look at leopards roaming the Serengeti in David Attenborough documentaries; another species altogether.

'I'm only joking,' Griff said.

Siân passed the bag to Andy. 'You'd better be,' she said, staring at Griff, play-acting reproachful. 'Six weeks you've been gone, and Niall started calling Bob the Builder *Dad.*'

'It wasn't like that,' Andy said, whispering into Ellie's ear. 'There weren't any girls.' But Ellie already knew that. She'd been to too many gigs, carried too many microphone stands in and out of clubs. She'd danced on too many empty dance-floors; pretended not to know the band. Andy was no Keith Richards. But Siân was paranoid about groupies. Her days slipped away between school runs and fish fingers, and Griff was convinced he was God's gift to starved pussy. Andy put his arm around Ellie, surreptitiously cupping one of her breasts. Ellie used her elbow to lock his hand in place. She enjoyed the warmth of his broad fingers; had missed him more this time than ever before. At night she'd woken up on the hour, every hour, waving her arm over the bedside table, searching for a pint of water that wasn't there. He used to take one to her last thing at night, turning the lights out with his little finger. Without him around her, food was tasteless. Her sense of smell was defunct. But now she could smell the sweet fug of the rushed sex they'd had before leaving the house less than an hour ago. She imagined the ringlets of his protein swimming around inside her, life seeming once more like its happy, Technicolor self.

'Are ewe takin' any of that?' Rhiannon said, pointing at the baggie in Andy's lap.

Andy looked down at it, blond eyebrows scrunched to a frown. 'Don't you think we're getting too old for it, Rhi? It's full of toxins, you know.'

Rhiannon leaned over Ellie's lap and grabbed it. She licked the inside of the bag, purple tongue thrashing against the cellophane. When it was clean she threw it in the ashtray. Everyone watched, eyes hopeless, as it slowly mingled in with the dust and dog-tabs, their first taste of phet for over a year.

Rhiannon lifted her wineglass. 'Well, don't look so bloody worried,' she said. 'Plenty more where that came from.'

2

It was a little after ten when the speed kicked in, dopamine rising to greet it; the time of night when life seemed full of possibility. Ellie was beginning to believe she was some sort of chemical Cinderella, blessed with wit and mystique. Big Barry was three-quarters of the way through the set-list Sellotaped to his sound desk. He'd been using the same one since he'd started the job in the late Eighties, only ever deviating to play the current number one. Rhiannon sprang to her feet when the piano intro to 'I Will Survive' began, drink splashing out of her glass. She headed for the walkway in front of the stage, extended chest bouncing against her ribcage. She stood facing the DJ, tight skirt preventing any real dancing, go-go boots slipping on the carpet, the other customers glaring at her. Generally, people either tolerated or detested Rhiannon. Any friends she'd ever had, she'd pissed off years ago.

'Come on, girls,' she said, shouting back at the table. She clapped her hands, the brass wall plates behind her shaking. This was the way Rhiannon moved; eyes screwed closed in devotion, hands held an inch away from her face, fatty palms smacking together, the slapping noise reverberating around the room. She stole Big Barry's microphone and held it in her clenched fist. 'Come on, girls,' she said. 'I wanna fuckin' dance.'

Siân lowered her eyes and sipped from her half-glass. 'It's *your* turn,' she said, hissing across the table at Ellie.

Ellie shook her head; she didn't want to dance, not with Rhiannon. A gust of energy had just detonated in the small of her back, driving tiny particles of euphoria around her throbbing bloodstream. She was having a lovely time just sitting down; she didn't want to waste a minute of it.

Siân pushed herself out of her seat. 'I come out at night to get away from the kids, not look after her. Why has it always got to be me?' She flicked her long hair, folded her arms, walked slowly towards Rhiannon.

A small blonde woman came in carrying a chair from the games area. She placed it at the edge of the table, struggling not to hit anyone with any of its stocky legs. Ellie didn't recognize her. She'd never seen her before. But Marc obviously had. He was beckoning her with his waving hand, smiling and shouting into her ear, using a folded beer-mat to wipe Rhiannon's wine spills from the table. Soon, a man followed, a tall, skinny man with a mop of dark, tangled hair. He sat next to the woman and nodded perfunctorily, eyes the colour of coal. It was hard to tell how old he was; mid-thirties – older than Andy, younger than Rhiannon; a scattering of black stubble around a pouting, mauve mouth. There was a thick silver belcher chain resting on his collarbone and dark circles under his eyes, the colour of smudged kohl. Ellie gawped at him until he opened his cigarette packet and counted what he needed for a flash, running a clean fingernail along the top of the corks. He threw some on the soggy surface of the table and balanced a further two in the V of his fore and middle finger.

'Anyone?' he said – an accent, not Welsh, but familiar. He looked quickly at each of the faces around the table, but if he thought anything at all about them, his stoic face hid it. Ellie waited until all of the loose cigarettes were taken and then clipped one from his hand. She thanked him, but he ignored her, tossing the last one into his mouth, holding it between alabaster teeth while he

8

lit it with the ferocious flame of his chrome Zippo. Ellie suddenly felt conscious of her appearance. She was no Cinderella. She had a round, plain, pale-skinned face, framed by dull brown hair, not platinum-blonde like her siblings or even golden-blonde like the woman he was with.

Rhiannon reappeared, jostling against the table, tipping more drinks. 'What's the matter with ewe, ewe fuckin' sourpuss?' she said. She slammed her body into the space next to Ellie. 'That's what speed is for, mun, dancing.' She pointed at Andy. 'Cheer up,' she said. 'E's home now. Ewe can get ewer oats tonight.' She lifted the egg cup to her moustachioed mouth and downed the modicum of wine left inside. 'Next time he goes away, ewe wanna tell 'im to leave ewe a dildo. Marc bought me iss massive pink rampant rabbit, din't ewe, love? Wouldn't fit in ewer 'andbag, El.'

Ellie blushed, embarrassed not by Rhiannon's crudeness, but by her memory of her quickie with Andy, the pair of them scrambling around the bedroom, tripping over one another's clothes. The thought had seemed heady a few moments earlier, but now it felt like a burden.

Rhiannon turned to the new faces at the table, looked the strange man square in the eyes, said, 'Where's my fag 'en, mush?' He took another cigarette out of his packet and passed it across the table. Rhiannon grabbed it and popped it into her mouth, leaned forward and waited for him to light it for her. She dived headlong into conversation, her screechy monotone blaring over the music, her twisted body preventing Ellie's joining in. It was useless to try to talk over Rhiannon, so she sat back on the bench, stole intermittent glimpses of him as he answered Rhiannon's relentless questions, his lips swiftly fastening and unfastening. Rhiannon was still leaning towards him, head inclined, steadily pushing her cleavage into his view. After a while she started touching, smoothing her hand along his forearm, slowly at first, and then faster, squeezing at his skin. Siân was staring at him too, her forefinger hooked in her mouth, stupefied by his beauty or his oddness or his audacity, it was hard to tell what. Nobody new had turned up at the Pump House since the last Millennium.

After a while Ellie became impatient, hungry for the man's attention. She thought up jokes to tell him. Something her friend Safia had said at work the day before had amused her, not for its content but for Safia having repeated it; something about Jeremy Beadle measuring the size of his penis. 'He decided it wasn't very big,' Safia'd said, 'small in fact; although on the other hand it was effing massive.' Ellie'd almost pissed herself. It was obviously something Safia had heard the print boys say, and without fully grasping its meaning had memorized, intending to impress Ellie. But was it good enough? Maybe if she thought of an alternative character – she didn't want to admit to ever having watched someone as naff as Jeremy Beadle. Ordinarily she wouldn't admit to owning a television, but she couldn't think of anyone who was cool *and* had a shrunken hand. Suddenly Andy coiled his arm around her shoulder, and pulled her close to him. They stared at one another, the balls of their noses touching. His eyes were lovely: irises a cocktail of blue gemstones, sapphire and topaz intertwining. But Ellie quickly wrestled away from Andy, looked back at the ebony eyes of the outlandish foreigner.

He was still busy with Rhiannon, head cocked towards her unintelligible banter. Ellie gave up on the joke idea, thinking he'd laugh at her, not at it. The anxiety was creeping in. The amphetamine high was over. She could feel the comedown lying in wait, bad blood pumping through her veins, and she submitted to it, began to contemplate the overflowing ashtray.

Before the bell rang for stop-tap, the blonde woman leaned over the table and said something to Rhiannon, the white strobe light revealing a crater-shaped patch of pockmarks on her cheekbones. Ellie hoped she was issuing some kind of reprimand, but she knew she wasn't when Rhiannon put her hand on the woman's shoulder and pointed at the door on the other side of the room. 'Down there, love,' she said, 'turn left.' The woman walked timidly, head bowed. When she'd disappeared behind Big Barry, Rhiannon turned to Ellie. 'Fuckin' English!' she said. 'Ey're like bloody rats. Ewe're never a mile away from one an' 'ey just keep on breeding. With a bit of luck she'll be in the men's now.'

There was a queue in the lounge so Ellie went into the bar to buy drinks. Two old men sitting on the ripped benches amidst the shabby flock wallpaper. The barman was hiding behind a tabloid newspaper, crude headline about the death of Saddam Hussein's sons splashed across the front page. She ordered four house vodkas and two cans of Red Bull. It was a ritual Rhiannon had started when the band was in Poland. She'd come back from an impromptu visit to the bar with three trebles, and placed them on the table in front of Siân and Ellie with a rebellious wink. She'd only been with Marc for a few weeks and Ellie knew now the drink buying had been an attempt to procure the girls' friendship. Rhiannon put too much faith in money and thought she could buy relationships; gift giving was a staple in her control-freakery. But back then she seemed charming and, when the boys had returned, the vodka custom had prevailed; a peculiar proclamation of their union, like a Freemason's handshake.

Ellie balanced the cans in the crooks of her arms, the glasses hooked in her fingers. As she turned to walk away, she stepped into somebody, her stiletto heel stabbing the rubber toecap of a basketball boot. Instinctively, she knew it was the stranger. She jolted backwards, the weight of a glass falling from her grip. Then, in her bewildered attempt to catch it before guessing which direction it was going to take, she jumped back at him, stepping again on his foot.

'Whoa!' he said, catching her, his arms stretched out like

Jesus, as though trying to counter all eventualities. He smelled of musk and petrol and faintly of smoke. The glass landed on a beer towel, the liquid trickling out, forming a small dark patch on the Terylene. The barman caught the glass before it rolled off the edge.

'Sorry,' Ellie said, cheeks beginning to burn.

'It's okay,' he said. 'Want another one?' He let go of her body and stepped backwards, the sudden absence of his touch sending an amphetamine rush through Ellie's spine. It smashed against her cranium like a pinball he had triggered. Something about him activated a weird animalism in Ellie, an acute hunger in her abdominal walls. Immediately, she wanted to touch him again, to feel the sensation one more time. She stepped away. 'Where are you from?' she said. She wasn't from Aberalaw either. She knew what a difficult time he'd have settling in.

He picked the empty glass up, gripping it with his bony, icicle-like fingers. 'Cornwall,' he said, sniffing it. He put it back on the towel. 'Did you want another?'

Ellie thought about the West Country accents that had surrounded her throughout her three-year stint at Plymouth University. She was homesick suddenly for nights out at the Pavilions, for morning strolls along the Barbican, for lunchtime editorial meetings at the student magazine. When she had lived in Plymouth, she had never been homesick for Wales. 'If you don't mind,' she said, remembering herself. 'That one was for your girl-friend anyway.'

The man smiled affectionately at her. '*She* is not allowed to drink vodka,' he said.

Andy daren't tell Ellie what she wasn't allowed to drink. Around here, the women wore the trousers, not because Welsh women were in any manner advanced in feminist thinking, but because Welsh men were so indolent; too dozy for domestic altercations. She couldn't decide if the man's dominance over his girlfriend's choice of beverage was sexist, or exotic. She smiled weakly, shrugged her shoulders. She walked back to the lounge, her arms scrunched around herself like wings, the cold glasses clutched against her prickly skin. *She is not allowed to drink vodka.* 'What a wanker,' she thought as she kicked the lounge door open, knowing even as she thought it that what she was experiencing was not abhorrence. It was allure. This was girl meets boy, big style; the token of acceptance she'd been about to present to his girlfriend was bankrupt, common sense pirouetting into the middle distance, vanishing like the spilt liquor.

The rest of the night slipped away between a long, drawn-out stomach-ache and ephemeral spasms of jealousy. The amphetamine high dulled to a dreary pain, winding leisurely around her stomach, like a washing machine on a wool cycle. All night Rhiannon wouldn't stop talking to the man. She jabbered perpetually, head bobbing like a buoy on choppy water. Every time she touched his emaciated wrist, accidentally, but more often intentionally, Ellie felt envy solidifying like a lethal tumour, deep inside her. Occasionally, the man caught Ellie's stare, his onyx eyes glassy now from the smoke. They rested on her for a few seconds, alert and apologetic, but then quickly moved on to his drink, or, unbearably, on to Rhiannon. But Ellie didn't stop looking at him, not even when Andy tried to kiss or speak to her. And what she noticed, just before the couple unexpectedly stood up, waved and left, was that everyone else in the pub was staring at them too, craning their necks and gawking, because this was a south Wales valley village, and nobody ever left, and nobody new ever arrived. They were like aliens, that couple, swanning in with their accents and their pockmarks. They might as well have arrived in a silvery saucer-shaped spaceship. Nobody outside of their own table attempted to speak to them, to ask where they were from or what their business here was, again because this was Aberalaw, a south Wales valley town. Instead, the other customers peered, and peered, like a mob of meerkats standing on hind legs. Then, when the couple had gone, they all turned to one another and made up their own stories.

3

On Monday, Ellie boarded her 7 a.m. train with the usual commuters: a middle-aged administrator at Ponty College and a bricky working down the Bay. They were the only three people awake in Aberalaw at that time in the morning. At 7.55 she alighted at Cardiff Central Station, the nearby Brains Brewery coming to life for another sun-soaked shift, the pungent stench of the hops saturating her twenty-minute speed-walk to Atlas Road. There she sat in a stifling workshop, sticking stickers on mugs while the rush hours whizzed past the yellow bricks of the city.

There was a crisis going on with the Alton Towers batch. They needed another five hundred by the end of summer but the Ceramics department couldn't get the colour right. Ellie was bored of the stupid picture: a navy turreted castle with red fireworks in the background. The mugs were orange and the castle kept coming out purple. It was because the kiln was set at the wrong temperature. Everybody on the floor knew it. But the management were adamant it was Safia and Ellie's fault. Jane was trying to stop them using hand cream, stop them eating crisps in case they got gunk on their fingers; all sorts of screwed-up rules it was illegal to instate. The desks were stacked with tray upon tray of orange mugs, all waiting for quality control. They even had a mini-skip in which to throw the rejects, smashing each one first in an attempt to prevent light fingers. Ellie had jokingly offered Jane a majority

15

percentage in a spot of bent trade but Jane had threatened to report her. Jane, who was Ellie's sister, had been the Ceramics manager for seven years. She was obnoxious to start with, but the job had pushed her to the edge. The factory floor was a breeding ground for paranoia. You had to keep watching your back because everyone around you would do almost anything to defend their own menial position, bereft of the courage to go and try something new. It was like a prison cell; the guy next to you initially appearing to be another hapless fool, then twelve months later turning into a loathsome psychopath whose face you dreamt about mutilating with a craft knife you stole from the art studio.

Safia threw a chewing gum at Ellie. It hit her on the cheekbone then landed at the bottom of her glue trough with last week's tacky scraps of paper. Ellie fished it out and threw it back at Safia, a new layer of gloop staining the sleeve of her crisp white blouse.

Safia laughed. 'Yous have a good weekend?' she said. She was a tall Pakistani girl with clumpy mascara. She'd ambled into the factory and sat at Belinda's desk, a week after Belinda had walked out. For the first five days she'd complained that the transfers sent in from the cover-coaters were too thin, or too thick, that the mugs were chipped and discoloured. Ellie'd liked Belinda because Belinda danced incessantly to the music in her headphones, ignoring everything Jane said. She'd had the words *Fuck Work* inscribed across the bust of her tabard. But Safia was pedantic.

One stormy Tuesday morning following a bank holiday, Safia and Ellie were the only daft cows who'd turned up for work. Forced to sit in the workshop together at lunch, chewing oily tuna sandwiches from the newsagent on the corner, Ellie reluctantly warmed to Safia's worrisome and naive nature; the way she thought she'd never get over her first love, a U2 fan from Caerphilly. She was born and raised in Cardiff, the essence of the city audible in her nasal words. Her family had sent her to Manchester for two months during a perplexing adolescence and her mother had taken her to Pakistan once to meet her grandmother. Safia had cried to come home long before the four weeks were spent; screamed on the first day, scared shitless by lizards climbing up the living-room walls. She was struggling to balance her life between her Muslim family and extended Western social circle. A difficult situation arose every time someone mentioned going to McDonald's for lunch or offered her a glass of white wine, endless bickering at home about trouser suits, uncomfortable conversations elsewhere about engagement rings and suntans.

Ellie shrugged now. 'Fine,' she said.

Safia copied the gesture contemptuously, unsatisfied with the answer.

'Fine,' Ellie said, again. 'Went out, got pissed. Same shit, different day.' She didn't have the energy for a discussion about it. Her head was still fuzzy with the phet comedown. She hadn't done powder for years, wasn't used to the dizzying after-effects.

She picked a new mug from the pile and gently ran her fingertips along the circumference, feeling for imperfections. She peeled a decal from its backing and wound it around the mug, squinting at it as she ironed the air bubbles out with her tongue-shaped smoother. Gavin dropped a mug on the floor and Ellie looked up to see if it had smashed. It had, but he continued to work regardless, struggling with the direct print machine. He was a solid man with a girlfriend he didn't like and twins on the way. He made mistakes and stuck by them, held his head high, took the bacon home. He was wearing a Cardiff City football T-shirt, the season fixtures printed on its back. It was a reject from the T-shirt department. Nobody wore their own stuff to work unless the only seconds out were England sweatshirts. She knew the fixtures now by heart. They'd both worked overtime fourteen days in a row. Gavin was saving for a double buggy and Ellie had to make-up Andy's half of last month's rent.

In the beginning, Ellie had been impressed by The Boobs. Andy

17

was adamant that they were going to make it and Ellie had no reason to doubt him. Ambition was written through her own bones like a stick of Porthcawl rock. She knew what it was to want rabbling cities and hectic skylines, to have dreams about seeing the back of the valleys. So when she moved in with Andy, only to discover their joint income didn't stretch to the lease, not even on a crumbling two-bedroom in Aberalaw, Ellie was happy to quit freelancing in favour of a steady income. She figured that when the hard work was done, she'd be one half of an über-couple, renowned for throwing vegetarian dinner parties at their chic Greenwich Village brownstone. That was over a year ago, and she felt as though she'd stuck enough stickers on mugs to last four lifetimes.

'Bastard!' Gavin said as another mug spun out of his grip. It shattered on the concrete floor. He bent down to retrieve the fragments, throwing each one into the mini-skip with an expletive.

'Are you going to tell me about your weekend?' Safia said, eyes narrowing to slits. 'I thought Andy was coming home on Saturday.' Safia didn't have a social life. She spent most of her leisure time cooking pasanday for her family. She watched *Coronation Street*. She meticulously clung to the details of Ellie's existence like a tabloid journalist unearthing the secrets of an A-list celebrity.

Every day, Ellie ran through an inventory of the things she'd done since she'd last seen Safia: what time she'd got home; what she'd eaten for dinner. Safia's favourite subject was Andy. If he and Ellie had had sex, Safia needed to know the position, the point of orgasm, the colour of the sheets. Over time Ellie had begun to embellish these little narratives, so that she'd eaten scallops instead of battered cod, worn negligees instead of fleece pyjamas, got twenty minutes of cunnilingus instead of nothing. It was inevitable: Safia's appetite for romance was insatiable, but Ellie had lived with Andy for a long time – they sometimes couldn't be bothered to have sex. And today she wasn't thinking about

Andy at all; her mind's eye was busy with the stranger's image: his chaotic hair, his treacle-black eyes, his lily-white teeth.

It made something in her tummy swell, like a fist of dough in an oven. She was wondering why his girlfriend wasn't allowed to drink vodka, wondering what his name was, wondering what the hell he was doing in Aberalaw. These little mysteries were far more compelling than anything to do with Andy, more compelling even than the idyllic fantasy life she had created for herself and conveyed on a daily basis to Safia. The stranger arrived seamlessly in her consciousness. One minute she'd been missing Andy; the next, there was some long-haired extraterrestrial who had materialized from thin air.

'El?' Safia said, as if from some distance.

Ellie sighed, annoyed by the interruption. She considered telling Safia about the stranger, but then quickly dismissed the idea. Safia was as chaste and delicate as the foil on a new coffee jar. She was religious. She'd been conditioned to ignore temptation, neglect her own feelings, banish any rebellious thoughts that accidentally found their way into her head. She wouldn't understand Ellie's predicament.

'Yeah, Andy's home,' Ellie said. 'And the band had some good news. A Radio 1 DJ liked one of their demos. He wants them to go on his show.'

'Wow,' Safia said. 'They're going to be famous!'

Behind her the fire exit opened. Jane appeared, heels clicking on the concrete. She stood next to their adjoining desks; hand on hip, counted the trays of mugs piled up from the floor. She noted the total down on her clipboard, her glasses slipping down her nose. 'You know we need a whole new batch of these packed and shipped by the end of August, don't you? Save your chitchat for your coffee break.'

4

At six on Wednesday night, Ellie was on her way home from the factory. The sun was reflecting on the bronze statue in the middle of Aberalaw Square. It was a Dai-capped miner, one arm clutching his Davy lamp, the other curved protectively around his wife and babe-in-arms. It was hard to distinguish one limb from another, especially if Ellie had been drinking in the Pump House. As Ellie got close to the pub she saw Rhiannon standing on the doorstep, talking into her mobile phone, a pair of pinstripe bell-bottom under her white hairdressing tunic. Ellie began to walk faster, trying to dodge her, scurrying past the statue towards the safety of Woodland Terrace. But a metre away from the pine end, Rhiannon's voice rang through the village like a marauding police siren. 'Oi, mush, come back by yere a minute.'

Ellie reluctantly turned around and walked back to the pub, her duffel bag jerking on her shoulder. She stood in front of Rhiannon while Rhiannon finished her conversation and flipped her phone shut. 'Kelly's gone to the dentist to get her rotten teeth out,' she said. 'Too many fuckin' sweets or somethin'. Fancy comin' in yere with me for a drink or what?'

Rhiannon was bordering on alcoholism, carried half-litre bottles of spirits around in her handbag. But she always needed someone to drink with. Misery loves company. Kelly was her teenage assist-ant at the salon; usually they went out together every night after work. Ellie picked at a glue stain on the thigh of her khaki cammos. Andy didn't like her drinking on week nights; he didn't like her drinking without him.

'Well?' Rhiannon yapped.

Ellie jumped.

'Ewe 'avin a bloody drink or not?'

Ellie followed Rhiannon through the pub and into the games area. Rhiannon sat at her table, the surface of it obscured with wineglasses full of Liebfraumilch, the house white. She picked one of the glasses up and gave it to Ellie, then took a sip of her own. 'I've got a game of pool on the go,' she said, pulling a worn cue out of the umbrella stand. 'I'll break if ewe don' mind.'

Dai Davies looked up from his newspaper. 'Go on, bach,' he said, shouting across the pub, holding his beer stein up in the air. He was a fixture at the Pump House bar, a retired cat burglar who delighted in malicious hearsay. He was also Rhiannon's uncle.

Rhiannon held the cue against herself, the tip burrowed between her double-D breasts. She squinted at it and puffed on the chalk then ducked at the edge of the table, one leg kicking out at the rear, her cropped bell-bottom revealing a thick band of brown skin. 'Italian coloured,' she called herself. But she wasn't Italian. Her parents were as Welsh as they came; career criminals from the Dinham Estate. The man who Rhiannon swore was her father, despite his being white and her clearly being mixed race, had been murdered in his prison cell when she was a kid. But not before giving her some cock-and-bull history lesson about south Walians originally being naturally dark-skinned, a story she still used to defend herself whenever someone from the estate called her a nigger.

The white ball rolled into the pocket without hitting any of the colours. Rhiannon passed the cue to Ellie. 'What d'yew reckon about this radio show?' she said. 'Ewe know about stuff like that, El. Am I gonna be rich next week or what? Cause I've had it with

that bloody salon, I 'ave. Ewe can catch all sorts of shit messing with people's 'air. Nits, skin diseases, 'alf of those inbreds from the estate got AIDS. I should get danger money for what I do.'

Ellie shattered the virgin balls, exposing a purple stain on the green felt where Siân had tipped a pint of cider & black a few months earlier.

'I tell ewe,' Rhiannon said, 'when 'ey make it I'm gonna have a big bloody mansion built on Pengoes Mountain, a big bloody electrocuted gate to keep the scum from the estate out.' She clapped her hands, like a seal doing tricks for a piece of fish. Pool games with Rhiannon were not meant to be won. They played by loitering around the table for three-quarters of an hour, talking about what-ever Rhiannon wanted to talk about, taking it in turns with slow, aimless strikes. Ellie daren't put any effort into it. She was afraid of beating Rhiannon, afraid of what Rhiannon's reaction might entail. If Rhiannon was anything she was a sore loser, so Ellie saved her concentration for pool games with Griff. Nothing annoyed Griff like losing a pub game to a girl.

'Bloody tired I am,' Rhiannon said. 'Marc's fault it is. Came home wanting six weeks' worth of nooky in two days.' Ellie cringed at the mention of *nooky*. Rhiannon was always fraught to portray herself as a hip, 20-year-old fashion aficionado. She read articles in Kelly's magazines about John Galliano and Stella McCartney, was always dripping in fake haute couture. But her vocabulary perpetually belied her disguise. Words like *nooky* and *mush* and *Billy Whizz*. Her voice came straight from the estate.

'Three times in one fuckin' night,' she said. 'That run in the family or wha'?'

Andy and Marc were brothers, Andy the elder by a year, which meant that Ellie and Rhiannon were very nearly sisters: sisters by common law. There was a time when Ellie could stand Rhiannon, when she didn't cross the street to avoid her, when she thought she was a suave and quick-witted *femme fatale*. Marc had met her eight months ago at a gig in Penmaes Welfare Hall, one of those ones where The Boobs stood in for the resident cabaret act, a glam-rock cover band called The Poseurs. As soon as the locals worked out that Andy didn't know any T-Rex riffs, The Boobs got bottled off. One dour Sunday afternoon, a black woman had appeared on the dance-floor, strutting around on her own, a miniature bottle of Moët in her fist, a luminous pink straw, shaped like a treble clef, sticking out of the top. She was wearing a tiny yellow A-line dress and a pair of fishnet stockings, the black lace bands at the top of them exposed. Her accent was *so* Welsh, so cordial and melodic, it would have seemed foolish to interpret it as anything other than endearing.

Ellie clearly remembered thinking that she could do with a friend like Rhiannon. It gave her hope to think that such a sophisticated specimen of being existed in a place so overcrowded with rednecks. Of course that was all positive prejudice. Rhiannon turned out to be the most bigoted person Ellie'd ever met: a brainless, reckless tart. There was no champagne in that bottle. It was just something she used to carry around in her counterfeit Prada handbag, one of her good-time-girl props. But she'd given Marc a lift home in her red sports car and he'd never been the same since. Ellie always joked that she must do something really special in bed.

'I mean,' Rhiannon said, swallowing a big gulp of wine, 'does Andy *have* to shag ewe every night?'

'He would if he could,' Ellie said. For the most part, Andy and Ellie's libidos worked on different time zones. His was on Greenwich Mean Time; hers was on Central Daylight. They hardly ever converged. 'Every night I hear him brushing his teeth in the bathroom with his electric toothbrush. That means he wants it. He told me once that it is a family trait; that it comes from his mother. Gwynnie. Can you imagine? Apparently she's a real goer.'

Ellie expected Rhiannon to laugh but she had already lost

interest in the subject. She was standing in front of the mirrored beer advert, arranging her hair so it stuck up like the head feathers of an exotic bird, her wineglass held in the air as though she expected an attendant to come and fill it. She hadn't expected an answer. She thought she was the only person in the village who had sex, and was therefore the only one qualified to speak of it.

They left the game half finished when Rhiannon decided she was too tired to play. She propped the cue against the wall and it immediately fell and crashed on the parquet floor. She rolled her eyes as she plonked herself down on the stool. 'It's that powder as well, see,' she said. She curled her hand around her jaw, hiding her mouth from Dai Davies's eye-line. 'A couple of dabs on a Saturday and I'm not right till Wednesday.'

'You took quite a lot of it,' Ellie said, safe in the knowledge that sarcasm went right over Rhiannon's head.

'Bloody good stuff it was,' Rhiannon said. 'I'd like to know where 'e got it from, El. Eighteen bloody months I've been trying to get hold of some whizz like that. Nothing!'

'Scotland,' Ellie said. She knew Rhiannon wasn't the sharpest knife in the drawer, but it was obvious. 'Marc brought it back from Glasgow.'

'No,' Rhiannon said. She shook her head, sprigs of her carefully placed hair falling flat. 'Marc din't have enough money to get home. Griff's asked 'is mammy to put a loan in his account for petrol. They'd still be on a fuckin' motorway somewhere otherwise. I bought the speed, from that English bloke, with the long 'air. 'E was in yere on Saturday with 'is missus. Just moved yere, 'e 'as, sold 'is farm in Devon or somethin'. Bloody good stuff it was, El. I don't wanna be lining some English twat's pocket, do I? Whass 'appenin' in Cardiff? Anything about?'

Rhiannon was talking about the stranger. 'He's not from Devon,' Ellie said. 'He's from Cornwall. There's a difference.' She looked

24

Rhiannon straight in the eyes, something she didn't do very often. 'Are you sure you got it from him?'

'Yes!' Rhiannon said. 'I saw 'im on the square on Saturday morning. 'E was doing a deal with a kid from the estate. I went right bloody up to 'im, asked 'im what 'e 'ad. He's got disco pills too, he told me.'

That's how Rhiannon knew him. That's why she kept touching him on Saturday, as if he was her pet dog. He didn't look like someone who sold drugs. Street pushers wore baggy, food-stained jogging-bottoms. They lived in unfurnished flats on the Dinham Estate. Ellie quickly imagined what kind of job her ideal man would have. He would be a painter or an architect, someone with a pencil in his hand. But this was Aberalaw and drug dealing was as good a job as anyone could hope to get. 'What's his name?' she said.

Rhiannon snuck a glimpse at Dai. He was reading the local newspaper, studying the 'Look Who's Been in Court' column, looking for stories he could exaggerate. Jenny Two-Books, the assistant from the betting shop on the High Street, had just arrived to collect her extra takings. She ran her own service for the alkies who were too drunk to walk to the shop. 'Johnny,' Rhiannon said. 'Johnny somethin'.'

'Where does he live?'

'I don't bloody know, El. What's it to ewe anyway?'

Ellie felt her cheeks redden. She looked down at the assortment of wineglasses on the table, trying to hide her face from Rhiannon, but Rhiannon had already detected something in her enquiry. 'Ewe don't fancy 'im or somethin', do ewe, El?'

'Don't be stupid,' Ellie said, not looking up from her drink. 'I love Andy.'

Rhiannon lifted the egg-cup-shaped glass to her mouth, peering intently at Ellie over the rim. 'Aye,' she said. 'I love Marc an' all. I love Marc as much as ewe love Andy, don't think that I don't. An' if I 'ear anyone saying I don't love Marc, I'll fuckin' batter 'em.' Whatever that was supposed to mean. Ellie shrugged and reached for her glass.

Rhiannon beat her to it. 'I'll get ewe a fresh one,' she said, giggling, the angry smirk on her face fading from the bottom up. 'But ewe'll 'ave to remember 'ow many ewe owe me. I can't afford to keep us both in wine. Things ain't *that* good at the salon.'

Dai Davies folded the newspaper down on the bar. Accidentally, Ellie caught his eye. He grinned at her lecherously, made a creepy clicking noise with his slick tongue. Ellie shivered. They were psychopaths, the whole family.

5

On Fridays the village smelled like chip fat, smog clouds from the deep-fat fryers oozing from kitchen windows. Ellie was at home, in Gwendolyn Street, a Victorian terrace overlooking the rest of Aberalaw. From her bay window she could see past the terraces in front, down to the square and the statue in the centre. A couple of pear-shaped women were unpegging their faded bedclothes from the washing lines, the men driving from the electronic factories on Pengoes Industrial Estate to the Pump House or the Labour Club. Her living room was bare, save for Andy's huge television. The fitted carpet had been a fixture since 1973; floral swirls bursting into explosions of satsuma and choco-late-brown every few square metres. The satinette sofa was covered with a cream linen throw-over, but it continually slipped away, revealing patches of mauve and royal blue. The block colour thinned the oxygen, made the atmosphere seem perpetually constipated. Buying expensive things for a rented property was negative equity, Andy said.

She was flicking through a copy of the *NME* when he came in; she was skim-reading stories about bands less talented than The Boobs written by journalists less talented than her. He stripped down to his denim cut-offs and T-shirt, left his paint-stained overall on the floor. He went straight to the tiny kitchen to wash his hands with antibacterial soap. Ellie put the magazine down and followed him. She sat on the chipboard worktop. 'Good day was it?' she said.

'Not bad, babe.' He whipped the tea towel from its handle and scraped his fingers in it, his skin pink with toil and hot water. He and Marc had laboured at his father's decorating company since they were 15 and 16 years old. They probably always would.

'It's Friday,' she said cheerfully, trying to alert him to the onset of the weekend. Six days and counting since Johnny-Come-Lately had turned up. Ellie would have liked to go to the Pump House in the hope of meeting him again. But Andy'd always exercised a dreadful Puritan work ethic. He didn't like drinking all that much. It was difficult to imagine how he filled his time on the road; cooped in a Transit van saturated with lager farts, a couple of dipsomaniacs for company. 'Do you think Marc and Rhiannon are going out?'

Andy pretended he hadn't heard her. He opened the fridge, unleashing the sweet stench of decaying food. He picked a lettuce up by its unopened packaging and tossed it in the swing-top. He took the potatoes out of a plastic grocery bag and began to peel and cut, his blue eyes squinting at the stabs of the vegetable knife, his tongue poked out in application, the starchy water sloshing out of the basin and landing on the floor tiles around his bare feet. An abnormally big bumblebee hurtled against the window, hit the pane with a thud, then dropped out of view.

The couple ate their dinner in the living room, at either end of the sofa. Andy was watching a rugby match, knife-handle seized in his curled fingers, head tilted towards the television; a physical mannerism he'd inherited from his father. Moving images hypnotized him. Commentators spoke to him in a seductive language that left him deaf to live words. Occasionally he looked away, hurriedly piled a handful of chips into a slice of bread and quickly gnawed at the sandwich, the grease collecting in the crooks of his mouth. At the sound of the half-time whistle, he turned to look at Ellie.

'Now that I'm home,' he said, pausing to ensure he'd got her attention, 'we should fix a date for the wedding.' He folded a piece of bread in half and mopped the egg yolk up from his plate.

Ellie put her own plate on the floor, setting her cutlery at the rim. It was eighteen months since he'd first asked. She was on her way home from work, stepping off the train in Aberalaw station when she noticed something strange about the mountain behind their house. Initially she thought it was a flock of sheep that had accidentally arranged itself into some uncanny correlation. When she got to the square she started to decipher the words. 'MARRY ME ELIZABET,' it said, vast characters spelt out against the moss green bracken with hundreds of smooth grey pebbles. Andy was standing on the doorstep, a nervous twist in his grin. 'What do you think?' he said, voice quivering. 'I nicked them from Merthyr Mawr in the old man's tipper. Weren't enough to do the last H.' She agreed, immediately, emphatically, because, even if she hadn't wanted to marry him, she thought she would grow into wanting it, the way she'd grown into her sister's hand-me-down clothes. Two days later, embarrassed by the attention it was attracting, she asked him to go back to the mountain and take the stones down. He'd bought her a nine-carat gold diamond solitaire, the only diamond she'd ever owned, and she'd spent days scraping her knuckle against the bay window, trying to slice the pane. The ring was dull now, with time and glue from the factory. They didn't get married because they didn't have the money to pay for the wedding. They still didn't have the money.

'My aunty'll do the cake,' Andy said, stretching to retrieve her plate, scraping the chips she'd left into his own dish.

'Why don't we go abroad?' Ellie said. 'Tobago or Cancún.' It was the only way she'd escape interference from Andy's relatives. There was a quagmire of customs to observe, a trail of conventional nonsense that kept all of their family traditions intact. Andy being her first son, Gwynnie demanded a church wedding. Ellie was petrified of walking into St Illtyd's only to find the groom's side bursting with jubilant spectators, her own pews entirely empty. She didn't want to marry his family; she wanted Andy all to herself. 'That's what people do now,' she said. 'The bride and groom go away on their own. It's more meaningful, don't you think?'

'We can't do that,' Andy said. 'My mother and father could never afford the flight.' He popped a chip into his mouth and sidled closer to Ellie, sliding across the settee.

'What about a winter wedding?' she said. It was August now. She was buying time, hoping she could change his mind, or that he'd forget about it all over again. 'February. We could serve hot toddies instead of Cava. I could wear diamantés instead of pearls, a Cossack instead of a veil.'

'The fourteenth?' Andy said.

'Valentine's Day.' Ellie sniggered. 'That's just tacky.'

'It's romantic.' He clambered on to her body, bunching her wrists together, holding them like a bouquet above her head. Ellie bucked and screamed, the sharp screech breaking into peals of laughter. 'Get off me,' she said.

Andy kissed her, his keen tongue pushing into her mouth. After a moment, she started to kiss back hungrily, looking for something that had been there two years ago when they'd met, that had been there six days ago when he'd come back from Glasgow; something that wasn't there now. All she could taste was the rust that had worked its way between them, months of widening water. His saliva was cold. An abrupt fatigue seeped through Ellie's body. Her lips froze, her own tongue slumping back into her throat. As Andy pulled away she glimpsed the scar on his neck, four centimetres above his collarbone, a sunken white-blue tear shredding through his wheat-coloured skin.

'What's the matter?' he said, voice doleful, eyes flickering in the last of the sunlight from the window.

'Nothing,' Ellie said. 'Nothing.' She waved his concern away with a chop of her hand, instructing him to continue. He began to work on her button fly. 'Stop,' she said pushing him away. She'd had an idea. She wriggled out of her jeans and then her pink cotton knickers, kicking them across the room. She flipped on to her naked belly and rose up on all fours. 'I've been waiting for this,' she said. It's what she always said. Sometimes he beat her to it, and asked the question, especially if he was just home from tour. 'Have you been waiting for this?' he'd say. 'I bet you have.'

She could feel him behind her, on his knees, the heat coming from him. She pressed her face against the arm of the settee, breathing the musty odour from the throw-over deep into her lungs, scrutinizing it for an iota of smoke, petrol; something that smelled like that man whose name was Johnny.

He placed his hand on her hip, getting closer.

'I've been *aching* for this,' she said.

6

Rhiannon weaved through the tables in the restaurant, winking at people she recognized. 'Hiiiyyyaaaa,' she said, wriggling out of her jacket. She sat down next to Gwynnie.

Gwynnie was a big woman with a permanent expression of terror splashed across her face. Nothing in her life had been easy and she expected her cycle of misfortune to persist until the death. Her skin was mottled with anxiety, her bones arthritic with exertion, her mouth quick with over-zealous counsel. Her demeanour was comical, her head constantly bobbing about in a frantic convulsion, gigantic sweat patches under her arms. Ellie often caught herself laughing at Gwynnie when she wasn't trying to be funny. 'We can order now,' she said, waving at Andy's father. 'Where's the waitress, Collin?'

'*Where's the waitress, Collin?*' Collin said, mimicking his wife's panicked voice. 'How the bloody hell should I know, Gwyneth?'

Eating at the Bell & Cabbage was a relatively new experience for the Hughes family. Gwynnie used to cook Sunday dinner in her own kitchen; pork with roast parsnips and fresh vegetables served in her best bone-china tureens. Collin hurtled from the bedroom to the dining table in one fell swoop, his naked stomach riding out on the chair around him. Afterwards, Gwynnie did the washing-up, the pots falling from the draining board with a clang and echoing into the living room, like smites aimed at the girls' sloth. 'Shit!' she'd say, sharp as a blade. At Easter the girls had booked a table for six in the carvery, encouraged by Gwynnie's resentful sideways glances whenever they talked about steak they'd eaten at the Bell, or salads at fast-food joints. 'There's nice,' she'd say, 'there's lovely,' as if it was lobster bisque at The Dorchester. Her idea of a day out was a ramble through the car-boot sales in North Cornelly, spending her paltry income on labour-saving junk – old bread-makers and sandwich-toasters, stuff most people saw fit for landfill. When the day came, Collin sat in his reclining armchair, his hands crossed over his belly, as if trying to protect it from anything that wasn't home-cooked. He refused to leave the house. Rhiannon managed to coax Gwynnie into her car, but at the restaurant she sat in the corner weeping, fretting over Collin's non-attendance, the waitress staring as she set the gravy boat on the doily.

Collin turned up with the carrots, his comb-over hair blown out of place by the wind. He ate his food in obdurate silence, frowning over every mouthful, Rhiannon and Ellie secretly smirking at one another.

Marc put Rhiannon's wineglass on the table now.

'Is it clean?' she said, twisting it in the light from the window. 'There was some bugger else's lipstick all over it last week.' She was wearing a grey sweater with glittery pink writing across the bust. Her face was made up, her eyelids licked with bold blue eye-shadow.

'Go down the club last night?' Marc said, pushing the potatoes towards his father.

'Aye,' Collin said.

'Artist any good, Gwyn?' Rhiannon was playing with her peas, squashing them to a paste with the base of her fork, her wine held to her mouth, her voice echoing in the glass. Gwynnie quickly chewed a fatty morsel of beef, her head bobbling. 'Two women,' she said. 'They were good but I think they were lezzers. They didn't have no wedding rings.'

Collin stopped eating and glared at his wife. He commonly regarded women with a mixture of bafflement and trepidation. Ellie often caught him purposely avoiding eye contact, the way someone with a phobia of cats avoided a stray tabby. When he was sure she'd turned away, he'd peep furtively at her, as if ensuring she hadn't moved any closer, or grown any bigger. He hated women. His only pleasure lay in trying to make their lives as miserable as his was.

For Ellie the feeling was mutual. She abhorred the control he had over Andy. He was absent for his childhood, locked in a prison cell for tax evasion. He missed his first word, his first footstep, and because he hadn't witnessed these developments with his own eyes, he seemed to believe that they had never occurred. He treated Andy like a two-year-old, a fate Marc had somehow managed to avoid. He'd tell him to order the lamb instead of the beef, buy diesel-powered vehicles instead of petrol; put a patio in the garden instead of a lawn. When Andy and Ellie moved into Gwendolyn Street, Ellie asked Andy if they could go shopping for a couple of knick-knacks to make the place look like a home. Collin took it upon himself to play chaperone. Ellie'd been holding an Angelo Cavalli canvas, a beautiful black-and-white photograph of the Flatiron Building, when Collin swooped on her and plucked it out of her hands. 'Ugly, isn't it?' he said, discarding it. 'What about this?' He passed her a Claude Monet print, *Bridge over a Pool of Water Lilies*. 'Do you like that?' he said. Ellie concurred, afraid of offending him. So he nodded and put it into their trolley.

When he was sure Gwynnie'd finished her sentence, Collin turned to look at Marc. 'Heard about this new yobbo in town then, boy? I was talking to old Dai last night. Said he's been hangin' round the House, a scruffy lookin' one.'

'Are you talking about Johnny?' Marc said.

A carrot split and fell from Ellie's fork. It landed in the watery vegetarian gravy, driving a beige-coloured splatter across her plate. She kept her head down, eyes fixed on the food. The question mark lingered in the air of the restaurant for a time, utilizing her head as its period. She could feel the weight of Rhiannon's stare.

'I don't know 'is name,' Collin said. 'Killed a fella, Dai said.'

'Killed a fella!' Marc laughed. 'Honest Dad, you're like a pair of washerwomen when you get together. Why do you think anyone who comes from somewhere else is a criminal? He can't afford to live in Cornwall any more, that's all. Tourists forcing the cost of living up.'

'What's his last name?' Gwynnie said.

'Frick,' Rhiannon said, the word bursting proudly from her lips.

'Frick?' Gwynnie said. She shook her head, features quivering. 'I don't know of any Frick families round by here.' Gwynnie knew everyone who lived in Aberalaw, all nine hundred and fifty-one of them. She'd lived there her entire life. She'd never dreamt of moving away from the street in which she grew up, or of doing anything more ambitious than raising her children to be honest and hard-working. She was the kind of woman who'd use the word 'eccentric' to describe anyone who'd read a book. But there was a fine line between naivety and ignorance. She'd called the Asian shopkeepers 'a pair of suicide bombers' when their grandson won the bonny baby competition in the local paper. Behind Rhiannon's back, she called her 'half a darky'.

Andy sighed, bored with the conversation. He obviously had no interest in Johnny. 'I've got some news,' he said squeezing Ellie's knee. 'Me 'n' Ellie,' he paused for a moment, deliberately duping Gwynnie into thinking that Ellie was pregnant.

Her mouth fell open; her head leant attentively to the side.

'We've agreed on a date for the wedding, Valentine's Day 2004.'

Gwynnie started rummaging around in her handbag, pulling out a crumpled tissue. Rhiannon slumped against the back of the bench and studied the fringes of the tablecloth, considering the implications. For a day at least she would not be the centre of attention.

'When?' Collin said.

'February,' Andy said. 'February the fourteenth.'

'Bloody strange time to get married – you should do it in October. A marriage licence is cheaper in October. That's when me and your mother got married.'

'Ellie wants a winter wedding,' Andy said. 'Don't you, babe?'

Ellie wanted to plunge her knife under the table and puncture Andy's hand. Everyone was gawping at her, waiting for her to start gibbering on about bridesmaids' dresses and seating plans. Her muscles solidified, rooting her to the chair. Her cheeks glowed scarlet. 'That's okay isn't it?' she said. 'A winter wedding?' She smiled self-consciously, the skin of her lips cracking as they stretched across her teeth.

'Your auntie Maggie's away in her caravan in February,' Gwynnie said. 'I'd have to do the sandwiches on my own. And flowers! They'd be extortionate that time of year. Whenever the boys have bought flowers on Valentine's Day—'

'Mam!' Marc said, scolding her.

Gwynnie stopped. She covered her mouth with her shrivelling fingers.

'I don't expect you to do *all* the food,' Ellie said. She didn't expect her to do any of it. 'We'll get caterers.'

'But it's tradition,' Gwynnie said, starting again.

Rhiannon yawned loudly, half covered her mouth with her hand. She ran her forefinger along the rim of her empty wineglass, waiting for someone to notice her, lipstick still in place.

'Are you going out somewhere today?' Ellie said.

Rhiannon realized that her wish had been granted. She fluttered her eyelashes. 'Out?' she said.

'Yeah, out,' Ellie said. 'Drinking. It's just that you've got make-up on.'

7

After lunch, Ellie and Andy left Gwynnie and Collin in the carvery. They followed Rhiannon and Marc through the High Street, their bellies stuffed with profiteroles, an ice-cream van playing *Für Elise*. At the junction, Rhiannon pointed out her new range of professional styling products lined up on the salon windowsill. 'Fifteen quid for the intensive light-reflecting conditioner, El,' she said. 'Only a two per cent mark up for ewe.' It was the only window in the street not hidden behind a graffitied zinc shutter. Andy tried to catch Ellie's hand but she brushed him off, reaching into her back pocket for a crumpled packet of ciggies. He watched her as she lit one, his mouth a single chisel-blow in pale flesh, clearly puzzled by her inclination to go out on a Sunday. Usually she sat in bed all afternoon, a magazine on her lap, a bar of chocolate on the bedside cabinet. Sometimes they had sex.

The Pump House picnic tables were set up around the mining statue. Griff was slouched behind a flat pint of lager and lime. Siân was sitting on the kerb, her orange ankle-length gypsy-skirt lying like a sheet over her legs, her hair scraped back from her face. She'd kicked her mules from her feet. One of them was on the pavement in front of the old YMCA, the fish-scale sequins sparkling in the sunlight. When Ellie'd moved to Aberalaw, Siân wore boob-tubes and hot-pants. With every new child, her tastes became more conservative: pastel blouses and woollen twinsets.

It was a shame to think of her smooth skin buried beneath several layers of cotton. A butterfly momentarily hovered at her throat and then danced into the ether, high above America Place.

America Place was a small street, a row of miniature fascias and hanging baskets erupting with tufts of orange pansies; a rare sight in a village marred by broken glass, concrete, used syringes, dog shit. The inhabitants had been having some sort of flower-growing competition for two years on the run. 'Know why America Place is called America Place?' Ellie said as she sat down on the kerb. Early in the nineteenth century, the whole street had decided to emigrate en masse. They'd appointed a chairman to book the tickets and collect the savings they'd accumulated over eight years. But he did a moonlight flit. The residents renamed the street, and called the old pub at the entrance to the estate the New York, New York. Siân knew the story. Ellie'd told her umpteen times, and on each occasion wondered why Siân didn't find it as intriguing as she did. Ellie was besotted with anything to do with America.

'Yeah, we all fuckin' know,' Rhiannon said. 'Ewe never stop bloody tellin' us, do ewe?'

'Have you ever seen a film called *In America*?' Siân said, spitting a chewed fingernail out of her mouth. 'What it is, it's about an Irish couple who go to New York with dreams of acting on Broadway, but end up in a stinking block of flats. Nobody's taken it out yet.' She worked in the video shop and watched each new release when it arrived, sitting at the counter with a packet of chocolate biscuits.

'Have a good bloody look at it, El,' Rhiannon said, ''cause it's the closest to America ewe'll ever get. Like them lot,' she pointed at America Place. 'Ewev'e already missed the fuckin' boat.'

There was another thing that interested Ellie about America Place, something she never talked about: Andy's ex-girlfriend, Dirtbox. She lived in one of the converted cottages but Ellie'd forgotten which. He'd taken her to a party there once, a few weeks into their courtship, before he'd admitted that Dirtbox was his ex-girlfriend. He introduced her as his 'friend', the clumsy air around the word divulging a sense of mischief Ellie couldn't quite define. The three of them had stood in the kitchen, gazing at her potted herbs. Then Andy pointed through the French doors at the prize-winning Lionhead rabbits leaping around in their pen. 'That's Flossy,' he said, 'and the other one is Thumper. Shag like bunnies they do.' Something in *that* sentence revealed the true nature of his and Dirtbox's relationship. Ellie hadn't imagined that Andy'd had a life before she'd arrived, and the realization had hit her like a juggernaut doing ninety. She'd immediately fled, the soles of her motorbike boots bouncing on the cracked pavements of America Place, then Dynevor Street, then the dogtooth tiles of the railway station. Andy'd followed, coins dropping out of his pockets and rolling down on to the track. As he'd reached her, the Ystradyfodwg train appeared, its brakes screeching. Andy fell at her feet, tears streaming down either side of his nose.

'Don't leave me,' he said tugging at the hem of her gingham dress, like a bad actor in a cheap made-for-TV film.

The electronic doors parted with a computerized bleep.

Ellie prised his fingers from her skirt, one digit after the other.

'I'll kill myself if you go,' he said, skin claret.

Ellie stepped on to the train. She didn't go in for emotional blackmail then; that self-confident, post-Plymouth period of her life which felt like an aeon ago.

'I'll get the round in then, shall I?' Andy said now, ambling into the pub.

Marc picked up a newspaper, opened it to a black-and-white photograph of George Bush. '*US admit guerrilla warfare*,' the headline said. He quickly flipped the page to a large colour photograph of a topless blonde model with generous, upturned nipples.

Rhiannon sidled closer to Siân, brushing her plump fingers

through her long ponytail. 'Feels a bit dry, love,' she said. 'I've got some new conditioner. Why don't ewe pop in the shop this week?' Her voice the honeyed adaptation she used to flatter people she didn't really like. Siân pulled her hair away from Rhiannon and smoothed it on to the opposite side of her neck.

Andy came out carrying drinks on an aluminium tray. 'Dai just told me that Gemma Williams is up the duff,' he said. 'Williams the Milk's daughter. She's only fourteen.'

Rhiannon opened a compact and stared into the mirror. 'Stupid likkle slut,' she said, plucking a hair from her chin with a pair of steel tweezers.

'Is there anybody else in there?' Ellie said. She thought Johnny might have been here, smoking his abundant supply of cigarettes, buying beer for his girlfriend, telling the bar-staff that under no circumstances were they allowed to supply her with vodka. She thought he might have been coming here for weeks; that's why she'd come.

'No,' Andy said. He shrugged. 'Why?'

Ellie ignored him, glanced around the square. The pine trees on Pengoes Mountain stretched up behind the sagging rooftops of the terraces, their branches thick with foliage, their tips piercing a cornflower sky. A car thudded over the cattle-grid, the sound echoing across the valley.

Suddenly Ribs came out of the pub. 'What the fuck are you doin' yer?' he said blinking at Andy. 'Never see 'im on a Sunday do we?' Ribs was a closet transvestite. He lived on his own in a house in Dynevor Street. He used to share a flat with Griff in the YMCA. Sometimes he forgot to remove his make-up before he left the house and he'd sit at the bar in the Pump House for two hours, a greasy film of red lipstick staining the rim of his pint glass, cheap blue mascara slithering down his cheekbones. There was some speculation about his sexual orientation because he'd tried to kiss Collin once, after a lock-in on a New Year's Eve.

'What songs shall we do, Ribs?' Griff said, 'for the John Peel session on the radio?'

Ribs was a big fan of The Boobs. He'd been around since Marc started the band at the age of sixteen, supported them through the garage days when they practised in an abandoned allotment behind the industrial estate. He still went to every local gig, but didn't know one song from another. He stood in front of the stage, his mouth flapping open and closed like an atheist holding a hymn book at a funeral. He wiped a sheet of sweat from his forehead, a coat of peach-coloured foundation disappearing with it. 'It's nearly bank holiday again,' he said. 'What are you going as this year?'

Some of the villagers wore fancy dress for the annual August bank holiday pub crawl, because this was Aberalaw and they had to make their own fun. Ribs's proudest moment came whilst wearing shocking pink stockings and red stilettos, pissing in a litter bin in the High Street, his back to the road. 'Show us your tits, love,' a bunch of joyriders had yelled at him through a car window.

'I'm going as a copper,' he said, 'a female copper.'

Ellie was looking at America Place again, and remembering that her grandmother had had wild pansies growing in her front garden, an exquisite purple colour. She had a funny name for them. 'Johnny Jump-Ups!' she said, thinking aloud. 'That's what my nanna called pansies, Johnny Jump-Ups.' There, she'd said it. It had been balancing on her lips for a week and now it had slipped out accidentally, like a burp.

'That's that English bloke's name ini?' Ribs said. 'Johnny?'

'He's a drug dealer he is,' Griff said. 'Dai told me, fallen out of favour with some big shot up in England.'

'Dai's a prick,' Marc said.

Ellie was thrilled with the response. If she couldn't have Johnny there, the next best thing was listening to people talking about him.

She liked the idea of him being some sort of fugitive, escaping Cornwall under the cover of darkness, his passport wedged in his back pocket. That image turned her nipples hard.

Rhiannon snapped her compact shut. She looked at Ellie, brown eyes turning to brass. 'Very funny, El,' she said. 'Johnny Jump-Ups? What did she call carnations?'

'Carnations,' Ellie said, playing ignorant, the familiar sting finding its way to the sides of her face. Rhiannon laughed her fat, fake laugh. She dropped her compact into her bag, fastened the zip and pushed the bag aside. 'Why don't ewe tell everyone ewer special news, then El?' she said. She slowly eyed everyone at the table and then after a moment, said, 'Ellie and Andy are getting married next year, Valentine's Day. Ain't that romantic?'

'No way!' Siân said, throwing herself at Ellie.

Rhiannon drained her wineglass and put it on the ground, the glass ringing on the concrete. 'Yep,' she said, voice saccharine. 'I take ewe, Andy, to be my lawful wedded husband, to 'ave 'n' to 'old, from iss day forward, in sickness and in 'ealth, to love and to cherish till death do us part: I 'ere to pledge my *faithfulness.*'

'And ooh are ewe callin' a prick?' she said turning to Marc. 'That's my uncle ewe were talkin' about. Ewe can buy me a drink for that, butty boy. Dai *is* a prick, about as much use as a cock-flavoured lollipop, but only I'm allowed to say that.'

Marc nodded, stood up, headed towards the pub.

Rhiannon nudged Ellie. 'I'm watching ewe, El,' she said.

8

The phone at the reception desk was ringing but Rhiannon didn't move to answer it. She was looking at herself in the giant mirror, staring at the dark fuzz on her top lip. She hadn't been to the beautician for weeks, not since she'd asked the girl behind the counter, the skinny one with a ski-slope nose, how to go about getting rid of dull skin. Rhiannon's face was a dingy, grey colour, like a cup of Marc's mother's coffee, nasty German stuff from Lidl. Eat more fruit, the girl had said, eat more bloody fruit. Fuck that. Rhiannon didn't have time to muck around with fruit. She wanted Botox, a chemical peel or something. There was a chrome fruit basket on the shelf, full of fresh green apples. She'd only put it there to complement the colour scheme. She didn't like apples. They were something she hadn't grown up with. The only things she'd eaten as a kid came in watery tomato sauce – baked beans, baked beans and sausage, out of a bloody tin. She didn't know what apples tasted like. Cider probably. She was going to get a new beautician.

'Ouch!' the woman sitting in front of her said.

'Sorry, love,' Rhiannon said. She pulled the tongs away from the woman's head and a ginger ringlet jumped out, the scalp underneath glowing red. 'I din't hurt ewe, did I?'

Rhiannon didn't like doing weddings, and this fat woman was a bride. She was from a party of six from the Dinham Estate,

44

all of them wearing chunky gold sovereign rings on their manky, tobacco-stained fingers. It was a wonder they could afford to come *here*. Rhiannon charged through the nose, but the scum from up there always found a way, nicked money off their parole officers or something. They were all desperate to look like some-body else, would spend their last quid on trying to buy a new identity, something Rhiannon understood perfectly well. She'd spent most of her life wishing her arse was skinny, wishing her skin was white, wishing her hair was straight. From the age of eleven she'd spent her evenings at her uncle's kitchen table sharing her auntie's homework from the local Christmas trim-ming factory, dipping baubles in a vat of glitter. For every hundred she got 1p. She was saving to go to the salon on City Road in Cardiff. It was the only place in Wales with ammonia strong enough to relax her Afro-Caribbean kink. The customers worshipped the woman who ran it, treated her like a priestess; practically curtsied when they gave her a massive tip. With Rhiannon's head for business it didn't take long for her to realize that sort of power was worth a fortune.

She'd been a hairdresser for nineteen years and she took pride in her work. She'd only ever had one complaint, from Kylie Beynon, a stroppy little bitch from the top of Gwendolyn Street. She'd sent a solicitor's letter to the salon, demanding compensation for a couple of hair extensions that had supposedly fallen out. *As if*. Five hundred quid she wanted. Rhiannon rang the Williams twins; a couple of smackheads from the estate. They'd do anything for a bag of ten. She told them to hand-deliver the letter back to Kylie with a can of petrol and a lighter. They were only supposed to warn her off, burn the letter up in front of her face. Kylie was washing her porch carpet with flammable shampoo. The useless pair of twats dropped the letter on the floor and the whole bloody house went up. Cut a long story, the ambulance rushed Kylie to Morriston with third-degree burns and the twins swapped life in nick for the address of their drug dealer. Kylie's still wearing a bloody wig. The best form of defence is attack.

Rhiannon checked the woman's blister. It wasn't anything special. 'Ewe'll be OK now,' she said, giving her fat shoulder a little squeeze. 'A bit sore, I'll just get somethin' to soothe it for ewe.'

On the other side of the salon, Kelly had tipped tea over the maid of honour. She was a big, no-nonsense peroxide blonde, sitting with her legs wide open, steam rising out of her jogging-bottoms. Lesbian probably. Kelly was on the floor, wiping the tiles with a worn tea towel. Rhiannon kicked her with the toe of her black Mary Jane's. 'Clean it up!' she said. 'And get the lady another cup.' Bloody teenagers; all they fucking did was hang around looking young, smoking Lambert & bloody Butler, sending text messages to their pre-pubescent boyfriends. Rhiannon only put up with Kelly because Kelly was too young for the minimum wage; she gave her fifty quid on a Friday and told her to fuck off if she didn't like it.

Rhiannon noticed a toddler in the corner, drawing on her leather appointment book with a chewed crayon. She crouched down beside her and said, 'Ewer a pretty likkle thing. What's ewer name 'en?' While it was looking for its voice, Rhiannon yanked the book out of its hands.

It instantly started screaming, spit running down its chin, snot dribbling out of its nose. Rhiannon turned on her heel and eyed her customers. 'Tired is she?' she said, trying to trick one of them into claiming it. None of them bloody moved. Rhiannon hated kids, didn't understand why anyone would want to replicate their wretched lives; take all the things they despised about themselves and give it to someone else to despise all over again, especially the inbreds from the estate. But those are the ones who multi-plied fastest. It was one mistake that she was never going to make. Businesswoman she was. 'Do ewe want some council pop, sweetie?' she said, turning back to the kid.

'Give her some Coke,' Kelly said, leaning over Rhiannon's shoulder.

'We haven't got any Coke!' Rhiannon said. She was fucked if she was going to start giving Coca-Cola away to the losers from the estate; it was over a quid a bloody bottle. 'Make urgh stop crying,' she said, nudging Kelly in her flat 15-year-old tit. She went back to the fat woman and daubed a dollop of Vaseline on her head. 'Are ewe nervous about tyin' the knot 'en, love?' she said as she replaced the cap. 'I would be. I'd be shittin' my bloody kecks.'

'No.' The woman shook her head. 'It's only a vow-renewal cere-mony. I've been married for seventeen years. Are you still married? You're not wearing your ring.'

Rhiannon bit down on the hairgrip in her mouth. 'I ain't bloody married,' she said. But she was married, to a chartered surveyor from Barry Island. She'd met him there in 1984, in a pub called the Pelican. She'd been sitting in the beer garden on her own, wearing a Kiss-Me-Quick hat, drinking tap water because the boyfriend who she'd gone on the day trip with, some fucking no-mark from the estate, had run away with her purse. A fella in a cream suit cut through her blurred vision, approaching her with two glasses of sparkling wine, a pink handkerchief in his breast pocket. He looked like some bloody film star. Bob Stone his name was. They got hitched a fortnight later. But nobody else knew that. And she was up shit creek without a paddle if Marc ever found out. He'd asked her to marry him again, since Ellie and Andy had announced their date, said it was about time she made a commitment to him, said he fancied a double wedding with his brother. *As fuckin' if.* The last thing she'd do was share her wedding day with that couple of Muppets, even if she could get married. The woman was grinning at her through the mirror and there was a tattoo on her bottom gum, beneath her sunken teeth. 'DEB', it said. Rhiannon vaguely remembered a Deborah, a girl who had

47

babysat for her a few times when her father went to Wormwood for the post office job. 'Ooh told ewe that?' Rhiannon said.

'Your mother told me,' she said. 'I saw her last week in the chemist in Penmaes. I asked her if you were still hairdressing. She said she hadn't seen you since you got married when you were twenty.'

Rhiannon leaned on the woman's shoulder, pressing it down with the weight of her whole body. 'Ewe don't wanna listen to my mother, love. She's as senile as a cunt. Don't know urgh arse from urgh elbow one day to the next.'

Rhiannon's mother was a liability, interfering all the time. Cut a long story, she was jealous, because Rhiannon had made it out of the estate. Rhiannon had never had to stand in a queue in the post office to cash a giro and everyone from up there hated her for it. It was like she'd let the team down by having the cheek to better herself. Any more lip from her mother and she'd have to send someone up there to batter her, make it look like a botched burglary.

She looked around at her shop, at the chrome shampoo bottles and glass shelves, the apples that no fucker ate. This wasn't Curl Up & Dye on Dynevor Street. This was a proper professional salon, like Vidal Sassoon or Toni & Guy, and she was going to put a sign up in the window that said, 'No DSS'. She put her tongs in the holster, said, 'Ang a banger, love. Just going outside for a bit of fresh air.' As she started towards the door she got an idea and turned around. She looked at the woman, said, 'Did Kelly mention the price increase? It's another ten per cent. Cost of the products, love. Iss out of my 'ands.'

In the doorway of the old ironmonger's she reached into her tunic, took a quick slug of rum from her silver hip flask, then lit a cigarette. There was a meat wagon parked outside the butcher's opposite. The drivers were carrying the carcasses into the shop. Ellie'd have a coronary if she could see that. She was a veggie, one of those awkward bastards, had 'Meat is Murder' written in felt-tip on her duffel bag. One Boxing Day, at Marc's mother's, she'd seen a group of fox-hunters in the street and got up from the table, went screaming blue murder at them, didn't say boo to a fucking goose usually. But she had a crush on Johnny, Rhiannon could tell by the way her little blue eyes lit up whenever some-body mentioned his name; as if a man like Johnny'd have any interest in Ellie. She was an olive short of a pizza, that one; had some really fucked-up ideas about not taking Andy's name, about it being the MFI who flew the planes into the big buildings; read too many of those bloody fat newspapers.

The lorry indicated out of the kerb and Rhiannon dropped her fag butt, crushing it under her heel. She was about to light another when she noticed a blue BMW slowing to let the lorry out. It was only Johnny's BMW. Well, talk of the devil! '*Oof*,' she said to herself as a stem of heat ran up the back of her legs. '*Oof*.' She waved at the car as it pulled up alongside her, music blaring out of the stereo.

Louisa poked her head out of the window. 'Is this where you work?' she said, voice all English. 'Are you a hairdresser?'

Rhiannon looked at the chrome nameplate shimmering in the sunlight. She'd named the shop after its own postcode, CF25. 'Yeah,' she said. 'I'm a stylist.'

Johnny was looking at her tunic, his eyes following the white piping at the edge of her lapels down to the dark pit of her cleavage, fingers drumming on the steering wheel. Something in her chest snapped at the thought of him touching her, long fingers pressing on her buxom flesh. An electrical current shot straight from her throat to her snootch. *Oof.* There was a man who could turn profit out of cunning, who could afford to buy her a new pair of Manolo Blahniks. There weren't many men around here like that, not since Rhiannon's dad had died. Marc thought nicking a muffin from the Services was adventurous.

She panicked when the car began to roll away. 'If ewe ever want ewer 'air done,' she said, pointing at the plate-glass window, 'on the cheap, like. I own the shop.' Louisa smiled, but didn't seem interested. She lifted an apple to her mouth and bit into it.

What Rhiannon said next was the first thing that came into her head. 'I'm organizing a picnic on Saturday, at the park in Pontypridd,' hand curled around her mouth, her voice strained. 'They 'ave bands down there on the weekend. Ewe're welcome to come along. We'll be meeting in the Pump House at lunchtime.'

Louisa nodded and waved, the wedge of fruit jammed between her teeth.

Rhiannon stood in the doorway until the car had gone, her blood still pumping ten to the bloody dozen. She took another quick slug of rum and went into the salon. 'Ewe're working on ewer own on Saturday, Kel,' she said. 'Somethin's come up.'

Kelly grunted.

Rhiannon smiled anew at the woman in the hydraulic chair. 'So, where are ewe goin' on ewer 'oneymoon, love?' she said.

9

On Thursday night, Ellie closed her desk drawer on three mugs she was planning to steal later. She walked with Safia along the main road, cutting through the Riverside area, the quickest way back to the city. They passed a schoolyard where children were playing football, little red jumpers tied to the steel railings. There were only two white kids among them, and one little black girl, hair braided into chunky cornrows. Safia stopped to chat to the tutor, a man in a long taupe cloak. Ellie patiently listened to their mysterious language as it ebbed and flowed, hurrying Safia along Wood Street when the conversation had ended, past the Japanese and Bangladeshi shop-fronts.

At the Millennium Stadium, the low sun was boring down on the commuters who scuttled like ants around the pavestones in Central Square. Two men sat on the bus-station floor, black T-shirts faded to slate grey, their emaciated pet terriers yapping at one another. Ellie waited with Safia until her Tremorfa bus arrived, admiring the cut and thrust of the disparate metropolitan lives that moved hurriedly around her, listening to the brisk tunes of the human traffic. She loved the anonymity of the city; faceless pedestrians coiling through the walkways like one long centipede. She didn't know their names, their secrets, didn't know who their mothers were. In the city, anything seemed possible.

When the bus arrived Safia climbed on to it, waving through

the dirty glass as she walked towards the back. Ellie ventured into the city centre, running along the wide pavements of St Mary Street and into Castle Arcade. Her breath quickened as she climbed the stairs to the Victorian attic. She could hear the resonant Zzz Zzz sounds of the violin doctor tuning a cello. The aroma of coffee and garlic from the cafeterias blended into a steam cloud lingering above the balcony. She walked to the end of the narrow landing and stood in front of the office door, staring at the white letters on the glass. **The Glamour**, it said, some of the u and the r flaking away. The man inside swivelled around in his old captain's chair. It was Jamie Viggers, one of the staff writers. 'Elizabeth,' he said, beckoning her inside.

'I wasn't sure I'd catch you,' she said. She walked over to the empty chair next to him and sat down. 'I've come straight from work, a mug factory in Canton.' She folded her arms around her waist and then unfolded them to brush an imaginary speck of dust from the thigh of her combat trousers. She glanced around the room, at the bubbling white paint, the colourful stacks of books and CDs, the splodges of coffee stains on the vinyl floor. There was a half-eaten seafood fajita on one of the computer desks, the flotsam of busy city living. 'Andy's been really busy with the band. They've been touring a lot. I had to find something which paid the rent, and freelancing didn't.'

When Ellie was fresh out of Plymouth University with a belly-button bar and a prescription for the combined pill, she'd come back to Wales with the blind intention of becoming a rock music journalist. She was a neurotic, depressive, frustrated romantic who loved everything from bubblegum pop to grating industrial noise, and her prose could piss all over Julie Burchill's. She'd discovered this talent quite by accident when her friend who edited the student magazine had asked her to review The Cardigans' concert at the Pavilions. Her plan was to part the Atlantic like Moses did the Red Sea; beat a path all the way to *Rolling Stone*, where the critics *were* the pop stars. But she'd had to start at *The Glamour*, where the critics were socially challenged computer geeks. One of her first assignments was an interview with The Boobs. She met them in a greasy spoon off Womanby Street where a horde of workmen were slowly demolishing the Arms Park. She'd ordered tea and death-by-chocolate and was about to devour the first forkful when the band filed into the café; valley bumpkins hiding behind swear words and ripped jeans. She was a ballsy self-assured über-feminist who scowled at monogamous relationships and housewifery, and then she'd looked up from her fat wad of cake and seen Andy, his cerulean eyes already trying to thaw her thick wall of resistance. Death by calculated erosion was how it had turned out.

She looked up at Viggers. 'How come you're still here?'

'I'm the editor now,' he said, his tiny eyes magnified by the thick lenses of his glasses. 'I'm here till gone seven most nights.'

She hadn't really been referring to the late afternoon, but wondering how, in two years, Viggers hadn't moved to London, or at least on to the *Western Mail*, like all Cardiff University graduates eventually did. 'Can I lighten the load?' she said. 'I can take the books that nobody else wants. Or write some art previews.' Ellie loved art as much as music. At university she often snuck into other people's art history lectures, just to listen to the erudite lecturers gushing about the tortured lives of Kandinsky and Munch. Pop art was her favourite, Jasper Johns, Roy Lichtenstein, Claes Oldenburg. 'Is there anything on at the museum?'

Viggers slapped her leg. 'I can do better than that,' he said. 'You've heard of The Needles, haven't you? We're doing this thing, paying tribute to the big Welsh bands. We're doing one every month until we run out. It's perfect for you because Gareth's gone back to college to do his MA. It's the January cover feature. What do you think?'

'I don't know,' Ellie said. She only wanted something trivial to keep her mind off Johnny-Come-Lately. Thirteen days and counting since he'd turned up. They were the longest thirteen days of her life. Like a frantic disciple in search of the great redeemer, she saw the shape of his face amidst the floral patterns in the front curtains, then she'd lose ten minutes staring out of the bay window, wondering where he was, heart brooding, pulse thumping. She *needed* to see him again, to look into his sooty eyes. Saucepans boiled over. The bath overfilled. She tripped over her own toes. Andy had caught her once, his father's binoculars pressed against her face. She was looking at the beer garden on the square. She said she was looking at an eagle.

'It's probably a kestrel,' Andy'd said.

Eventually the frenzy thawed into embarrassment. It was ridiculous, she'd only met him once, shared five, maybe ten words. But the hysteria always returned, sporadic, but inevitable, as though he himself was the drug, and she was already dependent. 'Have you got anything smaller, a gig review or something?'

'It's only two thousand words, El. What's that, a half-hour interview? I've got a press pack somewhere. The deadline isn't until December. That's four months away.' He pushed himself out of the chair and walked to the other side of the room, stood in front of a giant-sized poster of Rhys Ifans. He rummaged through a pile of paperwork on a desk. 'You'll enjoy it,' he said, squatting to open a drawer. He held a pack of CDs bound together with a rubber band. 'Will you do it, yes or no?'

Ellie shrugged. 'OK,' she said.

Viggers approached her, dropped the bundle of CDs into her hands. He pinched her chin and then swivelled back to his workspace, his fountain pen waltzing across a page of foolscap.

On the landing the heat had relented. The cafés were closed, the arcade doused with disinfectant. She walked back to Central Square, the city around her empty and expectant, some of the club doormen clocking on for their twilight shift, leaning in the doorways wearing dinner jackets and bow-ties. Platform Six was unmusically quiet. Ellie stood amongst the pigeons waiting for the Ystradyfodwg train. Going back to the valley always made her feel jaded, an hour journey feeling like a mammoth shift backwards in time. Aberalaw was full of resentment. The whole village disapproved of anyone it collectively deemed atypical. All the columnists in the broadsheets ever talked about was how community was dying, and what a detrimental effect its death was having on Great Britain. But in Aberalaw it wasn't dead, and Ellie wished that it was. Community was a tyrant when your face didn't happen to fit. Ellie was impatient now for escape, her belly like a wishing well, heavy with copper pennies, every coin representing some unfulfilled dream.

She sighed and opened her purse, took her train ticket out. Behind it was a clipped photograph of Siân and Rhiannon, herself in the middle; their arms weaved chaotically around one another. She'd forgotten that it was there; almost a year old, taken on a rare night out in the capital. Ellie and Siân had wanted to go to a roller disco in Bute Park. Rhiannon insisted on some strip club she knew of, a dank basement bar hidden under a Queen Street department store. She'd spent the whole night acting the big I Am, stuffing five-pound notes into the dancers' thongs. The flash from the camera had penetrated their lipstick and glitter. Or it had already worn off. They looked like three little girls, the little girls they must have been before they grew up, before they discovered plastic surgery, sarcasm and narcotics, all the stuff that numbed the pain. Round faces and bug eyes. Rhiannon's fat purple tongue was poking out. God knows she must have been through some crazy shit to turn into such a psychotic bitch. She seemed to think the world revolved around her, that she was playing the lead role in some elaborate stage play. Most people grew out of that when they were thirteen. Siân's alcoholic father had beaten her mother senseless; kicked her, pregnant, down the stairs, cut her hair, burned her with cigarettes, and when she was in hospital, Siân bore the brunt. Siân had told Ellie all about it when she was blotto on cheap champagne, the whole three bottles that were left after Niall's christening. Ellie hadn't had it easy, but nothing like that.

Funny how those three faces should end up in the same club, in the same photograph, all damaged and searching for some kind of affirmation. But then nobody from the valley was a model citizen. Even Andy with his idyllic nuclear family was plagued with insecurities. They were branded into him, something he could never escape, like the ridges in his fingertips. He couldn't have a shit without consulting his father about what brand of toilet paper to use. He was the sanest person Ellie knew and he floundered through life, waiting for the next instruction, unable to utilize his own mind.

10

At the same time, in Aberalaw, Siân was trying to apply foundation, squinting at her reflection in the mirror nailed under the open stairs. It was the only mirror in the house, something James had made at nursery. He'd painted pasta shells gold and silver and glued them messily around the oval frame. Siân cherished everything the kids made, but between the three of them it amounted to fifteen crayon drawings a day. One time she'd tried to slip a stack into the transparent recycling bag, hiding them between two cereal boxes. Immediately she was overwhelmed with guilt. She'd pulled them out again, filing them neatly on the shelf under the coffee table by subject: cats, Daddy, guns and houses.

She squeezed a splodge of the gooey, honey-coloured make-up on to her palm and tilted her head towards the light. She almost didn't recognize her reflection, had always imagined herself as the blurred, worried-looking image she saw in Niall's pupils; a doting, fretting mother, clammy red cheeks, a band of sweat at her hairline. But in the mirror she looked close to human. She brushed mascara on her lashes with brisk strokes, stabbing herself in the eyeball when she heard her daughter shriek.

'Angharad!' she bellowed, flinging the kitchen door open, the mascara wand still clenched in her fist. Her adrenal glands opened, her heartbeat hopping. 'Angharad? What's wrong?'

James was sitting at his plastic drum-kit, pounding on the bass pedal, the force of each blow sending his orange fringe into the air. He was four years old, a sober child. When he was newborn, Siân worried he was mute. He lay in his cot, staring at the Artex ceiling, no reaction to touch or to noise. Infancy brought an occasional scrap of conservative speech.

Angharad was leaning against the edge of the table, slugging cherryade, one of the legs of her sky-blue dungarees rolled up to her knee, an impish glint in her emerald eyes. A robust and outgoing three-year-old. When the social worker called on her at two years, asking about her speech patterns, Angharad pointed at the bar of Dairy Milk poking out of the woman's satchel. 'Come on, lady,' she said, licking her lips, '*everyone* has to share.' She put the cherryade down on the table and let go of a long burp, stared brazenly at Siân. 'James punched me,' she said.

Siân reached for the kitchen roll and broke a sheaf away, dabbing it against her streaming eye. The shock was wearing off, the pain returning, like a hot poker stabbing into her pupil. 'I think you're lying again,' she said, though she couldn't quite remember the last time her daughter had lied. There were no lies in Siân's house. There were fibs, like when Auntie Rhiannon came around in a miniskirt that didn't hide her saggy, orange-peel skin, and they all told her she looked very nice. Siân threw the tissue in the broken pedal bin. 'I don't think James hit you,' she said. 'He's been drumming nonstop. I was listening to him. I think you're after attention again.' Since Griff had gone to Scotland, Angharad had become abnormally clingy, unwilling to let her mother leave the room.

Siân opened the fridge door and glanced over the contents: Chantenay carrots and florets of broccoli stacked neatly in the glass vegetable box. There were six cans of Coca-Cola lined up on the top shelf, faces forward, a gap the width of a centimetre separating each. She placed the tip of her index finger into one of the lovely spaces and ran it along the edge of the cold aluminium. It gave her an immense sense of satisfaction, doing that, knowing something was in order. She had no control over the mountains of clutter in the rest of the house. However early she got up to polish and organize, Griff and the kids were always a step ahead of her; frenzied mounds of greying underwear on the bedroom floor, rowdy torrents of toys jumping out of their numerous toy-boxes. Secretly, she envied Rhiannon, who had lie-ins on Sundays and went for aromatherapy massages in white-walled beauty parlours. What it was, Siân had never had a massage, and God knows she deserved one.

There was half a bottle of Chardonnay next to the huge carton of skimmed milk, something Rhiannon had left behind. Rhiannon made a quick exit whenever the kids were about because Rhiannon hated kids. Siân poured some of the wine into a beaker and lifted it absently to her mouth. 'Come in the living room with Mammy and Niall,' she said, offering Angharad her spare hand.

Angharad leapt to catch it, springing over the tiles as though over some imagined jungle ravine. Siân stood in front of the mirror again and wiped her left eye clean. She reapplied the make-up, sweeping at her lashes with the mascara brush. She popped the top off a brand-new scarlet lipstick.

'What are you doing, chick?' Griff said. He was standing in the doorway, a black silhouette blocking the sunlight from the street. He came into the house, scratching his head with the stem of his van key.

Siân stood still, the red lipstick frozen in mid-air. She wasn't sure how long he'd been there watching her. 'I'm getting ready,' she said, 'for work,' though she knew it was more than that. She'd woken in the morning with a sudden craving to look like a glamorous mother, like the ones she saw every day in the films. It was pressing on her like an iron. There was a time when every man in Aberalaw noticed her. At eighteen she could stroll across the square in a shift dress and a pair of slingbacks and the boys outside the Pump House turned to stone. Only their eyes moved, like the eyes in old oil paintings. Now she could probably run through the town in her nightdress and no one would bat an eyelid. She was 28, but she could have been 82. On her way home from the school she'd nipped into the chemist on the High Street and bought the lipstick. She nearly didn't, because it cost four pounds, and a mouth her size needed a lot of lipstick, but the name of the shade was *Desire*, and that seemed right. 'Did the van pass the MOT?' she said. She ran the colour across her lips quickly, like a tick.

'Yeah,' he said, 'just. I saw Marc in the garage. He was buying a tartan blanket. He said Rhiannon's organizing a picnic on Saturday. He asked me if you'd bring a few things from the takeaway.'

Siân groaned. She'd be able to get *some* things, cold curry samosas and pancake rolls, but she'd need to buy the salad and bread rolls. She'd need to sterilize the plastic Tupperware too. 'Like I haven't got enough to do,' she said.

Griff shrugged, paused, said, 'You don't usually dress up to go to work, do you?' He picked Niall up and held him to his chest, breathing in the yeasty smell of his skin. Angharad slipped her hands around Griff's waist, still vying for some affection. They were a tangle of different-sized limbs, three pairs of the same sea-green eyes, all staring at Siân. She wished the kids had inherited her complexion. They were all freckles and sunburn. In this weather she was always smearing their shoulders with tomato guts because she couldn't afford factor fifteen lotion. They smelled like jars of chutney. She shrugged. 'Just wanted to see what I looked like with lipstick on,' she said.

'You know what you look like with lipstick on,' Griff said. He looked at the lipstick on her mouth and then the lipstick smudge on her glass. 'Is that wine?' he said.

Siân looked at the amber liquid in the glass. It looked like wine.

She knew it was wine but couldn't actually remember pouring it. She ran her tongue around her mouth, tasting it for the first time. 'Yes,' she said, 'it's wine.'

He put Niall on the settee and went into the kitchen, huffing as he brushed past Siân. She heard the breath of the kettle as he switched it on. She followed him and stood in the doorway, a deluge of contempt streaming through her waters as she watched him set two mugs on the counter and spoon instant coffee granules into them, the metal clattering against the china. Whilst attempting domestic chores, he made a lot of mess and a lot of noise, deliberately performing them badly in the hope she'd never ask him to do them again. James was still drumming. Siân whipped the plastic sticks from his hand, waved him into the living room, but he stayed where he was, sitting on the miniature stool, eyes vacant.

'Did I say I wanted coffee?' Siân said, surprised by her own insolence. Typically she would have drunk it, thankful he'd done *something*. But she was angry, in a way she'd never been before. She could feel it swimming around in the pit of her stomach, a fuming cloud of black. She picked a mug up and threw the granules in the sink.

'What's the matter with you?' Griff said, gawping at her. 'You don't even like wine. Are you pregnant again?'

'*Iesu mawr!*' Siân said, which was Welsh for Jesus Christ. 'All you had to say was that I looked nice. I'm not pregnant.' There was a magnificent sense of relief in the words, and in her raised voice. She'd never heard herself shout so loudly. Nobody in the house had. It was magnificently still, the only sound Siân's own harried breathing. She felt more of the boisterous disdain wedged in her throat, fighting its way out. Before she could stop herself, she cried, 'I can't be pregnant, can I? Because I was sterilized! Because you wouldn't get a vasectomy!'

Now there really were no lies in her house. She'd kept it quiet for two years, because she knew it'd break Griff's heart. He wanted as many children as possible; refused point-blank to get seen to, like a stubborn bull who thought his manhood was in his testicles. It was hard work looking after kids, looking after them properly. Two was enough for anyone and she hadn't planned Niall. She fell pregnant again before she had chance to organize contraception after Angharad. She couldn't cope with four, not with two jobs. She was already scuttling about like the beheaded hen she'd seen at her mamgu's farm. Another baby would've killed her. So when they told her she was entitled to tubal ligation she signed their form of consent, out of worry, not spite. Still, the news hit him like an uppercut. He was silent, his hand trembling as he dropped sugar into his mug.

'The doctors advised me to have it,' she said, staring at the floor. 'They said I couldn't provide more than three children with all the financial and emotional support they'd need. I'm not Wonder Woman, am I?' She took a deep breath, disappointed by the last statement because she wanted to be Wonder Woman. 'Anyway, I don't sit in those shops every night, getting ogled by alkies so that you can pay for MOTs and drive around Scotland sleeping with Scottish groupies. I do it for the kids we've got.'

'Siân!' Griff said. 'That money is for us to go to London. It's our big break. Besides,' he glanced sideways at her, 'if you don't want to get looked at, why would you put all that muck on your face?' He gave the kettle a smug grin, pleased with his snappy comeback.

'Piss off,' Siân said, bereft of a clever retort. She passed the drumsticks to James and he took them tentatively, his mouth a big O. She took her bag from the hook behind the door. 'There's curry in the pot,' she said not looking at anyone. On her way out she swigged the last of the repellent wine. She dropped her new lipstick into her handbag.

11

At lunchtime on Saturday, Andy and Ellie were five miles west of Aberalaw, in Pontypridd, the local market town; one high street with a Boots and a Woollies where people from the valley went to buy luxury goods, birthday presents for fussy teenagers, leather shoes for court hearings. Every other week they came, to stare at things they couldn't afford, to spend time. In Marks & Sparks Andy fingered the cuff of a suit jacket, stroking it like money. 'I like this,' he said. Before Ellie had chance to get near it, a middle-aged woman squeezed between them and joined him in his approval, squinting at the buttons over her half-moon spectacles, heaps of plastic bags hunched under her podgy arms. After a minute she seemed to remember that she had no need for a man's suit. Perhaps her husband was dead.

Ellie looked at the jacket. As she did she realized why Andy'd been so eager to get to the men's department, marching in military step towards the formal wear. He was looking for a wedding suit. 'It's OK,' she said, dread gripping her by the buttocks. She moved away from him, along the aisle to look at the silver cuff links. They were all packaged in little blue velvet boxes, one pair fashioned on a spirit level with a bead of purple liquid that swam around inside the transparent vials. Ellie was drawn to sparkle. She liked new, shiny things. At university she'd collected stainless-steel colanders and woks and hung them on the kitchen racks in the St Jude's student house. She liked the way they looked when they caught the morning sun from the patio. She never used them. She never cooked. Her housemates did, and when the utensils burned or grew dull, she threw them away and used her pitiful student loan to buy more, too lazy to set to work with a scouring pad.

'What about this?' he said. He was holding a black shirt with a beige tie knotted around its collar, the whole cellophane package pulled close to his proud chest, his pupils broad like a kid on its first ecstasy pill.

'Beige?' she said, wrinkling her nose. 'I don't think it'd complement my bridesmaids,' though she had no idea what colour her bridesmaids were going to wear. At some point in her life she must have wanted a white satin gown, a pearl-encrusted headdress, a horse-drawn carriage, ice sculptures, cake-toppers, champagne fountains. Most little girls did. But not Ellie, not now; now when she saw a wedding car her instinct was to shout 'Don't do it' at the bride. She'd recently seen an advert for perfume on Andy's big television, a film of a woman sitting at her dressing table on the morning of her wedding day, then cut to the same woman strutting along a catwalk, one silk winkle-picker in front of the other, ear-splitting applause from the crowded auditorium. The voiceover said, 'For the happiest day of her life', or something equally fey. That's all Ellie wanted: a big dress rehearsal. Her appetite for married life had fallen by the wayside; what she wanted was a life.

Outside it was hot, the street thick with the smell of sweat and anti-perspirant. Tarpaulin market stalls lined the road, the Asian traders standing behind clothes racks, arms folded, as adolescent girls jumbled through the stock, their mothers wincing at their choices. All around, shoppers reluctantly handed over dog-eared five-pound notes and walked away with gauzy blue plastic bags. Behind the traditional market, the booths of the French travelling bazaar wound around the corner into Taff Street, the vendors packing wine and olives in brown paper, the tricolour draped behind them, the lower half of the town immersed in the stench of Roquefort like bags of rotting rubbish.

Gangs of teenagers were skateboarding around the tax office, their wheels scraping on the concrete as Andy and Ellie walked back to the car park, cutting through the dilapidated precinct. 'When my mother and father got married they had the reception in their own garden,' Andy said. 'They had to call my mother away from the oven to cut the cake!'

'It's two thousand and three, And!' Ellie said. 'And I'm not your mother. I can't buy a metre of tulle from a fabric stall and conjure it into a veil. It doesn't work like that. Weddings cost a fortune. We could do Route Sixty-six before we put a deposit down on a cold finger buffet. And who wants a cold finger buffet?'

Ynysangharad Park opened up in front of them, the music from the bandstand drifting over to Bridge Street. On summer Saturdays the council provided free entertainment. 'Can't we do that instead?' she said. 'Go travelling? That's a commitment. It's a bonding exercise.'

Andy wasn't listening to her. He was pointing through the railings of the park, at a ginger-haired boy kicking a football against a tree trunk. 'Look!' he said, 'it's James.' He started walking towards the boy, through the ornate park gate. 'Griff must be here somewhere.'

They were *all* there, Griff and Siân, Marc and Rhiannon, Johnny and his girlfriend, on the bank in front of the stage, their bodies propped around a tartan blanket. Johnny was sitting cross-legged, at the edge of the gathering, his messy black ringlets hanging limp between his shoulder blades. His girlfriend was lying next to him, blonde hair fanned out on the ground. Ellie's nerves began to ring, vibrating against her spinal cord; she wondered how he'd got there, without her knowing about it. She tried to swerve towards them, but Andy gripped her wrist, pulling her towards Marc and Rhiannon. She sat down next to her sister-in-law, said, 'What are you doing here? I thought Saturday was your busiest day.'

'Nah,' Rhiannon said. She was wearing a stupid white rah-rah skirt, her hands slotted between her fleshy legs. 'Din't have much on. Kelly's there. Best way to teach urgh is to chuck urgh in at the deep end. She don't listen to a word I bloody say. I deserve some time off, anyway. It's hard work running a top company, El. Not like workin' for someone else.' She grinned; bared the fleck of gold in her molar. It must have had something to do with her, this cosy little set-up. Ellie wanted to ask her outright what Johnny was doing here, but Rhiannon's fat face would curdle as soon as Ellie uttered the first J. She had to wait for the mystery to unfurl of its own accord, or resort to listening to Dai Davies.

'El?' Marc said. He was holding a plastic bag open, presenting her with four cans of lager.

She took one. Andy shook his head, and then by thought association patted his jeans pocket to check his car keys were still there.

'Have some food,' Siân said, waving at the Tupperware boxes. There were salads and chicken kebabs, hot-dog sausages stuffed in fresh finger rolls, a bottle of mustard seed dressing fallen on to its side. Andy picked a salad bowl up and started gnawing at a slice of cucumber. 'Been looking at some outfits for the wedding,' he said as he chewed, a rivulet of juice dripping from his lips.

Ellie rolled her eyes. 'It must have taken you ages to prepare this,' she said, hoping Siân would reveal the origin of the picnic.

Siân shook her head. 'Chan gave me the kebabs last night. I threw the rest of it together this morning.' She packed some of the used Tupperware into a cooler bag, said, 'So did you find anything you liked? There was a wedding at St Illtyd's this morning. I saw it when I was leaving. What it was, the bride in cream, the women in coffee. What colour are you thinking about, El?'

'Yeah, El,' Rhiannon said, flipping on to her belly. She picked up one of James's stray miniature cars and threw it into Siân's cooler bag. 'What colours are ewe 'aving? Tell Auntie Rhi. Bet ewer gonna do somethin' really *unconventional*.'

'No,' Ellie said. She knew she should say something about shoes, rings, jewellery; something that sounded convincing. The last thing she wanted was to give Rhiannon the impression that she didn't want to marry Andy. But she was aware of Johnny sitting mere feet away. Her nerves were still fluttering, cells colliding with one another, pushing microscopic waves of panic through her veins. 'Ivory,' she said, glancing at him. He wasn't listening but she tried to change the subject anyway. She pointed at the stage, said, 'Who's this band, then?'

'The Water Babies,' Griff said. He opened a can, sending a spray of white foam across the grass. 'They're shit. Don't know how they got this contract – probably related to someone from the council. Wait till the Peel session goes on air, El. Fuckin' bunch of Muppets'll be too shamed to show their faces.' He twisted the metal tab from the can and flicked it at Andy.

'Wanna get her off the pill now,' he said, pointing at Ellie. 'Wanna start as soon as you get hitched if you wanna catch up with us. Me 'n' Siân are going for the soccer team.' He looked at Siân but Siân was looking down at the blanket, her eyes fixed on a blue criss-cross in the tartan, her bitten fingers lodged in her mouth. Ellie noticed her lipstick: vermilion red; the colour of blood.

'I'm sure she's pregnant anyway,' Griff said, 'the way she keeps crying in front of films that ain't sad.' He spat a glob of lager on the ground. As he did, the atmosphere changed, the sun sliding behind a cloud.

Johnny stood up, his long, skinny frame stretching into the heavens. Everyone watched as he brushed grass blades from his clothes and stooped to offer his girlfriend his hand. She took it and straightened up, the grey T-shirt that had ridden up her flat torso falling down over her taut waist. For a second, Ellie had spied her belly button, big and hollow, wedged in the centre of a size eight stomach, the colour of an unripe peach. She looked down at her own pierced navel; flesh plump around the steel belly bar. She was a size twelve on a good day.

'Sorry, everyone,' the woman said, gesturing at the food. 'Johnny wants chips so we're just going for a walk into town. We won't be long.' Ellie felt her heart sink, her oesophagus constrict, like someone with a nut allergy who'd just swallowed a whole sugared almond.

Rhiannon sat up. 'There's a good fish shop on Taff Street,' she said. 'Does Clark's pies an' that. Want me to show ewe?'

The couple didn't answer her. They were already on the path leading out of the park, walking shoulder to shoulder, their foot-steps concurrent, like policemen searching for evidence. They were stick figures on the other side of the railings when Griff said, 'Who does he think he is? Arrogant English bastard. There's plenty of food here, but that ain't good enough for him, is it?'

'Fuckin' 'ell, Griff,' Marc said. He was inspecting an elon-gated mustard stain down the front of his Liverpool shirt. 'It doesn't cost anything to be friendly. We only invited 'em because they don't know anyone else. They only just moved here for God's sake. Have some tolerance, will you? We'll keep a welcome an' all that.' He spat into his hand, massaged the saliva into his chest.

Ellie smiled slyly to herself. It was Marc who'd invited Johnny, ergo it was Rhiannon who'd invited Johnny. The cunning cow fancied him herself – that's why she'd made such a hubbub about being in love with Marc. At the Pump House, when Ellie had asked for his name, Rhiannon knew what Ellie was thinking because she was thinking the same thing. Ellie stole a quick peep at her. She was turned towards the railings, looking at the park gate, a nervous hum skimming out of her curvilinear lips. She was waiting for him to come back.

Griff ripped a grass stalk out of a big clump growing next to him, threw the wheat-coloured seeds on the breeze. 'You don't know what it's going to cost yet,' he said. 'He could be a fuckin' yardie for all we know. Dai said—'

'Yardies don't come from Cornwall,' Rhiannon said, cutting him off. She kicked him in the ribs, showing everyone her black lace M&S knickers. 'Bloody thicko! 'Ey come from Jamaica.' Griff stared at her for a moment, but said nothing. He turned to look at the stage.

The band had already finished. The only sound was of children splashing and screaming, the noises from the swimming pool reverberating across the park.

Exactly eight minutes later, eight minutes that seemed to go on for eight years, Johnny came back, creeping towards the gathering like an insect on its stick legs. The girlfriend sat next to Siân. Johnny sat next to Ellie, his thighs hitched up to his chest, a polystyrene tray balanced on his kneecaps. While he'd been gone, the fire in her nerves had waned, but the moment he sat down it instantly came roaring back. Her heart pumped so fast she was sure everyone could see it, pounding against her ribcage, pushing the material of her blouse out, then pulling it back in again. She held her breath and watched from the corner of her eye as he lifted the chips to his mouth and shoved them inside, one after the other, chewing them regimentally. He caught her eye and held the tray up, offering her one.

Ellie shook her head and turned away. There was an anti-war demonstration trampling along the path on the other side of the park, fifty-odd people holding handmade placards aloft. 'No More Blood for Oil,' one said. As long as she could feel his awesome gaze on her face, she kept her eyes fixed on the demo.

'You ever heard of the petro-dollar?' he said as he put the

polystyrene tray down on the ground. Ellie shook her head again, colour rushing to her face. She was so tense her jaw had locked. She was incapable of speech.

'The petro-dollar is the cause of this war,' he said. 'Oil from the OPEC countries is always paid for in American dollars, right? So if Japan needs oil it needs to get some Yankee dollar.' Ellie couldn't quite meet his stare. He was something to look at: run-of-the-mill face and infolded lips, but large iron-oxide-black eyes, darker than carbon. She couldn't understand a word he was saying for being fixed by those strange eyes. She quickly swallowed the well of saliva building up in her mouth and it went down like double-edged razor blades. 'So to get American dollars,' he said, 'Japan needs to sell goods to the American economy. Let's say it sells them a Honda, right? The Federal Reserve prints dollars and gives them to Japan.'

As he spoke, Ellie could feel the warmth of his shoulder against the hot flesh of her cheek, his height was cosseting her; setting butterflies free in her tummy. Nobody had talked to her about anything she cared about since the day she'd left Plymouth. He was supposed to be a drug dealer, a comprehensive school drop-out with a string of petty convictions and a frothy-mouthed pit bull terrier. But he knew what Ellie was thinking. A chord plucked in her stomach.

'When Iraq decided it was going to start selling oil in euros, Uncle Sam did his nut.' He reached into his pocket, took a packet of cigarettes out. 'Notice how the first thing the troops did was secure ownership of the oil wells?' he said. He lit a cigarette and passed it to Ellie. She took it with trembling fingers and watched as he lit one for himself, the Zippo's flame dancing in the wind. She took a long drag on the cigarette, filling her lungs with the delicious nicotine.

'That's the first thing they did,' she said as she exhaled, 'stole the Iraqis' oil.'

70

'Hang a banger, mush,' Rhiannon trilled. 'Let's chill out a bit, is it? Who's gonna do a joint? We don't talk about politics round 'ere.' She took a lump of pot out of her bag and tried to pass it to Johnny. Johnny looked blankly at Rhiannon and then turned back to Ellie. 'It's tantamount to a war crime,' he said.

Rhiannon's mouth had fallen open, a hunk of violet tongue perched on her bottom lip. For a fraction of a second it looked as if she was going to cry. She said, 'Fuck ewe 'en,' her whole face turning into a snarl. She rummaged through her bag, looking for fag-papers. Under her breath she said, 'I'll do it my fuckin' self.'

'Have you finished that can, babe?' Andy said, tapping Ellie's leg. 'Because I've got to go, I've got the car.' He might have sensed the malice in the atmosphere, but more than likely was offended by the mention of cannabis. He wouldn't condone drug use in a public place, not in a children's park. Ellie wanted to stay, but any excuse she made would sound suspicious. She shook her lager can, realizing she'd finished it without noticing. He took it out of her hand and threw it in a black bag that Siân had reserved for the group's litter. He took Ellie's hand and lifted her up. Her body felt weightless, as if it wasn't a body, but a soul, cleaving away from its carcass, leaving its shell on the ground.

'See you,' Johnny said, disappointed. 'See you again.'

'Bye then, El,' Rhiannon said, waving at her, the bracelets on her wrist jangling. She was jovial now, dimples forming in her chubby cheeks as Andy towed Ellie away from the gathering. But for a moment she'd been rattled.

A spark of peppery rapture warmed Ellie's belly as she realized that Rhiannon had been jealous of *her*.

12

Wednesday morning. Rhiannon was on her way to the salon when she saw the French market setting up on the High Street. One of the trestle-tables was covered in little cloth bags, markers sticking out of the top of them with the names of spices written in fancy joined-up script; *Turmeric, Paprika, Oregano*. She'd heard the words on cookery programmes on the telly but she didn't know what they were for. Siân would have known; Siân made her own sponge cakes instead of buying them from Kwik Save. She used real flour and icing sugar, even made her own bloody gravy. But if you gave her a penny for her thoughts you'd get change back. She spent too much time in the house, trying to be Delia bloody Smith, toddlers hanging around her feet. She should have been out in the real world, in the company of adults. She bit her finger-nails, a disgusting habit in a grown woman. In fact, she bit them until they bled. If she ever went to the cosmetic section in Boots she'd realize you could buy a packet of French manicured falsies for a fiver. Rhiannon wished *she* had the time to hang around in her kitchen, working out how the garlic got into the middle of a chicken Kiev. She was too bloody busy. A bloody businesswoman, she was.

A man on one of the stalls was arranging bread rolls; white knots of dough, tiny green specks sticking to them. She could tell he was French from a mile off. His skin was blue-white. Welshmen had red skin, fat cauliflower ears and tattoos. There was a scratcher in Ystradyfodwg who'd write 'Art by Jim' on your arse cheek for a quid. Marc had something on his shoulder. She'd never paid much attention to what it actually was. Rhiannon didn't like tattoos. Her father didn't have any tattoos; said they were too much of a giveaway in a robbery situation. The man stopped working to stare at Rhiannon's tits. She pressed them together and winked at him. They bloody cost her enough, why shouldn't she show them off? 'Ooh lah lah,' she said as she walked toward the shop. She'd never banged a Frog. She did a Spic once on her honeymoon in Lanzarote. She'd caught herpes off the dirty sod. Cut a long story, they did it on the beach, behind a cocktail bar, while Bob Stone was in the treatment room having a pedicure. All he wanted to do was hang around in the spa getting holistic massages, listening to dolphin noises. Poof probably. A girl deserves some time with a man who can get it up on her bloody honeymoon.

It's not like Rhiannon was a slut, like her mother, or a prostitute who stood next to the Custom House in Cardiff, like some people from the estate she could mention. But there was a bit of you-scratch-my-back, because with her head for business it didn't take her long to realize that most men would shell a couple of grand for the sniff of a warm snatch. She'd only fucked that Spaniard for fun, she didn't do it for money again after she married Bob Stone; didn't need to. He was rolling in it, had a five-bedroom semi-detached in the Vale of Glamorgan, wore diamonds in his shirt-cuffs, bought her a red Alfa Romeo Spider for her twenty-first birthday and didn't even want any nooky, just wanted to talk about birds all bloody night: sparrows, buzzards, goldcrests, red kites. She could see his face now, grey eyes screwing out of his wrinkles. The old bastard had to be getting on for a hundred and he still hadn't fucking died. She couldn't marry Marc until he died and even then she'd have to think about it. The Alfa was old now, covered in scratches. Some jealous fucker from the estate sneaked down to Chepstow Road once a month to key it across the bonnet. And Marc couldn't afford to buy her a new Porsche Boxster.

Kelly was standing on the salon doorstep, mobile phone in one hand, fag in the other. She had an orange tidemark around her hairline where she hadn't blended her foundation in properly. Myra, Dai Davies's ex-wife, was wearing a woollen cardigan, flaps of leathery skin hanging from her jowls, coughing like a machine gun.

Rhiannon opened the door. 'Ewe shouldn' be smokin' in front of the shop,' she said, pushing Kelly inside. 'We're trynna attract professionals.' She directed Myra into the chair in front of the washbasin. 'Cuppa tea for the lady, is it?' she said.

'I don't mind a cup of tea,' Myra said, pulling a strip of toilet tissue from the sleeve of her cardigan. 'But I'll have none of that bastard French stuff from over there. Got a cheek coming here with their cappabloodychinno's or whatever the hell they're called.'

Rhiannon fastened an overall around her neck.

Myra wagged her craggy finger. 'Too high and mighty to eat our beef but it's OK for them to park up over there and sell their disease-ridden cheese. Gets on my tits it does. They're worse than the bastard Eng—'

The wind chimes jingled as the salon door opened. Louisa was standing on the welcome mat, her tiny eyes darting around the shop. Rhiannon waited for Johnny to appear. The last time she'd seen him was at Ponty Park. He was talking about the oil prices in America, Ellie gazing up at him, fluttering her eyelashes like a little fucking girl. Stupid cunt thought she was in with a chance, him talking to her like that. As fuckin' if. Rhiannon had dibs on Johnny: she'd seen him first, selling drugs on the square. She'd never forget the way he first looked at her, like he'd wanted to rip her clothes off, and do her right there on the pavement. After a moment she realized Johnny wasn't with Louisa. 'On ewer own, are ewe, love?' she said.

Louisa flicked her hair out of her eyes. 'I want my roots done,' she said, voice all English. 'Would I need to make an appointment?'

'Don't be silly!' Rhiannon pointed at the hydraulic chair and walked Louisa to it, leaving Myra at the washbasin. She took a comb and began to brush through her long blonde locks. 'Shame ewe din't bring ewer old man with ewe,' she said, shivering as she imagined herself touching Johnny's scalp. She looked at Louisa's face through the giant mirror, yellowy skin, cheeks dotted with blackheads and moles. 'Iss an 'airdresser thing it is, love. We can't bear seein' men with long 'air.'

She started mixing the bleach, stirring the lilac powder into the cream until it turned to a thick paste. 'See that?' she said, showing Louisa the peroxide bottle, pointing at the label. 'Specially designed for pastel toning and colour baths, best stuff on the market, costs a bloody small fortune. Bring ewer roots up a treat, it will, go with ewer blue eyes.' She snatched the bottle back, before Louisa saw the Proctor & Gamble emblem at the base. She parted her hair with the tip of the highlighting brush. 'Love to 'ave eyes like ewers, I would,' she said. 'A boy at school told me once that lookin' into a brown eye is like lookin' into an arsehole.' She didn't tell her that she'd provoked him, stabbed him in the shoulder with the point of a compass. 'Not very nice, is it?'

'No, that's not very nice,' Louisa said. 'I think brown eyes are handsome.'

'Came from my father,' Rhiannon reached for a strip of foil. 'Dead now, he is.' She peeped at Louisa, trying to gauge the amount of sympathy she'd managed to generate, but Louisa was staring down at her knees. She looked like a Daddy's girl, one of those toffee-nosed English bastards who had a pony in a stable. It was easy to be sophisticated if you had a father who cared about you.

Cut a long story, Rhiannon's was murdered in 1974, beaten to death by his cell-mate over a packet of tobacco he'd hidden in his mattress. He was the only fucker on the estate who gave a shit about her. Her mother didn't. Rhiannon's first memory was of robbing Christmas trimmings with him when she was four years old. He had the keys to the decoration factory, had a temporary job there. She remembered sitting on his shoulders, her pink dolly-bar shoes dangling down his chest as he threw packets of baubles into a black bag. They were the same ones she had to make at Myra's table when she was thirteen. She still had one of them in a box under her bed. At Christmas she put it on the top of the tree. Every year, the dusty smell of trimmings coming down from the attic reminded her of her father running away from the factory, the dead blackberry bushes behind the warehouse coated in ice, the winter sun turning the frost into millions of white gemstones. He'd still be alive if her mother hadn't pressured him into the post-office job. He wanted to go straight but she couldn't live without her fur coats and Cognac. Rhiannon heard them having arguments about it at night.

Louisa lifted her head. 'I'm sorry to hear that,' she said.

'Oh, love,' Rhiannon said. 'It's not ewer bloody fault.' She brushed some of the mixture along one of the hair shafts and fastened the foil together. 'How're ewe settling in anyway? What part of Aber are ewe in?'

'On the square,' Louisa said, 'by the pub. We've bought an old block of flats. Johnny's been tarting the place up. It was atrocious when we got there, but we got a bargain. We paid with cash.' She looked away from the mirror, as if scared of the sight of herself.

'The YMCA?' Rhiannon said. 'No shit, Siân's husband used to live by there! It's about time ewe had an 'ousewarming do, innit? I wanna see ewer old man's 'andiwork. That place was a bomb site the last time I saw it.' She twisted Louisa's remaining locks of hair into a coil and pinned it with a bulldog clip. The neck underneath was as thin as a pipe cleaner. She could have fitted one hand around it and strangled her in a minute. Everything about Louisa was small. She looked like a little elf. 'Shouldn't be too long now, love,' Rhiannon said. 'Twenty minutes and we'll wash ewe off.'

Kelly had washed Myra's hair. She was sitting at the workstation waiting for it to be styled. Rhiannon squeezed a marble-sized ball of mousse into her palm, waited for it to grow to the size of an orange and then slapped it down on her crown. Myra spluttered into her toilet tissue, wriggling as she pushed it back into her cardigan cuff. 'What part of England is she from?' she said, tossing her head in Louisa's direction. 'She wants to be ashamed of herself coming here, buying our property. They wouldn't have this in the North, see? Burn it down, they would, with her inside it. There ain't nothing wrong with protecting your territory. More of that we need.'

Myra had married Dai because she was impressed with an arson conviction he had for setting light to a Cardiff mosque. Before that she'd been married to a KKK wizard from Ponty and her kids were all Combat 18. Rhiannon glanced at Louisa sitting in the waiting area, face buried in one of the magazines, legs crossed too tight, and then at Kelly who was waiting for a glimpse of the postman she wanted to shag, face pressed against the plate-glass window.

'Shut up, Myr,' Rhiannon said. 'Cornwall she's from. Iss not in England, iss in Wales, Ellie told me. She knows, she's got a bloody degree. All ewe've ever done is sat in that Ystradyfodwg bingo hall, listening to gossip.' She poked the butt of the tongs between Myra's shoulder blades. 'And she says there's no such thing as a border, says people can go wherever they want. She's going to New York when the band makes it.'

'Huh,' Myra said, 'fat chance of that.'

Rhiannon sprayed her head with a thick cloud of lacquer,

deliberately aiming some of it into her crinkly eyes. The best form of defence is attack. When, after her third cup of tea, Myra left, Rhiannon made a sly V-shape with her fore- and middle finger, pointed it at the back of her head.

'Ewe don't wanna listen to her, Lou,' she said, beckoning Louisa into the now empty seat. 'She's a tough old bitch. Most people round yere are lovely.' Louisa giggled sheepishly and sat down on the revolving stool. It took twenty minutes to blow-dry her hair, the drone of the hairdryer preventing any conversation. 'There ewe are, love,' Rhiannon said when she'd finished. She patted Louisa's shoulder. Louisa glanced in the mirror and nodded. She rummaged about in her corduroy handbag and pulled out two twenty-pound notes. 'How much do I owe you?' she said, voice all English.

'No!' Rhiannon said, slapping her hand away. She watched the purple paper slip back into the bag and she walked Louisa to the door. 'Remember the 'ousewarming party,' she said, the chimes ringing above them. 'I'll bring a bottle or ten.'

Louisa waved timidly and started walking towards the stalls of the French market. Rhiannon moved to the window and watched until she'd disappeared behind a tarpaulin. 'Why didn't you charge her?' Kelly said, joining Rhiannon at the window. 'I've never seen you do that before. Was she a health inspector?'

'Because!' Rhiannon said. She noticed the shape of a human face printed on the glass with Kelly's greasy tangerine-coloured make-up. 'Iss none of ewer business. Clean this off here, NOW. And wash Myra's cup out, and wash her overall as well. And do me a cup of tea. I'm bloody knackered. And blend ewer foundation in properly. Ewe look like a fuckin' baked bean.'

13

It was the middle of August and most of the operatives from the Ceramics department were away on their summer holiday. The sun burned through a hole in the roof of the ramshackle unit. It was too hot to work. Safia was filing her nails with an emery board, her fingers spread out on her desk. One of the advantages of being in the decal division was having good fingernails: the calcium in the girls' glue troughs turned keratin to fibreglass.

'Andy wants to book a date for the wedding,' Ellie said, opening her drawer.

Safia looked up at her, caramel face warped with a triumphant smile. 'When?' she said, breathlessly. 'Does your sister know yet?'

Ellie glanced at Jane. She was sitting at the manager's desk, writing something on a piece of paper. Ellie shook her head, discouraging ostentatious announcements. 'February,' she said, whispering. 'He's got his mother doing the sandwiches, his auntie doing the cake. It's a nightmare, Saf.' She took two Maltesers out of her packet and slid one across the desk.

Safia picked it up with a frown. 'Whassamatter?' she said. 'Yous been engaged to him for months. You knew what was coming.'

The printer whirred, the noise vibrating across the factory floor. 'I'm not ready yet,' Ellie shouted. Safia knew nothing of Ellie's fixation with Johnny, or her growing dissatisfaction with Andy. As far as Safia was concerned, Ellie had a perfect life; she'd never mentioned her overbearing in-laws or any resentment of Andy's cringing trepidation, and it was all too much to explain in one go.

Safia's predicament was worse, of course. Her elder brother was trying to arrange a marriage for her. He stood to inherit the family four-bedroom and he didn't want her left there when he did. He was ashamed of his sister because she worked in a factory and wore make-up, like a common white girl. By the time his ship rolled in he'd have her hitched to an Urdu-speaking computer analyst. 'Any news on your wedding?' Ellie said.

Safia's face turned sour. 'It's not funny,' she said.

'I didn't say it was.' Ellie had only broached the subject to make herself feel better. 'You don't have to marry anyone you don't want to,' she said, continuing in an attempt to repair the damage her flippancy had caused. 'You can contest his choice. I did a course about it at university. "Feminism and Culture: Theoretical Perspectives from Postcoloniality to Psychoanalysis".'

Safia loaded her trolley with a tray of mugs and wheeled it out into the aisle. 'Contest your choice then, El,' she said as she walked away.

That night Ellie worked an hour overtime, watching the clock behind Jane's desk. She was meeting The Needles in town at half past seven, interviewing them for the cover's feature. The radio was stammering quietly in the background, the cloying heat sticking to her skin. Gavin's phone rang and she turned around, remembering him.

'The Mrs,' he said, shrugging. He pressed a button, rejecting the call.

'How do you cope, Gav?' Ellie said. 'Living with a woman you don't love?'

Gavin threw his phone in his bag and turned the print machine off. 'There's no such thing as love, El,' he said. He peeled his T-shirt from his sweat-damp chest and threw it into his makeshift locker. 'Perhaps there is for a woman, but not for a man. A man needs a woman to do his cooking and his cleaning and he goes for the one who loves him most, because that's the one who'll do the best job. I could go out tonight and find me the best-looking bird in Cardiff, but she wouldn't be any good at doing my sandwiches in the morning; she'd just treat me like shit.' He took a fresh T-shirt out of the bag and put it on. 'See you in the morning,' he said, throwing the bag over his shoulder. Ellie smiled, impressed with his ability to not want what he didn't already have.

At seven o'clock she stood in front of the vindictive mirror in the women's toilet and checked her clothes for glue stains. She folded her T-shirt and tabard into neat squares and left them on top of her desk. The city was restful, the last of the rush-hour buses crawling back to the suburbs. The woman from the café on the Hayes was stacking chairs and carrying them into her hut. The members of The Needles had already arrived at the bar. Bleddyn Griffiths, the front man whom Ellie recognized, was sitting in the centre of a small gathering of men, bottles of beer fixed to their faces. She waved and rushed inside. It had been a while since she'd orchestrated a band interview and she was nervous. She never used to be, she used to be cocksure. But she'd spent so long living in the valley, working in a factory; she'd learned to hide her aspirations and get along with the brain-dead. Act like a dumbshit and they'd treat you like an equal. She glanced around the room, at the crimson walls dotted with miniature batiks, the polished wood floor. Two luminous yellow posters in the windows said: ALL SHOTS **FREE** FOR WOMEN WEARING SKIRTS. The barman cracked the top from her bottle. She scrambled through her purse for change, her fingers trembling.

She walked to the table and the men moved, making space to let her in. She shook their hands and took their names, forgetting them as soon as she'd moved on to the next. There were five of them in all: softly spoken west Walians. 'I heard they're re-issuing the first two albums?' Ellie said. It was something she'd read by chance in a day-old copy of the *Echo* left on the train. She didn't have access to the Internet or the microfilm she had once used at the office; she couldn't do any real research.

Bleddyn put his bottle down. 'They're out of print in the UK. Kids are buying Japanese imports for twenty or thirty quid. It's about time really.' He picked a wooden cocktail stick out of the cruet set and stabbed an olive, directing it into his mouth.

'Tell me about the new album,' Ellie said, pulling her notepad out of her bag.

'It's not like anything we've ever done before. It's got a harmonium, an orchestra and even a trumpet on some tracks. We recorded most of it in a tiny studio in Andalusia, and you can hear the Spanish influence in the sound. We even had siestas in the afternoons, absorbed the whole *mañana* culture.'

As he spoke, Ellie scribbled his words on to her page. Her questions were hackneyed and his answers were glib. Fifteen minutes into the interview, she became more interested in the world going on on the other side of the window than with the experiences of the Welsh celebrities sitting around her table. Eventually one of the men ordered a round of tequila. 'What about it?' he said, nudging Ellie, as if sensing her agitation. The barman carried two trays to the table, holding them in the air above each shoulder, six shot glasses balancing on one, six lime quarters on the other. He took the salt-cellar from his shirt pocket and knocked it on the table.

Bleddyn poured some into the webbing linking his thumb and index finger. '*Barod?*' he said, talking in Welsh.

Ellie knew that it meant 'Ready?' There was a girl from north Wales at Plymouth University who used to say it as they left the toilets of a club, quickly smudging their lip-gloss in the mirror, preparing for another session on the dance-floor. Ellie couldn't speak Welsh. Amid the coal boom, the mine-owners had demolished all the Welsh-language schools, and any kids caught talking their own language got the Welsh knot, a big wooden pendant tied round their neck, designed to humiliate them into accepting the lingua franca. Now the valleys were a cultural no-man's-land, derided by England for being Welsh and reviled by the rest of Wales for being too English. Siân could speak a bit of Welsh, though. Her mother was from Carmarthen. That's how her father got away with beating her to a pulp; her mother didn't have anyone she could tell. She didn't make any friends in Aberalaw because the people in Aberalaw didn't like outsiders; they started rumours about her being a practitioner of the occult.

Ellie swallowed the drink, the scorching sensation travelling from her oesophagus to her gut. Defying Andy's petty rules about alcoholism felt like a little victory, the heady combination of rebellion and liquor making her feel instantly drunk. Bleddyn wiped his lips with a paper serviette and lifted his empty glass, waving it at the barman.

'Who are we going to offer this tour slot to?' one of the other men said, playing with the salt. The question was for Bleddyn, but Ellie picked her pen up. 'What's this?' she said as the barman arrived at the table dispensing fresh shot glasses.

'Oh, we're touring this album in Europe in the spring,' Bleddyn said. 'The management want us to support local up-and-coming talent. That's fashionable now. But I don't listen to any other Welsh music. I want a Spanish guitar band.'

'Have you ever heard of The Boobs?' Ellie said. 'They're a punk band from the valleys. They're doing really well at the moment. They've got a Radio One session soon with John Peel.'

'I've heard of them!' one of the men said.

'Do you know them?' Bleddyn said.

'Kind of.' Ellie could feel herself blushing but there was no trace of the telltale pink stains in her reflection in the window. It was an idea she'd carelessly blurted out, but now she was realizing its significance. Securing a support slot for The Boobs on The Needles' European tour would mean postponing her and Andy's wedding. She'd be alone in the house for a few months, with Johnny-Come-Lately living just around the corner. It'd be like killing three birds with one rock. She smiled at her ingenuity.

'Send us one of their demos then,' Bleddyn said, brushing her off.

Ellie nodded. 'So,' she said, squinting at her notepad, pressing the nib of her pen on the paper, 'do you think your solo project has had a negative effect on the rest of the band?'

After the interview she took a short cut back to the station, ambling through the crowds in Caroline Street. The kebab spits were starting up for the night. A pisshead in a pastel shirt was urinating on the doorstep of the Blue Banana, singing 'What's New Pussycat?' to himself. At the junction she saw a man with a scruffy ponytail hanging down his back and her thoughts turned again to Johnny. It was twenty days and counting since he'd turned up, and after alcohol her infatuation grew to the size of a blue whale, ate any other thoughts in her head.

'Excuse me?' she said, confidence buoyed by tequila, and the possibility of getting rid of Andy for a few months. The man turned around to face her, but it wasn't Johnny. 'Sorry,' she said sourly. 'I was hoping you were someone else.'

14

Andy and Ellie were on their way home from the potato stall in Ystradyfodwg Market, the back of the truck loaded with the monthly sack of Maris Pipers they split with Andy's parents. At the traffic lights at the end of the town, Andy turned left and reversed up Ellie's mother's drive.

'What are you doing?' Ellie said. She could see the front of the awful house, the red door ajar, evening sunlight reflecting in the brass screw-on number 2. She squinted at the garish net curtain, trying not to imagine what was going on inside.

'Don't go mad,' Andy said. He took a deep breath and released his seatbelt. 'I want to ask your father for your hand in marriage.' He held his palm aloft in an effort to forestall Ellie's barrage of dissent. 'I know you'll think it's chauvinistic but I want to do it properly. It's only manners, common courtesy. I want to get things off on the right foot.'

One of the kids ran out of the house next door, its scream reverberating along the lane, its mother chasing it with a studded football shoe. Ellie sneered as she pushed herself out of the truck. She clenched her fist and rapped on the front window, knuckles white and taut. 'You're so wide of the mark it's actually *embarrassing*,' she said, hissing as she pushed the door open.

Ellie's mother and two sisters were sitting around the television, watching the National Lottery, roaring in time with the canned applause, hair as blonde as Nordics. By the clock on the mantel-piece it was three fifteen. It had always been three fifteen in that living room, the grooves in the velour sofa trapping the smell of boiled vegetables and laundry. 'Hello,' her mother said. It was more of a question than a greeting. She was looking sideways at Ellie, her eyes tight slits, the crow's feet pressing out. Andy sat between Sarah and Jane. They simultaneously crossed their legs, pointing their knees away from him. Ellie stood in the centre of the room, fists clenched. 'Is my father here?' she said, the word rusty on her tongue. 'Andy wants to ask him something.'

'No, Elizabeth,' her mother said. 'You know he goes to the Biz Club on a Wednesday.'

Ellie hadn't been near the place for two years. She didn't know anything. Apart from a vague recollection of the faint veining of grey in his hair, she couldn't remember what her father looked like. 'Andy wanted to tell him that we're getting married,' she said. She enjoyed the admission more than she'd thought she would. It was probably the only instance in which she would get any fulfilment out of it. Her mother had thrown her out of the house for taking Andy there on the day she'd interviewed The Boobs. Nobody saw him go in. Ellie'd sneaked him up the spiral stair-case, avoiding the creaks on the third and penultimate treads. But the whole house heard their lovemaking, the single headboard flapping repetitively against the crumbling plaster.

Her mother was gardening when Ellie let Andy out of the house the following morning. She waited until he'd turned the corner at the end of the lane and then called Ellie a slut. 'You're no daughter of mine,' she said, stabbing her trowel into the earth, 'and your arse is getting fat.'

Ellie had packed a bag and followed Andy to Aberalaw. They'd lived in Gwynnie and Collin's before they found the house in Gwendolyn Street. With her ire, her mother had inadvertently turned what would have been a one-off, one-night stand into an eighteen-month engagement. Now Ellie had vindicated herself.

'You're not pregnant are you?' Jane said, before quickly clapping her hand over her mouth. Her comment wasn't meant to be offensive, but it clearly revealed the contempt in which she held Ellie. She was thinking about the factory and its health and safety regulations. Ellie had signed a disclaimer agreeing to report pregnancy immediately. Compounds in the adhesives were detrimental to unborn foetuses, and Jane took her job too seriously, stalking around the workshop, management ID card clipped to her suit jacket. In her spare time she read textbooks about printing and organized the production schedules. At work, the closest she'd come to nepotism was to ask Ellie, one idle lunchtime, for a look at her magazine. She thought it was *Cosmopolitan* and she wanted to see Jennifer Lopez's wedding dress. When she realized it was the *NME* she apologized and walked away.

The way they conducted themselves at the factory was nothing more than a continuation of their behaviour at home. Since they were teenagers they'd ignored each other because dialogue never failed to morph into physical violence. Their periods didn't synchronize, like most sisters'. When Ellie opened the bathroom cupboard, tens of boxes of tampons and pots of eye-gel came spilling out. Blood and tears, that's what that house had been full of.

'Of course I'm not pregnant,' Ellie said. 'He's marrying me because he *wants* to, in February, in Saint Illtyd's.' Why she felt the need to lie about the church she wasn't sure. They hadn't discussed venues yet.

Ellie's mother sat up and turned her reading lamp on. 'You didn't want to borrow money off him, did you?' she said, the question landing on Andy.

Andy scratched his leg and stared at the worn carpet. 'No, Mrs Evans,' he said. 'We'll pay for the wedding ourselves. My family are going to help out where they can. We just wanted to let you know, invite you properly . . .' His speech trailed off pathetically.

Ellie stormed out, fighting the urge to slam the door behind her. She waited for Andy on the concrete path, staring insolently at the face of the house. A dead string of ivy hung like a reptile's tail from her mother's windowbox. Her fists were still clenched. When Andy appeared she waved them at him. 'I can't believe you made me do that.' She stomped to the truck, the sound of her sisters' laughter ringing again in her ears. 'She's not even my mother! He's not even my father!'

And they weren't.

Ellie was adopted. When she was ten, Jane had told her that her real father was a drunken Irish man with no teeth. That he'd gone to jail for stealing whiskey. That her mother was a drug-addled prostitute from Cardiff Docks. That they were coming back for her as soon as the man escaped. That they were taking her on a ship to Dublin where they were going to sell shoe polish out of a broken pram. Ellie had imagined that she was the secret love child of Shirley Bassey and Shane McGowan.

On her thirteenth birthday, her mother had called her into the master bedroom and patted a space on the pink bedspread. Ellie approached it tentatively, knowing somehow that what her mother was about to say would irrevocably change her life. Her real parents were too young to cope with a baby like Ellie, she explained, a baby who constantly demanded attention with her big kissy mouth and too-long legs. Ellie's mother wanted her children in a clump, all at once, like a litter of puppies. After Jane there was no rumbling in her tummy. Impatient, she picked Ellie, two years old, like a fresh cauliflower from a grocer's rack. The day they'd brought her home Ellie had broken the Betamax video, trying to feed it a biscuit, and five years later Sarah was born.

She'd never looked at Ellie any differently, her mother said, any differently to Jane and Sarah; even though Ellie was hyperactive.

Ellie knew it was a fib or she wouldn't have had to say it; she could still remember her mother's pointed fingernails clawing into the cotton as she lied through her stupid teeth, Ellie nodding beseechingly like the urchin she was.

Even before Jane had started with the rumour-mongering, Ellie had guessed that something was wrong. In the summer when she was seven, she'd been sitting next to a sandpit in her grandparents' garden, playing with her grandmother's nail polish, painting a gnome an unsuitable crimson colour when Jane came around the corner with Sarah in her pushchair. Jane's fists were stuck to the handles with caramelized sugar, one white sock up, the other down, her dress tucked into her knickers. She was ramming the pushchair against a brick, her strength not enough to go over it, her sense not enough to go around it, the baby wobbling all over the place. 'You don' know your times-tables,' she said, glancing at Ellie. 'We do, don't we S'ah?' She started to chant the twos, stopping eventually at twenty.

Sarah was so impressed that her tremendous smile shone through the melted chocolate smeared all over her face. She picked a dandelion, handing it ceremoniously to Jane.

Numbers were Ellie's Achilles heel, but everyone in the Evans family was mathematically adept. After work her father sat at the dining table copying figures into his accounts book, running his fingers through his fringe after every three zeros. Her mother was a pharmacist who sat in the dusty back room of the chemist's, counting and noting every pill that fell into a brown plastic bottle, and at night Ellie heard Jane count and separate her copper coins, the dull clunk of their weight tapping on her bedside table. Ellie couldn't add eight and eight together. However many of her drawings or stories the primary school teacher put up on the classroom wall, her mother still grimaced when on Saturday she took her daughters to buy gobstoppers in Ystradyfodwg Spar and Ellie was always a few pence short.

At fourteen she gave up trying to figure the whole sorry mess out. She still stared at people in supermarkets, examining the shapes of their faces, squinting behind their earlobes for evidence of a small brown mole, like hers. She watched contestants on game shows and wondered if they were her cousin or her brother, a hot prickle shooting through her solar plexus when there was a resemblance. She thought she needed to know something about her real family, to know who she was. But she wouldn't ask Jane where the shoplifting story had originated, would not give her the satisfaction. Besides, Ellie didn't want to meet those people. They had to be arseholes, whoever they were, giving their own kid up like that.

One Boxing Day, Ellie's mother found the heads of Sarah's Barbie dolls hanging from the ash tree in the garden, tied to the skeletal branches by their long white hair. The bodies were buried under shingle and mulch, glitter-caked gowns dappled with brown mud, nothing but orange pegs between their plastic shoulders. Ellie didn't remember doing it, but they assumed it was her. They sent her to a counsellor in Pontypridd, an obese cherry-haired woman who specialized in adoption cases. Every fortnight for four years Ellie spent an hour sitting in her L-shaped office, staring at the taupe walls, the woman insisting that Ellie was a good girl who was only trying to be bad, Ellie maintaining that she was trying to be good, but was, deep down, intrinsically bad. At first, she did it for argument's sake, but after a year of the futile rhetoric, the tedious to-ing and fro-ing, she began to believe herself.

She dealt with her lack of identity by rubbishing all of the values the Evans family tried to implant. Every Saturday there was a visit to a farm shop in Brecon to buy meat for the Sunday roast, so Ellie became a vegetarian. Jane left school at sixteen to start work, so Ellie made a very special effort to go to university. Ellie's father had friends in the Welsh Conservative Party, so Ellie joined the student Labour movement. Jane didn't have boyfriends, or at least she didn't bring them home, so obviously Ellie did. Everything Ellie was, was founded on everything her adoptive family were not.

'I told you, didn't I?' she said, as she hauled herself up into the cab. 'You think you're doing the right thing but you don't know what the right thing is. Not everyone is like you, Andy. Not everyone's family is happy.' She lit a cigarette.

Andy ignored her wrath. He smiled at her. 'Hey, fag-ash Lil,' he said, pointing at the window. 'This is my old man's truck, remember? He'll die if he knows you've been smoking.' He put the key in the ignition and stared at the windscreen, said, 'You could be happy if you tried. You don't try, El. You don't even speak to your sister at work.'

Ellie was silent, never talked about her childhood for fear of ridicule, though she knew most people had guessed. She knew Gwynnie and Collin talked about her behind her back, the way they talked about Rhiannon. Because it was all speculation, they had no idea about the reality of the situation. They thought Ellie should be grateful for having been claimed at such a young age, but that was exactly what gripped her balls. She'd been lied to, made to believe she belonged somewhere, but the belonging had gradually unravelled. Her relatives were a pretence; a beautifully wrapped gift box, empty inside. She didn't want to be part of anybody's family – not her real one, her joking one; not even her in-laws'. She definitely didn't want her own family. Family was for people who didn't have their own lives.

Andy had asked her once if she wanted children and she'd said yes. She knew that was what he wanted to hear. They'd just moved into Gwendolyn Street and Ellie was trying to please him. But she didn't want children, not here in the valley where their father would be a feeble painter and decorator, their grandparents over-powering and ignorant; a place where talking about your own personal problems was anathema but talking about other people's was a form of entertainment. Ellie wanted American children, who sat in strollers and hollered, ate peanut-butter sandwiches at picnics in Central Park. But Andy wanted Welsh children. Welsh children were the least he'd expect. She wound the window down and flicked her cigarette butt into a clump of stingy-nettles.

Andy started the engine and the cassette player came alive with the horrible sound of The Boobs a piercing and discordant rumpus. The production was terrible.

'Is this your new demo?' she asked.

'Yep,' Andy said. He squashed the gearstick into first.

Ellie reached for eject, caught the tape as it jumped out of the machine. She dropped it into her duffel bag.

15

One morning mid August, Ellie woke to Andy's alarm clock. A news reporter was announcing the death of at least seventeen people killed by a suicide-bomber targeting the UN headquarters in Baghdad. She shuffled into the bathroom and plonked herself down on the toilet, body heavy with sleep, pyjama bottoms pushed down to her shins. Andy was getting ready to leave for London, standing naked in front of the sink, the water gushing from the tap and spitting at the splashback. He was fair enough, broad shoulders tapering into a narrow waist, a straight nose, an oblong face. The receding hairline that had claimed Marc's fringe had yet to bother Andy, but his once round, pert buttocks were gradually turning square. Ellie was close enough to reach out and touch one, but she didn't. A few hours earlier, in bed, his fingertips had crept over the brow of her hipbone and tap-danced towards her vagina. She'd recoiled, flown to the edge of the mattress.

'What?' he'd said resignedly, as though he'd been expecting rejection.

'I'm sleeping,' Ellie'd said. She'd sipped from her pint glass of water and secured the string of her pyjamas.

Now their bodies were disjointed, out of bounds to one another.

Andy's razor blade caught the light as it fell into the day.

'Watch you don't cut yourself,' Ellie said. She meant it with concern but as soon as the words hit the air they found a sarcastic quality. One year earlier, Andy had tried to kill himself with the same kind of disposable straight blade. Ellie had received a phone call from a nurse at Abertach Hospital, two hours after she'd fled Dirtbox's America Place cottage. He was asking to see her.

She caught the late bus and found him in Ward 9, lying on a metal frame bed in the corner. His knees were raised under a mint-green waffle blanket, the top of it pulled up to his chin. There were thick yarns of white bandages wrapped around his slit wrists. Ellie saw the Borough Council's insignia stamped on the undersheet; a dark green creature that was supposed to be a dragon but looked more like a cantankerous swan. It was a familiar symbol, the same one she'd seen printed on the paperwork at her counselling sessions.

'You're supposed to cut lengthways,' she said. 'Everyone knows that.'

Andy forced a smile that didn't reach his blue eyes. Ellie felt a prickle of guilt for having left him on the railway station. He'd threatened to do it. She hadn't believed him. 'So why did you phone me?' she said, 'not Dirtbox?'

'I didn't tell you about her because I didn't think it was import-ant,' he said, voice coarse. 'I had an affair with her before she got divorced, two years ago, long before I met you. It wasn't serious. It didn't mean anything. She was only using me to get at her husband.'

As he spoke the blanket slid down his throat. There was a chunky wad of paper, like a cheap sanitary towel, stuck to the inflamed skin of his neck, secured at either end with a strip of medical tape. He'd cut his throat as well.

'You won't tell my parents, will you?' he said. 'I don't want them to know.'

Now Andy dipped the razor in the water, found her through the mirror with the corner of his eye, a smudge of foam left near his earlobe. 'I won't cut myself,' he said. 'It's London today. Nothing can go wrong today.'

A horn sounded outside and he ran into the bedroom, came out dressed a few seconds later, crouched to peck her cheek. A surge of relief washed through her as the front door slammed beneath her. She supposed it was the same kind of feeling over-worked parents got when they sent their children on school trips for the weekend. She loved Andy, the way Siân loved James and Niall; had felt that way for more than half of their relationship. During the soporific minutes between sleep and wakefulness, and a few times when she was drunk, she'd thought about leaving him, secretly quitting her job and catching the first eastbound train out of Cardiff Central Station. Those thoughts calmed her, quietened any anxiety she was feeling at the time. In the cold light of morning she pushed them to the back of her head, afraid she'd have to spend the rest of her life with Andy's death on her conscience. Besides, Andy was the only person who loved *her*, and she owed herself to him for that. But Ellie didn't know how to love. She only knew how to rebel. She flushed the toilet, stood in front of the basin and stared at the assemblage of blonde stubble clinging to the base of the ceramic bowl. A sliver of bright, oxygenated blood twisted through it like the Thames.

At quarter to seven she left the house and headed to work, trudging down Gwendolyn Street. The entrance to the estate was cordoned off with police tape. A WPC was standing guard. On the opposite pavement a man was walking three dogs, Doberman pinschers, two black and tans and one fawn. He sucked on a tab and flicked it skilfully into the gutter, then rearranged the dogs, winding their chains around his wrist and pulling them into his legs. Ellie was parallel with him when she realized it was Johnny. He was wearing a baseball cap, his hair tied in a ponytail, a posy of greasy curls tucked into his collar. There was an intrinsic grimace in his features, mouth open, teeth clenched. Johnny. Fuck.

This was destiny, surely. She scanned the street, looking for witnesses to this bizarre incident. The policewoman was staring at her wristwatch, oblivious.

'Hello,' Ellie said, shouting across the road, her heart soaring into her mouth.

Johnny looked up, startled. 'Well,' he said, face softening, 'fancy seeing you here.' He changed direction, started to walk towards her. They met in the middle of the road. 'I didn't know you had dogs,' she said. There must have been hundreds of things she didn't know. 'Dobermans,' Johnny said. He scratched one of the dog's heads and nodded at the Dinham Estate. 'What's happened there, then?'

'Mortar attack probably,' Ellie said. 'We call it Little Beirut.' She looked at Johnny, said, 'I went to Plymouth University, you know. I've been to Cornwall a few times. I don't understand why you'd leave there to come *here*.'

Johnny laughed. 'You obviously didn't go to where I'm from,' he said, voice furtive, a cruel smile playing on his lips.

'Where's that?' A few days earlier she'd found her old *Rough Guide to Devon & Cornwall*. She'd skim-read it before she'd gone to sleep, pored over the coloured photographs of Polperro and Penzance, scanned columns about tin mining and the beast on Bodmin Moor, anticipating conversations like this.

'Falmouth,' he said, 'or close to it anyway, a small village on the coast, full of tourists, holidaymakers coming and going all the time. It's where I learned my art.'

'What art?' Ellie felt obliged to ask.

'Seduction,' he grinned, and then began to walk away.

Ellie's whole body told her to follow him. But she was already late. She could hear the train zipping through the valley, echoing against the walls of Aberalaw Bridge. She ran to the station, feet rhymeless and heavy.

On the train she stared at herself in the double-glazed window. Her reflection looked as though it belonged to a ghost, as if she wasn't really there. She fingered the outline of her mouth, checking that she was. In the dirty glass she saw her hand, but the face behind it was a cloudy blur. She felt stupid for insinuating that everywhere in Cornwall was idyllic, knew really that it wasn't; it had the lowest-paid workers in the whole of England. When she told people she came from Wales they conjured images of mountains flecked with daffodils, golden beaches stretching around the Gower. They didn't think of sink estates or queues at the dole office. But she was upset by something *he* had said too. Johnny's reference to his romantic experiences with tourists had been an attempt to impress her, she knew that. But there was something patronizing about it as well. The word casually spitting out of his mouth, smooth and flat, as though 'seduction' was something he intended to try on everyone he encountered, not just her. His nonchalance was charming, and repugnant. She was disappointed that her unexpected brush with fate was not preordained after all – had not produced any instant bombshells. Johnny hadn't collapsed at the sight of her. Ultimately, he had walked away and, in reality, that was hardly surprising. She couldn't imagine making much of an impression on anyone, not with Siân and Rhiannon around; Rhiannon, the man-eater, silicone in her chest and a bell in every tooth, and Siân, all sweet mother's milk. Compared to them, Ellie was mousey – a little vagabond. She spoke when she was spoken to and, more often than not, did as she was told. She was a subservient factory girl, traipsing to the city in her dowdy work clothes, her nerves weakened by her fiancé's fears, her heart emptied of its ambitions. She had the kind of relationship that constantly required patience, a love that demanded endeavour. She wanted the sort of love that would set things on fire, the sort of love that made you think you could rule the world, the sort of love that made you think you *already* ruled the world. She wanted somebody to take her away from the valley and everything that was festering in it. She wanted somebody to take her to New York.

She wanted Johnny to take her to New York, because like all orphans, Ellie was insatiable.

At work she went straight to the women's toilet and looked at herself in the water-blackened mirror. The fluorescent strip light highlighted the blue veins mapping her forehead. There was a cluster of premenstrual spots above her jaw. Every day, Andy told her that she was beautiful. It was the truth, his truth, but she never believed it. She wasn't unattractive, she believed that. But if she stayed in Aberalaw any longer, the despair embedded in the place would find its way into her features – wrinkles, thread-veins, saggy, swollen skin. Before she knew it, she'd be one of those women who roamed around the outdoor market in pyjama bottoms and scuffed heels, buying bad vegetables. She'd be like Gwynnie, a banshee who stood in her kitchen hissing cuss words that nobody heard. And no one was immune to it. Rhiannon was almost there. She kept the worst of it at bay by visiting a beautician every week. Even Siân, handsome as she was, would turn ugly in a mental hospital like Aberalaw. But, when it happened to Ellie, she never would have been one of those blithe, effortlessly good-looking women, who men desired and women feared, who aroused suspicion wherever she turned. The reason Ellie had overreacted at Dirtbox's cottage, and then run so quickly away, although she'd never admitted it aloud, was Dirtbox's glorious face. She was devastated, not by Andy having a past, but by Andy having a past with such a pretty girl, a petite, blonde-haired nymph. There wasn't an honours degree in the world that could compete with *real* beauty. Fact. Even the woman's fucking rabbits were beautiful.

The toilet door opened and Safia came in panting. She dropped her handbag on the vanity shelf. 'Missed my bus,' she said as she twisted the lid from a tube of mascara. 'I had to get a cab. That cost me two hours' wages.' A stick of concealer fell out of her bag and rolled into the steel sink. Ellie picked it up. The liquid was brown and greasy, designed for dark skin, but she squeezed a drop into her palm and kneaded it into the sunken flesh beneath her eyes.

Safia peered at her. 'Whassamatter with you, El?' she said. 'Yous look kind of *fierce*.'

'Do you think I'm fat, Saf?' She was staring at her profile in the mirror.

Safia roared. 'Fat? Yeah! As fat as a budgie's flippin' leg.' She pinched the stick of concealer out of Ellie's hand, threw her bag over her shoulder and rushed into the workshop.

Ellie took her box of contraceptives out of her duffel bag and popped a red pill from its dent in the foil card. She was about to swallow it when she decided it was the very thing that was making her plump. Oestrogen caused weight gain, she'd read it in the paper a hundred times. She spat the pill into the basin and washed it away. It didn't matter. She wouldn't be having intercourse until Andy came back from London, probably not even then. She counted the pills left in the card, four, and then she threw the whole thing in the bin, watched it flit through the intricate obstacle course of toilet-roll carcasses.

16

The band came back from London in the early hours of Sunday. They all went to the Pump House in the afternoon. Andy and Ellie were the last to arrive. The other girls were already sitting in the recess behind the front door; Siân was wearing her new lipstick, face a blank sheet with a vivid slash of red cut through the middle. Rhiannon was sitting with her back to the bar, holding a cigarette between fingers adorned with false nails, not the usual milk-coloured French manicure, but elongated talons that curled at the ends. They were painted bright turquoise, an intricate gold pattern stamped on the tips. There were four cans of Red Bull on the table.

'Want one?' Rhiannon said.

'Bit early, isn't it?' Ellie looked at the marcasite watch Andy had bought for her birthday; a pearl face with tiny rubies for numerals. It was the first time she'd worn it. The girls had never seen it and they were looking at it too. It was quarter to five. 'Go on then,' she said.

Rhiannon stubbed her cigarette out and marched to the bar. She stood next to Dai Davies, who was sitting on his barstool as though he'd been there all his life (and had).

'Where are the kids?' Ellie said, sitting down next to Siân. She reached to touch one of the glass beads hanging from Siân's throat but Siân lifted her hand to her breastbone, shielding the necklace from Ellie's fingers. 'They're up Griff's mother's,' she said. Rhiannon appeared again, a shot glass in her hand. She slammed it on the table in front of Ellie, hard enough to crack it.

On the other side of the room, the boys were drinking stout. Their pint glasses looked like plastic props – perfect white heads balancing on the glutinous black beer. They were talking about a strip club on the Tottenham Court Road, someplace someone from the John Peel production team had suggested; an idiotic grin splashed over Griff's mug, as if he'd never seen a woman in the nude before. 'I'm going to get one of those chrome poles for Siân to dance on,' he said. He hadn't shaved and the origins of a bushy, carrot-coloured beard seized the lower half of his face. He caught Siân's eye for a moment, sniggered. 'Actually,' he said, 'I won't bother. I'll just get a lifetime membership with my record company advance.'

Marc picked his drink up with a flourish, eyes bulging. 'Yeah, I think it's gonna kick off, boys,' he said. 'It's how Teenage Fanclub got signed. A John Peel session. The show went on air at half eight, by ten their phone was ringing. The contract was already typed.'

'What d'ewe think, girls?' Rhiannon said. 'Think 'ey got it in 'em to get signed? Think 'ey'll make us rich?' She laughed her acerbic laugh.

'So long as it's enough for a one-way ticket out of here,' Ellie said. She didn't care about money. She cared about getting out of Aberalaw. 'Know what a fanny is in America? An arse. They call bum-bags *fanny-bags*. Isn't that funny?' She threw a gulp of vodka at the back of her throat.

'Will ewe shurrup about ewer bloody American dreams for a minute?' Rhiannon said. 'Bloody rude awakenin' ewer gonna 'ave when ewe realize ewe can't get a green card.' She flashed her smile, revealing half a tube of tooth whitener and a speck of gold. 'What *d'ewe* think?' she said to Siân.

'Oh, I don't want to tempt fate,' Siân said.

'Anyone can get a green card,' Ellie said. From the corner of her eye she noticed Dai Davies and quickly added, 'Anyone without a criminal record.'

'Seriously, Siân,' Rhiannon said. 'If ewe 'ad a windfall, a nice bit of cash, what would ewe do first?' She pursed her lips, a blue ribbon of smoke twisting out of her cigarette.

'Nothing fancy.' Siân picked the empty glasses up, arranging them in a neat row at the furthest edge of her table. 'Maybe a cleaner or a nanny or just an au pair. I love housework, I do, but I can't leave Angharad alone for a minute without her scribbling on the damn wall.'

'Too much television,' Ellie said, reaching for a can of Red Bull. 'Kids' TV is the capitalist's favourite tool. It's all a big advert for junk food and toys. Television schedules are designed to keep the working classes down. The same reason the government brushes heroin statistics under the carpet. They'd rather we kill ourselves with drugs than protest about the war.'

'What do you know about bringing up kids?' Siân said. She pointed at herself. 'Three kids, two jobs and a husband who thinks he's Liam Gallagher. I'd give you twenty minutes before you reached for the remote control.' Siân used to have the patience of an angel but in a matter of weeks the flashpoint on her temper had plummeted. Ellie was stunned that Siân would talk to her like that; she knew that Ellie didn't want kids.

'Know what I'd do?' Rhiannon said. She tugged at her face, pressing her skin taut over her cheekbones. 'The whole lot: facelift, eye lift, nose job, collagen, liposuction.' She grinned and gestured at her crotch. 'I'd even get downstairs done. They can reduce the size of ewer labia, tighten ewe up. Ewe could have that done, Siân. Three kids! Griff must feel like he's fucking a bucket. A designer vagina ewe want. They can make ewe into a virgin again!'

The barman came to the girls' table and collected the dirty

glasses. 'Heard what happened on the estate?' he said to nobody in particular. 'One of those Williams twins got beaten up. Gang of them left him for dead. They booted his jaw into fifteen pieces. He's in the old intensive care.'

Dai Davies wriggled, his backside writhing around on the seat of his stool. 'Another fight caused by a woman,' he said as he drove his forefinger into his right nostril. The tattooed L under his knuckle had shrunk into an I. 'The wives started it all, see, arguing about the ground rent on their caravans in Trecco Bay.' He stared at the yellow bogey on the end of his tobacco-stained finger then popped it into his mouth.

The barman shook his head. 'It used to be the salt of the earth sort living up there. Now it's attracting all kinds of bad elements.'

Johnny's girlfriend walked through the door, as if on cue. Johnny followed seconds later; legs going up to his neck, every bone and sheaf of sinew distinguishable under tight black denim. He was bad all right: bad from his mud-stained basketball boots to his tousled black ponytail; looked like he'd tried every dirty thing four times and smiled like butter wouldn't melt. He sauntered towards the bar and leant against it, arm's-length away from his girlfriend. Immediately, the atmosphere thickened. The boys stopped talking. Dai Davies retched and spat a glob of saliva on to the chipped floorboard. For a few moments Ellie forgot to breathe. When she'd gathered enough courage to look at Johnny's face, she realized he was looking right at her. He nodded at her glass. 'Drinking vodka again?' he said.

'Yeah, an' Red Bull,' Rhiannon said. She plucked the can out of Ellie's reach and pointed at its list of ingredients, tapping her nail against the aluminium. 'Ewe shon't be drinking Red Bull, El. It's got bull's spunk in it an' ewer supposed to be a vegetarian. Look! Taurine! That's bull's spunk and ewer not woman enough to handle it.' She grinned at Johnny and poured the remainder into her own glass.

'Technically it's not bull's spunk,' Johnny said. 'There are traces of taurine in bull's semen and urine but the stuff in those energy drinks is synthesized. *I'm* a vegetarian. It's safe. I've checked it out. It corrodes your teeth though,' he said. He smirked and exposed his own lovely teeth.

The telephone rang and the barman jumped. Ellie watched as he answered it, the receiver held to his chin. He spoke in cagey monosyllables, without moving his mouth. 'I'll have to shut up,' he said, glancing around the bar when the phone call had ended. 'There's no one to work the evening shift and I've got a darts match.' He shook his head apologetically. 'If you could all finish your drinks.'

Griff stood up, drained his beer with a slurp. 'Come on, chick,' he said to Siân. 'We can go home and watch one of your rom-coms, make the most of having a babysitter. We can make more babies.' He stood next to Johnny and stamped his empty glass on the bar, ginger eyebrows parallel with Johnny's nipples.

Rhiannon gave the barman the evils. 'Oi, mush,' she said, pointing at him. 'A bloody public 'ouse, this is. Ewe can't decide to close just 'cause ewe feel like it.'

'Hang on,' Johnny said. 'I only live a couple of minutes away. Why don't you all come over? Help me christen the place? A house party?' He shrugged casually. 'Fancy it?'

17

The sky was the colour of milky tea. Johnny strode over the steps of the miner's statue and down again, stalking across the square. Ellie noticed he walked like the troublemakers at her old comprehensive school, the boys who carried knives and smoked dope behind the gym; a buoyant, self-assured swagger. They were never far away from the remedial classes, those kids, but they had a certain charm that ushered them through life. Fourteen-year-olds covered in shag-marks, destined for jail cells. She'd had a bit of a thing for Kristian Brightman. He had an anarchy symbol tattooed on his wrist, had done it himself with a sewing needle and Indian ink. What she wouldn't have given for one night with him. The students in her own form knew everything about *Hamlet*, nothing of their own bodies. Since adolescence she'd been looking for someone who could set her libido alight *and* blow her mind. There was no antidote to the age-old quandary of good girls falling for bad boys. Not then. Not now.

Johnny stopped in front of the YMCA and fiddled with the blue door. Ellie wondered what he was doing. Then, as he opened it, she realized that's where he lived. A grey, double-fronted building with pebble dash coating the first floor. It used to be a block of bachelor flats. Ribs had rented a room there. So had Griff. Ellie hadn't noticed the For Sale sign go up or the Sold sign comedown. She hadn't noticed the new Venetian blinds appear.

He had been there all the time, amongst them, like a lost ten-pound note nestling in the lining of a discarded handbag.

Ellie followed the others along a narrow corridor and up a murky stairwell. On the landing, Rhiannon stopped and pointed at a canvas hanging on the wall, a plump red mushroom with big white dots on its cap. The paint was acrylic, a glowing riot of colour. 'Look at this, El,' she said, pawing at it. 'Iss good ini?'

Ellie stared at the painting. 'Very Dalíesque,' she said.

Johnny came by, just as her eyes had begun to wander over the fraction of the bedroom visible through the chink of the open door. 'Do you like that, girls?' he said, the soft of his coat brushing against Ellie's arm. 'I did it myself.' He was an artist. She *knew* he was. He coiled his arms around their shoulders and coaxed them away from the picture, his hand falling on to the small of Ellie's back. He guided them into the sitting room at the front of the house. It looked like a photograph from Gwynnie's catalogue: smooth, linen-coloured walls, black leather settees, huge dried flower arrangements on the windowsills.

There was a print on the back wall, a huge colour photograph of the World Trade Towers, the aerial on the east tower piercing a feathery cloud. Ellie clapped her hand over her mouth. 'That's an Angelo Cavalli,' she said, remembering the Flatiron print that Collin had forced back on the shop shelf. She quickly squinted around the room in search of family photographs. There weren't any. No mothers. No fathers. No siblings. No cousins.

'This used to be where my bunk was,' Griff said. 'Remember, Siân? Right here where I'm standing! He's taken the wall down.'

There was a gargantuan television tuned to MTV, the sound turned down. Rhiannon stood in front of it, obscuring the image on the screen. 'Ever seen one this big before?' she said, pupils wide as pound coins. 'It must 'ave cost 'im a fortune. A bloody fortune it must 'ave cost!' Siân ran the tip of her bitten ring-finger along the top of it, looking for dust, her fingertip coming back clean. Andy was rifling through a stack of DVDs.

'See that statue?' Johnny said, walking towards the window. He gestured at the mining statue in the middle of the square. The streetlight cast an ochre blush on the wife's face. Ellie thought about herself sitting next to it a couple of Sundays ago, talking about him. Perhaps he'd seen her. Perhaps he'd heard what she'd said. 'The artist who sculpted that thing made the wife and baby for free. The council commissioned it to represent the coal industry. But they only paid for the man. The artist said that was only half of the story, said he was doing the woman too, if they paid him or not. Did you know that?'

'No,' Ellie said, shocked that she didn't.

Siân pushed between Ellie and Johnny and stared wistfully out of the window. 'That's a lovely story,' she said. 'Lovely.' Rhiannon accidentally-on-purpose kicked Siân in the shin, cackled her signature laugh, said, 'If ewe look at it from the window in the women's bogs it looks like she's fistin' 'is arsehole.'

'Look at the craftsmanship on this,' Marc said, alerting everyone to the walnut coffee table in the centre of the room, the legs carved into mermaids, their tail-fins sinking into the carpet. There was a baggie of pills sitting on the glass surface. Johnny laughed. He picked it up and emptied the contents into his cupped palm, offered the yellow tablets around as if they were chewing gums. The boys stared at him, eyes unblinking. 'Go on,' he said, nodding encouragingly. 'I'll be offended if you don't.'

Ellie was the last to take one.

'Drinks now,' Johnny said, heading into the long, cupboard-lined kitchen, the women following. He opened one of the melamine doors, presenting them with a hotchpotch of spirit bottles: vodka, whisky, gin, tequila, rum, liqueurs, the multi-coloured glass competing for shelf space. 'Think we can do something with this?'

he said. The whole house was a bizarre amusement park; a play-ground for debauched grown-ups.

Rhiannon grabbed two bottles, bashed them base down on the worktop. 'We'll 'ave a few Black Russians,' she said.

Siân picked the Tia Maria up and set it back on the shelf. 'That's not how you make a Black Russian,' she said. 'You need a bottle of Kahlúa.'

Rhiannon glowered. 'What d'ewe know about it, Siân? Ewer paralytic after 'alf a bloody cider.' She retrieved the Tia Maria and began to pick at the cellophane around its neck. 'Remember that time in the Pump House, El? When she tipped a glass of black-currant on the pool table? We nearly got bloody barred because of that.'

'I worked in the Bell and Cabbage, remember,' Siân said. 'Before James was born. A Black Russian is two parts vodka, one part coffee liqueur.' She snatched the Tia Maria from the crook of Rhiannon's arm. 'I'm telling you, Rhi. You can't get me on cocktails. I'm an expert, I am.'

Johnny put two clean tumblers down on the worktop. 'Sex on the Beach,' he said. 'Know how to do that?' He reached into the cupboard for more glasses. Siân lifted her hand to her mouth and giggled, a speck of dried blood under her chewed fingernail. 'One part vodka,' she said, 'one part peach schnapps, one part fruit juice.' Johnny put more glasses down on the worktop. 'What about a Slow Wet Orgasm?'

'Malibu, Irish cream, vodka, milk.'

'She's good, isn't she?' Johnny said.

Rhiannon tsked. She made a lunge for the Tia Maria, seizing it from Siân's grasp. 'Watch this,' she said. She flung it at the ceiling. The bottle did a somersault in the air and came down belly first. She caught it awkwardly, the bottle-top protruding from her armpit.

Siân stole it from her, face sour. She tossed it blindly into the air. It hit the corner of the fridge and smashed, the treacly black liquid dripping in thick rivulets down the mirrored door. 'Look what ewe've done now, Siân,' Rhiannon said. 'Clean it up, ewe dozy cow.'

Siân stood motionless in the middle of the room, biting the inside of her cheek. The mood was hysterical, threatening, jealous and sexual, as if each of the individual women harboured a mildly irritating component but together they were flammable and volatile; a Molotov cocktail to which Johnny was the spark.

After a moment his girlfriend appeared in the doorway, a dustpan in her hand. 'What's broken?' she said, walking towards the gathering, eyes apprehensive.

Johnny took the dustpan out of her hand. 'I'll do it,' he said. 'Come on, girls, lighten up. No use crying over spilt milk.'

Later they were sitting around the wooden picnic table on Johnny's patio, the tangled fairy lights in the sycamore tree turning the whites of their eyes to warm amber. Andy was lying in a hammock on the lawn. Johnny's girlfriend had plugged a CD player into an extension lead and carried it out into the garden. It was playing 'Tapestry' by Carole King. Rhiannon was humming along in a toneless drone.

'How old are you, Johnny?' Ellie said. He was sitting opposite her, pushing a roach into a joint with the nub of a matchstick. He smiled at the wooden surface of the table but didn't answer the question. 'Johnny?' she said.

Johnny's girlfriend sighed. 'I'm twenty-eight,' she said. 'He's ten years older than me.'

There was fifteen years between Johnny and Ellie. Something in this new awareness of his age, along with the MDMA in her bloodstream, made Ellie's desire for him all the more critical. She found his foot under the table and pressed her own foot down on it. 'Do you like America?' she said. 'I saw your picture of the Twin Towers.'

Johnny looked at her. 'Yeah,' he said. 'I love New York. I love it, in films, when you see people on the sidewalk, arms full of brown paper grocery bags, steam shooting up from the subway. That's so romantic.' Rhiannon was trying to open the ring-pull on a beer can without breaking her false nails. Accidentally-on-purpose, she elbowed Ellie in the chest. Ellie would have flown off the edge of the bench had she not quickly put her foot back on terra firma. 'What's the matter with you, Rhi?' she said. 'I thought you didn't like beer. I thought you only drank wine. I thought you were a lady.'

Johnny passed his spliff to his girlfriend. 'I've got wine,' he said. 'What do you think I am? Some kind of savage? What d'you fancy? Pinot, Merlot? I've got some Ukrainian Riesling.' He stood up and walked into the house. Rhiannon jumped out of her seat and followed him. 'Anything but red,' she was saying when they disappeared behind the door.

Louisa tapped the reefer on the table and twisted the end of the paper. She picked Johnny's lighter up and lit it. A tiny orange ember jumped out of the flame and landed on the table. Andy began to snore, a respiratory pant, like Darth Vader. Louisa scoffed at him. 'Tell him about it when he wakes up,' Ellie said, rolling her eyes. 'I've told him a million times. He doesn't believe me. I even taped him with my Dictaphone. He said I taped it off the telly.'

'That's what I've got to put up with on tour,' Griff said. He kicked the hammock.

One of the Dobermans lying under the table licked at Ellie's wrist. She pulled her hand away and caught a sneeze, her eyes filling with allergy-induced tears. She wiped her wrist on her thigh, noticing the face of her watch, the rubies shimmering in the fairy lights, her vision blurred. Rhiannon and Johnny had been gone for more than a minute now. She stood up suddenly, glancing around the garden. 'I'm just going to the loo,' she said. As she entered the kitchen, the harsh light showed Rhiannon leaning against the oven, hands clinging to the towel rail. Johnny was next to her, still, not doing anything. 'All right, El?' he said, too quickly, an acidic trait to his voice.

There was a bottle of Chardonnay on the worktop; a corkscrew plunged into it, metal arms at half-mast, an air of waywardness in the room. Rhiannon stood up straight and wiped her mouth with the back of her hand, peering vapidly at Ellie. Johnny turned to the wine bottle and started twisting the corkscrew. It was obvious that they'd been up to something, but it was nothing that Ellie could prove. She coughed and walked slowly past the pair of them, a gobbet of annoyance and discomfiture. clotting in her throat. As she reached the corridor she sensed the arrival of another person in the kitchen. She turned and saw Johnny's girlfriend walk in through the door. She stopped next to the sink. 'What's going on?' she said, the question stale, as though she'd already asked it a hundred times. She was glaring at Rhiannon, blue eyes electric.

Rhiannon lifted her wineglass and sneered before taking a sip.

'Nothing's going on, Lou,' Johnny said. 'You silly thing. I was only getting the girl a drink.'

Louisa's face cracked. She leapt at Rhiannon, whipping the wineglass out of her hand, sending it soaring through the air in a long, seamless arc. It landed on the chessboard on the windowsill, the flax-coloured liquid spitting over the chess pieces. A rook and three pawns toppled on to their sides.

'Get out of my house,' Louisa yelled.

Rhiannon studied the apple-white walls for a few moments. She took a deep breath, her huge breasts rising and falling. She turned to face Louisa. 'Fine,' she said. 'I didn't want to be 'ere anyway. Nutter ewe are, love. There's someone in Bridgend eatin' ewer bloody biscuits.' She turned and walked steadily to the door.

Ellie stepped aside to let her pass. As she did, Rhiannon slapped her on the shoulder. 'Go and get my bag, El,' she said irritably. 'And remember my pot. Tell the others we're leaving. I'll 'ave a party in my own bloody 'ouse.' She turned and squinted at Louisa. 'An' ewe ain't fuckin' invited.'

18

At ten the next morning Ellie opened her eyes to the sound of bells clanging. It was Holy Communion at St Illtyd's. She stretched her throbbing legs over the arm of the settee, the cushions beneath her moist with perspiration, the sun screaming into the room. Rhiannon was cleaning the coffee table, a duster in one hand, a can of polish in the other. She looked like what she was: a woman hitting middle age, dark shadows around her eyes, muffin top spilling out over the elasticated waist of her *Playboy* jogging bottoms. Ellie blinked. She'd expected to see Dai Davies's ex-wife. Rhiannon never attempted anything domestic. She paid Myra to come around once a week, had only been talking about it on Johnny's patio the previous evening; said her best vibrator had gone missing and she suspected Myra of taking it. That's why when Ellie first heard the hum of the vacuum cleaner several hours earlier and had felt the weight of somebody's gaze on her face, she'd kept her eyes screwed closed.

'Rhi?' she said, a hint of astonishment in her voice.

Rhiannon smiled and then disappeared into the kitchen.

Andy was cooped in the rocking chair, holding a mohair bolster to his stomach, his eyelids the colour of raw beef.

'Coffee?' Rhiannon said, returning. She put three mugs down on the table, knelt down in front of the fireplace and pulled one of them towards her, cradled it with both hands. Some of her false nails had vanished and her own fingernails were rough and brittle. She lifted the coffee to her face and blew on it, then put it down again, gently running her index finger around its rim. She began to pluck orbs of fluff out of the sheepskin rug that she sat on, rolling them up in her hands and throwing them into the wastebasket. She picked at it until there was no loose fuzz left, tersely ripping fat clumps from out of its papery skin. 'Look at this,' she said, holding some up, 'Slut's wool, my mother called this.' She sipped her coffee, spluttering when it burned her mouth.

Marc popped his head around the door, a plastic spatula in his hand. 'I'm doing breakfast,' he said. 'What do you want, El? Egg on toast?'

Ellie held her hand over her mouth until the threat of vomit sank. Her brain was pounding. It felt dirty. She wished there was some way of lifting it out of her cranium and swilling it, like a tea towel. Ecstasy was not her drug of choice. It always put her in mind of Manchester clubs, rammed full of sweat-soaked navvies, people who hated each other by day, adoring one another by night; strangers putting their tongues down each other's throats.

'I'll just do you some toast then,' he said. As he turned around, Ellie noticed a fresh love-bite on his neck, deep purple and shaped like a fifty-pence piece.

When he brought the food into the living room, the margarine had already penetrated the bread, turning the toast soggy. Ellie turned a slice over to check it wasn't charred on the base – one of Gwynnie's tricks. Andy and Rhiannon scrambled over the coffee table, procuring knifes, forks, ketchup. Marc sat on the settee, bursting his yolk with the puckered end of an over-cooked sausage, sending it haemorrhaging into the baked beans. 'Saw some fireworks last night, didn't we?' he said. 'That Louisa's a queer fish.'

Andy rolled his shoulders around like oars. 'What happened?' he said.

Rhiannon was sprinkling pepper over her tinned tomatoes. 'Louisa did,' she said. 'I was only getting a drink. Johnny was pouring it for me. Out of nowhere she comes in throwing glasses about like Xena Warrior Princess, mad fuckin' bitch.'

'Why?' Andy said. Andy'd always been suspicious of Rhiannon, worried about what her business was with his brother. He came home from the building sites with stories he'd heard about her, urban legends about women who kill for money, speculation about one of her ex-husbands dying in mysterious circumstances. But Rhiannon owned the house. Marc didn't have any money to get swindled out of. He seemed content to suffer Rhiannon's exploitations. She'd have him redecorate every six months, paint the windowsills peach, then white, then peach again for no good reason. One time they'd called there unannounced and caught him cooking pasta for her in the buff, one of the apron strings wedged between his buttocks.

Marc licked the edge of his knife. 'Thought they were up to something, didn't she?' he said. 'She probably smoked too much pot. Paranoid, mun. We'd been at it since teatime.'

That must have been the line of reasoning Rhiannon had used when Marc had asked her for an explanation. '*Don't be silly*,' she would have said, unclasping her bra, baring her big comedy tits, clamping her teeth on his neck like a frenzied teenager. By the time Andy and Ellie had got back to Rhiannon's house on Chepstow Road last night, Rhiannon was already in bed. Marc was standing on the doorstep, a bottle of wine and two glasses in his hands. 'Help yourselves to anything,' he said as he pummelled up the stairs, like a cheetah on a promise.

Rhiannon was playing with her baked beans. '*Oh yeah*,' she said. 'Course I was up to somethin'. E's bloody 'ansome, that Johnny. I could run away with 'im, I could.' She flashed Ellie a quick, knowing look, as though she'd seen what had gone through Ellie's head as she'd lain there in the murky morning light; had been a spirit watching her walk a tree-lined Greenwich Village street, hand in hand with Johnny. 'All that long hair an' skin and bloody bone, I mean, *as if.* I din't do nothin'. 'E only poured me a glass of fuckin' wine. Ask Ellie, she was there.'

Ellie chewed her toast. She let the silence hang over the room until she'd swallowed a mouthful. She put the plate down on the table and picked her cold coffee up. 'Do you think she gets paranoid, though?' she said. 'Louisa? I mean, she lives with a drug dealer. Wouldn't she become . . . immune?'

Rhiannon's knife fell out of her hand and clattered against the edge of her plate. 'I don't know what the fuck she is,' she said, retrieving it. 'Mental, by the looks of things. She's lucky I din't batter urgh. Accusin' me of kissin' urgh ugly bloody boyfriend, funny cow.' Her plate was still loaded but she pushed it away from herself, lit a cigarette. '*As fuckin' if.*'

So far, nobody had mentioned anything about kissing. Ellie wasn't certain that that was what she'd seen. In fact, she had discouraged her mind from going down that particular route, convinced her psyche that what she'd seen was Johnny pushing Rhiannon away. Now Rhiannon had confirmed her worst fears. She felt an overwhelming urge to force Rhiannon's fat face into the breakfast she'd left on the plate. She glanced sideways at her, said, 'Why *didn't* you smack her then, Rhi?' After all, she'd stabbed people for less.

Rhiannon flicked a crumb of ash on to her plate. 'Pills, El,' she said.

'Yeah, El,' Marc said, rushing to Rhiannon's defence. 'They've got the only stuff around, and they were top quality, weren't they? It's best to stay on the right side of them, for now at least.'

Ellie had a fight on her hands. She had done since the day he'd washed up. The moment he'd walked into the Pump House, offering cigarettes and drinks and narcotics, like some great self-made philanthropist, it had been every woman for herself.

'I quite like her,' Andy said, seemingly from nowhere.

'What?' Rhiannon said.

'Louisa,' he said. 'I think she's a nice girl. She said something weird to me when I was leaving, though. She touched my elbow, really gentle. She was crying. She said, "I have to tell you, you snore."'

19

A few weeks later, Ellie was on her way home from work, purposely adding ten minutes on to her journey in order to pass through the square; she did it every day now. There was a bunch of wild fuchsia growing through the rotting fence at the pine end. She'd rip handfuls of it away and play 'He Loves Me/He Loves Me Not', diligently removing the petals and letting them fall behind her until only the stiff red bud remained, jutting like a bloated clitoris. She made sure she always landed on 'He Loves Me'. She'd glance up at the YMCA windows and the blinds would always be drawn.

That day, there'd been a sun shower in the afternoon. The cracked pavements were still wet. The air smelled of earth and moist foliage. Occasionally, like an afterthought, a starburst of rain hit the cars lining the kerb. There were two obese women standing at the junction, blocking Ellie's view of the square, talking with loud, mealy voices.

'That Williams twin is dead too,' one said.

'Ooh, so it's a murder investigation now,' the other said, tongue flicking around her lips. Ellie tried to sidestep them but one of the women recognized her. 'Hello, love,' she said. 'You're Gwynnie's daughter-in-law, aren't you? How's that husband of yours doing? I heard all about that radio show in London, aye. Nice to see someone from round 'ere doin' well, isn't it? They'll be on that

Top of the Pops 'fore you know it, like that Shakin' Stevens. Land of song we are, see.'

Ellie smiled reluctantly and plodded on. As she reached the square she saw the YMCA, blinds and front door open, Johnny's BMW parked on the forecourt. Louisa was leaning into the boot, thick wisps of hair spinning around in the wind. Ellie's pace slowed as she watched Louisa toying with something in the trunk, one of the Dobermans sitting on a yellow blanket on the back seat. As she approached, she feigned surprise. 'Louisa!' she shouted cheerfully.

Louisa looked up, a heavy terracotta plant pot in her hands, a spiky red yucca inside. 'Ellie,' she said, propping it protectively on her hip.

For what seemed like minutes, they eyed one another silently. Then, 'I just got back from Cornwall,' Louisa said. She tucked a strand of hair behind her ear and gestured at the open boot. 'This is the last of our stuff.' She offered Ellie a pithy smile, her mouth revealing a cluster of pinprick holes in the enamel of her front teeth. She turned into the house.

'Do you want a hand?' Ellie said tentatively, a hot stab of excitement pricking her gut as she spied the dark corridor. It was Johnny's corridor.

Louisa was halfway up the stairs. 'No, no, I'm OK,' she said, her voice echoing. Ellie peered around the square, noticed the petals she'd dropped on the Dynevor Street pavement and hoped that Louisa hadn't. She looked at the things left in the boot, a plastic grocery bag full of paper, fragments of earth from the houseplant scattered over the champagne-coloured carpet. There was a black bin liner full of clothes, a rip in its stomach exposing the colours and textures, all squashed and tangled together. Ellie hurriedly pressed her face against the tear and breathed through her mouth and her nose, hoping for the faintest reek of petrol, a hint of Johnny, but she could smell only damp. As she lifted her head, she saw one of the old women walking past, giving her a dirty look.

Louisa thumped down the stairs, car keys in hand, surprised to see Ellie still there. 'That's enough of the humping and dumping for now,' she said, slamming the boot locked. She let the dog out of the car and cajoled it into the house, slapping her hand against her thigh.

Ellie looked at the film of condensation on the windows of the Pump House. 'Do you fancy a drink, Louisa?' she said. She wasn't any good at small talk, or girl talk, but if you couldn't cook, and Ellie couldn't, the best way to a man's heart was through his girl-friend.

Louisa frowned.

'Just one?' Ellie said. She gestured at herself, at her frayed working clothes. 'I'm on my way home from the factory,' she said. 'I'm not planning on being long. Andy'll wonder where I am.'

Louisa didn't seem convinced.

Suddenly, Ellie had an idea. She ripped the Velcro of her duffel bag open, lifted the wedding magazine out. There was a photo-graph on the cover of a redhead in a fussy, butter-coloured meringue. 'You could help me choose one of these.'

Louisa shouted up into the darkness of the flat, 'Just popping over to the pub, with Ellie.' She banged the front door closed. The fucking fairy-tale wedding: did it every time.

Dai Davies was at the bar, mumbling to himself. Ellie carried the drinks as far away from him as it was possible to get, behind the jukebox in the games room. She gently placed Louisa's white wine on a brand-new beer-mat. As they sat down, their knees touched. Ellie jumped away as if she'd touched blue flame, conscious of her impiety. Louisa didn't notice, so Ellie edged back, close enough to distinguish the citrus scent of Louisa's deodorant, to study the pockmarks on her face. Louisa toasted Ellie with the wineglass, with Rhiannon's egg-cup-shaped wineglass.

'Remember that other Saturday?' Ellie said.

Louisa squinted at her.

Ellie lowered her voice. 'That incident with Johnny and Rhiannon. Rhiannon doesn't mean any harm. She's just an old flirt; likes to think everyone would sleep with her if they could. She's like that. Vain.' It was in everyone's interest to keep Louisa sweet. If Louisa trusted them, they only had each other to deal with.

Louisa laughed sharply.

'Oh, you don't really think there was something going on?' Ellie said, dejected. 'You don't think they were necking?'

Louisa put the glass down. She crossed her skinny legs. 'Probably,' she said. 'But it wouldn't be Rhiannon's fault. It's Johnny I worry about. He'd fuck anything with a pulse. I have to watch him, Ellie. He'll stick his fingers in the dog if I'm not looking.'

Ellie stared at Louisa, her mouth moving, no words coming out. She didn't know what to do. Defend him? Defend herself? Defend Rhiannon? Sympathize with Louisa? 'Still,' she said finally, changing tack, 'Rhiannon's insane. She needs all the love she can get. She doesn't mind where she goes looking for it either. She used to be a prostitute, that's what some people say. Nobody's actually asked her though: scared she'd slaughter them. She set fire to one of her customer's houses once.' Ellie stole a glimpse at Dai Davies. Arson must have run in the family.

'She's not much of a hairdresser, is she?' Louisa said, grabbing a tuft of her blonde hair. 'I had highlights with her last week. You wouldn't know the difference.'

Ellie giggled. A year earlier, Siân had wanted her hair dyed magenta. She'd paused the video in the shop and matched a swatch to the lead actress's curls. She took it to CF25 and came out two hours later, hair the colour of orange peel. She tipped Rhiannon a fiver and spent the afternoon crying in front of Ellie's bathroom mirror.

'I hope she didn't charge you,' Ellie said. 'Curl Up & Dye on Dynevor Street is where me and Siân go.'

Louisa was looking at the magazine. She paused on a photograph of the redheaded cover girl, sitting on a stile, surrounded by chestnut trees and daisies, wearing a revolting ballerina dress. She pointed at it. Ellie ignored the gesture. She was still reeling from Louisa's revelation. 'Why do you put up with Johnny, Louisa,' she said, 'if he's like that?'

Louisa shrugged, turned the page. 'Force of habit,' she said. 'I've been with Johnny for fourteen years.' She paused, let the words impact on Ellie. 'I've seen all of his flings come and go. In the end, they always go, but he's always stayed with me. I'm the only family he's got. He's the only family I've got. My mother walked out when I was thirteen. A year later I met Johnny.' She stopped at another page, an advert for wedding rings. 'You'll need a pair of these,' she said, pushing the magazine across the table.

Ellie took it, but she was still looking at Louisa's face. 'My mother walked out when I was thirteen months,' she said. 'I'm adopted.' A rush of blood came with the words, the words she'd never used so facetiously before.

Louisa nodded attentively, drained her wineglass.

Ellie took it from her. 'Another one?' she said.

Louisa snatched it. 'No,' she said. 'No thanks.' She stood up. 'I'll have to get his dinner on.'

Ellie's elation drained away as quickly as it had come. Typical of the English, she thought. You say 'one drink' and they think you mean it. As Louisa disappeared, Ellie began to feel unclean. She'd used the truth to fabricate a lie, to try to garner sympathy and affection from Louisa. And it hadn't even worked. She swallowed the last of her watery lager, one hand held aloft in a static wave as Louisa slipped through the door.

20

It was the middle of September, and it was getting chilly at the Chinese takeaway. Siân took her two-bar electric fire to work and plugged it in behind the counter. She sat in front of yesterday's local paper, the heat glaring at her ankles. It was the same age as her, that fire. She remembered it on the icy floor of the house, its lead snaking behind the cooker, her mother's laundry rack pinching all the heat.

One time, her father held her mother's fingertips against the top bar for a whole minute because she was wearing pink nail varnish. 'Who do you think you are,' he'd said, 'that Davies slag from the estate?' Rhiannon's mother was the talk of the town because she'd had a black kid and Mr Davies was white. Siân cowered under the kitchen table as her mother's face twisted into a knot of red skin.

Afterwards, there were hard yellow calluses on the tips of her fingers. She never wore nail varnish again and she kept playing a horrible Tammy Wynette song on her boxy record player, something about not wanting to play house because it made somebody's mother cry. That Southern American drawl went right through Siân, so whiny and self-pitying. Siân couldn't remember how she ended up with the fire. It had dents in it, thrashed, like everything from that house, and she turned it towards the wall and started to chew a broken sliver of skin next to her thumbnail.

Through the plate-glass window she saw her co-worker, the Boy Racer, pull up and approach the shop. He came in with his pen balanced behind his ear, his bright-white trainers shining against the rough horsehair mat. The phone rang and they both jumped to answer it.

The boy got it. 'Hau Kung,' he said.

Siân hated the way he answered the phone. She hated the way he walked about with his nose in the air, as if he was better than everyone else. He had a sticker in his back windscreen that said, 'How's my Driving? Ring 0800 Eat Shit.'

She'd tried to explain to Chan how rude it was, how it would affect his business. What it was, Chan stood in the steam for eight hours cooking Szechuan beef and prawns in oyster sauce, special Thai and Cantonese dishes. But the people in Aberalaw preferred Wong's in Ystradyfodwg where they got free chips with the chicken omelettes.

She couldn't understand how he could afford to employ them both. He wasn't making enough profit to pay for the phone calls to his wife who was waiting in Beijing. The last thing he needed was that lazy upstart. 'This is youth, Zhan,' he'd say. 'One day, he grow up. And you not leave, Zhan, I need you.'

It was the easiest money she'd ever made. When she wiped the counter with antibacterial spray and a dishcloth, he'd come in from the kitchen shouting at her. 'Not your job, Zhan. You write order down is all you do.' It was the boredom that was killing her, thinking she could be at home cleaning when she was in the shop doing nothing.

'Where's that again?' the Boy Racer said, his little finger stuck in the curls in the telephone cable, a jet-black arch of dirt under his fingernail. Siân pulled the notebook away from him and struggled to read his childish handwriting. It was an order for sesame prawns on toast, beef in black bean sauce and chicken and spring onion with Singapore rice. It was going to 1A Aberalaw Square.

124

'Who was that?' she said when he'd put the receiver back in its cradle.

'What am I?' he said, rearranging his baseball cap, 'a fucking mind reader?' He tried to snatch the paper out of her hand but Siân held on to it stubbornly.

'We don't take names, do we?' he said eventually. 'Some English bitch it was.'

In the kitchen, Chan was washing a wok by boiling washing powder inside it, the smell putrid. Siân knew the Boy Racer was taller than her but she held the order above her head, the way she did with James and Angharad's sweets. 'I want to do this delivery, Chan,' she said.

Chan scratched his black cow's lick, shook his head. 'Too cold,' he said.

Siân pinned the paper to the cork board. 'I'm doing it, Chan,' she said. '*He* doesn't know the address. I do, it's my friend's house.' Chan nodded casually, turning back to the wok. Siân smiled at the boy.

'Please yourself,' he said, smiling back, 'but you ain't using my car.'

Chan turned to face them again, aiming his metal skimmer between the boy's eyes. 'Zhan gets the car,' he said. 'That's what I pay you for, that noisy, loud car. You watch phone. Favourite thing now, hey?'

There were five pine-tree air fresheners pinned along the top of the windscreen to combat the smell of food. Siân couldn't help thinking about that horrible scene in the Brad Pitt film, where a serial killer kept a man rotting for a twelvemonth in his apartment and tried to disguise the vile stink with hundreds and hundreds of the things, all fastened to the ceiling. In his spare time, the boy probably entertained girls here. She expected that thought to make her feel sick, too; instead it excited her a bit. She'd never done it in a car. She didn't have matching underwear, had never tasted a blueberry-flavoured condom, had never used a vibrator – unlike Rhiannon, who was very open about all that kind of stuff. Siân had only ever slept with Griff, missionary position usually, doggy-style one time when she was heavily pregnant.

She put the meal on the passenger seat and started the engine with the bunch of keys the Boy Racer had thrown at her. She left the drum 'n' bass throbbing out of the speakers. On the way she stopped at her own house on Dynevor Street. Griff was asleep on the settee, three empty cans of lager on the table in front of him. He'd hardly spoken to her since she'd confessed to the sterilization. But in front of the others, in the park and at the pub, he'd mentioned having more kids. The words were deliberately designed to hurt her, the way her father had bullied her mother, using his mouth instead of his fists.

James was lying next to him, his eyes open. He watched her as she pulled the worn pumps from her tired feet and waddled into her four-inch red stilettos. As she tiptoed out of the house she thought about telling him to go to bed, but sooner or later she knew that Griff would put her son to bed.

There was no knocker on the door of the YMCA. She used the letterbox, hitting it ham-fisted against its frame. It made a shrill clapping sound, like Rhiannon. When Griff had been there, there'd been an intercom, but the door was always open. There was a never-ending party in the common room. Anyone was welcome. One time, she'd caught them trying to boil eggs in the electric kettle because all their saucepans were dirty from stewing cannabis leaves. It was around that time she'd asked Griff to move in with her, because Siân had always wanted to play house, always wanted 2.4 children, always wanted what Ellie called a 'nuclear family', like it was destined to blow up.

The light in the passage came on. Johnny opened the door in a pair of jeans and a polo shirt. Bare feet, long, clean toes, veins jumping out of his skin like squiggly blue bridges. The greying hair at his temples coiled into kiss curls.

'Oh, it's you,' he said, leaning against the doorframe, inspecting her from head to foot, cool as you like. 'I haven't long ordered Chinese.' Siân lifted the paper bag into the air, the handwritten order stapled to the handle. 'I am your Chinese.'

'Look who's brought our food,' Johnny shouted as he climbed the stairs. Siân walked carefully, trying to keep her balance. Louisa was taking a plate out of a wall cupboard, a white one with a black stripe through the middle, holding it in front of herself like a shield. 'Siân!' she said, relieved. 'This is a small village isn't it?' She put the plate down, took the bag from Siân's hand. Johnny gave Siân the right money, a twenty-pound note and a one-pound coin, cold fingers pressing it into her warm palm.

Louisa plucked the lid from one of the containers. 'I thought you were a stay-at-home mum,' she said. 'That's all you ever talk about, your kids. Do you get a night off, ever? You and Griff should come around, eat takeaway with us.' She shook the prawns on to the plate.

'No, you two should come over to ours,' Siân said, ignoring the 'night off' comment. Mothers didn't get nights off. 'We only live in Dynevor, just around the corner. I don't eat Chinese. I see what goes into it. I'll cook for you.' Siân always longed to throw grand dinner parties, like the ones in Richard Curtis films: posh people sitting down to salmon en croûte and vanilla crème brûlée, cloth napkins and three sets of silver cutlery. Besides, it was hard to find babysitters. 'I'm a good cook,' she said, 'even if I do say so myself.'

'Of course you are,' Louisa said.

Johnny saw Siân out. When she reached the door, her fingers clamped on the handle, he pulled her hair, a short, sharp yank. She wasn't sure if she wanted to turn around and slap his face or giggle and throw her arms around his torso. There was something about him, something disarming. He'd turned Rhiannon and Ellie agog. Siân had noticed the way they looked at him, and winning his attention with the cocktail mixing had driven Rhiannon crazy; wound her right up like a pocket watch.

She turned and looked at him, leaning boldly in the doorway. He wasn't good looking in the traditional way. In fact, she could have called him ugly, but he was confident, so flipping sure of himself, he could ask for the moon and some poor bitch like Rhiannon would bend over backwards trying to give it to him. 'Good night,' he said, his tight lips stretching into a half-smile. He was waiting for something. Siân said nothing. She slammed the car door and turned the ignition on, indicated out of the square.

When she pulled up outside Hau Kung, she fumbled around on the floor, searching for her pumps. There was a lone sesame prawn on the mat beside her left shoe. She opened the glove box, shuffling through the paperwork and CDs until she came across an empty sunglasses case. She put the prawn inside, and then quickly snapped it shut, hid the case behind an old can of de-icer. The Boy Racer stared at the red shoes in her hand as she walked across the waiting area of the shop. She threw his keys at him. 'Your car absolutely stinks,' she said. 'How can you drive around in that? It smells like gone-off meat.'

21

On Friday night in Gwendolyn Street, Ellie sat cross-legged on the worktop in her kitchen, flicking through the dusty, onion-skin pages of *The Conscientious Wife*. It had been an engagement present from Gwynnie a year earlier, a bulky 1950s housekeeping manual. She laughed aloud at the foreword on a chapter called 'Love & Marriage'. 'Every normal man and woman tries to find the true mate and wants to make a success of marriage,' it said. She'd dug the book out in search of a recipe. For as long as anyone could remember, Gwynnie's sister Margaret had always baked the family wedding cakes: square, three-tiered fruit cakes covered in white icing. The uppermost tier was always wrapped in grease-proof paper and stored for the first baby's christening. Too bad Ellie didn't like fruit cake. Too bad Ellie was never going to have a baby with Andy. Too bad she was going to make her own cake, chocolate-flavoured and shaped like the Empire State Building.

There was a chapter called 'Cakes for Special Occasions', but the only recipe listed was for a square, three-tiered fruit cake covered in white icing. She read the information anyway, imagining she could modify it to suit her own needs. 'Cream the butter and sugar,' it said. 'Add the beaten eggs gradually, beating well, and adding flour towards the end if the mixture shows any signs of curdling.' It was a different fucking language. How did she *cream* the butter and sugar, and how would she know if it

129

showed any signs of curdling? She was going back to an earlier chapter, simply called 'Cakes', when the phone in the hallway rang.

There was a man's voice on the line, polite but officious. 'Could I speak to Elizabeth Evans?' it said. Ellie thought of Johnny but she knew Johnny wouldn't have called her *Elizabeth*. 'Speaking,' she said.

'Ian Lewis,' the voice said, 'The Needles' manager. I'm ringing because the band listened to the demo you sent us. They'd like The Boobs to join them on the French leg of their tour. I don't have a contact number for any of the band members. I understand you know them personally?'

'Are you serious?' Ellie said, thinking someone had got wind of her time-buying scheme. There was a pause on the line and then, deadpan, the voice said, 'Yes. This is Elizabeth Evans, isn't it?'

It was past stop-tap. The Pump House door was locked. Ellie thumped on it, the rapping echoing around the stagnant village. She peeped around the square and noticed that it had rained. The beads of water on the YMCA windows glistened in the moonlight. She heard the bolts on the back of the pub door unfasten. The barman stood against the jamb. 'You know you can't come in if you haven't been drinking here since ten,' he said.

Ellie squeezed past him and burst into the bar. The first thing she saw was Rhiannon, eyes blunted by drunkenness, flanked on either side by Johnny and Louisa. Rhiannon usually went to the Labour Club with Kelly on Fridays. They started drinking alcopops at six and watched the resident blues band – four grizzled old men who used to back Tom Jones. Rhiannon got a cheap thrill when they winked at her between songs or bought her drinks in the interval. But somehow she'd wormed her way into the pub, and back into Louisa's affections, the rain marbling her eye-shadow and flattening her hair in the process, like a Black Widow spider spinning her fine and intricate web.

Andy was a bit further along the bench with Marc and Griff, the white cotton lining of his trousers pocket drooping out. He was puffing on a fat cigar, pretending to enjoy it. Ellie slumped down next to him.

'What does this look like, El,' Griff said, 'a flipping discotheque? Friday it is, mun. The bar is no place for a woman on a Friday. You should be in the house, looking after the kids, like my missus. Good girl Siân is, not like you lot.' He waved dismissively at Rhiannon and Louisa, plucked the cigar out of Andy's mouth and lodged it between his own lips.

Ellie glanced around the room, at the old men lined on the barstools, swaying precariously to hymns and arias. Their skin was all wildlife, blurry tattoos of dragons and bluebirds, work-stained denim rolled to the elbow, all partaking in some implicit competition of who could shout *cunt* loudest, as if that made them men. The place looked like some shit-kicking Southern barroom, mining lamps hanging on the panelling instead of cow skulls. 'Listen,' she said, 'I need to talk to you about the band.'

'Want a drink?' Andy said, noticing her. He slid his half-finished pint of flat lager towards her and started on the house whisky that waited next to it.

'What about the band?' Marc said, looking at her from beneath his eyelashes. It had been four weeks since the John Peel session had aired and nothing had happened; no phone calls, no letters, no contracts. Marc was despondent. He'd cancelled weekly rehearsal, preferring to spend the time drinking in the Pump House. Talking about The Boobs had become taboo.

'The Needles want you to support them on the French leg of their European tour in February,' Ellie said. 'I've been writing a feature about them for *The Glamour*. I gave them a copy of your demo. The manager phoned just now.'

'Fuck off,' Rhiannon said, shouting. She stood up, tottered around on the heels of her go-go boots, waving her wineglass around, throwing a trickle in the general direction of the band. 'Watchin' ewe three trynna make it is like watchin' a bunch of retards trynna fuck a doorknob.' She fell back on the bench, skilfully guided by Louisa, who was holding her by the back of her halter-neck top.

'The Needles?' Marc said sceptically.

Ellie teased the manager's phone number out of her pocket and pushed it across the table. Marc stared at the digits scrawled across the back of a grocery receipt. 'He's going to ring you in the morning in any case,' Ellie said. 'I gave him your number.'

'Thanks El,' Marc said, a quaver of emotion in his voice. He went to the bar and ordered a bottle of champagne. Griff picked the receipt up and stared at it, his carrot-coloured eyebrows knitting together, face shaped like a pear. 'You better not be lying, El,' he said. He burped, then crumpled the piece of paper up and stuffed it into his own pocket.

'Ain't we supposed to be getting married in February?' Andy said. The cigar was in his hand again, the burnt-out ginger butt embedded between sausage fingers, a rim of carnation pink around his blue eyes. Forgetting he'd just given his lager to her, he picked it up and started drinking.

'Don't worry about that,' Ellie said, trying to brush him off, the way Bleddyn had done with her. 'We can get married when you come back. Hopefully we'll be able to *afford* a wedding when you get back.' A young, disabled man, one of the Friday-night regulars, struggled past the table on his aluminium crutches, legs slow and twisted. 'Oi, mush,' Rhiannon said, pointing at him. 'Ewer more pissed than I am!' The man continued walking, writhing laboriously through the gangway. 'I'm not drunk,' he said. 'I've got spina bifida.'

Rhiannon shook and then hung her head, silence punctuated by her booze-soaked hiccups. Johnny quickly circumnavigated the table and sidled up to Ellie, nudged her furtively with his shoulder.

'You've managed to postpone your wedding,' he said, voice low and playful, his breath on her neck. Ellie looked at the black sprigs of stubble sprouting from his angular face, the sharp, chalk-white incisors set in the middle. 'I'm not getting married,' she said. 'Just humouring him, that's all.'

Marc appeared with four glasses of warm wine on a plastic drinks tray. He was holding it in the air, a beer towel draped over his forearm. He put one down in front of Ellie.

'Not much fizz in that, is there?' Johnny said. He smoothed his hand across the top of the glass and dropped something inside, then swiftly moved his hand away. A crumb of powder at the base of the glass sent a blast of bubbles to the surface. 'People like you and me aren't meant to be tied up in shackles,' he said. 'Are we?'

'To The Boobs,' Marc said, raising his wineglass.

Ellie was about to lift her glass when she noticed Rhiannon glaring at her, the yellow strip lights reflecting in a ribbon of sweat across the bridge of her broad nose. She picked Marc's tobacco tin up from the table and aimed it at Ellie's glass, knocking it on to its side, the liquid dripping into Johnny and Ellie's laps. The tin bounced on the floor, the tobacco spilling into the grooves, stray fag papers soaking the liquid up.

'Sorry love!' Rhiannon said, lifting her hand to her breast. 'I'm pissed as a bloody parrot, I am. Ewe know I thought that tin was a beer-mat!'

Suddenly, a few yards away, Ribs fell backwards on his barstool. He lay sprawled along the floorboards, a stream of urine snaking down the leg of his jeans, blood from his head bleeding into the tobacco, one false eyelash fluttering.

'I'm going to invest in a bag of bastard sawdust for this place,' the barman said, arriving with his dustpan and cloth.

22

It was almost Bonfire Night and Johnny and Louisa were on their way. Siân had paid the mortgage that week and didn't have enough money to buy steak and brandy for bourguignon. She was hoping party food was going to suffice. She folded tinned tuna flakes into homemade mayonnaise, the starchy smell of baking potatoes drifting from the oven. She wiped her hands on her mother's old cotton apron. Angharad left her lollipop stick on the counter and stood idle in the doorway, licking her fingers. Siân picked the stick up, catching sight of Griff through the kitchen window. He was hacking at the dead brambles with a machete, tossing them on to a pile of mulch in the middle of the garden, holding them at arm's length, like a girl.

'Hey Ang,' Siân said, summoning her daughter. 'Is there anyone at nursery that you like? A little boy?' She held the stick under the cold tap. Angharad approached, face sombre. 'I don't like boys,' she said. She fondled the hem of her mother's overall. 'I like Emily Richmond.'

Siân chuckled. 'That's no good, *cariad*. It has to be a boy. I'll show you a love spell. Go 'n' get your crayons.' She wiped the stick on her apron while Angharad wandered into the living room. 'What you do,' she said, flashing it at her daughter as soon as she'd come back, 'is write your own name on one side, and the name of the one you love on the other.' She leaned over the stick, her black hair falling down over the counter as she struggled to write her name with the waxy green crayon. On the opposite side she scrawled the word 'Johnny'. She smiled at her daughter. 'Then,' she said, dropping the stick into a glass container, 'you cover it with honey.' She took the canister from next to the kettle, tipped a heap of white sugar over the stick and sealed the jar. 'Clear your mind of everything except the boy's face and say, "Sweet, sweet thoughts of me, you will think constantly." Come on, say it with me, "Sweet, sweet thoughts of me, you will think constantly."'

Angharad wasn't interested. She took the crayon from her mother's hand and quietly mooched away. Siân hid the container behind the Coke cans in the fridge, before Griff came in from the garden and stamped a dirty footprint on one of the clean tiles. '*Iesu mawr!*' Siân said, sucking air over her teeth. She took the van keys from the worktop and threw them at his fleshy torso. 'Go and pick the boys up from your mother's, will you?'

Griff held the keys clenched in his hand. 'Can leave them up there for a while?' he said. Siân turned the tap on, a volley of furious water hissing out. She pulled a scrubbing brush from the cupboard. 'What are you talking about, Griff?' she said. 'We're having a family party. We bought the fireworks for the kids.'

'I don't want the kids around when Johnny's here. He's not family, is he? I don't trust him, chick. Not as far as I could chuck him.'

'And that's not far, is it?' You can't put the rubbish bags out on Sundays. How're you going to lift a man of six foot?' She knelt on the floor and scoured at the tile, the bristles scratching frantically against the old porcelain. Griff stood watching her for a minute but Siân ignored his presence, breathing heavily over her work.

When he'd gone she dismantled James's drum-kit and stood on Angharad's bed, pushing the plastic pieces into the attic door, the weight of her body creating ripples in the duvet cover.

Downstairs, in the living room, there was a stack of clutter on the coffee table: plastic farmyard animals, a half-eaten custard-cream, two exercise books. She threw it all into a toy-box and frenziedly polished the table top. From the kitchen doorway it looked like other people's living rooms, but when she peered too long she noticed the ballpoint pen on the walls, the folded highchair and packets of nappies in the alcove, the safety gate attached to the stairs. She looked at the clock. It was four forty-seven. They'd be here in ten minutes. She opened the fridge and found the wine that she'd hidden beneath the vegetables, its gold screw-top poking out of the carrots. She guzzled straight from the bottle, before setting it on the patio table with plastic tumblers.

Soon she heard Griff coming in, the television going on with a ping. He was lying on the settee, his Nike trainers balanced on the surface of the clean table. Niall was sleeping in his pushchair. James was hauling a football from the toy-box.

'Get your feet off that table,' Siân said, voice vehement. This was her opportunity to show Johnny and Louisa that she was a competent human being, a Domestic Goddess capable of keeping a beautiful home, holding down two jobs, expertly raising three children whilst still being attractive; all the things the television reckoned a woman of her age should be. She retrieved the remote control and pointed it at the screen, her hand trembling. *The Weakest Link* evaporated, the screen turning black. 'They're going to be here any minute,' she said, 'so for God's sake don't start going on about having more kids.'

'Siân?' Griff said, sitting up.

'I know what you're trying to do,' she said. 'You're trying to torment me into getting a reversal, but I'm not getting a reversal until you get a job.' She'd thought carefully about her predicament and made a decision. If Griff continued to mock her infertility, she'd start on about his sheer laziness. The doorbell jingled its pivotal ding-dong, the battery going flat.

Johnny stood on the doorstep wearing a long-sleeved black shirt. He grinned at her, his oversized teeth reminding her of a pantomime horse. 'Hello,' Louisa said, diminutive eyes burnishing through a layer of matte foundation. She spied into the house. 'Nice place you've got,' she said, tart voice failing to mask her dishonesty.

'You're early!' Siân said, stepping back to let them in. 'We're out in the garden. Come on, follow me.' She guided them through the kitchen and out to the collapsible camping chairs, grabbing the pushchair along the way and parking it on the decking next to her seat. Johnny plonked his six-pack on the table, the cans bound by their plastic handcuffs. Louisa pulled one free, handing it to him. Siân hooked her toe under the pushchair and wheeled it back and forth, smiling at her sleeping toddler. Griff came out of the house and headed for the garden while James came to the table to scrutinize the visitors. He peered at Johnny. 'He's got hair like a woman,' he said, patting Siân's knee.

'Some men have got long hair too, James,' Siân said.

Griff snorted and pricked at the unlit bonfire with a pitchfork.

Siân shook her head. She smiled at Johnny, then Louisa.

Johnny snickered. He looked at James. 'Do you like guns, mate?' he said. 'Because I can get shot ring caps, the ones you can't buy from the shops.'

'Of course he doesn't like guns, Johnny,' Louisa said, aghast. 'He's only—'

'Four,' Siân said. 'Actually, he loves guns. Next-door's cat got shot with an air rifle last weekend. Now it's blind in both eyes. Every time it walks into the wall the kids' sides split.'

She'd tried to discourage it, if only for Ellie's sake. Ellie hated toy guns more than she hated real ones. But guns were all over the place: on the news, in the films, in the cowboy outfits they sold in the costume shop on the High Street; accepted by society as if they were part of everyone's daily life. You had to think hard about it before you realized they were unnatural. Like plastic surgery. On a couple of occasions, Siân had noticed Angharad staring at Rhiannon's chest. Whenever anyone complimented Rhiannon on her tits, her response was an unfailing, 'Why don't ewe get some 'en, love? All ewe gotta do is go to the doctor an' tell 'im ewer gonna kill eweself unless ewe get a pair of double Fs.' Sooner or later, that's exactly what she was going to say to Angharad. Siân imagined her four-year-old son standing in the middle of a forest, an Uzi under his arm like a miniature Rambo. She imagined her three-year-old daughter with enormous silicone breasts, standing on a sidewalk like Jodie Foster in *Taxi Driver*.

Griff lit the fire with a disposable lighter and a copy of the local newspaper. He poured a dash of petrol on to it and it erupted with a roar, the tapering flame swallowing the shredded phone bills and kindling. James ran towards it and Griff caught him before he got there. He drew a line in the earth with the pitchfork, said: 'Look, butty, you can't pass this line. If you pass this line you'll end up in casualty.' He gave him small pieces of wood to throw from a distance into the blaze. A flare on Siân's near-side burned incandescent as the fire caught the lead paint on the old wood. James crossed the line and edged closer to the fire.

'James,' Griff said. 'What did Daddy say? No crossing the line.'

James stepped back hesitantly, only to cross it again a second later.

'Who wants a sparkler?' Griff said, enticing him away from the fire. He ripped one from its paper sheath and James ran to him, grabbing it. Griff cupped his fist around James's hand and together they wrote their names in the air, the sparkler's yellow point dull against the slate-grey sky. It was still daytime, too light for fireworks, but that was the way that people with children lived their lives. They were always making compromises. When they wrote 'Niall', Siân noticed they left one of the Ls out.

'Come and see my alien,' Angharad said, seizing Louisa by her slender fingers. Louisa stood up, face paralysed with dread. Angharad tugged, dragging her towards the back door, Louisa allowing herself to be hauled away, her body limp with fright.

'She won't bite,' Siân said. Already she could feel Johnny's eyes on the side of her face. She picked her picnic glass up and swallowed a gulp of wine.

'I've been thinking about you,' he said, diverting his voice into her ear canal, out of Griff's earshot. Siân giggled. 'Were they sweet, sweet thoughts?' she said.

'What?' he said, long fingers fumbling around in his breast pocket. He pulled something out and held it in front of her. It was a pill with an emblem shaped like a butterfly pressed into its chalky face.

Siân hadn't taken a drug since the first blue line appeared on her home pregnancy testing kit four years ago. People hadn't stopped giving them to her though. She pretended to swallow them but what she actually did was hide them in an inside pocket of her handbag. That's what she'd done with the one he'd given to her in his flat. She brought them home and put them in her grandmother's ivory pillbox. It was lodged behind the electric meter, where the children had no chance of getting it. There must have been more than a hundred, two hundred perhaps. She was using them as insurance. She knew that if the drought went on any longer she could sell them from a tenner upwards.

'I don't want anything for it,' Johnny said.

Siân glanced around the garden. Niall was still asleep in the pushchair, his mouth pinched into a cherry-coloured bow. She didn't want Johnny to think she was square. He was a drug dealer. He must have liked women who were game for a party so she took the pill and placed it on the back of her tongue, quickly lifting her wineglass, scared that she was going to choke. She wasn't good at swallowing tablets. But what harm could *one* pill do?

'Thanks,' she said, reaching under the table and squeezing a pad of denim above his knee.

'Siân?' Louisa was shouting out of a gap in the kitchen window. 'I think something's burning in here.' She waved and reached up to the handle, pushing it wide open. 'I'll be there now,' Siân said, but she didn't get up. She turned to look at Johnny. 'Louisa's a bit uptight, isn't she? Does she like children?'

'I don't know what she likes,' Johnny said, shrugging. He tilted his can to his mouth and said, 'You work in the video shop, don't you? Have you ever seen a film called *Donnie Darko*?' Siân had a vague memory of the name, a hazy image of a jet engine colliding with the roof of a house, an old Tears for Fears song. 'I think so,' she said. 'What's it about?'

Johnny flashed his teeth; a smile like the estuary of a river. 'You know the main character's called Donnie Darko, right? And there's two Donnies in the story, right? One that's dead and one that's alive in a tangent universe. Some scientists think there are other worlds out there, full of people who made different decisions earlier in their lives, who took a different direction at a certain crossroad.'

Siân frowned at Johnny.

'What it means,' he said, the blaze reflecting copper in his pupils, 'is that if these scientists are right, there could be another Siân out there somewhere, the one who never got married or had children, and there'd be another me too. The one who never met Louisa. For all we know, me and you could be hooking up right now, over a couple of Slow Wet Orgasms, in a bar in Thailand.' He slugged at his lager. Behind him the fire crackled. The air smelled like gunpowder.

'I don't regret having my children,' Siân said.

'Of course not,' Johnny said. 'I'm just—'

Suddenly Angharad emerged from the house, wailing and gripping one hand in the other, little face sunburn-pink. She whirled

140

around and around, blaring, pausing intermittently to catch her own breath. Louisa ran on to the decking, her hand pressed on her forehead. 'I opened the oven, Siân,' she said. 'Your potatoes were burnt. She picked one up. I think she's hurt.'

'Angharad!' Siân said. She stood up but her legs were weak. She held on to Johnny's shoulder for support but slumped back into her chair. 'Angharad,' she said. She leaned forward, pushing the soles of her feet against the decking, striving for balance. 'Come here please. Show Mammy your hand.'

Angharad was still grizzling, standing on the path, face wet and terrified. Griff dropped his pitchfork and it fell ringing against the concrete. He flew at Angharad, scooping her into his arms and bringing her to the table. 'Come on, chick,' he said, slowly unrolling the child's fingers. He held her palm up to the dim light.

Siân strained to look at the injury, her vision foggy. There was a big ruby blister on the ball of her daughter's hand. 'You need to run it under the cold tap,' she said.

'No, I think it's a bit worse than that,' Griff said.

'We'd better go, hadn't we?' Louisa said. She was already at the back door, preparing to make her exit. Johnny stood up with a sigh and joined her reluctantly.

'Yes,' Griff said. 'Siân, get your things. We'll have to take her to Abertach.'

'Griff,' Siân said, 'I feel a bit faint.' The orange flames of the fire were a blur against the silver horizon. In her entire lifetime she'd never taken an E that had made her feel like this. She tried to lift her arm but her effort was futile. She felt her muscles ripple but her arm was still next to her side.

'You're not ill, Siân,' Griff said. 'You're drunk.' He propped Angharad on to his hip, holding her by the backside. 'James,' he said, his voice echoing across the row of terraced gardens. 'You can come with us. Come for a ride in the van.'

Siân felt a pressure on her neck, Griff holding her chin in his hand. One side of his face was illuminated by their neighbour's security light, his eye mean and accusatory. 'Think you can look after Niall until we get back?' he said, voice impatient. 'Think you can do that?'

He let go of her and her head lolled on to her shoulder. 'Yes,' she said, the word not quite coming out. She could see her empty wineglass on the table, the stem of it seemingly tilted at a 60-degree angle. She was alone now, apart from Niall asleep in the pushchair. She could sense her own solitariness. She stamped her foot on the decking, surprised by the feel of the wood against the sole of her shoe. She tried it again for good measure and then struggled out of the camping chair. She staggered to the house in a zigzag pattern, her weight lunging from one side of her body to the other.

A few moments later she emerged, a stack of crayon drawings clutched under her elbow. She reeled towards the fire and threw the papers at it, retreating haphazardly back to the patio to watch them burn. She managed to lift the wine bottle to her lips and take a sip, but didn't like the taste of it. Somewhere in the back of her mind was the feeling that she should be worried about something, but the only thought she could concentrate on was that, in another world, she'd be on a beach, rising out of the sea in a white bikini, like Ursula Andress in *Dr No*.

23

Early in November, Ellie was walking to the bus stop on the High Street, on her way to the Labour Club where the band were playing a gig. The trees on Pengoes Mountain were sticking up like furious black fingers. There was already a plastic notice outside one of the cottages on the square that said, 'Santa, please stop here.' In the YMCA the blinds were open but there was nobody at home. The driveway was empty. By the time she reached the club, the band had finished. Mogg, a committee man who was shaped like a barrel, directed her to the lounge in the basement.

It was decorated entirely in red, the velveteen benches burgundy, the piebald carpet tiles claret. The band was sitting in the middle of the room, Andy and Marc playing fifteen-card brag, a game they'd started in 1991; faces obscured in the half-light of the winter afternoon. Griff was asleep, head on the table, old cigarette butts rammed into his nostrils. Ribs looked up from his pint, a vague trace of blue make-up above the cirrhosis-yellowed whites of his eyes.

Someone approached Ellie from behind, their fingers covering her eyes, blocking her view. 'Where've you been?' he said. She could feel the heat of his tall body close to her back. She breathed the tang of petroleum deep into her lungs and spun around to look at him. She hadn't seen him for weeks. She'd been waiting for this moment, waiting for him to change her life.

'It's been like an old working man's club here without you,' he said, pupils swelling as they landed on her face.

'Where's Louisa?' Ellie said.

'Cornwall.' He walked her to the table, a grin streaked from jaw to jaw. 'Her father had a nasty accident on his motorbike, broken both his legs. She's visiting him in the hospital in Saint Austell.'

'No!' Ellie said, a hint of delight escaping with a gasp.

'Yep!' Johnny said, sensing Ellie's irreverence.

'OK, babe?' Andy murmured, looking up fleetingly from his cards.

Johnny poked Ellie in the ribs. 'You fancy a game of pool?'

They both stood up, as quickly as they'd sat down. They made their way to the pool table on the other side of the room. There were two balls left on the crimson felt. In the corner was a gawky, artificial Christmas tree, plastic moons and stars clinging to the sparse branches as though the whole committee had stood a few feet away, wearing blindfolds, and bunged the decorations in the general direction of it.

'Got any change?' Johnny said, flicking through a fat wad of purple notes.

Ellie put two twenty-pence pieces into the slot at the base of the table, pushed the lever, watched as the balls came exploding out of its bowels. She still couldn't look at him properly, something subversive behind his chilling black eyes.

'I've got a present for you,' he said, crouching down next to her.

The closeness of him made something in Ellie's physicality react. She could feel her blood racing to her face. She focused on his lean wrists. He produced a bag of powder and pushed it into her cupped hand. Slowly, she opened the bag, sucked the tip of her finger before dipping it inside.

'Careful though, El,' he said. 'It's not speed. Pure Columbian Marching Powder, that is.' As she swallowed, a metallic aftertaste remained balancing on the back of her tongue, like a buoy. Ellie smiled at their nefariousness; they were hiding behind the pool table, doing drugs like a pair of teenagers, her fiancé mere feet away.

'There won't be much call for this around here,' she said, passing the baggie back, trying to appear confident and nonchalant. 'Nobody in Aberalaw can afford cocaine.' As she stood up she unhooked one of the star-shaped baubles from the tree and passed it to Johnny. 'A present for you,' she said. Johnny laughed as he pushed it into his pocket. He rolled the plastic triangle along the felt.

She'd made the mistake of letting him break and had to watch as he stalked the table, measuring, setting his yellows up against the pockets and effortlessly dropping them in. 'Have you heard about the American Chinook that came down?' he said, body stretched the length of the table, one leg pushed out behind him. 'Surface-to-air missiles in Fallujah. I'm telling you, El, it's Vietnam all over again. Nobody learns anything from history, do they? Then again, war isn't about making the world better; it's about retaining order. Make sure the poor stay poor and the rich stay rich.' She nodded in agreement but said nothing. Her mouth was watering and she could feel the liquid gathering at the back of her throat, her gums and lips numb. She looked at the blond hairs standing up on her forearms. If he kissed me now, she thought, I wouldn't even be able to feel it.

A few minutes later, Mogg brought a huge piece of hardboard to the table. 'Sorry Elizabeth, love,' he said, resting it against the side cushion. 'It's karaoke on a Saturday.' Another committee man followed, wheeling a shopping trolley with an amplifier inside. 'Sorry,' he said, grunting at Johnny. He took one end of the hard-board. 'It's karaoke on a Saturday.' Together, the two men set it on top of the table.

'Can we finish our game first?' Johnny said, agitated.

Mogg looked at his watch. 'No, it's six o'clock now.'

Johnny waved his arm around the room. 'But there's nobody here but us.'

'Sorry,' he said. 'You'll have to call it a draw.'

Johnny shook Ellie's hand, his long fingers pinching at her skin. They were on their way back to the others when Rhiannon turned up, tits bursting out of her bustier like a pair of nut-coloured airbags. She uncoiled her silk scarf and took a bottle of white rum from her bag. She whacked it on the table. As if she could sniff something troublesome in the atmosphere, she stopped abruptly and stared at Johnny. 'Where's ewer missus, mush?' she said.

'Cornwall,' Johnny said, gaze planted on his basketball boots like a child that'd been caught stealing lollipops. Ellie looked at the space on the table in front of him, searching for the Christmas bauble, something that laid claim to him. It wasn't there. But she noticed her knee was touching his knee, their nerve endings numbed with nose candy.

Rhiannon glowered at Ellie. Plonking herself down next to Marc, she reached for the box-file the committee man had left on the table. She began to run her fingernail along the list of karaoke songs, intermittently glancing at Ellie. After a minute, she shouted across the table. 'Look El, I've found somethin' we could do together, that 'Summer Nights' song from *Grease*. It suits ewe down to the fuckin' ground that does, shy likkle Sandy thinkin' Danny's in love with urgh.'

Ellie'd made too much progress to be intimidated into submission. She was bored by Rhiannon's threats. 'What does that make you, Rhi?' she said. 'Rizzo?'

Rhiannon's face buckled, eyes demonic. She picked the file up and carried it over to the karaoke machine. She stood next to the compère and prodded something written on the sheet. He gave her a microphone. The music began with a couple of sombre piano bars. Rhiannon stood with her legs spread defiantly,

146

the microphone at her chest. '*I hear him, before I go to sleep*,' she sang; voice flat and stony. It took Ellie a while to work out what it was. The lyrics were inaudible. Then, as the chorus started she realized it was 'The Man with the Child in his Eyes'.

Marc slapped his cards face down on the table. 'Not again?' he said. He plucked the fag butts out of Griff's nostrils and plugged them into his own ears.

'She couldn't have picked a worse song,' Ribs said, eyelashes fluttering in amazement. Three women had just arrived and were queuing at the bar. They stood in a huddle, cackling and pointing at Rhiannon. 'Fucking hell, Davies,' one of them shouted. 'Get some fucking singing lessons, you tone-deaf tart.'

Andy shook his head, drained his pint, stood up. 'I think she needs some help,' he said. He walked over to the karaoke machine and asked the compère for a microphone. Andy loved karaoke. He jumped into the song at the beginning of the second verse, his sturdy baritone drowning Rhiannon out.

Ellie turned to Johnny. 'Done much painting lately?' she said.

Johnny's eyes lit up as if it was the question he'd been waiting for. 'I'm working on an installation,' he said. 'A Goya-type of thing, insects fighting each other, English insects fighting Cornish insects. Want to come and see it?'

'Having a party later, are you?' Ellie said. 'Would Louisa approve of that?'

Johnny drained his glass. 'No,' he said, laughing. He took his coat from the back of his chair. 'I'm going now. Come with me if you want.'

Ellie glanced about. Rhiannon and Andy had started another song, 'Don't Go Breaking My Heart'. Marc and Ribs sat rigid, watching them, mouths agape. Griff was still asleep. 'Well, won't we need to book a taxi?' she said, shaken by the abruptness of his offer. She'd always tended to believe that seduction was a long drawn-out process, not a casual, one-night thing. That was the way ordinary, unremarkable people did it; people like her and Andy.

'I've got the BMW,' he said. 'I drunk drove.' He beckoned her with a swoop of his hand. 'Make a decision, El,' he said. 'It's a yes or no answer,' a catch in his voice, at odds with his playful smile.

Without another thought she promptly followed him up the stairs and out of the door. The car park was shrouded in a thick layer of hailstones; for a moment it looked like snow, tinted amber where the streetlights reflected on it. Johnny opened the passenger door for Ellie and a shelf of the slushy matter fell from the car and crashed to the ground. He strode around the back of the car and got in on the driver's side, plucking the silver star-shaped bauble seemingly from mid-air, and tying it to the rear-view mirror. 'I hate Christmas,' he said, squinting at her. 'I don't usually trim up but I'll make an exception for a present from you. How do I get back to the square?'

'Straight ahead,' Ellie said, getting into the car. 'Turn right at the junction for the High Street and left on to Dynevor.' The bauble swung from the mirror as he started the engine and reversed out of the car park.

Along the road, snaking through the industrial estate, two parallel tyre tracks cut through the hail where many a drunk driver had gone before. Ellie hoped that at some point the paths would converge, though she knew they never would. In the car it was warm and silent. 'Johnny?' Ellie said, glancing at him. His eyes were focused on the road. 'Can I ask you what you're doing here in Wales? People are saying you've run away from a gangland boss, or that you have something to do with the Williams twins, that you're on a witness protection scheme, or that you killed someone.'

'Killed someone?' His hand fell from the steering wheel and landed with a slap on her leg. He laughed. 'Look at me, El. Eleven stone on the nose. I couldn't kill an ant. People talk a lot here, don't they?'

'Of course they do!' she said. 'This is Aberalaw. What else are they going to do? Someone like you turning up, that's like a goose laying the golden egg. You should be careful, you know, dealing. Someone'll grass you up, especially when you're driving around in a Beamer, looking so proud of yourself.'

He pulled up alongside the YMCA and tore the key from the ignition, but he didn't get out of the car. His hand was moving slowly up her thigh. It was quiet again; the only sound, the engine ticking down. Ellie felt like she was going explode, a suicide bomber without the bomb, about to burst into blood-saturated slivers.

'I've got a confession to make,' he said. 'I haven't started my installation yet. I'm going to do it though. I've got it all planned.' For a moment Ellie had thought she was going to be privy to some classified information, that he was going to trust her with a secret, but he only told her what she already knew; that he'd brought her here to have sex with him. She began to worry about her bikini line. Since she'd stopped taking the pill she'd only bothered to run a disposable razor over the parts she could see, sitting upright in the bath. Johnny lifted his hand and placed it around her neck, holding her head, his thumb pressing on her chocolate-stain mole. Ellie was static with pleasure, waiting for his next move.

'Not shy now, are you?' he said, making *shy* sound like some sort of disorder. The car alarm's red light was flickering on the dashboard. 'That stuff I gave you is good for shyness.' Ellie thought of Rhiannon likening her to Sandra Dee from *Grease*. 'I'm not shy,' she said, affronted. 'And that stuff you gave me doesn't mean shit. Pills, speed, coke, I can take it or leave it. That's not why I came with you.'

'Good.' He opened the car door and stalked towards the YMCA. 'Come on, slowcoach,' he said, rubbing his hands together. 'It's cold.' *The YMCA*, Ellie thought. If that building had ever been a Christian institute, God was long gone. Satan had moved in and he was turning it into a seditious playground, recruiting fallen angels to play tag.

Johnny began climbing up the dark stairwell. Ellie followed. Halfway up, through a fissure between his legs, she deciphered a figure on the landing. The blunt light stuttered, and then, in full view, she saw Louisa standing on the top step, wearing saggy peach pyjamas.

'Ellie?' she said, voice treacly with sleep. 'What are you doing here?'

Shit. 'The party,' Ellie said, stammering. 'Johnny said he was having a party. The others are on their way. I didn't know you were in bed, Lou. I didn't want to disturb you. Sorry. I'll go.' She turned around on the stair.

'I'll see you out,' Johnny said.

Louisa coughed abruptly. 'No,' she said. 'No, you stay right here.'

24

Ellie's first instinct was to run as far from the YMCA as it was possible to get, out of Louisa's demented, glass-throwing reach. The hail had thawed and the water squelched beneath her feet. At the entrance to Woodland Terrace she realized she was safe, for the moment at least. She stopped running.

A joyrider careered over the cattle-grid on Pengoes Mountain, the noise echoing through the valley like a gunshot. As the cold air began to lick at her arms she realized she'd left her coat at the Labour Club. She lit a cigarette. She glanced around at the ribbons of terraced houses. The lights were out now in the YMCA. What the hell was Louisa doing there anyway? He'd told her she was in Cornwall. Ellie's gilded coach had turned to a festering pumpkin and she turned to walk home, dawdling along the wet pavement of Gwendolyn Street until she reached her own gate. She lifted the cracked strawberry planter next to the doorstep, retrieving the spare key. She was home, and she knew she had a limited amount of time in which to construct a credible excuse for having left the club with Johnny.

She was lying in the bathtub when Andy came in, the steam gathering on the blackened ceiling. She decided on a bath because she couldn't get rid of her cocaine throat. Twice she brushed her teeth, the second time forcing the bristles so far back she'd gagged. Still, a little blood-flavoured bubble hovered above her epiglottis. She heard his footsteps on the stairs, then moving across the landing.

'There you are,' he said, feathery blond hair damp and clinging to his head. He was holding Ellie's pea-green coat in his arms like a baby. He sat on the edge of the tub, pushing the soap-dish into the water. 'Where've you been, babe?'

Ellie squeezed a splodge of shampoo into her palm. 'Here,' she said happily. She imagined her ability to tell a successful lie depended on her ability to retain as much of the truth as was feasible, in case an eyewitness refuted it later. Louisa, for instance. 'I wanted to come home. You were busy with the karaoke and Johnny was driving back, so I got a lift with him.' She worked the shampoo into a lather. Through its residue she felt the outline of her mole, relieved to find it still there, as though Johnny could have made it vanish with the tip of his magical finger.

'You were in a rush though,' he said. 'You left your coat.' He was still holding it, broad fingers clawing at the viscose. He lifted it, presenting it to her.

'Yeah,' she said. 'He was going there and then.' Ellie was sure that if Andy embarked on an affair she'd see it coming a mile off, women's intuition and all of that. But Andy wasn't particularly perceptive. All she had to do was ride it out. She leaned back into the tepid water and stayed there a while, the foam fizzling around her head. If Andy had been less conservative, she might have been able to confide in him about her adventure. She couldn't help feeling that her recent experience with Johnny deserved a less gentle ending. She wanted to talk about it. Eventually she sat up.

'But you didn't tell me that you were going,' Andy said.

'You were in the middle of a song.' Something bleeped. It was her mobile phone. It was in her coat. She reached into the pocket and rummaged around with wet fingers. She brought the phone out, holding it away from the bathwater. There were eight missed calls, six from Andy, two from Rhiannon. 'I'm not a kid, And,' she said. 'You and her, you think I need to be looked after, but I'm more responsible than the two of you put together. I lived in Plymouth for three years on my own. I learned to look after myself at the age of thirteen . . .' something Andy'd never given her any credit for.

'She thinks you're having an affair with him,' Andy said, voice casual.

Ellie flipped her phone closed and put it down on the floor. 'What?' she said.

'Rhiannon. She thinks you're having an affair with Johnny. She said she caught you playing footsy under the table at that party of his.'

Ellie laughed. 'Rhiannon?' she said. 'Is that the same woman Louisa caught kissing Johnny in the kitchen? That woman you call a gold-digging hooker? Footsy!' She imagined punching Rhiannon's mouth, sending her whitened teeth, bloody and chipped, spraying in three different directions; the one with the gold filling skidding into the gutter outside the pub. She could feel herself blushing. She threw a spurt of water at her face, smearing it on to her cheeks with her open hands.

'Oh, it's not you,' Andy said. He was staring at the pile of clothes she'd left on the carpet, her inside-out bra balancing on its cups, like a W. His lip curled to a scowl. 'It's him, the slimy bastard. You can't turn around without him staring at your arse.'

Ellie quickly turned her face to the row of cracked tiles lining the wall and smiled at this revelation; she didn't know she had the kind of arse that men tended to stare at. She'd never really thought about her own arse. Perhaps Johnny wanted to get caught. Perhaps that's why he'd been so flippant about luring her out of the club. He'd said something once about him and her being tied up in shackles. Perhaps *he* was trying to escape with her, because Andy and Louisa, they shared a trait: they both clung to their partners like magpies who'd found gold. She straightened her face and turned back to Andy. 'That's not my fault, is it?' she said. 'He's a womanizer. Look what happened with Rhiannon. And have you seen the way he stares at Siân? If you're going to marry me you have to trust me.'

'I don't want you encouraging him,' Andy said. 'You hardly spoke to me. You were with him all night, playing pool, giggling together in the corner. When I looked up you'd both gone.'

'You never spoke to me,' Ellie said. 'You were playing cards with Marc. Then you started on the karaoke with Rhiannon. I hate karaoke. You know I hate karaoke.'

She was getting tired of the argument now. It had been a bad idea to go back to the YMCA. Discretion was essential. She was engaged to a man with suicidal tendencies and she was scared of her murderous sister-in-law. In any case, extramarital liaisons should be conducted in hotel rooms, neutral locations, not aligned to either party. Next time she'd tell him to book a room at the Cardiff Hilton. 'It's only because he's English, isn't it?' she said. 'You wouldn't have a problem if I got a lift with a Welshman. You're xenophobic. It isn't easy for them, moving to a place like this, you know. It helps if people are friendly.'

'But not too friendly,' Andy said. He dropped her coat and sidled along the edge of the tub, lowering his hands into the water, slowly moving them up her back. He began to massage her taut shoulders. Ellie started thinking about an observation she'd made unwittingly, in the heat of the exchange; the way Johnny stared at Siân. In the pub and in the park, she'd seen him gawping at her, black eyes broody, facial expression on the brink of an extreme fury that never manifested itself. Ellie had seen it, but she'd never really noticed it, until now.

She could feel Andy's hands wandering down her back. They were under the waterline, the surface rippling lightly around her. Suddenly he touched her coccyx, his forefinger steering into the chasm between her buttocks. Ellie jumped. She turned and splashed water into his face. 'For God's sake, Andy!' she said. 'You can't accuse me of being the village bike and then jump on me yourself!'

25

Sunday afternoon, Rhiannon's birthday. She was sitting in the Pump House with Marc. 'Look! It's Mrs fuckin' brain,' she said as she spied Ellie arrive. 'What brings ewe yere?' The last time she'd seen her was in the Labour Club, just before she'd made off in Johnny's BMW, the sly cunt. As if Johnny was interested in that fucking bint. Ellie was the kind of girl who'd piss herself if a stranger pinched her arse. Probably carried a rape alarm around in that ugly little duffel bag. All she ever did was bang on about America, feminism and animal bloody rights. She was about as sexy as a set of dentures. If Johnny had screwed her it must have felt like he'd dipped his cock in a dead fish.

'Happy birthday,' Ellie said. She slapped an envelope down on the table. Rhiannon opened it without looking at her. It was an old-fashioned card, a bunch of lilies on the front. 'Sister-In-Law,' it said in red writing. 'Ta,' Rhiannon said. She threw it on the shelf without reading the message inside.

Johnny arrived a few minutes later. 'Whose birthday is it?' he said, squinting at the cheap birthday card from Ellie. The chain around his neck was thick as rope, worth a monkey at least. His arms filled the tops of his sweatshirt as he leaned down on the back of an empty chair.

'Mine,' Rhiannon said. She pushed her cleavage out.

'Oh,' Johnny said, eyes landing on her tits. 'How old are you?'

'Ha ha,' Rhiannon said. 'Ewer not supposed to ask a lady urgh age. Some gentleman ewe are.' Louisa arrived at the table, carrying the drinks. She was always ten paces behind him, like one of those immigrants you saw in Cardiff, drenched in black and traipsing after their husbands.

'Twenty-nine,' Rhiannon said, looking at Johnny. 'Twenty-bloody-nine, I am. Bet ewe wish ewe were twenty-nine again, uh, tiger?' She was desperate to be alone with him again; hadn't seen him properly since that party in his flat in the summer. Cut a long story, he'd been staring at her all night, sitting in the garden, a string of Christmas lights hanging from a tree. He'd kept rubbing his own arms, peering at her over his spliff, touching her hand for too long when he passed it to her. When he'd got up to fetch her a glass of wine, she knew it was an invitation. She made some excuse about not liking red wine – she didn't anyway, it was foul that bloody stuff; only pikeys drank it. She followed him into the house. She'd never been backward in coming forward, not like Ellie, the dumb cow.

He'd been standing by the cupboard, a wineglass in his hand, his square nails spread around its enormous bowl. 'There's a big one,' she'd said.

Johnny'd laughed. 'Are they real then?' he said.

Rhiannon had held her cleavage up, offering it to him, her flesh warm under her Donna Karan camisole. They weighed a bloody ton: breakfast, dinner and everything in between. 'Guess,' she said. Johnny'd reached for a nipple, tweaking it through the material. 'I'm not sure,' he said. 'I'll need to see them naked, check for scars.' His breath smelled of alcohol and skunk. Rhiannon leaned against the cooker, stood up on tiptoes, his hands all over her body, her legs heavy with lust, the metal of his belt buckle digging into her stomach. 'Course, Ellie had to come in and ruin it, skin of her arse on her freckle-splattered face. She was on her way to the bog to have a cry about the state of the world, or whatever the fuck

157

it was that made her so pissing miserable. And then Louisa, spitting chips, accusin' her of all sorts.

Two weeks later, Rhiannon had seen Louisa in the pub. She was standing at the bar, looking up from the money in her hand. Rhiannon had expected the cold shoulder but Louisa smiled, and waved at her like a spastic. 'Orright?' Rhiannon had said, puzzled by Louisa's sudden change of heart. Louisa crept up to her and whispered in her ear. 'I'm sorry about my little outburst before,' she said, voice all fucking English. 'I get a bit silly when I've had too much to drink.'

'Yeah,' Rhiannon had said. 'Ewe do. Ewe wanna count ewer lucky stars, love, 'cause I've lynched people for less; and I got no interest in ewer boyfriend, beaut, I got my bloody own.' They were friends again but some of the trust had been lost in the crossfire. Louisa wouldn't leave Rhiannon alone with Johnny for any length of time. Still, he was always making eyes at her, still whispering sexual innuendos into her ear.

Dai Davies was coming over now, a glass of Scotch in his hand, his little tobacco-stained finger sticking up, as if he was posh or something. As if. 'How old are you now, bach?' he said, spit forming in the corner of his mouth. 'Thirty-five? Thirty-six?' He looked around at the others. 'I didn't think she'd live this long, the way she pined for her dad. I thought she'd end up doing something stupid. Cried for him day and night she did.'

'Course I fuckin' cried,' Rhiannon said. 'I was eight years old. My father'd just fuckin' died.' She remembered her mother at the funeral, walking through the cemetery in a stupid black-feather fascinator. Her new boyfriend, some low-life from the estate, waiting for her in a gold Escort parked at the entrance. She must have cut an onion up to make her eyes all puffy like that. Rhiannon took the glass out of Dai's dirty hand and downed the whisky in one. It was a trick she'd learned somewhere along the way, you had to open your throat and take a deep breath at the same time, pour the liquid steady and slow; useful for a few other things too. She could do deep throat like a Kirby vacuum cleaner. She gave the glass back to him, waved at his face, shooing him away like a fly. She looked at Johnny. 'Fuckin' demented old bastard,' she said. 'Twenty-bloody-nine, I am.'

Suddenly the music from the jukebox stopped. The barman was aiming the remote control at the TV, turning the volume up. 'They've found Saddam Hussein,' he was saying, everyone turning to look at the screen. Some tart of a newsreader was babbling on about the war, then a blurry homemade video of some Paki, a big white emery board in his mouth. A man standing behind a dais in the White House came on and said, 'Ladies and gentleman, we got him.'

Rhiannon gripped the stem of her wineglass and tried to steer the attention away from the TV. 'Ewe'll never guess what Marc did iss morning,' she said. 'Sappy bastard only woke me up at ten, standin' naked at the bottom of the bed, holding a giant bottle of bubbly in front of 'is pecker! Sprayed it all over my Egyptian cotton sheets, din't ewe, love?'

Marc nodded.

She didn't go on to mention the proposal. He'd asked her to marry him again and she'd agreed. She'd told him they'd go to Gretna Green when she could get some time away from the salon. She had to tell him something. Bob Stone wasn't ever going to grant her a divorce. She'd emptied his building society account in 1986, two days after she got her City & Guilds, one day before their second wedding anniversary. It was only a measly sixty grand. By the time she'd paid for the operation and bought the salon there wasn't enough left for a fortnight in Ibiza. The way he went on about it you'd think it was bloody millions. He only would have frittered it away on a bloody conservatory to watch the starlings. The minute she advertised CF25 in the Yellow Pages, he was on the blower, threatening to contest her petition.

'Can you believe that?' Johnny said. He was still staring at the screen, amazed by the news. 'I didn't think they'd find him. I really didn't.'

'I knew they'd get Saddam,' Ellie said. 'It's Bin Laden I worry about.' Johnny stepped back a few paces to be next to her. 'They'll never get him, El,' he said. 'Didn't you know? He's George Bush's cousin!' The pair of them started laughing like a couple of fucking drains.

'Oh, get a fucking room,' Rhiannon said. She could feel her control of the situation ebbing away, a pang of adrenaline shooting up her forearms. This was her pet hate, not being listened to. All her life she'd suffered from a recurring night-mare in which she found herself standing naked in the middle of the High Street, shouting at the top of her voice. Hundreds of people kept walking past. Nobody even looked at her. They just kept on milling by.

'Oi! Mush!' she said, yelling at Johnny. He turned to look at her, an unlit cigarette dangling from his lips. She lifted the hem of her blouse, deliberately flashing her tits. She was wearing the Ted Baker bra Marc had bought for her birthday, pink with black polka dots and a lace trim. Ribs was walking to the toilet and he stopped dead in his tracks, said, 'Woo, Rhi, that's *gorgeous*. Where did you get *that*?'

'Nice inni?' Rhiannon said. 'Marc bought it for my birthday.' She let her top fall back down to her waist. She winked at Johnny. He smiled as he lit his cigarette but then turned back to the TV. Rhiannon could taste blood in her mouth. Her vision was blurred, a murky film in front of her eyes, as if she was trying to focus on Johnny from underwater. She pushed Marc aside and sprang up from the bench. 'It's *my* fucking birthday!' she said, shouting. She picked a chair up and threw it at the jukebox.

A leg smashed through the coloured frontage, shards of glass exploding over the pool table. The chair landed on the floorboards with a thud.

Rhiannon slumped back on to the bench, relieved. Best form of defence, she thought.

26

Collin was late getting back from the Welfare Hall in Penmaes. He practically fell through the living-room door and landed on his seat at the dining table. 'Shut up mun, woman,' he said without looking at Gwynnie. She was snivelling because the butter on her new potatoes had congealed. 'I'm home now, in I?' He hummed a tune as he chaotically carved the pork, eyes blunted with drunkenness.

'It all needs reheating now!' Gwynnie cried. She jumped out of her seat and snatched the Pyrex jug, still wearing her flour-stained pinafore, her hands shaking. A stripe of gooey gravy splashed across the plastic tablecloth.

'Leave it, Mam,' Marc said, seizing her swollen wrist. 'It's warm enough.'

Ellie had been to Andy's parents' house for Christmas dinner three times in a row. It was the same every year. She looked away from the uncomfortable scene at the table, to an oil painting behind Rhiannon's head, a clipper ship with cream sails, balancing on a malicious blue wave. It was the only piece of art in the house and it was ugly as hell. It had been given to Collin as part-payment for a decorating job, and he'd put it up because he could. He reckoned it was seventeenth century and worth a bit. Ellie knew it was impossible to get hold of that ultramarine colour before the Industrial Revolution because lapis lazuli or azurite gemstones were too expensive for artists to buy. It was a modern reproduction, the canvas dipped in tea, worth about fifty pence. Andy's parents didn't realize that art was its own reward.

Marc opened the bottle of Lambrini that Rhiannon had brought and poured some into each of the women's glasses. 'Drink up, ladies,' he said. Instead of his usual red football jersey he was wearing a short-sleeved navy shirt, pop art pictures of John Lennon's face plastered all over it. He picked up one of Gwynnie's cheap crêpe-paper crackers and held it in Ellie's direction. Ellie pulled at it grudgingly. It burst and spat a slip of yellowed paper on to the roast potatoes.

'Where do astronauts leave their cars?' Marc said, reading from it as he picked it out of the grease.

Nobody answered him. Andy was shovelling heaps of cold cauliflower on to his plate. Gwynnie and Collin were glaring at each other. Rhiannon's wineglass was stuck to her face, like a clay plate inserted into a tribeswoman's lip.

'At parking meteors,' Marc said, passing the hat to Ellie.

'Come on, Ellie,' Collin said. 'It's Christmas, mun. Put your hat on.'

Ellie glanced at Andy, hoping he'd issue some sort of reprieve, but he was grinning inanely, unaware of her discomfort. She secured the hat against her temples with a sigh of defeat, the thin paper rustling against her conditioned hair, blood rushing to her face.

'*Very* nice, El,' Rhiannon said, sniggering. As she spoke her mobile started ringing. She shuffled around in her handbag, took the handset out and glanced at the screen. 'Excuse me,' she said jovially, gripping the stem of her glass and shooting out of her seat. She took the phone call into the passage, closing the door behind herself. Ellie stared hard at the door panels, trying to decode Rhiannon's words, but she only fathomed the frequent rounds of her thunderous laughter. A few weeks ago, on her birthday, she'd had a tantrum in the Pump House and thrown a chair at the jukebox. She'd failed to explain the motive for it, just sat on the bench, cool as a cucumber, claiming that she'd suddenly seen red, the workload at the salon pushing her to the edge. The other patrons fussed over her, stroking her forehead and massaging her shoulders, offering her sugary tea and Malibu and milk. The jukebox was a write-off but the management didn't ban her. She was too good a customer for that. The woman was like fucking Teflon.

After a few minutes, Ellie began to contemplate her dinner. Dinner in the Hughes household inevitably included meat; roast pork and stuffing, roast potatoes and gravy, all of it stodgy with pig fat. Gwynnie always overlooked Ellie's vegetarianism. She thought it was something Ellie could switch on and off. She couldn't comprehend the fact that Ellie hadn't contaminated her body with animal flesh for over fourteen years. For Ellie the only edible things at the table were peas, carrots and new potatoes.

Rhiannon breezed back into the room. 'Only Kelly wishing me a Merry Christmas,' she said shrugging. Like anyone believed that.

'Who's for pudding?' Gwynnie said, mood lightened with half a glass of perry and the straightforward pleasure of feeding her sons. 'Two for the price of one in Kwik Save, back in October. I made my own brandy butter.' Everything Gwynnie bought was carefully budgeted for. She started clearing the table, noticing Ellie's plate. 'You girls,' she said disappointedly. 'You haven't eaten a thing. Come on, eat your veg. You need the folic acid, for when you conceive. I'll be dead by the time I get grandkids otherwise.'

Rhiannon sneered. 'No chance of that 'ere, Gwyn,' she said. 'I bloody 'ate kids, I do. I'm gonna get my tubes tied. In fact, that's my New Year's resolution. No ugly likkle critters comin' outta my bits!' She pushed her plate away and poured herself another glass of wine.

Gwynnie's eyes brimmed with water. She must have had tear

ducts the size of the North Sea. So much of her future happiness relied on Ellie and Rhiannon's reproductive organs, but neither of them wanted children. 'Iss orright, Rhi,' Collin said slurring. 'We don't want tar babies anyway. We want proper ones: white, like.' He laughed at his own malevolent joke, belched and then heaved a stringy spray of vomit on to his dinner plate. Looking up, he said, 'Get your brandy butter out of the fridge then, Gwyneth.' He rubbed his hands together. 'I love Christmas, I do.'

Ellie hated Christmas. She'd hated it from as far back as she could remember, when her skin burned crimson with envy as she watched her sisters rip the ludicrous Barbie dolls out of their baby-pink packaging. She thought it was something she might grow out of. Now she realized that even in normal families Christmas was all about highlighting the sheer ghastliness of everyday life, hopelessness with bells on.

On their way home, Andy gripped Ellie's hand, the sky above them the colour of teeth. There was one kid on the square, pummelling down Dynevor Street on a quad bike, his father standing on the doorstep smoking a tab. Ellie sneaked a glance at the YMCA. The blinds were closed. The drive was empty. She assumed they'd gone to Cornwall for Christmas. The last time she'd seen Johnny had been at the Pump House on Rhiannon's birthday. He'd failed to explain what Louisa was doing at his flat on the night he'd tried to seduce her, but Louisa was unusually civil, had even shrugged off an allegation from Rhiannon claiming Johnny and Ellie were planning to elope. If only that was the truth. The uncertainty of their relationship was driving Ellie insane, a perpetual itching on the roof of her mouth that she just couldn't scratch; her tongue too smooth, fingernails too sharp.

'What's wrong?' Andy said, pulling at her.

Without noticing, she'd slowed to a standstill. 'Nothing,' she said, speeding up. She didn't like being so insincere. Insincerity was the eighth deadly sin. She'd often thought about telling him that she was having an affair with Johnny, but that wasn't true. Apart from the transient spells of jealousy, the sporadic ripples of paranoia and the constant and insatiable desire to be in Johnny's company, she didn't know what she was having. You couldn't help who you fell in love with.

Back in Gwendolyn Street, Andy laid on the settee, the throw-over bunched around his chest, the remote control gripped in his fingers. Marc had given him a DVD for Christmas. There was a photograph on the cover of an obese Mancunian comic, holding a pint of stout, the image faded in one corner where the printer had run out of ink. It had been procured from the woman with a club foot who sat at the bar in the Pump House every Sunday, selling contraband from her handbag. 'Come and watch this with me,' he said. He patted the burgundy cushion. 'Come on, let's have a Christmas *cwtch*.'

Ellie was folding towels, limbs heavy with Rhiannon's cheap wine, feeling cheated out of her day. She balanced the stack of towels on the arm of the chair and reached for the bottle of Bailey's Andy'd bought her. She perched on the edge of the settee.

As the opening credits began to roll it was immediately apparent that the DVD had nothing to do with comedy. *Gang Bang Bitches 58*, it said, pink letters dancing on the black screen, *directed by Wicked Uncle Ernie*, the ecstatic bleating of a woman in the throes of orgasm echoing in the background.

'What's this?' Andy said, as curious as he was surprised.

They both stared deadpan at the screen as a spray-tanned blonde in a whalebone basque materialized. It had been more than a month since Ellie had rejected Andy and she'd sensed his sexual appetite developing, like the constant whirr of a generator projecting pressure on to her auditory nerves. Now, she was surprised to find she was as frustrated as he was. From the corner of her eye she spied his erection. She deliberately tipped some of the liqueur over the crotch of his jeans.

'What did you do that for?' he said, voice irritable.

Ellie kicked her shoes from her feet. 'So I can lick it off,' she said.

Their copulation was over before the end of the film's first scene. In the paroxysms of Ellie's climax, she was visited by a wonderful moment of clarity, in which she realized Johnny, like all men, was susceptible to womanly persuasion. She just had to tell him what she wanted, and make him want it too.

27

On Boxing Day it snowed. Ellie and Andy were on their way to the Labour Club, turning out of Tallis Street and into the square. 'It snows in New York,' Ellie said. 'It's a built-up city. It freezes in the winter and stews in summer. Autumn's nice though. Hundreds of tourists go upstate just to see the colours of the leaves. Wouldn't you like to do that?' She was looking at the ivory sky, catching snowflakes on her tongue.

'Do you know what they do to tourists in New York?' Andy said. 'They mug them, rape them and kill them. What stupid bugger would go all the way to America just to see a flipping tree? Nothing wrong with where we live. We could be in Ethiopia, El.'

Something in the distance caught Ellie's attention. The BMW was parked in front of the YMCA. Johnny was sitting at the wheel. A kid from the estate was sitting in the passenger seat, a hoodie pulled up over his head. Ellie knocked her arms against her sides like a child, watched as they got out of the car and slammed the door. The boy waved at Johnny and headed for Dynevor Street, his hand balled into a fist, the right side of his face freckled with red pimples. Andy and Ellie were close enough now to see the chassis shudder as Johnny stepped away from the car, the silver bauble tied to the rear-view mirror swinging back and forth.

'All right, you two?' Johnny said. He was wearing a grey blazer,

168

snowflakes clinging to the sleeves, his coal-black pupils trained on Ellie's face. 'Going out this afternoon?'

'Yeah, we're on our way to the Labour,' Andy said.

Ellie was staring at Johnny, her head involuntarily inclined.

Johnny smiled kindly at her. 'We are too,' he said nodding at the pebble-dashed fascia. 'Lou's just getting ready. Do you want to pop in for a drink? We can go over together.'

Andy coughed. He stuffed his hands into his pockets. 'We'd better not,' he said. 'I want to have a drink with my brother and the club closes at four. It's Boxing Day. It's tradition.' He made to walk off but Ellie stayed.

'You can see your brother later,' she said. She smoothed the toe of her shoe along the edge of the kerb. 'It's too far to walk anyway.'

Johnny locked his car and stood on his doorstep. 'Yeah, man,' he said. 'Who cares about tradition? Live dangerously for once.' He stomped up the stairs leaving the front door open, the sound of his keys jangling. Ellie was in the YMCA before Andy got chance to speak.

Upstairs they stood at Johnny's window drinking stumpies of cold beer, watching the snow sprinkling over the pavement. It was starting to stick to the statue, a heap of it perched on the crown of the Davy lamp. 'This is rare in Cornwall,' Johnny said, pulling a sheaf of fag papers out of a packet. 'The air from the Gulf Stream is mild. We never get snow.' He licked the edge of a cigarette and plucked the tobacco out, sitting on the edge of the coffee table.

'Why did you come here then?' Andy said.

Johnny was looking down at the joint, smoothing his fingers along the length of it, his shock of black hair hiding his expression. 'Supply and demand, And,' he said. The flame of his Zippo caught the paper and turned blue. He sucked from the roach. 'You didn't have any of this before I came here, did you?' He passed the joint to Andy and knelt down in front of the Christmas tree. He opened a tin of Quality Street, took one for himself and

169

gave a handful to Ellie. 'New York is the place to see snow, though,' he said walking back to the window. 'What do you reckon, El? Christmas in the Big Apple, ice-skating in Central Park, the boys from the NYPD singing 'Galway Bay'. What's that stuff the Yanks drink on Christmas Eve?'

'Eggnog,' Ellie said, scraping a shard of toffee from behind her front tooth.

Louisa came in with the smell of newly sprayed deodorant. She was wearing a pair of black stilettos, her hair wet. 'Merry Christmas,' she said, her gaze landing on Andy. 'Or Boxing Day, anyway.'

It was dark when they left the flat. The streets were empty, the lights casting an amber tint on their skin. The snow was turning to slush. Louisa's heels made a shrill *ssshhing* sound every time she took a step. It was too late to go to the Labour Club so they walked straight to the Bell & Cabbage, Johnny and Andy ahead, Louisa and Ellie behind. The card bingo had just finished. The barmaid was collecting the cards, dropping them into a dusty biscuit tin. A black terrier was sniffing around the chair legs, a garland of green tinsel tied around its thick neck. Ellie opened her compact and applied a new layer of lipstick, a thick rosy colour. It smelled of cherries, the sweet fragrance momentarily triumphing over the smell of farts and dog piss. Johnny bought a round and brought it to the table on a beer tray.

After a few minutes the others arrived, Rhiannon shrieking, loud as a dry-ice bomb. 'Ere ewe are!' she said, the whole pub turning to look at her. She was standing in the gangway, drunk as a lush, wearing a denim miniskirt, a black bra and fishnet singlet. She'd drawn a mole on her face with the tip of a brown eyeliner pencil. She loped towards the table, stamping on people's feet with the soles of her boots. She dived into a space on the bench next to Louisa. Marc was a few feet behind her, head bowed. Behind him, Siân and Griff were skulking in, looking as if they wished they'd stayed at home.

'Guess what Marc had for Christmas,' Rhiannon said, voice purposely raised. She whipped a bottle of rum out of her bag and said, 'A threesome! 'E's always wanted a threesome, keeps on about it all the time. So for Christmas I got Kelly to come over. Gave urgh a gram of speed and a bottle of poppers and she was at it like a whippet, the dirty likkle cow.' She took a slug of rum and shouted over to Marc. 'Loved it din't ewe, love? We started with a nice slow sixty-niner in front of the fire and then—'

Marc put a glass of wine down on the table in front of Rhiannon. 'Shh Rhi,' he said. 'Keep your voice down. Kelly's auntie's in the lounge.'

Rhiannon took a big gulp of wine and looked at Johnny. 'You can come next time if you like,' she said.

Siân slapped Rhiannon's thigh. 'Have you got to be so crass, Rhi?'

'Oh, shut up Siân,' Rhiannon said. 'Just 'cause ewe 'aven' 'ad a cock since nineteen ninety God knows! Doesn't mean we all gotta act like fuckin' nuns, mun. I've got photos as well,' she said, giggling. She opened her bag. 'Kelly brought her Polaroid. Wanna see?' She took a picture out and threw it on the surface of the table.

'That's disgusting!' Siân said. She flung the photograph back at Rhiannon without looking at it. 'Put it away, Rhi!' She looked at the others, said, 'It's getting beyond. She's depraved.'

'No,' Griff said, seizing it in plump fingers. 'I want to see.'

Ellie watched the exchange, aware of Johnny sitting opposite her, his eyes focused on her face, her heart beating manically. He kicked her shin to get her attention. His face was genial and patient. He didn't say anything, just looked at her zealously, the way women in Cardiff looked at shoes in shop windows.

She felt obliged to fill the silence, said: 'I've got a bit of a crush on you.' The understatement of the century.

Johnny sighed. 'Yeah,' he said. 'I've been thinking a lot about you lately too.'

Ellie stole a look at the others. They were still squabbling, the Polaroids scattered across the table. In one Rhiannon was wearing black underwear and a Santa Claus hat, a cocktail glass in her hand. William the Milk was standing next to the table, unashamedly gawping down his gin-blossomed nose.

'I'm not the kind of girl who plays games,' Ellie said. 'With me it's all or nothing. Either we're going to do something about it or we're not. I'm not going to share you with Rhiannon or Louisa. I'd want you all to myself.'

'Who said anything about playing games?' Johnny said. 'You're the one who's engaged.' He bit his bottom lip, his mouth shrinking to a paper cut. 'I'm trying to get to know you but this lot are always around.' He rolled his eyes over the others, squinted quickly at Rhiannon's dirty photographs. 'We need to find some time, some quality time. Give me a chance to sort something out.' He lifted his glass to his mouth, staring over it at her, eyes wide with desire.

Suddenly Ellie felt a grip on the hem of her T-shirt. Rhiannon was lifting her off the bench. 'Oi, mush,' she said, clawing. 'Come with me, we're gonna dance.' She prised the lipstick out of Ellie's hand and threw it on the bench, dragging her towards the dance-floor, Ellie's rigid knuckles clicking. It was a Meatloaf song, 'Paradise by the Dashboard Light'. Rhiannon writhed against the amplifier, head undulating. Ellie stepped from side to side, legs stiff, her movements belying her inner delight. She felt like a lottery winner on acid – she was having a bona fide affair with him now, and there was nothing Rhiannon could do to stop it.

28

The playground in Aberalaw was a patch of broken concrete nestled between the forestry and the housing estate. It had a bright orange roundabout and three rubber swings, but it wasn't suitable for small children. The local drug addicts had claimed it: used syringes on the ground, misspelled graffiti scrawled over the railings. But Siân needed to get out of the house. James wouldn't let her take the trimmings down until 5 January and it was impossible to clean around them, coils of grey dust glazing the papier-mâché angels and homemade cardboard garlands.

On the doorstep she crouched in front of Angharad and put the new fur-lined mittens on to her hands. 'How does that feel?' she said, squeezing them gently. Angharad wrinkled her nose. 'Oright,' she said listlessly. It was below 4°C but summer freckles still smothered her face.

Siân kissed her forehead. She stood up and tied her scarf into a knot, kicked the brake from the buggy free. 'Come on then, *plentyn bach*,' she said. She wheeled the pushchair towards the estate, trying to ignore the family-filled people-carriers on their way to shopping outlets to spend disposable income at the January sales. Siân didn't have two beans to rub together. James hung back a few yards, tapping the terraced windowsills with his plastic drumsticks. Angharad was singing 'Onward Christian Soldiers' at the top of her little voice. As they reached the gate, Siân saw the back of a stick-figure sitting on the swings. He was surrounded by his three Dobermans, the chain loose in his hand. Instinct told her to flee but Angharad was already past the threshold, pushing the heavy gate open, the stiff hinges squealing.

Johnny spun around and waved at them. His face a mixture of apprehension and glee, his mouth turned down at the corners, his eyebrows arched.

Immediately Siân worried about her own shrunken frame. Since she'd last seen him she'd lost a lot of weight. Griff's parents had bought heaps of expensive Christmas presents for the children; a Silver Fox BMX with rear stunt pegs for James, a Barbie tri-scooter for Angharad, a Fisher Price baby-walker with seven hundred integrated melodies for Niall. She knew they meant well but it undermined Siân's ability to provide for her own children; she wanted her kids to appreciate the modest things she'd saved for – a set of Roald Dahl paperbacks, a flower-planting kit, a faux Steiff teddy bear; the kind of gifts that were ignored while the house was brimming with packets of Duracell batteries and shiny, multicoloured plastic.

As usual, Siân cooked her way into her family's affections: pigs in blankets, mince pies, Christmas cake, Pavlova, Bara-Brith, chocolate meringue, cream éclairs, jam tarts, orange cake, Scotch eggs, sweet pickles and pea and ham cawl. What was unusual was that she hadn't sampled any of it. Throughout the holiday she'd been consumed by an awesome hunger, but not for food. The only thing that gratified it was the stash of capsules crammed in the ivory pillbox. She took an ecstasy tablet every day because it made her feel slightly vague, as though she wasn't quite there, as though she was perpetually on the brink of being somewhere else. She'd taken the first one two weeks before Christmas, whilst trimming up the tree with Angharad. Her daughter insisted on placing the baubles at the end of the branches, before they added the tinsel. She tied all the chocolate coins to the base where she knew she'd be able to reach them later. Siân realized two minutes into the task that she'd need to get up in the night and do it all over again. She'd wanted a little something to ease the constant accountability of being a mother. Now she didn't need to eat and her clothes hung on her bones. Luckily she was wearing her big double-breasted coat and it covered most of her emaciated body.

'Would you mind putting your dogs on the lead?' she said as she approached the swings. 'I know you think they're harmless but children are always getting savaged by *supposedly* tame dogs,' her contempt for Johnny spitting out with the consonants in the words. 'I've got to be careful,' she said. She was suspicious that what he'd given her on Bonfire Night wasn't ecstasy, but Rohypnol or GHB, some kind of date-rape drug. Not that he'd be able to assault her with Griff lurking about like a big silver-backed gorilla, but whatever it was had rendered her nervous system helpless, preventing her from caring for her children. Perhaps he was trying to cause a rift between her and Griff because ultimately that's what he'd done. She'd woken up on the settee the next day, her face glued with drool to the scatter cushion, Griff pretending to vacuum, the bumper of the upright cleaner hammering repeatedly against the skirting board. Angharad was sitting at the kitchen table trying to eat a bowl of cereal, right hand swaddled in bandages.

Siân sat down now, leaving one swing empty between herself and Johnny. He fastened the chain around the dogs' necks and tied it to the metal frame.

James and Angharad raced one another to the roundabout.

Johnny fixed Siân with his determined stare. 'How are you?' he said. 'All right? That Boxing Day knees-up was a bit of a disaster, wasn't it? That friend of yours, Rhiannon, she's as mad as bats.'

Siân laughed bitterly. 'Yeah, she's mad all right,' she said.

'She's black, isn't she?' Johnny said. 'You don't see many black people around here, nor in Cornwall, not the villages.'

'Half-caste,' Siân said, before she remembered it was what Ellie called a 'derogatory term'. Ellie worked in Cardiff and was up on those kinds of things, but Siân didn't have any use for that knowledge so it slipped out of her mind. 'Mixed race, I mean. Her mother's white, her father was black, her real father. He was a sailor from Tiger Bay. Everyone knows but Rhiannon still denies it.' She watched her children playing on the roundabout, Angharad lying face up, James pushing it as fast as it would go. 'One time,' Siân said, 'Angharad came home from her grandparents and asked me what a "Paki" was. I said, "That's a bad word, sweetheart. Some people use it to describe people with dark skin, but you won't, will you? Because it upsets people." Angharad looked up at me, innocent as a dove, said, "Does that mean Auntie Rhi's a Paki, Mam?"'

Johnny laughed through his nose.

'Don't go too fast, James,' Siân said, shouting over at him, 'or your sister'll fall off. He's finding his feet now,' she said, turning to Johnny, explaining her alarm. 'He wanted to play Joseph in the school nativity but the teacher wouldn't let him. She made him the innkeeper. Come the night of the performance, Mary and Joseph walk up to the little prop door and knock. James comes out. Do you know what he said? "You can come in, Mary but Darryl Thomas can fuck right off."' She sighed. 'You don't know what you and Louisa are missing. Kids fill your lives with so much joy.' She crouched over the transparent cover of the buggy and blew Niall a fat air kiss.

Johnny was laughing again, petting one of the dogs. After a moment he said, 'It must be tough though, three kids and two jobs. I can hardly look after myself; couldn't imagine having young 'uns as well. Deserve a medal, you do.'

'No, it's pretty simple,' she said. 'It's natural. The second they put the baby in your arms, the instinct kicks in. I wish that my mother had lived to see them, though. She died five years ago. I was pregnant with James but I didn't know it then.'

176

Johnny was gawping at her, unsure of a response. Siân didn't know why she'd raised the subject, especially in Johnny's company. She didn't think about her mother often. Her grief had been so quickly absorbed by her love for her firstborn. Still she decided to continue, so that Johnny wouldn't think she was nuts. 'What it is,' she said, picking at her fingernail, 'they see a lot of Griff's parents. But that's only half of their history, isn't it?'

'What about your father?' Johnny said.

Siân shook her head, dismissing the question. She said, 'My mother's mother, Gu, she had a pig farm in Llanpumpsaint. Welsh pigs mostly, for bacon, but a couple of Tamworths. I would have loved for them to see it, nature, grass, fresh air.' She looked around at the ramshackle park. 'All they've got here is concrete. But we had to sell it in the end. Turned out she was up to her eyeballs in debt.'

'I used to have a farm,' Johnny said. His long legs were stretched out in front of him, fingers gripping the chain-link cable of the swing. He looked like a boy, light and narrow. 'There were a few chickens there when I bought it, and ducks, but Louisa was scared of them. Have you ever seen duck shit? Glowing green! We gave them away, to another farm down the road.' He pushed backwards, working the swing into a pendulum, his shins gyrating.

'That's crazy,' Siân said. 'Have you ever tasted omelette made from duck egg? I'd love to live on a farm, grow veg, live off the land. That's my ultimate dream.'

Angharad had abandoned the roundabout and she was on her way over to the Dobermans. She stood in front of one, hand held up in the air. The dog bowed before her, allowing itself to be stroked. Angharad patted its temple. 'Goody doggy,' she said, slipping her hand out of the big mitten.

'Don't . . .' Siân said, but it was too late. The glove was lying on the uneven cement, Angharad's hand bare, the strawberry-shaped burn on the ball of her hand clear in the magnolia daylight.

Johnny didn't seem to notice but Siân broached the subject anyway. 'You know that thing you gave me on Bonfire Night was dodgy,' she said, voice low. 'It was spiked with codeine, wasn't it? It made me bard.'

Following the incident, Griff had refused to speak to her for a month. He wallowed around the house trying to cook his own food, leaving singed saucepans on the draining board. Every day, a scorched fragment of a child's drawing turned up on the coffee table. He borrowed money from his mother to put petrol in the van. When communication was essential he used the children: *'Go and tell Mammy that the bathplug is clogged.'* In the end Siân had felt so guilty, she'd found him in James's bedroom playing 'Sonic the Hedgehog' on a handheld console. *Okay*, she said, *I'll get the reversal.* But Griff had laughed at her. *What's the point?*, he said. *You can't look after these three.* It wasn't long then before Siân was at the ecstasy. Secretly she craved the ingredient in Johnny's pill that had anaesthetized her parental conscience, had kicked the maternal instinct out.

'Really?' Johnny said. 'Never got any complaints before. How long since you last took one?' Siân shrugged. She let the accusation go. She was remembering the scene at the dinner table on Christmas Day. When she'd reached for the cranberry sauce, she'd tipped a glass of water over the table runner, her coordination flawed by all of the self-medicating she'd been doing.

'Whoops!' Griff's mother said. 'Been at the firewater again, have you, love? I'm beginning to worry about you. You don't know what to think when your son turns up late at night with your granddaughter's hand burnt to a cinder, do you? You'll be at the AA meetings next.' Griff hadn't been near the hospital! He'd only taken her to his frigging mother.

James had ventured over to the swings now too. He was hitting the empty rubber seat with his drumstick. Angharad was still stroking one of the dogs' heads. The dog rolled on to the floor,

revealing the eight teats lining its grey underside in two symmet-
rical rows. 'Her name's Salty,' Johnny said, smiling at Angharad,
a calm, temperate manner that had been absent in Griff and
Louisa's presence. 'She's an old salty sea dog.'

Angharad chuckled violently. 'James likes salt,' she said, 'on his
chips, and ketchup.' She pushed the dog's fur back against its grain.
One of the other dogs yawned and danced on its front paws, then
sat down, the outline of its back a smooth gradient. James
approached it slowly, looking as if he intended to mount it like
a horse.

'James!' Siân said, warning him.

'It's OK,' Johnny said, putting his hand up to quieten her. 'Arnie's
harmless, a total sook. Honestly.' James straddled the dog, his
hands clamped around its floppy ears. 'Vroom,' he said, twisting
them gently, as if they were the handlebars of a motorbike. 'Vroom,
vroom.'

Johnny smiled at Siân, a conspiratorial glint in his eyes. 'Looks
like he's made a friend,' he said.

29

There were only two hours left until the calendar year crumbled into history, Johnny's living room already reeking of skunk, a cloying mishmash of burnt sugar and sage. Andy was on his phone, wishing one of his cousins a Happy New Year, working through a laborious list of relatives before the mobile network clogged. He offered the handset to Ellie but she shook her head and walked over to the window. She opened the frosted sash and sucked on the cool air.

The square was dormant, the lacklustre streetlights reflecting on the wet pavement, a faint, far-flung clamour from the new-fangled jukebox in the pub. Ribs came out of his house wearing one of his mother's old blouses, black with white polka dots, a georgette bow tied at the neck. Underneath it, his stonewashed drainpipe jeans and big-tongued white trainers; the very clothes he was wearing when alcoholism took him in 1985.

'Ribs has made an effort for the occasion,' she said, bringing her head inside. 'He's just gone in the pub wearing a chiffon blouse.'

'Leave him alone,' Griff said. He was sitting against the skirting board, still wearing his leather coat, ginger hair gelled into three stiff peaks. 'You know his parents died when he was nine. He can't help it.' He took one more toke from the joint he was holding and passed it to Andy. 'We should have done that gig in Penmaes

Worky's, butt. Four 'undred quid they wanted to pay us: better than a boring house party.' He'd practically had a coronary when a stranger like Johnny turned up, but full-on transvestism from someone he knew was fine. 'It cost us forty quid for a babysitter, some slapper from the estate.' He sat back, face falling into a pout. 'Olds couldn't do it. They go down the Bell on New Year.'

Siân lifted her shot glass to her mouth. 'You could have stayed in and looked after them,' she said, 'instead of sitting there making the place look untidy, whinging all the flipping time.'

There was a mewing noise from the street and Ellie turned back to the window to see where it was coming from. Rhiannon was skipping through the square, wearing a pair of stilettos, shaking her big hips, humming a tune in falsetto. Johnny joined Ellie, their breath mingling as together they watched Rhiannon waltzing around the mining statue. Funny that they were already having an affair, and had never even kissed. At midnight they'd have to peck at least, Andy watching them guardedly, Ellie going red as a Coke can.

'Rhiannon!' Johnny said, shouting out of the window, his hand curled around his mouth. Rhiannon spied up, and then immediately toppled down the concrete steps, landing tits-up on the pavement, legs spread in opposite directions, her skirt hitched to her dimpled thighs. 'Rhi?' Marc cried, emerging from the darkness, darting towards her body.

Ellie turned to the others. 'Rhiannon's just collapsed,' she said, not quite resisting the urge to laugh. Ellie believed in karma and this was Rhiannon's comeuppance for throwing a wobbly on her birthday.

Johnny pulled the sash closed and stood waiting by the window until Marc had supported her into the flat. He deposited her on the settee and she sat up, an expression of perplexity on her face. She held her ankle clamped in her hand, a bloody graze on her knee. 'I'm OK,' she said, voice obstinate, eyes circling the dim room. 'Just twisted it is, that Achilles from where I broke it last time.'

'When you dropped that bottle of wine on it?' Siân said. A magnum of Lambrini had rolled out of Rhiannon's fridge last winter, landing on her foot, breaking two metatarsals.

'She walked around on it for a week,' Siân said, looking at Johnny. 'Too pissed to realize.'

'I weren't pissed, Siân,' Rhiannon said. 'Just didn't feel it. I'm hard like that.' She eased her shoe off and held it by the heel, showing everyone the Manolo Blahnik label on the insole. She caught Louisa's eye and said, 'I need to lie here for a bit if that's OK, an' a bag of frozen peas might 'elp.'

'Sure,' Louisa said, diving out of the armchair.

Johnny went to the entertainment system at the front of the room. He turned the PlayStation on. 'Now you're all here,' he said, 'there's something I want to show you. I bought it for myself for Christmas.' He was so damn exotic! Nobody in Wales bought presents for themselves. A vivid blue light filled the television screen, reflecting on the glass surface of the table. The screen was filled with a cartoon avatar: a girl in a white jumpsuit, rotund bunches in her yellow hair. She was dancing on a podium. Johnny unrolled a plastic mat and positioned it in front of the TV. 'A dance pad,' he said. 'These arrows correspond with the arrows in the game. All you have to do is hit the target with your feet, the same time the arrow hits the target on the screen.'

Ellie had seen something like it in the Barry Island arcade, an aluminium platform adorned with neon lights. It was on a day trip in the summer and there'd been a teenager with a Scouse accent bouncing erratically on the coloured panels. Andy had tried to stop and watch but Ellie was eager to get back to the car. It was a Saturday afternoon and they were going to the Pump House. She remembered hoping that Johnny was going to be there. She glanced around the room and the others were rapt.

Rhiannon was still holding her ankle, the whites of her eyes glistening.

'Sounds complicated,' Johnny said, unlacing his boots, 'but it's not. Watch me now.' Brightly coloured arrows flew across the screen in all directions, a drum-machine beat pumping out of the speakers. He skipped and jumped and pirouetted, trying to catch the cursors with his ungainly feet, his socks slipping on the plastic; too long legs, like a newborn giraffe.

'Wow!' Siân said. She glided towards the dance mat like a vulture towards carrion. 'Let me have a go.' She tapped Johnny on the shoulder, kicked her shoes off. 'I'll be great at it. I was disco-dancing champion in the Welsh youth-club finals.'

Johnny stepped away and stood aside, watching her, grinning as he lit a cigarette. Siân picked up where he left off, hitting every arrow in the sequence with the ball of her foot. The computer registered the change in player and sent a ticker-tape of praise across the screen. '*Excellent! Awesome! Keep it up!*' Soon she was raising her arms and performing unnecessary swivels and twists. Ellie noticed that she too had lost weight. Her hips had gone. Her body was a quadrilateral column, like the frame of a teenage boy. Through her diaphanous black dress, she could see her third rib, her breasts sunken; her skin like clingfilm on bone. *Bitch*, Ellie thought, already dreading being asked to join in. Her shyness turned pathological when it came to anything athletic. She was too tall to dance, too awkward to move without being ridiculously self-conscious about it. She'd never been as jealous as when she saw Rhiannon doing a continuous cartwheel along the length of the dance-floor in the Working Man's.

Siân did a scissors kick and glanced over her shoulder at Rhiannon. 'You should come and have a go at this,' she said, goading her. 'It's amazing, Rhi. It really is. I'll get one of these for the house, keep myself trim.'

'Does it fuckin' look like I can have a go at that?' Rhiannon said. Louisa was sitting on the edge of the settee with a bag of frozen chips and a strip of elasticated bandage, preparing to tend to Rhiannon's wound. Rhiannon drove her hand into the bag, grabbed a handful of the chips and flung them at Siân. Johnny stepped over them, opened a cupboard and took something out. 'Who's for a party-starter then?' He held a baggie of pills up to the light, an attempt to deflect the squabble. He flicked one at Rhiannon and it landed on the settee next to her.

'Cheers, mush,' Rhiannon said, pushing Louisa off the edge of the cushion as she writhed around searching for it. He flicked a second at Siân. He was thrusting his hand into the bag, reaching for more, when one of the dogs sat up and barked, an ominous, guttural growl. Johnny pressed the mute button on the remote control. The computer-game music dissolved.

All of the dogs began to snarl, their ears erected, the hair on their backs rising. A row of policemen marched into the living room. Even in the dark Ellie could see they were policemen, the light from the TV reflecting in the crests on their lapels. The living-room bulb came on abruptly. Everyone was still, sitting and standing in their various positions, Siân balancing on one leg, arm raised, hand curved; her body a child's impression of a teapot.

A policeman walked into the centre of the room, an Alsatian dog on a short leash. There was a flurry of noise as Johnny's dogs barked and lurched at it. Two plain-clothed detectives entered and stood in front of the television screen. One of them was the new police chief. He had a column in the local newspaper with a grainy photograph of his face above it: translucent-white bald head with a smattering of ginger freckles and cat's-eye spectacles. Ellie recognized him, but it was the other one who spoke first.

'Hello, Mr Frick,' he said, throwing his Cornish accent around the room as he quickly inspected the guests. He smiled acidly at Johnny, a familiarity in his glare, as though they'd dealt with one another before. He took a crumpled sheet of A4 paper out of his jacket pocket and threw it on the table. 'We've got a warrant, so you won't mind us having a little nose around. Now,' he said, 'I'd like residents to stay where they are and I'd like nonresidents to leave.' He pointed at the door. 'That way, one by one, nice and slow and calm. My colleagues will have a little chat with you on your way out.'

Siân let go of her awkward stance, her arms dropping to her sides. She peered around uncertainly, grabbed her shoes and handbag and scuttled out of the room.

When it was Ellie's turn to go she looked back momentarily at Johnny. He was sitting in the armchair nearest the window, his elbows resting on his knees, his head in his hands, his straggly hair hanging down over his eyes. The blunt light illuminated a tear rolling down Louisa's pitted face.

'OK,' Ellie said to herself resignedly as she turned into the passage and edged past the row of policemen. There was a WPC standing at the top of the stairs. She put her hand up to obstruct Ellie's path, said, 'Would you mind telling me what you're doing here?' She looked embarrassed as she quickly ran the back of her hands around the contours of Ellie's body, looking for some sort of contraband, her face close enough to lick Ellie's forehead.

'They're my friends,' Ellie said. 'It's New Year's Eve. It's a party.'

'You didn't come here to buy drugs?' the woman said.

Ellie shook her head.

'So I'll take that as a no, shall I?' She placed the edge of her hand into Ellie's armpit, Ellie aware of the warmth there. 'Have you ever bought drugs from Mr Frick?'

'No,' Ellie said, and it was the truth. She'd never bought drugs from Johnny.

'Go on then,' the woman said, tossing her head at the stairwell, visibly disgruntled with having to work a drug bust on New Year's Eve.

Outside, Siân was sitting on the steps of the statue. She'd smoked

185

a cigarette deep into its cork. When she saw Ellie coming she threw it at the gutter and lit a second. Ellie'd never seen Siân smoke before. 'You all right?' she said.

'Mad isn't it?' Siân said. 'I've never been in a drugs raid before. Except, one time, when I was buying pot for Griff.' She looked at the YMCA. 'He was living in there himself, but he wouldn't go out, 'cause he had this disease all around his mouth. Impetigo it was. He sent me to the Llewellyns's, the flat above the jewellers next to CF25. It's a Bargain Booze shop now. The door was open, which was strange. I was about to go in when I heard a crackle, a police radio. I turned around, tiptoed out.' She smiled subtly, pleased with her level of experience. Ellie was shocked. She'd almost forgotten that drugs were illegal. Unless you were injecting brown into your eyeballs and robbing old women of their pension books to get it, no one in the valley fluttered an eyelash. But Johnny was the only source of uppers in an eighty-mile radius; he wasn't shy about what he did and this was a place where word got around.

Rhiannon came out of the YMCA, slamming the door behind her. She was carrying her shoes in her hands, limping barefoot across the pavement, a strap of bandage around her ankle glowing white against her dark skin. 'Bloody fucking pigs!' she said, spitting. She hopped towards the pub door, stopping just before she reached it. She shouted over at the girls, 'Ewe comin' in 'ere with me or what, ewe dozy cows?'

Siân and Ellie stood up. 'Your foot okay?' Siân said.

Rhiannon scowled. 'I'll fuckin' live,' she said. She pushed the door open and went inside.

The atmosphere was claustrophobic with curiosity and cele-bration. Everyone looked the girls up and down a few times before turning to get on with their own business. The queue at the bar was three deep so they waited quietly at the end of it, too dumb-founded to complain, their bodies on autopilot. They were still queuing when the three boys came in together, breathless and paper-faced. 'They've got the carpet up now,' Marc said. 'They're checking underneath the floorboards.'

Without noticing it, Ellie had wormed her way to the edge of the bar. Now the barman was in front of her, waiting for a request. She ordered six house vodkas and two cans of Red Bull.

'I told you we should have done that gig,' Griff said.

It was quarter to twelve when they sat down, sharing chairs around the cocktail table behind the door. Dai Davies was standing at the window, his head poking through the slit in the curtains, his nose up against the glass.

'Look at that nosey old cunt,' Rhiannon said, pointing him out. As soon as she had, he turned around. 'They're bringing him out!' he said, shouting.

A mob of customers stormed the door and stood in front of the pub watching Johnny make his way towards an unmarked car, handcuffed and flanked by four officers. The girls balanced on the doorstep trying to cop a look. A squad car parked in Dynevor Street sent an eerie blue light revolving around the square. It seemed to light the threads of grey at Johnny's temples. One of the officers placed his hand on Johnny's head, guiding him safely into the car. His sudden vulnerability made Ellie feel sick.

'There ewe are,' Rhiannon said, voice so low and quiet that Ellie turned to see if her lips were moving. 'What'll we do now?' Ellie knew instinctively that Rhiannon wasn't talking about their drug supply running out. They might not ever see Johnny again. She looked at the sky. A premature New Year firework erupted, sending spirals of gold beads spinning around. She frowned at the rudeness of it.

30

The rain poured through the holes in the factory roof. The mid-morning news was babbling out of the radio. Ellie pushed her trolley through the corridors of the T-shirt department, then back down to Ceramics, picking up scraps of cardboard from the floor. Gavin was hiding behind the door of the tallboy, shouting into his phone.

'Got any rubbish?' Ellie said. He pointed at a pile of empty boxes stacked up against the print machine, and Ellie folded them and set them on the trolley with the rest of the refuse. It was January, month of new starts. There wasn't any work. Jane took the old porcelain bells out of the back of the cupboard. The women slowly streaked their bead-lines with a fine strip of gold, painstaking work that required an iron-steady hand. Ellie had already spoiled four of the damn things, which was why Jane had ordered her to collect the rubbish. She wheeled the trolley into the yard and threw the cardboard into the skip, the wind pulling it out again, her hair whipping her face.

A flock of seagulls swooped overhead, one of them bold enough to land a few feet away. It ate a soggy crisp, one malicious eye focused on Ellie, reminding her that she was in the city. Seagulls only ventured into the valley when the sky was cloudless, which wasn't often. She hurriedly took the magazine out of her duffel bag and sneaked another look at it. It was knockout: a photograph of The Needles standing in front of a concertinaed garage door. Bleddyn in the middle, head twisted left, baring his prominent Adam's apple. He was surrounded by the other four band members, eyes expressionless, legs spread, all wearing white like a quintet of archangels. Above it, the magazine's insignia: '**The Glamour**'. It fell open to her article and she saw the subheading that she'd already memorized. 'Fifth album *Romance Language* is set to be their most successful, but The Needles tell Elizabeth Evans why they still prefer golf to groupies.' She'd found it on her way to work that morning, staring out of the hundreds of other magazines on the newsstand in Central Station. Now it was here, in her hands, palpable proof that the ennui of the valleys had not beaten her *yet*. She still had dreams *and* she could still make them come true.

She folded it carefully, protecting it from the rain, sliding it back into her bag. As she did, something fell out. It landed in a crack in the concrete, a triangle covered in mint-green foil. It was a chocolate noisette, one of the Quality Street sweets Johnny had given her on Boxing Night. She wanted to pick it up and eat it so that the seagull couldn't, but it was soaked through. She hadn't seen Johnny-Come-Lately since he'd been arrested on New Year's Eve. He'd been sitting in the back of the silver Vauxhall Astra when it reversed out of the square. He'd put his head down and focused on his feet, purposely ignoring the people standing on the pavement watching. She and Siân had sat out on the steps until dawn, their drinks cradled in their laps, avoiding the fierce tittle-tattle of the pub, both secretly hoping the detectives would realize they'd made a terrible mistake and deliver him safely back to the YMCA. Between them they'd smoked two packets of cigarettes.

Johnny had been the main topic of conversation over lunch at the Bell & Cabbage yesterday. Andy's father reckoned he'd seen him that very morning, taking the dogs for a walk. 'Looked rough as ten bears,' he'd said, 'greasy as an Eyetie.' There was a half-baked story from Dai Davies doing the rounds, something about a cache of cocaine found buried on Cornish farmland. 'Nine years for intent to supply,' Andy had said, looking at Ellie as he spoke. 'He could go down for a long time.' It was as if he had a knife in her stomach and he was twisting it, slow and meticulous. It was as though he knew something.

'Well,' Marc said, 'if you can't do the crime . . .' and his sentence trailed into nothing. Ellie expected a sunnier outcome. Johnny was a drug dealer and he'd been arrested. Surely that was just an occupational hazard? He just needed to strike a plea-bargain, or do whatever it was he usually did, and they could get back to having a good old-fashioned extramarital romance.

Jane came out of the factory now, hand clenched around the handle of her leather briefcase. She froze momentarily on seeing Ellie. 'I'm just popping out,' she said, opening her umbrella. 'Doctor's appointment, I'll be back in half an hour.' She ran towards her parked car, dodging the puddles. Before she got inside she called back with an afterthought. 'Get inside, El, out of this blinking rain.'

Ellie stayed where she was until Jane pulled out on to Atlas Road. Then she entered via the packing department, leaving the trolley in the yard. There was a man in a suit standing in the corridor near Jane's office. 'My sister's asked me to do some photo-copying,' Ellie said without looking at him, and she slipped through the open door. It was a room the size of a two-man tent, with a window that looked out on to the red-brick wall. As she sat in Jane's chair, the dolphin-themed screensaver on the monitor evaporated. She double-clicked the Internet icon and typed two words into a search engine: 'Johnny' and then 'Frick'. She quickly scrolled through the results, the biro gritted between her teeth.

When the office door creaked and Safia's head peeped through the gap, Ellie spat out the pen. 'Don't, Saf!' she said. 'I thought you were . . .'

190

'What yous up to? It's break-time. I couldn't find you.' Safia sauntered into the room and sat on the edge of the desk. She craned her neck around the monitor and squinted at the screen. 'Who's Johnny Freak?' she said.

'Frick!' Ellie said. 'Frick, not Freak!' She swiftly cancelled the browser. 'He's this guy who moved to Aberalaw in the summer,' she said. 'He's been busted for drugs. I was just trying to find out if he had any other convictions. They reckon it's nine years for intent. They reckon he'll go down.'

'Not like yous to care about anything that happens in Aberalaw,' Safia said.

'I don't want him to go down,' Ellie said.

'Excuse me?' Jane said. She was standing in the doorway, mean eyes magnified by the lenses of her reading glasses, Ellie and Safia setting like a blancmange under her gaze. She plonked her briefcase on the desk with a thump. 'Safia Siddiqui,' she said as she removed her glasses, wiping them with a felt cloth. 'I might have known.'

'It's not Safia's fault,' Ellie said.

'But it's somebody's fault, isn't it?' Jane said.

Their punishment was sponge duty. Put to sit in the gangway of the Ceramics department, a washing bowl filled with soapy water placed on the desk between them. They scraped the fading, misprinted transfers off dusty pint glasses, buffing them until they were new and ready to be reused. It was a form of humiliation; cheaper to buy new glasses than it was to pay employees to wash old ones, and Jane knew Safia hated putting her hands in water. She had a phobia about her fingertips going wrinkly. Rhytiphobia, the fear of wrinkles was called.

'Looks like your days are numbered here, Saf,' Gavin said, breezing past. 'They only put people they're going to sack on sponge duty.' He pointed at Ellie. 'She'll be OK because Jane ain't going to fire her sister, is she? You though, I don't know.' He sniggered as he walked away.

Safia looked at Ellie. 'What were you telling me?' she said. 'In the office before Jane came in? It was something about that freak guy. You said yous hoped he wasn't going down. You were about to say something else.' Ellie knew exactly what she'd been about to say. The words were still reeling about in her trachea, angry because they'd been promised a freedom that never transpired. '*I don't want him to go down because he's lush.*' That was the word, *lush*, but she was glad now that she hadn't said it. It would have been like opening Pandora's Box. How could she explain it to Safia? Innocent Safia, who didn't know the difference between an aspirin and a diazepam. She shook her head. 'I can't remember now. Why?'

'Well, jail terms never last as long as they're supposed to, do they?' Safia said. Gavin was coming back, his chin propped on a sealed box of mugs, and Safia lowered her voice so it sprayed out in a hiss. 'Look at him!' she said. 'He was in Dartmoor three years ago doing a stretch for armed robbery. Twelve years cut to six for good behaviour.'

31

It was six at night and Ellie needed cigarettes. She'd been avoiding the High Street since Rhiannon had thrown the chair across the Pump House. The woman was utterly berserk and Ellie had reservations about being alone with her. She was heading for the newsagent's on Tallis Street.

It was late in January, the sky inky, the naked trees on Pengoes Mountain rattling in the wind. The newsagent was still open, its purple awning throwing a dim light across the pavement. Most people called it the 'Paki shop', but it was owned by Sikhs, two brothers in their twenties. Gwynnie wouldn't go there because the milk was expensive – two pence more than in Spar – and she reckoned that Mr Evans at number 68 was deliberately being overcharged for his papers. 'He's got Alzheimer's,' she'd say, 'and don't those bloody Pakis know it!' What Gwynnie didn't seem to know was that the entire valley had been created by immigrants: tin miners from the southwest, lead miners from north Wales, Irish, Scots, Italians, Poles. Andy himself had told Ellie that his mother's family originally came from France. Until the coal seam was discovered, Aberalaw was a couple of acres of farmland, used to grow corn.

As Ellie reached the shop she noticed Johnny's BMW parked outside, its tyres biting the kerb. She peered into the passenger window, checking her reflection. Her face was framed with wisps of brown hair blown loose from her ponytail. She blinked as she stepped inside. The atmosphere was disturbingly placid; the only sound, the refrigerator whirring in the corner. Instead of going straight to the counter she walked down an aisle, swiftly inspecting a solitary prawn sandwich, a pint of banana milkshake, a chocolate mousse that was already past its sell-by date. She saw Johnny when she turned into the second aisle. He was standing facing her, the strip light reflecting in his black hair, a giant tin of dog food in his hand.

'Hi,' she said, the word jumping out of her like a squeak from a cornered rat.

Johnny was staring at something on the shelf. Ellie summoned volume from deep in her gut. 'Johnny!' she said, then in a girlish, singsong tone: 'Earth to Johnny.'

'All right, El,' he said, voice lethargic. His black eyes seemed to be looking right through her, at the wall behind her head. Ellie waved, said, 'Are you OK? I haven't seen you since . . .' She looked at the grey flecks in the red linoleum. It was him who usually did the talking.

He sighed. 'Since I got arrested for drug dealing? I'm on bail until the case goes to court, April or May or something.' He took a tin of mushy peas from the shelf and read the ingredients. Ellie shuffled towards him, a cannonball twisting around in her belly. That was what love felt like, she thought, a big spherical object jammed in your intestines, pressing on your vital organs, your bladder, your lungs. It was always there when she thought about him, worse in his presence, an unbearable weight, depriving her of gracefulness. 'I know it's a bit awkward at the moment,' she said, 'with what happened on New Year's Eve, but I was wondering if you managed to sort anything out?' She was fiddling with the hem of her coat, still looking at the floor. 'On Boxing Night you said you would. You said you wanted to get to know me. You said we'd spend some time together.' She switched her gaze on to the tin in his hand. 'I still want to,' she said.

Johnny put the tin on the shelf and edged away from her, laughing as he went. 'Don't be silly, El,' he said. 'I was pissed on Boxing Night. I can't even remember Boxing Night.' He turned into the next aisle.

Ellie stayed where she was, watching him through the gaps in the shelves, too stunned to move. It was as if he'd punched her square in the face. She coughed self-consciously and walked slowly to the counter, asked for ten Lambert & Butler. She snatched them from the man's hand, leaving the coins on the counter. She marched out of the shop, something she regretted before the door had closed. She couldn't leave yet.

She sat on Johnny's bonnet and ripped the cellophane from the packet. She lit a cigarette, the heels of her boots wedged under the wheel arch. When Johnny appeared, the giant tin of dog food poised in the crook of his elbow, Ellie crossed her legs. 'If you were pissed on Boxing Night you were pissed on the day you washed up too,' she said. She took a drag of her cigarette. Johnny opened the passenger door and threw the dog food on the back seat. He sat down, one foot on the pavement. 'Get off the car, El,' he said. 'Seriously, I'll drive it. I don't care.' He stared through the windscreen at her.

'Just tell me,' she said. 'Tell me what I've done, please.'

'You fucking know,' he said.

'I don't fucking know,' she said. She took another drag of the cigarette and then threw it into the road. Johnny slammed the passenger door. He struggled over the gearbox and into the driver's seat, his long limbs thrashing. He started the engine. Ellie felt it tremble under her bones.

'Tell me,' she said, crawling into the middle of the bonnet. She knelt in front of him and stared through the glass. The terrible scenario reminded her of another time, early into her relationship with Andy when, after a day of watching rugby and drinking beer in the sun, she'd begged him to drive her to Porthcawl. He'd agreed, but Gwynnie had come out of the house and sat on the car, refusing to move until he gave up the keys. Ellie'd been in the passenger seat then, blitzkrieged, spangled, sparkling like the fourth of fucking July, which is where she should have been now, escaping all of that Welsh mam bollocks. Johnny's malevolence was making her dizzy.

He pressed his window down a few inches and shouted out of it. 'You know what you did, El. Always telling me to be careful, telling me they'd grass me up. Except it was you who grassed me up, wasn't it? Bubble on me one minute and then try to arrange a fucking date. It's serious, El. I could go down. You a bunny-boiler or what? Get off my fucking car.'

'Whoa!' Ellie jumped into the road. She clung to the edge of the window and peered in through the gap, eyes focused on his clean-shaven chin. 'Who told you that? Rhiannon?' As she said it she felt the truth in the name. There was a flicker of recognition in Johnny's eyes as he put the car into first. 'She's lying!' Ellie said.

Johnny pressed a button on the inside of the door. Ellie felt the edge of the glass push into her palms and she quickly pulled her fingers away, knowing her lack of strength would make resistance futile. 'You know she's lying!' she said, shouting defiantly. 'Why would I report you and then hang around in your flat waiting for the bust? Do you think *I* wanted to get done?' She rapped on the glass. 'That's ridiculous, Johnny. It's fucking ridiculous!'

Johnny shrugged; a look of helplessness on his face. He indicated left. Ellie stood aside, watching him drive away. She should have expected it, because Rhiannon's malice was inevitable. Like death and taxes: the fecund stink of shit-stirring.

196

32

A week into February and it was the band's leaving party at the Labour Club. Ellie caught sight of herself in the mirror as she charged into the women's toilet. She'd worn the shortest skirt in her wardrobe, the highest heels on the shoe rack. Siân was standing in front of the sink, looking like something out of a fashion supplement. A backless top held together with an elastic thong, two brown beauty pocks on the crest of her shoulder blade, like wet coffee granules on silk. Her make-up bag was a child's pencil-case. She took out a tube of mascara and held it to her eyelashes, her crotch pressed against the washbasin, her mouth falling open in application.

'That's a nice top,' Ellie said, still gawking at Siân's back. Her skin gave off a musky, slightly sour odour: the smell of babies. Ellie didn't know what she expected, an anthology of welts fashioned by her father's whip, at least an old chickenpox scar, not this constant bloody perfection.

'Ponty,' Siân said, voice aloof. She threw the mascara into the pencil-case.

Ellie had a feeling Johnny coveted Siân, a peculiar niggle deep down in her abdomen, something she'd tried for a while to suppress. What she never imagined was that his desire might be reciprocated. Siân idolized her children, which meant she idolized the father of her children too, but there was no other explanation for this sudden baring of so much divine olive skin. Ellie reapplied her lipstick, blotted it with tissue paper, said, 'I suppose it's for Johnny's benefit.'

Siân glanced through the mirror at Ellie's legs. 'And that's not?' She plucked a plastic baggie from the condom pocket in her skinny jeans, holding it up to the light: five or six white pills with the biohazard symbol stamped on their faces. Ellie hadn't seen them since the Williams twins were dealing. 'Where did you get them?' she said. 'Not Johnny?'

Siân shook her head. She took one out and flicked it into her mouth, washing it down with a gulp of orange alcopop. 'Mine,' she said, 'I've been saving them for a special occasion. Want one?' Ellie thought about it for a moment. She shouldn't really. Andy's parents were here. Everybody was here. 'OK then,' she said, 'yeah.' She threw her head back and swallowed it, noticing a streak of luminous green vomit on the beige wall tiles above the Tampax machine.

Out in the hall, Big Barry the Disco was late arriving, hastily unpacking his CDs, ribbons from the crêpe-paper backdrop tangled around his equipment. Ribs was chock-full of Valium, sitting on the lip of the stage, a pair of white leather platform boots poking out of his jeans. Gwynnie was stooped over the pasting table, peeling the foil from a dish of anaemic sausage rolls. She opened a packet of ready salted crisps and poured them into a polystyrene bowl. One whole row of tables was occupied by Andy's family, second cousins who'd come from Bristol, nieces and nephews from Penmaes. Griff's parents sat facing one another at the end of the aisle, two glasses of stout on the table between them, his mother dressed in a sunflower-yellow twinset, wishing she had a bigger nose from which to look down on everyone.

Andy and Marc were standing in the corner, gossiping about Johnny. There'd been a clipping in the local newspaper that week – 'Drug Accused to Face Trial' – in small print on page thirteen.

'We'll need to keep an eye on that Louisa,' Marc said, sipping from his pint glass, his eyes swiftly shifting around the room. 'She'll be stuck in the YMCA all on her own. Dai says it's a ten-year stretch, easy. We can have the girls take her out, to Cardiff and that. Maybe she'll carry on with the dealing.'

Andy smiled. 'She'd be better off without him anyway.'

'Haven't you got anything else to talk about?' Ellie said. She stood next to Andy, feeling tall in her high heels. 'You're leaving for Biarritz in the morning and all you care about are the rumours you're going to miss.' She was sick of hearing about Johnny. He was *her* obsession, but now everybody was jumping on the band-wagon. Every time she heard someone else utter his name she felt a little nauseous, like she'd eaten too many sweets.

Andy squeezed her, his hands pressing on her shoulders. He rammed his tongue into her ear canal, trying to kiss her earlobe. 'You look gorgeous,' he said, his thunderous voice rumbling into her head. 'I haven't seen these legs for years. I forgot how beautiful they were.' He snatched at her thigh, his breath smelling of hops.

Rhiannon arrived and walked towards an empty table, her hair glued into uneven black spears, going this way and that, like spines on a cactus plant. Her eyebrows were plucked and arched, her skin sore-looking. She was wearing a sequinned wife-beater and one of her too-small skirts. She smiled her fat, fake, rubber-lipped grin, the gold in her tooth glinting. Ellie felt a jolt in her stomach, a cascade of adrenaline. She wanted to punch her right there and then. She waved at Ellie, plump fingers wriggling anxiously, and Ellie remembered that she was just a silly little 40-year-old girl, vying for first prize in the popularity contest going on in her own head, hungry beyond measure for affection from anyone with a dick. Ellie nodded in acknowledgment but stayed where she was, watched Rhiannon plop herself down next to Kelly, her back to the entrance, her white-wine spritzer tilted towards her mouth.

Johnny and Louisa arrived ten minutes later, Johnny wearing his black shirt, eyes restlessly scanning the room. Ellie, embarrassed by his rejection, pretended not to notice. After the incident outside the shop she'd started to think he was playing with her. She'd scurried home that night, her face frozen in confusion, feeling like a zebra that had tried to mess with a lion, thinking Johnny and Rhiannon deserved each other anyway – wannabe Alpha male and female, liquid narcissism pumping through their veins instead of the old claret. Her face burned scarlet with the memory. But if it was a game, she thought, it was a game she didn't want to lose. That's why she'd worn the skirt and the heels. She imagined that she was still in the running. Louisa passed him a pint glass and he carried it outside.

Louisa sat in front of the toilets with Siân, the UV lights pursuing the lint clinging to her clothes. There was a gang of girls in the corridor, 11-year-olds wearing Ugg boots and Puffa jackets, waving at anyone who'd look at them. Kids from the estate were always trying to gatecrash parties in the Labour Club. They came for the free food and the unattended glasses, like gaggles of South African urchins begging at the feet of affluent tourists. Wales was, in many ways, a Third World country. After a few minutes, Ellie approached them. One of the girls thrust a birthday card up at her face, a basic design, a bunch of forget-me-nots in a powder-blue jug.

'It's a leaving party,' Ellie said, irritated with herself for paying them heed. It was Gwynnie's job, surely. 'Piss off or I'll call for the committee.' The girls ran halfway down the stairs and then lingered on the middle winder, cursing and giving her the finger. Then, 'All right El?' another voice from behind the door. Johnny was playing the one-armed bandit, luminous lights flickering across the screen. He was systematically tapping the same key, cool as ice cream, his untouched pint on the floor next to his feet.

Ellie's instinct was to run. She didn't want to feel last week's pain all over again. But the masochist in her prevailed.

'See your old man's off to Europe then?' A bunch of coins tumbled out of the machine. He stooped to pick them up, and then fed them back into the slot. Without looking at her he said, 'Sounds like you'll be spending a bit of time on your own.'

Ellie looked at the back of his stringy body, the arched muscles in his legs. 'What's it got to do with you?' she said. She could feel the swelling in her tummy now, like the firebrick in the kiln, absorbing the heat of her blood.

Johnny glanced sideways at her. 'My question exactly,' he said.

From the gap in the door, Ellie could see Rhiannon on the dance-floor with Kelly. They were straddling one another's thighs, play-acting slapping each other's cheeks, Rhiannon thinking she was chocolate, thinking that she was alive. Suddenly Ellie knew what would hurt her more than a clout. She looked back at Johnny. He was so handsome she didn't know what part of him to look at first. 'I didn't grass you up, you know,' she said. 'I can't believe you'd think that.'

'Well I don't know if I'm coming or going in this place,' he said. 'Every fucker here's talking about me. It's like I killed someone or something. There was a story about me in the newspaper last week. Can you believe that?'

Ellie saw a crack of vulnerability fracturing through his arctic facade, the one she saw on New Year's Eve when he was sitting in the back of the police car. He'd stayed in the corridor because he was uncomfortable with the gossip. She smiled at him. 'You know we could go outside right now,' he said. 'There's nothing stopping us, is there?'

The pill kickstarted her nerves. Johnny had just spoken the words she'd been waiting to hear, but this wasn't the way she wanted to do it. She'd fantasized about duvets filled with goose down, room service champagne, lingerie and cocaine. She'd imagined that fate would buy them time, privacy, luxury, not a rushed quickie in the car park of the Labour Club. 'Now?' she said eventually, voice hesitant. 'It's his leaving party, Johnny. He'll be gone in a couple of days. We'll have plenty of time then.' The bandit puked up another bunch of pound coins and Johnny stooped to collect them. As he did, Siân came rushing out of the hall, slingbacks tapping a tattoo on the lino. She grasped hold of the balustrade, looking at Johnny and Ellie in turn. 'I've got to go,' she said, voice breathless. 'The babysitter phoned. Niall's running a temperature. I'll see you later.' She started springing down the stairs where the girls were still loitering, squealing like ferrets. Siân's haste sent them scattering in three different directions.

'Wait!' Ellie said, quickly seeing her chance to stall fornication with Johnny. If she could get out of it now, she could arrange a night at her house next week, music and candlelight, Chilean Merlot and Grade A Candy Cane. 'You can't go on your own,' she said, leaning over the banister. 'It's late. It's dark. I'll come with you.'

Siân stopped on the penultimate stair and stared up at her, her hair curling into her cleavage. Her huge mouth was stretched open. She was about to say something. Ellie could see the fleshy hunks of her tonsils at the back of her throat. Johnny put the coins in his pockets and walked over to the top stair. 'No,' he said, 'I'll go with her. I feel like an exhibit at a zoo here anyway.' He shrugged. 'May as well help her.'

'Would you?' Siân said.

'Yeah, no problem.' He started skipping down the treads.

Ellie wanted to discourage him but she didn't know what to say.

'I'll see you later, El,' he said, shouting up. 'Have that pint if you want it. I haven't touched it.'

Ellie stood in the corridor, superfluous to requirements; spare cunt at a wedding. What did he think he was doing? He didn't even like kids. 'What a wanker,' she thought, and she kicked the pint glass over, the lager pouring across the floor and dripping into the foyer underneath, one of the girls from the estate trying to catch it in her dirty mouth.

33

Early on Monday morning, the band's wasp-yellow Transit van was parked on the Gwendolyn Street kerb. Griff was sitting in the driver's seat, arm hanging out of the window, fingertips drumming on the door panel. An eerie eddy of ground mist rose out of the gardens in Chepstow Road, the sky the colour of pewter. A cockerel from the allotment crowed.

Andy lifted Ellie off her feet and held her in the air, his hands pressing on her ribcage. It had been years since he'd had the inclination, or the strength, to pick her up. On her last inspection at the weighing scale in the chemist, she'd been nine stone two, two stone under the right weight for her height. Behind his head, hanging on the passage wall, she saw their Hau Kung calendar. He'd scored through his tour dates with a black felt-tip, the splodges of ink bleeding together to form a thick block, as though without him here, half of February and most of March didn't actually exist. He lowered her back down to the floor, kissing her crown, her forehead, finally her lips. 'Look after yourself, babe,' he said.

Griff beeped the horn. Andy threw his holdall over his shoulder and bounced down the steps. As he turned to walk around the van, he looked back at Ellie, eyes watery. His mouth fell into a rictus, face calcified with anxiety. The first time he'd gone on tour, leaving her alone in the house, she'd told him about the old adage:

that if you loved someone you should let them go, and if they came back they were yours. Until now he'd always come back, and Ellie had always been waiting, but they were rapidly growing apart, the distance palpable in their cautious demeanour. Ellie felt energized by the thought of his absence, looked forward to stretching lengthways across their double bed. She waved, then tightened the belt of her dressing gown, watching the Transit vanish behind the hedge in America Place, the village quiet as a domino.

She was still on the doorstep staring down at the square when the postman strolled into the street, a bundle of letters at his chest; the mottled brown envelopes of the giros clashing with his royal blue uniform. When he reached her he passed her the letters with a wink, an electricity statement and an application for a credit card, a plain white envelope from an arts magazine in London. She expected it to be a rejection letter – good news came by 'phone, bad by post. She opened it in the passage where she stood, struggling to read it in the dark. 'Dear Elizabeth', it said, and she took a deep breath, preparing for the worst.

Thank you for your recent letter and sample of your work. We are currently trying to expand certain aspects of our magazine and would be interested in talking to you about the possibility of a commission. Please contact me soon regarding this matter. I look forward to hearing from you.

Ellie read the letter twice and then turned the light on and read it again. She took it into the kitchen and read it while the kettle boiled. She poured herself a cup of instant coffee and read it while she sipped from the mug. She read it until she'd missed her 7 a.m. train to work.

By the time she was scurrying across the High Street, it was ten to eight. She was wearing blue jeans and a red blouse, her work clothes dirty. Her mouth threatened to rupture into a grin every time she thought of the letter, a euphoric chuckle simmering at the base of her larynx, like bubbles of oxygen in a warm pan. The railway station was still hidden under the morning fog, its flat roof poised above the mist like a magic carpet balancing on cloud. She was only half aware of a car pulling up next to her, its engine gurgling.

'Ellie!' Johnny was leaning out of the window, a lit cigarette pinched in his fingers. 'Where are you going? I'll give you a lift.'

Ellie's mouth slunk to a pout. Without a thought she walked around the car, opened the passenger door and got inside. She stared at her knees, the leather cold against her back. For minutes she said nothing, her expression the surly sulk of a teenager. Everything about Johnny made her feel like a teenager. Sex had been exciting when she was fifteen because of its newness, its danger, but over the past eight years it had become part of a routine; something she did because it was what Andy expected from his fiancée. As a grown-up, Ellie regarded the electrical thrill of her sexual awakening with a certain amount of nostalgia. She realized that she'd begun to pepper her existence with chocolate and alcohol and sex-toys and drugs, the small succours that everyone used to file away the edges of adulthood, to help them feel young again. But then Johnny appeared like an evil manifestation of her unspoken prayers, reminding her *exactly* what it was like to be fifteen. And it wasn't all taut flesh and orgasms. It was a desperate time, racked by jealousy, insecurity, fear. She'd been living on her nerves since he'd given her that first cigarette.

'Where are you off to?' he said.

'Nowhere,' Ellie said snappily, perturbed by his sudden appearance. In the beginning she'd spent months searching for a mere glimpse of him. Now he was omnipresent, like God. 'I was on my way to work, but I'm late now, so I won't go.' Her voice slipped into a mumble as she tried to explain herself. She tugged at the sleeves of her jacket.

Johnny took his hand from the steering wheel and quickly squeezed her wrist, his fingers butterscotch against her ivory skin.

Ellie brushed his hand away. 'You fucked her, didn't you?' she said. 'Siân! You slept with her.' She didn't think he had, but she knew he wanted to, which was just as bad.

Johnny giggled as he pulled into the road. 'Don't be silly, El,' he said. 'I walked her to Dynevor Street and spent the rest of the night playing "Grand Theft Auto" in the flat. Don't make me out to be some kind of Lothario; I'm just a weird-looking string of piss. I can hardly get Louisa into bed. If I told my brothers back home that I had a girl like you interested, they'd laugh me right out of the clubhouse.'

Ellie was pleased with this charm offensive but tried not to show it. She kept staring at the windscreen, not seeing anything beyond it. Johnny turned the stereo on and a metallic furore came clawing out of the speakers: the Sex Pistols' cover of Eddie Cochran's 'Something Else'. He reached behind his seat and produced an unopened bottle of vodka, plonking it in her lap. 'Want some of that?' he said.

'It's eight in the morning,' she said.

'Yeah, I know, but I keep it here because it's my office. I'm like a CEO with a bottle of Scotch in my drawer. You look tense.' She unscrewed the bottle top and swigged feverishly at it, its potency immediate. Johnny was driving past Pengoes Industrial Estate, the new sun thawing the frost on the corrugated zinc units. He turned to look at her, said, 'I've got five brothers, four sisters. I'm the oldest of ten. We were the poorest family in Cornwall, brought up on dinner tickets and clothing grants. When I was twelve I wanted an Adidas sweater so bad I painted three lines down the sleeves of my school jumper with a bottle of correction fluid.'

They turned right at the junction behind Dinham chicken farm, heading for Penmaes Mountain. Ellie guessed that she wasn't going to get a hotel room after all, but if she blew cold now, she knew

Johnny was as good as Rhiannon's. She could have invited him back to her house, but the idea of being dominated, of being *taken*, was quite appealing. She understood now why people had sexual fantasies about Nazi generals. Johnny's power was so pervasive it freed Ellie from the burden of trying to manage her own moral code. *He made me do it*, she thought as she slugged at the poisonous vodka. Suddenly she took an interest in the glove-box, opening it quickly in the hope of finding evidence of his involvement with Siân or Rhiannon. There was an insurance policy, a packet of Rizla and the Christmas trimming she'd given him in November. She slammed it closed. 'All day I dream about sex,' she said, pausing for a moment before adding, 'an acronym, of Adidas.' Something she'd learned in school, smoking Lambert & Butler's with the remedial kids behind the gym.

'Very good,' Johnny said, the tyres pressing on gravel as he pulled up next to a rotting picnic table. The new ferns were the colour of malachite, blisters of dying grass dotted around the outcrop, black moss adhering to the scree. 'How do you know about this place?' Ellie said suspiciously. 'You're not even from here. Bet you found it looking for somewhere to screw Siân.'

Johnny teased the bottle out of her hand and sipped from it, features twisting into a grimace. 'This is where I get my deliveries,' he said, rummaging around in his pocket. 'It gets left here and I get a phone call a few days later. That way nobody ever sees us together, me and my contact.' He was holding a money-bag, the words '*No Mixed Coins*' vivid against the white powder inside. He dipped a coke spoon into the bag and then held it, heaped, at Ellie's nostrils. She snorted and then wiped her nose.

'Are you getting in the back with me or what?' Johnny said.

They got out of the front of the car, and into the back, the thuds of the doors stinging Ellie's eardrums.

He hauled her on to all fours, tearing her jeans down to her knees, her blouse above her breasts. Her face was pressed against a box-weave blanket draped over the shoulder of the seat. She could see strands of black dog hairs tangled in the yellow fibre. They went at it in silence except for Johnny's sharp intakes of breath and a couple of Ellie's allergic sneezes. After a few minutes she had the sense to close her eyes, the winter sunshine burning on her eyelids, turning the inside of her head to the colour of a cayenne chilli-pepper.

34

Half an hour later the sun had slithered behind the vapour. The wind turned the pine trees to babies' rattles. The skin between Ellie's legs was tacky with patches of dried semen. She pulled her knickers up, sitting with her knees in the air, the vodka bottle hooked in her mouth, Johnny propped next to her, his head on her shoulder. He was staring at the roof of the car, eyelids heavy. Ellie could see now that his irises were the same colour as Coca-Cola, russet in the daylight.

'Have you been to prison before?' she said.

He picked the money-bag up and folded it into a neat, flat square, balancing it on his thigh. 'No,' he said, 'not going there this time neither. They've got nothing on me, those cunting tyre-biters.'

'But I read the story in the newspaper,' she said. 'Intent to supply is a minimum seven-year sentence. And you're not doing your-self any favours, carrying a class-A drug while you're on bail.'

Johnny's eyes skirted the mountainside. There was a flock of hardy sheep a few miles down, a bald patch in the forest where kids had set light to it last summer. He pulled away from her, yanking his jeans up to his waist, exhaling loudly. 'How are they gonna know, El? How are they gonna know what I'm carrying? They can't do me for intent. They haven't got no evidence, no witnesses. They found half an ounce of weed in my bedroom.

That's personal use. Most they can do me for is possession, which is all they could do me for last time. A fine, two years' probation, max.' He opened the car door, the smell of smoke and sex escaping on the breeze. 'They can't touch me.'

He sat in the driver's seat and waited for her to join him on the passenger side.

As they headed back to Penmaes, car snaking around the winding road, Ellie spied a jumbo jet ripping through the icy blue sky. 'America,' she said, pointing up at it. 'We're directly under the flight path for the Heathrow to JFK. You know I'd kill to be on that plane.'

'Why?' Johnny said. He was bearing on to the main road, the indicator ticking. Some of the workers from the shampoo factory were out on their fag break, middle-aged women wearing string hairnets, talking about housework and menstrual cycles, their fingers brown with nicotine. 'Look at this place,' Ellie said. 'It's disgusting! It reminds me of the psychiatric wing in a low-security prison. Ever see that Sixties series, *The Prisoner*? They filmed it in Wales and that wasn't a coincidence. It looks nice, yeah, but it's full of mentalists. I mean, what did you think when you walked in the Pump House the first time? I bet you thought you'd licked the bottom of the fucking barrel.'

Johnny laughed. 'I mean why America?' he said. 'You're against capitalism, you're against the war. You're against everything America's built on.'

Ellie's eyes were watering. She sneezed and said, 'I'm not against people trying to make a better life for themselves. They used to call the south Wales coalfield "American Wales", because mining here sucked in more population than it did in the whole state of Pennsylvania. We all came here to work, except, when the work went, we forgot to leave. America's already in the blood. And it's just a generalization to say it's a country built on Republican ideologies. It's a great country because whoever you

211

are, and whatever you want to do, there's a part of America that'll welcome you.'

'So long as you're not a drug dealer,' Johnny said.

Ellie sucked air over her teeth. She knew he had a conviction for possession and that he'd never be allowed to enter the States legally, but why did he have to state the obvious? 'Hmm,' she said. She stared at the black-and-white crash barrier so hard the paint merged to slate grey. When they turned into the High Street, the aluminium shutters were pulled up on the shop fronts. Ellie spotted Rhiannon standing in the doorway of the ironmonger's wearing her hairdressing tunic, batting her eyelashes at the butcher across the road.

'Shit!' Johnny said. 'It's Rhiannon. That's Rhiannon.'

Ellie pressed a button in the door panel, the window slowly lowering.

'Don't do that!' he said. He overrode her command, pressing on his own set of switches. But Ellie wanted Rhiannon to see them. She pushed her face up against the smoked glass, lips wet with anticipation.

'Don't!' Johnny said. He held Ellie by the scruff of her neck and pushed her head into her knees, one hand still gripping the steering wheel. Ellie was astonished by this sudden violence and she succumbed for a few seconds, the wiry weight of Johnny's arm balancing on the soft cleft of her shoulder.

'What did you do that for?' she said, angry as the devil when she'd managed to sit up. 'What would it matter if she saw us?' That was the whole point of the exercise. Ellie'd fucked Johnny because that's what Rhiannon wanted to do, and Rhiannon needed to be taught that she couldn't have *everything* that she wanted. She was just one little person in a big wide world.

Johnny was heading for Kwik Save. 'She's pretty friendly with Louisa at the moment,' he said, 'and I don't want to get caught. Not now. I'm in the doghouse as it is, with the bust and all that.'

He circumnavigated the car park, turning back out on to the main road. 'What street do you live in, El?'

'You're a real prick sometimes,' Ellie said, voice provocative, tired of Johnny suddenly. She'd used her ace of spades but the croupier still wasn't paying out. His indifference hurt and she wanted to stick her head in his face. 'I've got genuine feelings for you. I want to be with you. I'd leave Andy this afternoon. All you care about is how much pussy you can get: Siân, Rhiannon, Louisa, me. I told you I wouldn't share!'

She opened her duffel bag and stuffed the vodka bottle inside, hands shaking, teeth clenched, a dam building up behind her eyes. 'Let me out. I'll walk.' Johnny pulled up next to the Bell & Cabbage, but kept his gaze on the dashboard, eyes sooty. 'Sorry,' he said, but he didn't say what for. Ellie guessed she'd scared him with her incendiary rage. She'd scared herself, too. This is what life felt like when all of your dreams had come true but none of your nightmares had gone away. She shuffled out of the car and stomped to Gwendolyn Street, hot tears burning the rims of her eyes. Instead of letting them go she held them in her head, sniffling and muttering like a mad woman. At home she rang Jane.

'Yes?' Jane said, voice level, the hollow chatter of the factory machinery in the background.

'It's Ellie,' Ellie said. 'I can't come in today. I've got hay fever, can't hardly breathe.' Providence sent her a well-timed sneeze.

'Well, you should have rung the office,' Jane said. 'Just because I'm your sister, I can't run your errands for you. We're rushed off our feet here.' A mug smashed in the distance, the earthenware ringing on concrete.

'You're not my sister,' Ellie said. 'You're my boss.'

She put the phone down and went to bed fully clothed, pulling the duvet up to her chin. The top of it smelled of Andy's meaty breath. Guilt grabbed her by the tail and pushed up into her stomach, a pain like a stake going through her bowels. He'd only been gone a few hours and already she'd committed adultery, two years of monogamy ruined in a shot. Meanwhile, the smell of Johnny was still on her skin: the tart vinegar tang of his seed, a hint of petroleum from his Zippo.

For twenty-five hours she stewed in her own sweat, debris slowly building up around her; vodka bottles, toilet tissues, boxes of Ibuprofen. The plastic washing-up bowl was tucked under the valance, half full of vomit. Daylight nipped at her closed curtains and then rolled away again; day then night then day again. Late on Tuesday morning she crawled out of her self-imposed cell, deciding it looked a little like a Tracey Emin installation, and knew, even without thinking it, that she was going to try to screw Johnny again. It was as if she'd walked down part of a path that had fallen away under her feet. It was too late to turn around now. Nobody kills a pig for a *soupçon* of gelatine.

35

Early on Tuesday evening, Griff's mother was standing on her doorstep. Siân tried not to look at the mole on her chin. It was beginning to resemble a miniature brain, grey and rutted. 'They've had their tea,' she said stiffly. 'I'd prefer it if they didn't have anything else now.' Griff's mother had a drawer full of chocolate that she used to pacify the children, rather than reward. Sometimes she paid the teenagers next door to drive to McDonald's in Ystradyfodwg. Angharad would come home wired, crying for the half-eaten McFlurry left in her grandmother's fridge. Even as she spoke, Siân could see her request falling on deaf ears.

'Give over, gul,' Griff's mother said. 'We've got a slab of Battenburg for supper. I bought it especially.' Siân turned the buggy around, positioning the handles in front of her mother-in-law's fingers. 'You've got the number for the shop?' she said as she started to walk away. 'Should do, love,' Griff's mother said, 'the amount of flyers that Chink keeps stuffing through this letterbox.'

Siân was ten minutes late when she got to Hau Kung. The Boy Racer's hatchback was already parked outside. He was sitting on the bench, flicking through the local newspaper. 'Sorry, Chan,' she shouted, plonking her handbag down on the counter. He was frying beansprouts, the oil sizzling as they hit the wok. The Boy Racer looked up from the newspaper. 'He's well pissed off,' he said, nodding at the window. Over the winter, the mechanism in the aluminium shutter had seized and Chan was too weak to operate it. Siân opened it automatically, on arrival, but if the Boy Racer got there first, Chan had to ask him for help, something the old man was loath to do.

The telephone rang and Siân answered. The order was for delivery and she'd be glad to be rid of the boy for a few minutes. She wrestled out of her coat and wrote the numbers down on her notepad. Before she'd taken the whole thing, she saw Johnny slinking into the shop, his grubby basketball boots trampling over the lino. He stood in front of her, studying her face. Siân tried to concentrate on the voice in the receiver, the chewed pen-top going to her mouth. When she'd finished she stumbled into the kitchen and pinned the order to the board. Chan grunted in acknowledgement.

'What can I get you?' she said as she emerged, voice terse. She flicked her hair back on her shoulders and focused on one of Johnny's earlobes. He stared at the menu Sellotaped to the counter and gave her a list of dishes, loud and slow, as if they were clues to a puzzle she needed to solve. 'Lemon, Chicken, Special. Shrimp, Fried, Rice.' She scribbled the items down while the Boy Racer gawked at Johnny.

Chan came in and dropped a bag on the counter, its handles tied in a knot. The Boy Racer sighed as he whipped it from the shelf. He headed out of the door. Chan went back to the kitchen. 'Is that all?' Siân said.

'A couple of poppadoms,' Johnny said.

'I thought you were a vegetarian. That's what you told Ellie, isn't it? There's nothing vegetarian here.' She tore the top page away from the pad. Johnny leaned over the counter, three inches away from her face. 'Are you due for a break?' he said.

The last time Siân had seen him had been on Saturday at the band's leaving party. It tickled her, the way he'd been so eager to follow her down the stairs. She never thought she'd pull a trick like that off, never thought he'd choose her over Ellie. Ellie was intelligent; she could talk about things that were happening in the world: wars, conspiracies, music and art. A meaningful conversation with Siân revolved around the continuity problems in *Pretty Woman*, of which there were many. But Johnny *did* choose her, and Ellie'd been left on the landing, looking like the world was about to end.

Siân had led him around the back of the Labour Club. They'd sat on the concrete step of the fire exit, the window above them smashed and covered with a black bag. The sky was brassy with stars. She could see the Great Bear. 'Your little boy *is* OK, then?' he'd said worriedly, as though Siân was incapable of mischief. Siân laughed. 'Yeah,' she said. 'I just needed a bit of fresh air, five minutes away from Griff's parents. Did you see my mother-in-law?' Griff's mother was wearing the lurid yellow twinset she'd bought in a boutique on holiday in Las Vegas. Siân remembered the present she'd bought back for James, too: a blue LA Lakers T-shirt with the number 24 on the front.

Johnny had thrust his hand into the waistband of her jeans, his long fingers scrabbling around in the denim like an animal, his fingernails scratching at her knickers' gusset. She jumped away from him. Nobody had touched her like that for six months. The last contact her vulva had had with anything was a steel speculum, during a cervical smear, the nurse quickly swiping it with KY jelly before deftly driving it in. After Siân had got the children she'd wanted, sex with Griff was pointless. She always found herself in the wet patch, parboiled and wanting to say, '*Again?*' the way the children did during games of fishy-in-the-water. '*Again, please. Again?*' She used to wait for him to go to sleep before finishing herself off.

'Sorry,' she'd said, running away from him. She'd been embarrassed to find herself acting like a horny teenager, squatting on a step that smelled of piss. 'Stupid girl,' she'd said to herself as she put her key in her front door. She'd taken the old thermometer out of the bathroom cupboard, so that when Griff returned it'd look as though Niall really had been running a temperature. She'd sat next to his cot until she'd heard Griff coming in.

Now she pinned Johnny's order to the corkboard in the kitchen. Chan was standing at the Belfast sink, his back to her. An electronic flytrap held the papery bodies of two bluebottles. 'Do you mind if I go outside for five minutes?' she said, 'a quick cigarette? The shop's empty.' She knew she had to give in to Johnny's advances this time. She'd run out of pills.

Chan hit the draining board with a metal spatula, making her jump. 'A zhigarette?' he said. 'Didn't I tell you to take ginger?' He'd looked at her fingernails one time and diagnosed her with nervous exhaustion. He wrote an ancient Chinese remedy for anxiety down on a piece of paper: ginger, liquorice and peony. Siân had little chance of affording the ingredients, so she'd quickly forgotten about it. After a few moments of silence he waved at her. 'Yes, yes,' he said. 'Hurry up.'

There was a narrow alleyway at the side of the shop that led to a sharp descent. The railway track lay at the bottom. Often, Chan threw his vegetable peel down there. The neighbouring businesses were always complaining about the rats. She stopped walking halfway along the path and Johnny squeezed behind her, pushing the slings of her arms against the jagged brickwork. He yanked her pencil skirt up to her waist. She'd worn the skirt that night because she was dropping the children off at Griff's mother's. She'd wanted to look smart. Now there was no fly, no zipper, no buttons to hide behind. She could feel Johnny working his penis, sliding it up and down between her buttocks. He pushed himself inside. The brisk pain made her yelp.

'That's it,' he said as she submitted. She moved back against him. It didn't last long, and during the process she heard the telephone in the restaurant ring twice, saw the Boy Racer's car pull up, its lights skating across the walls of the alley. As Johnny withdrew he turned Siân around. She looked away from him, over his shoulder, scared there'd be traces of faeces on his dick. She'd never done it that way before. 'You all right?' he said as he buttoned himself up.

Siân nodded feverishly as she pulled her skirt down. 'You haven't got any Es, have you?' she said.

He was looking at her disappointedly, as if he expected something else. 'Sure,' he said, remembering himself. He took a small Ziploc bag out of his inside pocket. Even in the dark, Siân could see there were only three tablets. 'It's all I've got on me now. There'll be more next week, just pop in the flat.'

Siân smiled as she snatched it from him. 'Thanks,' she said. She drew away from him and stepped out on to the pavement. The door-chimes clinked as she turned into the shop. Johnny's order was on the counter, steam rising out of the bag. She moved self-consciously across the linoleum, thinking the Boy Racer could see that she was walking strangely; that he'd be able to guess what she'd been doing. 'Sixteen fifty, please,' she said, sliding the bag across the counter towards Johnny, face wet with perspiration.

'What about the crackers?' the Boy Racer said.

'What?' Siân was agitated as she slipped the baggie into her handbag. She scratched her collarbone, eager to feel the calm lull of the first pill.

'Free prawn crackers with orders over fifteen pound!' the boy said. 'Your idea, remember?' He flipped the flap-door open and took a bag of crackers out of the heater. He threw them at Johnny. Johnny caught them in the crook of his arm, some of the wafers snapping under his grip.

'Can't give them away, see, mate,' the boy said. 'Smell too much like women.'

Johnny snickered as he dawdled out of the shop.

Siân stared at the boy.

'What?' he said. 'What did I say? Your mother-in-law phoned by the way, said your little girl's puked all over her goatskin rug – ate too much tomato soup or some shit. Gross. She wants you up there to see to it. I told her you would; as soon as you'd finished flirting with the customers.'

36

It was half eleven, Monday morning; the Pump House still smelled of polish. Dai was sitting on his stool, squinting at the local newspaper. 'Filthy Perv Banged Up', the headline said. Rhiannon approached him with the cold roast dinner, a heap of slimy cauliflower and an anaemic-looking Yorkshire pudding protruding over the edge of the plate. 'Look what ewe've got,' Rhiannon said. 'Beef, look, I did it special.'

Gwynnie'd done it really. The band was in France and there was nobody to pay the restaurant tab. Collin had her back in the kitchen, chucking baking trays about like Frisbees. Rhiannon didn't fancy a rerun of Christmas day: Ellie sitting there, bony as Skeletor; Gwynnie begging for grandchildren. She told them she was stock-taking and she picked the meal up in the evening. Rhiannon had left it in the Alfa overnight and ordered food from Hau Kung.

'What is it?' Dai said. He cleared his throat with a retch and folded the newspaper down on the bar.

'Dinner,' Rhiannon said. 'Don't ewe want it? Marc's away. It'll only go to waste.'

Dai smiled at her, his top lip riding over his nicotine-stained teeth.

'They can put it in the microwave for ewe, can't 'ey?' she said.

She walked back to the car park and took the rest of the Tupperware from the passenger seat, piling the pots on top of one another. The rhubarb pie had been a last-minute idea, bought pre-baked from the deli counter in Kwik Save. That morning she'd cut it into four fat triangles and thrown three of them in the bin.

She'd tried to take a shit in the gravy, squatting over the plastic jar for ten minutes. But she couldn't squeeze anything out. Her bowel movements hadn't been right since she'd had colonic irrigation at St David's Spa. Instead, she'd managed a dribble of cloudy piss. She studied the gravy now as she carried it back to the pub. There was a frothy white film on the surface but Dai wouldn't notice. Stupid old bastard didn't know shit from Shinola.

Two new customers had arrived, twenty-somethings wearing Ben Sherman and Ralph Lauren. They had Cardiff accents. Rhiannon always winced when she heard that nasally twang for the first time. When she was eighteen she'd been walking through Splott, looking for a house party in Emerald Street, when a man in a balaclava dragged her into a lane. She was half cut and hadn't seen him coming. She remembered him holding her around the waist, her legs kicking; the way kids rode imaginary bicycles in the air. Cut a long story, she'd managed to pluck a nail file out of her handbag and stab him in the face, the dirty rapist cunt.

'They poofs or what?' Dai said, eyeing them. Dai liked to think of himself as the local hard man, a bare-knuckle street fighter who commanded fear and respect. *As if.* He'd never lifted his fist to a bloke. He was mean, though, sadistic like a woman. He found your weak spot and went for it. When Myra'd found the nerve to leave him, he'd put her cat in the tumble dryer, left it on the highest setting while he went to piss his giro up against the wall. Rhiannon was the one who'd found it, bits of its scorched flesh glued to the sides of the drum, one of its paws boiled clean off its body. She knew it was Dai who'd shopped Johnny to the fuzz.

'Ignore 'em, Dai,' she said. 'They're not doin' any 'arm, are they? They're only youngsters, mun.' She passed the pot of gravy to the barman, said, 'Eat ewer dinner. Ewe'll get ewerself killed one o' these days, ewe will, the amount of steroids the kids are doin' now.' One punch off a 'roider and he'd be dead in two minutes.

'I ain't afraid of no fuckin' 'roid 'eads,' Dai said. He shoved a carrot in his mouth, a loopy purple vein in his forehead quivering as he swallowed.

'But ewe're not as young as ewe used to be, are ewe?' Rhiannon said.

The barman arrived with the warm pot of gravy and tipped it on to the plate. It landed on the potatoes in a lumpy mass. Rhiannon snatched the fork from Dai's hand and raked it on to the veg. 'Come on, Dai,' she said, passing the fork back. 'Ewe gotta try my gravy.' She watched as he licked the edge of a new potato.

'Nice inni?' she said.

Dai looked surprised. 'Aye,' he said, slapping a slice of beef on his tongue.

Rhiannon picked a beer-mat up and scratched at it with her nail. 'By the way, Uncle Dai,' she said, glancing at him sideways. 'Those pictures ewe took of me when I was a kid. I want 'em back.' Dai stared at her momentarily, face frozen, a garden pea balanced in the dish of his mouth.

'People don't like 'ose sorts of pictures nowadays, do 'ey?' she said. 'I don't want 'em gettin' into the wrong 'ands. Ewe could get into trouble with 'em, ewe know.'

As she was speaking, Johnny strode into the pub. He walked to the games area and stood between the two boys from the city. She watched as he reached into his arse pocket. She'd seen him briefly a week after he'd been arrested, on the roadside by the salon. He'd had the yellowed remains of a shiner around his right eye. 'Roughed ewe up a bit, din't ey?' she'd said. She knew the way the filth operated. 'Ewe know it was Ellie who grassed ewe up, don't ewe?' she'd said. 'She acts all broad-minded and shit, but she's as square as 'ey come really.' Johnny'd nodded and walked off without a word. Now he was passing something to one of the boys, black eye gone. 'All right, Rhi?' he said, shouting across the bar at her. 'Want a glass of wine?'

Rhiannon left Dai on his stool and walked to him, concentrating on his beautiful hands. She remembered him tweaking her left nipple. 'How are you?' he said, passing her her glass, staring at her with his magpie-black eyes. 'I think the last time I saw you, you were trying to show me Polaroids of your Christmas *ménage à trois*. You got them on you now?'

Rhiannon laughed. 'Actually, mush, I think the last time I saw ewe, ewe were bein' escorted into a Black Maria.' She took a gulp of her drink and glanced at Dai. He was still eating his dinner. 'You 'ad Siân and Ellie in tears,' she said. 'Who do ewe think ewe are? Adonis?'

'No, that's what *you* think,' Johnny said.

'Follow me,' Rhiannon said, picking their glasses up. She walked into the women's toilet and propped the drinks down on the vanity shelf. It smelled of bleach, cold air blowing through the open sash in one of the cubicles. Johnny leaned against the tiles between the basins. 'Ellie says it wasn't her,' he said.

'She would say that, wouldn't she?' She knelt down in front of him, reaching up for his belt buckle. She unzipped his fly. He smelled of burned rubber as she took him into her mouth. She stared up at him, his pubic hair rough against her nose. She gagged as he gripped her crown, pulling at the short branches of her hair.

Rhiannon was reminded of the soft toys that people tried to win at the fairground, a metal claw clutching at the sides of their skulls. Her father had nicked one of those machines from the Stardust arcade in Porthcawl when she was six. She'd been trying to get a stuffed Bagpuss and every time she got near, it just slipped right out of the electronic grip. Her dad was drinking in the Dirty Duck in Trecco Bay, so when she'd run out of money she went to him. He'd taken her back to the arcade and unplugged the machine, walked straight out of the place with the whole thing perched on his back.

Now she washed her mouth out with wine. She led Johnny back to the bar where Dai was wiping his grey mouth with a paper serviette. Johnny tucked his shirt into the waistband of his jeans. He looked at the clock on the trophy shelf. 'Is that the time?' he said. 'Quarter past twelve?'

'*Eleven* minutes past twelve,' Dai said sourly.

'Shit,' Johnny said, face full of panic. 'I've got to go, I've got to . . .' He darted out of the pub. 'Nice one,' Rhiannon said. 'Give a guy a blow-job and not a by-ewer-bloody-leave.'

37

It was 1 March when Ellie went back to work. A troupe of children were marching into the primary school on Kitchener Road, girls wearing Welsh hats and shawls, boys in Dai caps, their mother's black eye-shadow smudged on their cheeks; big, clumsy daffodils pinned to their lapels. The factory's goods entrance was open. Ellie loped through reception and stamped her clock-in card. The girls were working on a new design: a fat, pea-green frog on a salmon-pink mug, a fiendish leer in its puffy, cartoon eyes.

'Stupid friggin' things,' Safia said. A hunk of dried mascara had fallen out of her lashes and landed on the soft flesh under her eye. There was a thin layer of perspiration on her nose. She lifted the mug from between her thighs and showed Ellie a crumpled piece of paper stuck to the base. 'Yous got to put a sticker on the inside and smooth it out with your brush. My fingers are killing me.'

Ellie's decal tray was empty. She dropped her duffel bag on the desk and took her water jug to the sink in the corner. Jane was kneeling on the floor behind her desk, shuffling through a stack of paperwork. 'Hello, Ellie,' she said without looking up. 'Have you seen the production reports yet?'

The notice board was a wash of white paper, a black bar chart stretching across three pages. It still smelled of ink. 'I'm just fetching some water,' Ellie said. She had no interest in Jane's trivial bureaucracy.

'Have a look,' Jane said. She stood up, a box-file under her arm. She walked to the notice board and pointed at the bar chart. 'See how Nicola and Maria hit a hundred and twenty per cent last month?' She tapped the corner of the notice board and it shook. 'You and Safia are at the bottom. You only did ten thousand mugs between you; ten thousand mugs in a whole month.'

A thousand mugs sounded like a lot. Ellie couldn't comprehend how anyone could do any more than a hundred per cent. She shrugged and turned the tap on, holding her jug under it, the water rattling as it hit the tin base.

'Do you understand?' Jane said. 'The success of the bonus scheme is reliant on everyone pulling their weight. The department missed the target. The other girls missed out, because of you, because of you and Safia. If you were wondering why the atmosphere in here is so awful, that just might be your answer!' Ellie glanced around the room. The other girls stared back, eyes frosty. The jug was full and the water spurted into the air, gushing down over Ellie's hand. She jumped away from the sink. She felt naked as she twisted the tap off at arm's length. '*I* didn't vote for a bonus scheme,' she said, and she made her way back to her desk.

'We can talk about it tomorrow,' Jane said, 'at your disciplinary hearing.' She put a piece of paper down in front of Ellie. 'A sick form. Fill it in and bring it with you. Three o'clock in the director's office.'

It was an hour later when the production manager came in, strolling guardedly among the desks as though he expected a wild animal to jump out and maul him. He picked up one of Ellie's mugs, holding it above his head as he peered at it. After a minute she realized he was waiting for her to acknowledge him. 'Is it all right?' she said. She felt the girls' stares homing in on her like a scold of crosshairs.

'Can you go through them again before they're dry?' he said. 'It's a new type of fixative. You've forgotten the decal on this one.' He passed it to her. 'Check them all if you can.'

As he turned into the print department, Ellie took her week-old letter out of her bag. She pulled it out of the envelope and carefully unfolded it, brushing imaginary flakes of dust out of her eye-line. She read it, though she already knew what it said:

Thank you for your recent letter and sample of your work. We are currently trying to expand certain aspects of our magazine and would be interested in talking to you about the possibility of a commission.

She hadn't rung the telephone number printed on the top right-hand corner yet. She'd convinced herself that she didn't need the pressure of another assignment, but that wasn't the real reason. The incident with Johnny had knocked the wind out of her sails. She felt her old crippling insecurity creeping back. If she wasn't good enough for Johnny, she thought, she wasn't good enough for London. All of her vim was focused on winning him. She was still expecting him to liberate her from her stolid marriage, to unfetter her from the confines of reality as if he was some prodigal, telekinetic sorcerer. She wasn't thinking about saving herself. She wanted the knight in his shining BMW. She wondered where he was now and imagined him on Penmaes Mountain with Rhiannon, his icicle-fingers reaming up under her miniskirt, his nose lowering into her spiky black hair.

After a while she decided that she couldn't do anything about anything while she was stuck in the workshop. She put the mug down on the desk and quickly stood up.

'Look at you,' she said to no one in particular, feeling the blood drain out of her face. 'You're grown women and you're sticking stickers on mugs! You're sticking stickers on mugs for the minimum wage.' She was incensed now and she felt her anger like a seam of coal under a harmless patch of earth. 'You're sticking stickers on mugs, for God's sake!' She pulled her top drawer out of her desk and tilted it into her duffel bag, old train tickets and chewing gum wrappers spilling out.

'What are you doing?' Jane said from behind her desk.

'I'm a freelance journalist,' Ellie said. 'I don't work here any more.' She began the long walk past Gavin, through the passage in the print department and out into the yard. She flew through the factory gate, running towards Atlas Road. There were two black cabs waiting in the tailback behind the traffic lights. She put her hand in the air, waving at them.

'Wait!' someone said, a voice from behind her. Ellie glanced over her shoulder, expecting to see Jane, but it was Safia hurrying after her, white cotton handbag knocking at her hip. One of the Hackney carriages pulled up next to Ellie. 'Where to, love?' the driver said, an old man with an old Cardiff accent. 'Central Station, please,' Ellie said. She got in the back, left the door open for Safia.

'Why did you do that?' Safia said as she climbed in next to her, a gummy glue stain across the back of her hand.

'Because I've got qualifications,' Ellie said, laughing at the truth in her lie. She'd walked out because she couldn't bear to think about Johnny with Rhiannon, just raced straight out of the place, powered by anxiety. 'You didn't have to walk out though, Saf,' she said. 'How're you going to manage now? What are you going to do for money?'

'Doesn't matter,' Safia said. 'I couldn't work there without yous, anyway. I'll get a job in the new Tesco on Glossop Road.' She looked at Ellie, said, 'Will that cause problems now at home?' Ellie didn't know what she meant. 'With your sister?' Safia said.

Ellie looked out of the window. They were on Cowbridge Road East, the taxi speeding past a row of Indian and Chinese restaurants. The fury in her guts had petered out. Her head was vacant, body exhausted. 'Jane's not really my sister,' she said, voice cutting through the stuffiness in the cab. 'Not even my step- or half-sister. I'm adopted.'

Safia nodded. She said, 'I thought yous never looked alike.'

For the remainder of the journey, the cab was heavy with their silence. The taxi driver sensed the awkwardness and turned the radio on, the high-pitched twitter of Radio Wales a welcome diversion. When they got to Central Square, Ellie paid the driver and opened the door, her legs caving as she shuffled out of the cab. She tried to cling to a lamppost on the kerb but her hands slid down the length of it. She hit the ground on her knees.

'Are you okay?' Safia was screeching, the clamour drawing attention from the commuters hanging around the square. Ellie jumped up quickly and leaned against a concrete bollard. 'I'm fine.' She'd been feeling spaced-out since that morning on the mountain with Johnny. She'd done a whole gram of coke. Her nasal cavity was still sore, the membrane burning perpetually. Her immune system was weak, her body run down. It was nothing that a soak in a warm bath wouldn't cure, a night or two off the pop.

'When was the last time yous ate something?' Safia said.

Ellie couldn't remember but she lied, said, 'This morning, tea and toast.'

Safia shook her head worriedly and rushed towards the Burger King next door to the station. She came back with a bean burger wrapped in greaseproof paper, her telephone number scrawled on the corner. 'You're not pregnant, are you?' she said, handing it over. 'That's what my friend was, when she started collapsing like that.'

Ellie laughed. 'Don't be stupid, Saf. Anyway, you haven't got any friends.'

Safia looked hurt, but she laughed anyway. 'You OK to goes up to the platform?' she said. 'Some guy over there says the Tremorfa bus is due.' She waved at the bus station across the road.

Ellie could see the Perspex shelters in the distance wobbling slightly. 'Yeah, I'm OK,' she said. 'I'll give you a ring.'

38

When the band got back from France they marked the occasion with drinks in the Pump House, as usual. The bar was packed with labourers, still wearing their working clothes, faces stippled with flecks of pink plaster. The April air was gluey. It was like trying to breathe honey. Marc was talking about a concert in Montpellier and the woman in the front row who'd kept baring her Brazilian. 'She didn't give a shit,' he said, voice bombastic, Welsh skin splashed with a hint of dusky European sun.

'Bet her armpits were hairy though,' Siân said, shouting over the football results. 'French women don't shave.'

'Shut up, Siân,' Ellie said. 'That's a fallacy. You know it is. Who told you that? Rhiannon?' Siân had been there since before Ellie had arrived, wearing a black camisole that shimmered with every move she made. Her scarlet lipstick made her mouth look like a wind-up toy, one of those chatterboxes that rattled across the surface of a table.

Rhiannon was at the bar with Dai Davies, the pair of them whispering conspiratorially over an A5 envelope. Ellie hadn't seen her for a month and her hair had grown. She'd shaped it into a stark, Mia Wallace bob. After a few minutes she put the envelope in her bag and came back to the table. All three girls had hardly said a word to each other all evening. It was as if they were strangers, the only thing linking them a gift from a duty-free counter on the Calais to Dover ferry; a Zircon jewellery set, two cubic stones set in the point of a five-sided star. Ellie wore the charm bracelet. Siân was wearing the earrings. Rhiannon had the necklace.

Ellie turned to look through the pub window at the second floor of the YMCA. She could see the outline of a Doberman but there was no Johnny-Come-Lately. She'd been looking for him since she'd quit her job, still getting up at six in the morning in the hope of catching him walking near the entrance to the estate. She couldn't knock on his door in case Louisa answered, so she did her shopping in the Sikh newsagent's on Tallis Street. One afternoon she'd even hiked to the top of Penmaes Mountain and sat on an ants' nest next to the rotten picnic table, made an HB pencil sketch of the view. She'd been living on the utility bill money she and Andy had saved and hidden in a copper tea canister at the back of the melamine tallboy. Andy didn't trust banks, so they kept their cash behind the old tins of ham and hotdog sausages, its container gummed to the shelf with spilt gravy browning. There was three hundred and eighty pounds on the day she'd found it; now there was less than a tenner. Two weeks ago she'd rung the arts magazine in London and a man with a voice like a shredded gearbox had answered. He was the editor, and half of his in-house staff had eloped to establish a new rival title with a chunk of pooled savings and match funding from the Arts Council of England. He'd given her a few book and CD reviews, but the fee wouldn't cover the overdue gas bill.

Andy had only discovered her change of career a few hours earlier. 'How's work?' he'd said, picking pairs of thrice-worn boxers out of his suitcase, throwing them on the bathroom floor.

'I quit last month,' she'd said. She was shovelling the dirty washing into the overflowing laundry basket, trying to look domesticated and useful. 'Had a bit of a quarrel with my sister about

233

her bonus scheme. It's OK. I've got some freelance stuff lined up. I'm going back to journalism.'

Andy had looked at her distractedly, his newly tanned forehead creased. 'That doesn't pay much though, does it?' he said.

Ellie'd shrugged. 'Neither does schlepping around France with no record deal.'

'We'll get a deal,' Andy'd said. 'The tour went well, babe. It's only a matter of time.'

Ellie didn't believe him. In the two years she'd been around the band, nothing had changed; the road to success was permanently under construction, like the slip road out of the valley. 'We'll have to rearrange the date for the wedding now,' she said in an attempt to appease him, cleverly directing the conversation away from money.

'Yeah we will, babe,' he'd said, stepping into the shower.

It was growing dark when Louisa arrived. A vast wave of relief washed over her face as she spotted them sitting next to the window. 'Thank God you're all here,' she said, hurrying towards the table. 'I hate walking into pubs on my own.'

Andy stood up. 'What do you want to drink, Lou?' he said. 'It's my round, I'll get it.' He plucked some of the empties from the table.

'Oh, a white wine please,' Louisa said. She sat down on Andy's chair.

'Where's Johnny?' Rhiannon said. She was staring at Louisa, her eyebrows shaped like crowbars.

'Well that's just it,' Louisa said. 'He's in the flat. The probation people put him on a home detention curfew. He can't leave the house after nine at night. A policeman comes by once or twice to check he's there. He was late reporting to the police station a few weeks ago. They reckon it's a breach of his bail conditions.'

'No shit,' Marc said, rapt by the admission.

Rhiannon looked as if she was about to spontaneously combust.

'Yeah,' Louisa said. She glanced around at the women, enjoying their disappointment. 'I just had to get out for an hour, get a change of scenery.'

Andy put a glass of wine down on the table in front of her. She took it quickly, their fingers touching briefly. 'Thank you, Andy,' she said; then, after a moment, she added, 'You're looking well, aren't you? I think you've caught a bit of sun.'

At stop-tap Rhiannon organized an impromptu party at the YMCA. If Muhammad couldn't go to the mountain, the mountain was going to him. She skipped across the square, jerk dancing like a chicken. Marc carried two plastic bags, heavy with take-outs, the others following like lemmings. '*I can feel my mojo working,*' Rhiannon sang in an abysmal American accent. When she reached the front of the building she rapped on the window-pane. 'Come out, Johnny Frick,' she said, shouting. 'It's the Aberalaw Police. We've got ewe surrounded. Come and meet PC Aunty Rhi.'

'Sshh!' Louisa said, ducking under Rhiannon's arm. 'I need to check if it's OK first. He might be asleep.' She put the key in the door and glanced over her shoulder, smiling impishly, as though she was part of the scheme, not the one being duped.

'I don't know about this,' Griff said, voice leaden with fore-boding. He tilted his head, peeping up at the first-floor windows. 'It's late and we've got a babysitter waiting.' He put his arm around Siân's shoulder, as though capturing her with a lasso. They started dawdling towards Dynevor Street, the sky above them indigo, the moon swollen between the tips of Ystradyfodwg Mountain.

'Come on then,' Louisa said, whispering through a narrow fissure in the doorway.

A crooked uplighter behind the armchair gave the living room a mute, tawny glow. Johnny was on the settee, face demonic in the half-light. One of the Dobermans was curled up next to him.

Ribs was on the chair, a can of lager in his hand, hair slicked back on his head, wearing a black woollen cardigan with gold piping around the cuffs.

'What are ewe doin' 'ere?' Rhiannon said accusingly.

'Keeping him company, aren't I?' Ribs said. 'He's locked in, mun.'

Rhiannon screwed her face up, miffed that he'd thought of it first.

'Where's Siân and Griff, then?' Johnny said. Nobody answered him so he lit the spliff he'd been rolling, said, 'There's not much to drink, a bit of vodka. Go and pour it for them, Lou.'

The surfaces were all heaped with used ashtrays and CD covers. There was a mirrored tile and a credit card on the coffee table. Andy and Marc sat on the floor and took cans out of the plastic bag. Rhiannon sat down next to Johnny and picked something up from the floor. 'Whass iss, mush?' she said, holding a pair of fur-lined moccasins in the air. 'Din't think ewe were the pipe and slippers kind.' She slipped them on to her hands, as if they were gloves, gave the room a muffled round of applause.

'You don't know everything about me,' Johnny said, snatching them from her. He threw them behind the settee. Ellie sat down on the opposite side of him and took a sip of the drink Louisa had given her, vodka with neat orange squash, the tart mixture burning the skin of her lips.

Rhiannon reached for the remote control and turned the volume on the television up. She clambered on to her knees and straddled the arm of the settee, dancing like a maniac, rubbing her undercarriage against the leather. 'For God's sake, Rhi,' Johnny said, taking the remote. 'We're trying to chill out.' He turned the volume down and changed the channel. Now Kelly Jones was singing 'Handbags and Glad Rags', the old Rod Stewart classic.

'Oof,' Rhiannon said, pointing at the TV. 'Look El, it's Kelly Jones. He's fuckin' gorgeous, ain't 'e? Wouldn't kick 'im outta bed for eating crackers, would ewe?'

Ellie shook her head.

'Nah, nor me,' Rhiannon said. 'Wait till I get 'old of the likkle bastard – smother 'im I will.' She pressed her plastic tits together, staring intently at Ellie. 'Who'd ewe think'll fuck 'im first, El? Ewe or me?' Ellie shook her head again, trying to dodge the question. She knew Rhiannon wasn't talking about Kelly. She pointed at the boys curled up on the floor, asleep now, or at least pretending to be, bodies hemmed by beer cans like cadavers outlined in white chalk.

'Me or ewe, El?' Rhiannon said. She seized a cigarette from out of Johnny's hand. Ellie sensed Johnny's body stiffen. He was biting the inside of his cheek, his lips sucked inwards. Ellie coughed. She glanced at Louisa, said, 'I heard he prefers blondes, Rhi.'

Rhiannon shot a look at Louisa. 'So?' she said.

'I could be blonde tomorrow,' Ellie said. 'All it'd take's a good hairdresser.'

'What ewe tryin' to say, El?' she said. 'That I ain't a good 'airdresser? Cause I'm the best fuckin' 'airdresser this village 'as ever seen.' She gawked incredulously at Ellie, waiting for an explanation, but Ellie said nothing. She hadn't been referring to Rhiannon's hairdressing skills. She'd been talking about her hair. It was Afro-Caribbean and notoriously difficult to bleach.

Rhiannon reached past Johnny and slapped Ellie's leg. 'Cheeky fuckin' slut,' she said.

'You're not a good hairdresser, Rhi,' Ellie said; an impulsive retort, designed to save face in front of Johnny. Already she was regretting it, but she had to keep going now. 'You dyed Siân's hair orange once, remember? And there was that court case about the extensions. I heard that certificate on your wall is a mock-up, that your uncle made it on his computer.'

Rhiannon jumped out of her seat, grabbing Ellie by the arm. She stood staring at her, her vodka gripped in her other hand. 'Am I a good hairdresser?' she said, the uplighter reflecting in the gold in her mouth. Ellie felt a flush of warm blood course through her body. She felt faint. 'No, Rhiannon,' she said, voice gentle, as if temperance could soften the impact. 'I don't think you're a good hairdresser.'

'Wrong answer!' Rhiannon said. She flung the drink into Ellie's eyes.

Ellie fell backwards, the small of her back landing flat on the settee. She opened her eyes, the liquid smarting. Rhiannon was trying to get at her, but Johnny was holding her back, her fingernails clawing at the skin of his forearms. The dogs were barking. Ellie sat up and tried to land a punch on Rhiannon's face. She missed and hit Johnny's shoulder. The Zircon charm bracelet slipped off her wrist.

'Listen,' Johnny said, shouting. He had Rhiannon's hands secured behind her back. 'I'm in enough trouble because of you already. The last thing I need is a female wrestling match in my flat.' He slackened his grip a little, testing her. Rhiannon stood still, listening to him, her eyes wandering around the room. He said, 'Leave Ellie alone, pick your things up and go. Come back when you're in a better mood.'

Rhiannon heaved herself free. 'Don't worry, mush,' she said, voice sore.

Ellie pulled her knees up to her chest, curling into a foetus, but Rhiannon walked straight past. When she got to the door she stopped and picked a mug up off the video cabinet. It was one of the tartan ones Ellie had stolen from the factory and given to Louisa. She launched it at Ellie but it hit the wall. It cracked into two pieces.

'Will you just go?' Louisa said.

Rhiannon lingered by the door for a few more seconds, then

said, 'Ewer banned from CF25 now, El. Ewe've pissed on ewer fuckin' chips.'

There was a collective sigh of relief as her footsteps faded across the square. Johnny passed Ellie his joint. 'Have some of that,' he said. 'Calm down.'

39

Siân put Niall in the high chair and pulled him to the edge of the patio table. He reached into the dish of pickled onions and grabbed a couple, squeezing them in his plump fist. He popped one into his mouth, and then immediately spat it out, green eyes mystified. She giggled as she pushed the pickles out of his reach. She wiped his face and hands in her gingham tea towel. '*Ych y fi,*' she said. 'Yuck.'

It was five on Sunday evening; too late to boil vegetables. She'd shredded an iceberg lettuce, peeled a cucumber, cut tomatoes into quarters, thrown a handful of potato wedges into the deep-fat fryer. The chicken was falling apart. She stole a flake of the breast meat as she went back to the house to call for the others. Angharad had returned to one of the old crayon drawings that was pinned to the fridge with a Bart Simpson magnet. She'd added a new being to the once-finished family of five: a stick figure with a flowing mass of purple hair. She was standing in front of it, examining her work. Griff was leaning against the washing machine, watching her, a bottle of beer in his hand.

'Come on then, you two!' Siân said. 'Dinner's ready.' Angharad's hair was still wet and curling into fat ringlets. They'd spent the day in Porthcawl, strolling along the promenade. Griff had suggested it early that morning, the April sun shining through the slats of the Venetian blind. He'd driven them there in the band's Transit van: Siân, Niall and Angharad sitting on the ripped seat next to him; James in the back, kicking the skin of the bass drum with the heel of his trainer. Griff led the way, over the zebra crossing, fingers clasped around the pushchair handles. Usually he attempted to keep the kids far away from the funfair, but today he'd headed straight there, had even bought them a bag of ring doughnuts at the entrance. Griff won an Elmo toy, tossing a ping-pong ball into an empty goldfish bowl. He gave it to Angharad and she insisted on taking it into the sea with her.

Siân stood on the beach watching, occasionally glancing around at the dilapidated esplanade. It had been the highlight of her childhood, of Griff's too. Now it was as tawdry as one of Rhiannon's one-liners. She saw a tattoo on a sunburnt bicep, a she-devil draped around a giant penis, her fork-tongue plunged into the eye. She shivered with revulsion and slipped her arms around Griff's waist, embracing him from behind. They'd stayed like that for a few moments, watching the distant freighters gliding across the Bristol Channel. It was the most physical contact they'd had in years and Siân was enjoying it, until the guilt had come raining over her like a cyclone.

It was over a month since she'd had sex with Johnny Frick, a rushed grope in the gulley behind the shop. She was still livid with herself. When she'd eventually got home that night, she'd put Angharad to bed with a glass of warm milk, half of a crushed paracetamol stirred in with a teaspoon of sugar. She ran a warm bath and sat in it for an hour, scrubbing herself like a rape victim, reflecting on how brainless her actions had been; trying to wash her idiocy away with a bar of coconut-scented soap.

She was terrified that the Boy Racer had seen her with Johnny, pressed up against the wall, and nothing stayed secret in Aberalaw for long. If he blabbed, her six-year marriage would be in jeopardy, over something she didn't even enjoy, her children's lives shattered by the brutality of divorce. She felt more like a cheap hooker than a glamorous mistress, turning a trick for a measly three pills. She'd already taken one, swallowed it dry as soon as Johnny had left. She'd needed it to cope with the instant paranoia; could not face Griff's mother with her intestines still full of another man's semen. She vowed to start her married life anew, and had. She'd gone cold turkey on the pills and bought a box of camomile teabags. There was no way she was going to demean herself again for a shoddy chemical thrill. Whenever Griff touched her she felt blessed *and* cursed: glad that she'd got away with it, and scared that the truth might still find its way out.

She caught Angharad's hand now and guided her out to the patio table. The stuffed Elmo was pegged to the rotary line, water dripping from its rump like a never-ending stream of urine. James was standing on the bench, squatting over the food. 'I just farted in the salad,' he said, jeering triumphantly.

'I'm not eating it now,' Angharad said. 'Not if he's farted in it.' She turned to her brother and slapped him. 'James, you stinking pig!'

'Don't be silly, Ang,' Griff said. 'Loads of people have farted in my salad and *I've* still eaten it.' He reached into the bowl and clawed at a pile of lettuce. Siân was about to pull him up on the banality of his statement when she realized it was probably true.

They'd almost finished dinner when Siân's phone trilled with an incoming text message. James was carrying a drum of strawberry ice cream to the table. She reached into her handbag and pulled the phone out, a flurry of miniature Welsh flags that the children had used for their sandcastles spitting out over her lap. She expected it to be from the phone company; a warning about her bill being due for payment, but the message was from a number she didn't recognize. She flipped the handset open.

'Fancy some fun tmrw? L going Cornwall l8r. House empty. Call in. Jx.'

She read it three times in two seconds, already wondering if the lace underwear set Griff had bought her for Christmas was clean.

'Who is it?' Griff said, leaning towards the phone, trying to read the message.

'No one,' Siân said. She pressed delete and clapped the handset shut.

'Did you just delete it?' Griff said. 'Why did you delete it? Who was it from?'

'No one,' Siân said. 'Ellie.'

'Yeah, right. What did it say?'

Siân couldn't think up a reason why Ellie would text her. 'Do I have to tell you everything?' she said. 'You go on tour to France for a month and you don't even phone. Are you going to tell me about that? Are you going to tell me about the girls in the front row? The nightclubs? The strip clubs? No. I get one text message and . . .'

Griff took a lollipop stick out of the pocket of his check shirt and held it up in the air. 'What's this?' he said, twisting it back and forth in the sunlight. Siân could see the words scrawled on the wood with green crayon, 'Johnny' on one side, 'Siân' on the other, the circumflex above the A reaching right off the stick. 'I don't flipping know.'

Griff made a face, his eyebrows converging. 'It was in a jar of sugar, in the fridge. Fairies put it there, did they?' He stared un-relentingly at Siân.

Siân could feel the fury in the lining of her belly, like black ink in an octopus. The stream of water pouring out of the Elmo had stopped, replaced by an unpredictable drip. James was hitting the bowl of his spoon on the bottom of the ice-cream dish, the clanging chafing at Siân's nerves. Finally, the anger reached her fingertips and quickly snowballed into rage. She threw the mobile phone at Griff's head, simultaneously emitting a gutsy primal snarl.

Griff moved aside, out of the object's path, and it hit Angharad on the temple. Siân saw it all in slow motion: Griff's muscles quivering as his shoulder arced backwards, a spurt of blood erupting out of Angharad's ginger hair, like an oil strike from sand.

'Shit!' she said, holding her own forehead.

Angharad started howling.

Siân stood up and stumbled towards her. She pressed her palm on her daughter's head to stem the bleeding.

'Get off her,' Griff said, shoving Siân aside. He picked Angharad up and galloped with her into the house. Siân went back to her seat. She looked at James. James glared back at her. Niall was smiling, excited by the commotion, splatters of mayonnaise smudged around his cupid's-bow mouth. She reached for the kitchen roll and broke a bit off, wiped his face, her hands trembling.

Griff came out of the house and bent down next to the phone. He put it on the table in front of Siân, placing the lollipop stick on top, Johnny side up. He lifted Niall out of the high chair. 'She's hurt pretty bad,' he said. 'I'm going to take her to Abertach. Come on James, come with Dad.'

'To your mother's, you mean,' Siân said.

Griff shrugged. 'Wherever,' he said. 'Not safe here, are they?'

'I'm sorry,' Siân said, but they were already in the house.

She threw her phone at the kitchen window. It ricocheted and fell clattering into the drain. She stamped to the line and ripped the Elmo off. She trampled on its face, a course of water pumping out with every step. Eventually she fell to her knees and held the soft toy at her neck, its nose pressed against her clavicle, her clothes sopping with seawater and tears. 'I'm sorry,' she said.

40

An idle Tuesday, four in the afternoon, rain pummelling on the pavement; Ellie rapped on Siân's Dynevor Street front door, stood studying the wrinkled skin of her fingers. Siân peered out of a two-inch gap, eyes vacant, as though waiting for a hard sell from a cold caller. 'Hiya,' Ellie said, expecting Siân to let her in. She didn't and the word hung in the air between them, lashings of rain unable to drown it. 'For a minute I thought you'd gone out,' Ellie said, 'taken the kids swimming or something. Do that on a Tuesday, don't you?'

'Stopped that ages ago,' Siân said sourly, 'too expensive.' Ellie glanced around the street, rainwater the colour of sewage curling into the gutter. 'You going to let me in?' she said eventually. 'It's raining out here.'

Siân shrugged and retreated into the house, leaving the door ajar.

'Haven't got any hand cream, have you?' Ellie said, following her in. 'I've never had to use it before. There was something in the glue at the mug factory, kept them moist, now they're dry as paper.' She recognized the smell of children, an amalgamation of chocolate and faeces, but the children weren't there. The house was deathly quiet. The curtains were drawn. 'Where's the kids?' she said.

Siân picked a bumper tub of Vaseline off the mantelpiece and

245

threw it in Ellie's direction. 'Griff's taken them,' she said, 'left me.' She stomped into the kitchen and sat down in front of a glass of white wine.

'No way,' Ellie said. She smeared the petroleum over her hands.

'Sunday,' Siân said. 'After dinner. Things have been bad for a while, since he found out I had my tubes tied.' Ellie stared hard at the marble-effect floor tiles, wishing her own tubes were tied.

Siân fixed her with a miserable stare, said, 'What it was, the final straw, a text message from Johnny. He was asking me to go to the YMCA because Louisa was away. Right there in front of Griff. Griff was trying to look at it so I deleted it straight away. He threw a big wobbly.' She looked guiltily at Ellie. 'I chucked my phone at him, just to shut him up, but it hit Angharad in the head. He gave me all that bad mother claptrap and buggered off up his mam's.' She sighed, said, 'I haven't seen him since.'

Ellie sat down at the table. 'Is Angharad OK?'

'Fine,' Siân said. 'It was only a scratch.' She slugged straight from the wine bottle, pushing the smudged glass over towards Ellie.

'Did you go to Johnny's?' Ellie said, sliding it back.

Siân scratched at a knot in the surface of the pine table. 'Yeah,' she said, 'yesterday morning, wearing nothing but a pair of ten-denier stockings and my mother's old leather raincoat. How mental is that?' Ellie thought it was a joke. She burst into laughter. But Siân was still scoring the table with her jagged fingernail. 'He wasn't there,' she said. 'That's Johnny all over, isn't it? Causes a big to-do and then he stands me up. I got my heel caught in the cobbles on the square as well. I had to leave the shoe there. There I am, naked as a flipping jaybird, limping home like an invalid.'

Ellie looked out of the kitchen window at a pile of dinner plates left on the patio. A lone magpie was clawing at a chicken carcass on the decking.

'What it was, I wanted pills.'

'Pills?' Ellie said.

'Ecstasy,' Siân said, 'to take the edge off. I take one now and again, when I'm feeling stressed. I've only got two left.' She took her handbag from the back of the chair and turned it upside down. She shook it so the contents spilled over the table: two lipsticks and a pair of kid's plastic sunglasses, a handful of miniature Welsh flags made from cocktail sticks, a pack of chewing gum; finally, a plastic baggie. Siân picked it up, showing Ellie the pills. 'Want one?' she said. 'Come on, one each, you used to love a pill.'

She dabbed at her fingertip and picked one out of the bag. It clung to her like an iron filing to a magnet. She placed it on her tongue and gulped it down with a swig of wine. 'I know we haven't been the best of friends, not recently, but we used to be. We used to look after each other. It's Johnny who's caused all the hostility. Things haven't been right since he turned up. Can you remember it, that night at the Pump House? It's like he's Jack Nicholson, El. It's like we're the witches of bastard Eastwick.' She paused for a moment, said, 'Rhiannon's always been nuts, hasn't she?'

'Yeah,' Ellie said, 'totally. Pistachio.'

'But she's got worse since he turned up, proper whacko like. Sixteen shades of crazy in the space of a bloody year.' She placed the remaining pill on the table in front of Ellie, said, 'See that skirt she was wearing on Saturday?'

'No,' Ellie said. She shook her head. She couldn't understand why Siân was suddenly purporting to be her best friend. They were only acquaintances, hurled together by circumstance, the wives and girlfriends of the band, like a pair of passengers on a long-haul flight. Siân was a mother of one by the time Ellie had met her. She pushed the pill across the table like a draught. 'What are you going to do about Griff and the kids?' she said.

Siân shrugged. 'They'll come back when they're hungry.' She laughed nervously. 'Worse frigging luck.'

Ellie smiled sympathetically. 'Why did you have children so young, Siân?' she said. She took a sip of the wine, just to be polite. It tasted of rotten wood, the bottle corked. Siân rolled her eyes, expecting one of Ellie's anti-family rants. 'I wasn't that young,' she said. 'It wasn't like I was a teenager, El.'

'No,' Ellie said, 'I know. That's what I came here to ask. I've been thinking about my mother, my natural mother. I've been thinking of looking for her.' It was a lie, and Ellie thought Siân would sense it.

She smiled, happy to talk about her children. 'It's because I wanted them, El. Why else? I wanted them so bad I lied to Griff about contraception. I used to flush the pills down the toilet and leave the card on the table where he could see it. He didn't want James, not until he was born, and then he couldn't get enough.' She bit the top of her little fingernail. 'A kid is a totally innocent thing, see,' she said. 'If you bring it up with love, it'll be lovely. My father was a dick, brought me up to be frightened, and I thought I could change all that, that I could stop the cycle. But I couldn't. If there's a speck of madness in your past it always comes back to find you. Because it's there, eating away at you. People only hurt others because they really want to hurt themselves, deep down inside.'

Ellie frowned.

'Look!' Siân said, shouting and scratching at her forearms, her eyes red. 'I've never laid a finger on another human being and then that English knob turns up and I'm throwing phones at my own daughter. It's the psychosis! It's in me!'

'Don't be stupid,' Ellie said.

'I'm not,' Siân said.

'You are,' Ellie said. 'You're panicking. Calm down and you'll be fine.' She stood up, the chair legs scraping on the tiles. 'Just sober up and ring Griff. Get your kids back, you'll be fine.'

Siân was sobbing but Ellie couldn't look at her. She'd come

here in search of innocence, had wanted to see the children colouring on the dining table, Siân tending to them like Mother Goose. She wanted proof that the idyllic conjugal family was a reality, not romanticism. Instead she'd found Siân alone and slowly losing her mind, confessing to liaisons with Johnny. The thought of her flawless body in stockings and suspenders, there for Johnny's taking. It was too much for Ellie. She marched into the gloomy living room, almost tripping over a toy car. She put the Vaseline on the mantelpiece, next to a half-empty packet of organic wet wipes. 'I have to go,' she said, feeling sick, not sure if her reaction was biological or psychosomatic. At what point in the proceedings did morning sickness commence?

'Wait,' Siân said. She came running into the living room, arms outstretched. She grabbed the shoulders of Ellie's pea-green coat. 'I told Griff it was you,' she said. 'The text message, I said you sent it. Tell him, will you? Tell him you sent it.'

'Of course,' Ellie said. She wriggled free of Siân's grip and ran all the way to Gwendolyn Street. In the passage she stood next to the phone stand, rainwater dripping on to the floor as she plucked a crumpled piece of paper out of her duffel bag, the telephone number of an abortion clinic in Pontypridd. 'I want to book an appointment,' she said, voice raspy, 'as soon as possible, please.'

The receptionist was silent for a moment, and then she said, 'We've got a cancellation, Thursday morning. Would that suit?'

41

The nurse was a big woman with a strawberry-blonde beehive, wearing powder-blue eyeliner and mascara, early fifties perhaps. Ellie put the used pregnancy test down on the desk.

She'd realized it was a possibility over Sunday lunch at the Bell & Cabbage, Rhiannon talking about her active menstrual cycle, telling the whole restaurant that she was bleeding like a slaughtered pig; informing anyone who might have suspected it that she hadn't hit menopause yet. Time was, Rhiannon and Ellie used to get their periods together, on the third week of every month. 'Jam-rag season,' the boys called it. At nine on Monday morning Ellie had bought the test, and by ten minutes past it had shown up positive, two sober, sapphire-coloured lines developing in the plastic window.

The nurse held it at arm's length, squinting at the result. 'Right,' she said, passing it back to Ellie. She picked up her clipboard. 'Do you take any recreational drugs?'

'Coke,' Ellie said. There was no point in lying, was there? 'Cannabis, ecstasy, a little bit of amphetamine.' The nurse glanced disapprovingly at her and ticked a box on her survey. After a few more queries about allergies and contraception, she put the clipboard down. 'I'll need to examine you now.' She stood up and secured the knot on a new plastic apron.

Ellie lay down on the bed, a square of kitchen roll placed over her pelvis, hiding her pubic hair. She winced as the nurse locked the speculum into place, felt the blood pumping against the taut walls of her vagina. Her muscles constricted around the clamp, resisting the sudden intrusion. 'Do your breathing,' the nurse said, pushing her palm flat on Ellie's stomach.

Ellie didn't know what she meant. She stared at the polystyrene ceiling-tile above, trying to keep her back pressed on the leather mattress underneath. 'What do you think we should put there?' the nurse said, following Ellie's gaze. 'I've got a lovely picture of Paradise Island in the house. My husband took me there for our anniversary last year. Do you think that'd loosen you up?'

Ellie shook her head. 'A picture of Johnny Depp,' she said, shuddering as the woman prodded at the neck of her womb. Afterwards she snatched her knickers from the chair and quickly wriggled into them, the nurse throwing her sterile gloves into the tin pedal bin.

Back at the desk, the verbal interrogation continued, the clincher arriving eventually, six or seven minutes in. 'Why have you decided to pursue this choice?' the nurse said casually, as though asking for Ellie's favourite sandwich filling, attempting to conceal the gravity of the enquiry under a frothy, orange-lipsticked smile.

'I don't want kids,' Ellie said, voice like an axe splitting wood.

The woman sighed. 'It's not an option you can take lightly, you know. It leaves no room for regret. Have you thought about it properly?'

'So I've snorted a few lines in my time,' Ellie said caustically. 'It doesn't mean I can't think.' She nodded dismissively at the consent form on the desk. 'Evans,' she said, prodding at the word scrawled across the top of it in blue biro. 'That's not my real name. That's my adoptive parents' name. They adopted me when I was two. I don't know what my real name is.' She stared at the woman's blue eye make-up. 'In a way I've been thinking about it for twenty-three years. I'm not having a baby just to give it up.'

The woman's face was spongy with pity as she nodded and began to sign the forms. The fucking Annie the Orphan routine: it did it every time. It wasn't the real motive, of course. Ellie hadn't had sex with Andy since Christmas Day. She knew the baby was Johnny's and that it was going to be born with his fiendish black eyes. She imagined Collin and Gwynnie leaning into the Moses basket for the first time, aware that Andy and Ellie's eyes were sky-blue, making a holy furore about the compromising of their stupid bloodline. Faced with this thorny predicament, Ellie had also quickly realized that Johnny was just a man, an extremely fallible man, not the seductive and enigmatic deity she'd been irrationally idolizing for the past eight months. There was no new life in the offing. He'd leave Aberalaw in a flash if she tried to trap him with the old pregnancy ruse.

'The gestation period is almost ten weeks,' the nurse said. 'It means you can have a surgical termination, with a general anaesthetic. I'll need to book the appointment for you at reception.' She pushed the consent form towards Ellie and walked out of the room. Ellie listened for a moment to the beat of the woman's heels along the corridor. She grabbed the pen and swiftly signed her name.

Two days later, Ellie was at the hospital in Abertach, sitting on the bed, a paperback open on her lap. It was Kerouac's *On The Road*, a few chapters in, where Sal Paradise and Dean Moriarty drive from North Carolina to New York. The words were jumping from one spot to another, bouncing like fleas. She couldn't concentrate any longer and in any case she knew the story by heart. She closed the book and stared at the green curtain surrounding her bed, tear ducts swollen with grief. Suddenly it whooshed open and a fat nurse in a navy uniform appeared. 'Should be about an hour,' she said, smiling sympathetically. Ellie took a deep breath, inhaling the disinfectant and talcum-powder smell of the ward.

The nurse gently tapped Ellie's knee, a kind gesture that Ellie found overwhelming. A stream of acid rain came running out of her eyes, burning the skin of her face.

She was still crying when a doctor appeared a few minutes later, a Chinese woman with a thick black plait that hung down to the small of her back. 'I just need to pop some tablets into you,' she said, leaning over Ellie's body. 'They need to go in here,' her hand already wrist-deep in Ellie's vagina. 'There,' she said as she withdrew, Ellie recoiling with delayed shock, the doctor's minty breath on her neck. 'Keep your knees up. In ten minutes there'll be an ache, just something that helps the process along.' On her way out she whipped open the green curtain.

Ellie was faced with the other patients on the ward, three middle-aged women, all staring back at her. She focused on the one with a bunch of yellow chrysanthemums on her side table, trying to guess the reason for her being here. Almost immediately she decided it was a hysterectomy. She tried to smile at the woman, feeling her dry lips crack as they stretched. After a minute the woman struggled out of her bed and approached Ellie, her hands pressed on her belly. She perched on the edge of Ellie's mattress, fiddling with the buttons of her quilted dressing gown. 'Do you know what you're having done?' she said, frowning at Ellie's tears.

What a stupid fucking question. Ellie bit the inside of her cheek. 'A termination,' she said, voice hushed, an inflection at the end of the word as though she was asking the woman, not telling, the way actors in Australian soap operas ended all of their sentences. The tears came back with a vengeance, salt water spitting on the painful cracks in her lips, throat as tight as a duck's arse.

'Oh,' the woman said. She reached for Ellie's hand and stroked the back of it, eyes flitting around the ward. 'It's a brave decision really,' she said finally. 'I've always thought that.' She picked the paperback up and squinted at the cover, then put it back down with a slap, as if it was the cause of Ellie's problems. 'A bit of light reading you want, love.' She scurried back to her bed to get a copy of *Marie Claire*. She put it down on the sheet and tucked a stray lock of Ellie's hair behind her ear. 'Don't think too much,' she said. 'It'll be all over soon, won't it? And you can go home and start your new life.'

In a corridor outside the operating theatre, an anaesthetist skilfully drove a needle into Ellie's hand. He pointed at the enormous wall clock in front of her. 'If you start counting now,' he said, 'you'll be asleep by the time you get to ten.' *One, two.* Ellie didn't believe him. She was terrified of not being able to go under, or of waking up in the middle of the operation and seeing the foetus in a bucket at the foot of the bed. She'd seen a midwife on the TV once, arguing against abortion. She said she'd seen babies plucked from wombs, fully formed and crying. Ellie stared hard through the window of the jade-green operating theatre. By seven she was unconscious.

The next thing she remembered was lying in the corridor again, two nurses standing over her, talking about liposuction. One of them wanted it for her forthcoming birthday. 'My friend had plastic surgery,' Ellie said, slurring, voice full of mucus. 'Now she looks like a fat blow-up doll.' The nurses laughed good-naturedly and handed her trolley over to a porter. When he'd wheeled Ellie through the hospital, he lifted her back on to her bed. She looked for the woman who had given her the magazine but she wasn't there. One of the yellow flowers had fallen out of its vase and landed on the table.

She looked at the ceiling, a polystyrene tile like the one she'd seen at the clinic in Pontypridd. '*This is not in vain,*' she said, talking inside her head. '*I promise I'll get away from Aberalaw, I'll make something of myself.*' There'd been enough destruction. Now she needed to create. It was time she tended to her own aspirations. Andy would have to understand.

After a while the nurse in the navy uniform was back. 'You can have a sandwich now if you're ready,' she said, voice enthusiastic, eyes wide, talking to Ellie as if she was ten years old. 'Tuna mayo, cheese and chive? What d'you fancy, lovely? I can't let you go unless you eat something.' She pointed conspiratorially at a clean sanitary towel on the side table. 'Just for a few days,' she said, whispering, dimples in her cheeks. 'And a paracetamol here and there if you need it.'

42

A week later, Ellie could hear the drone of Andy's electric toothbrush drifting in from the bathroom. She was sitting on their
mattress, red pen poised in her fingertips as she proofread an
album review she'd written the day before. He walked naked into
the bedroom, and sat down on his side. Ellie stared at the double-
spaced text, pretending not to have noticed.

'Maybe you *should* think about a job at the shampoo factory,' he
said. Earlier they'd been at his mother's sixty-fifth birthday dinner,
where Collin had suggested Ellie went to work on Pengoes Industrial
Estate. 'It cuts out all of the travelling and there's only my money
covering the rent at the moment. There's that eighty-pound gas bill
to think about. We had a reminder in the post today.'

Ellie smacked her papers down on the bedside table. 'That's
not a very nice thing to say. And,' she said, 'it's like me saying The
Boobs wouldn't know a good song if it hit them round the head
with a baseball bat. It's like me saying that *you* can't play guitar,
that the band will never make it and you may as well give up
right now. You may as well be a painter and decorator for the rest
of your miserable life. That's what you're saying.' As she spoke she
noticed a strip of white plaster on the bridge of his nose. 'What's
that?' she said, pointing at it.

Andy looked puzzled.

'On your nose?'

'Oh,' he said. He pinched it with thumb and forefinger, securing it in place. 'It's a new treatment for snoring. I saw it in the chemist yesterday. I thought I'd give it a go.' He scratched at his mound of blonde pubes, adjusted his penis. 'You know I'm only talking about in the meantime,' he said. 'About working somewhere you don't like until you find somewhere that you do.'

Ellie picked the papers up and waved them in his face. 'This *is* the meantime,' she said. 'If the editor likes it there's a chance of permanent work.' She gazed inquisitively at him for a moment, said: 'There's a hundred of those snoring treatments in the bathroom cupboard. I've been asking you to try them since we met. Why've you started now?'

Andy shrugged, nodded at her papers. 'But that job's in London,' he said.

'Of course it's in London,' Ellie said. 'That's where most of the publishing industry tends to be. You've only just come back from France. Before that it was Scotland. Do you know how much overtime I had to put in last year? No wonder I walked out of the mug factory. I was sick of the fucking sight of the place!' She started reading her review again from the beginning but stopped after two sentences, livid with Andy's selfishness. 'Give me a month, and if I haven't got a real writing job I'll go and make shampoo. Fifteen years it's taken your band to get *this* far, fifteen years and still counting. Give me a month and I'll bet I'll do it.'

'I'm sure you will, El,' he said. He stroked the knee of her jeans. 'I wasn't trying to insult you, babe. I was making a suggestion. That's allowed, isn't it?'

'Yes.'

He reached in to kiss her, his mouth cool with toothpaste. Ellie tried to back away but Andy ignored her protests, slowly rolling on top of her, his torso pushing into her midrib, her papers thrashing and dropping to the floor. He licked her shoulder, a streak of cold saliva moving across the top of her bra strap.

'I've got a headache, And,' she said, voice strangled by his weight.

Andy laughed. 'You can't say that,' he said. 'We're not even married yet.' He leaned back on his elbow and studied her face. 'Do you know the last time was about five months ago? Don't you fancy me any more?' His hand was on the waistband of her jeans, fingers stroking the hot skin underneath.

'It wasn't that long ago,' she said.

'Come on El,' he said, fingers moving towards her sex. 'Relax. You might like it.' He thrust two fingers into the cavity at the back of her vulva, nudging at her entrance, but then he quickly withdrew. He held his hand up to the light, his fingers outstretched. They were glazed with a thin layer of slippery, carmine-coloured blood. He tried to wipe it on the duvet cover but it clung to his skin like drool. 'Don't move,' he said standing up. 'There's something wrong with you. I'm going to call the doctor. My God.'

'It's just my period,' Ellie said.

Andy lurched towards the door, still staring at his hand, trying not to touch anything. 'That's not a period,' he said, 'and it's only the first week of the month.'

Ellie was curled on the bed, pillow bunched up under her grip, fingers between her lips. She knew she had to tell him now. 'It's OK,' she said, eyes closed. 'I had an abortion. Last Thursday. I can't have sex with you yet. I'm barely off the painkillers.'

'An abor, an aborsh, an . . .' He couldn't say it. 'What?'

'An abortion,' Ellie said. 'I'm not ready yet, am I?'

Andy cupped his hand around his mouth, a bloody imprint impressing on his jaw. He belched loudly and then ran to the bathroom, his retching echoing out of the pan. As his stomach released its contents, Ellie felt a cold trickle moving down her chest. She yanked her T-shirt up, pulled the cup of her bra aside. A rivulet of watery milk was seeping out of her nipple, nutrients that were destined to nourish nightmares. Nightmares and nothing else.

43

Rhiannon pushed her last customer out of the shop. 'See ewe next week 'en, love,' she said. She flipped over the *Open* sign. She reached for her silver hipflask and took a quick swig of rum. The floor tiles were littered with clumps of shorn hair, purple-rinse curls sticking to the wet patches around the washbasin. Kelly would have to clean it up in the morning. Rhiannon had sent her home an hour early, sick of listening to her relentless teenage drivel. She'd finally fucked the postman, and wouldn't stop going on about it; how he'd done her four times in one night on the foldaway bed in his father's touring caravan. Rhiannon hoped he'd given her chlamydia.

She wiped her Jaguar Loop scissors on a tea towel, popping them into their carrying case, the steel blades sparkling against the red velvet lining. They had been a present from Bob Stone. Every other month she took the whole set into the ironmonger's next door to get them professionally sharpened and cleaned. In the office she unlocked the desk drawer, pulling an A5 envelope out, carefully ripping it open with the tip of her false nail. She fanned the photographs across the surface of the desk. In the first she was sitting on Dai and Myra's big double bed, wearing a winceyette nightdress, her thick hair pulled into two chunky bunches. In another she was wearing a set of luminous pink underwear, the bra padded, the knickers too big, its bright, jazzy colour clashing with her chocolate-milkshake skin. The orange candlewick bedspread gave the date away. It was 1981. Rhiannon was 14.

Photography was Dai Davies's hobby. He had a big heavy Kodak camera that it took two hands to hold. The first time it happened she'd been sitting at the kitchen table, dipping Christmas baubles in a bowl of white glitter. Myra'd gone to bingo.

'Rhiannon, my little honey-pot,' he'd said, nudging her in the rib. 'Want to earn yourself a couple of quid? I wanna take some piccies of you, upstairs. It won't take long.'

Course Rhiannon was saving for a hair-straightening session on City Road, so she'd said yes, the daft bitch. Child pornography they called it now. Seemed like every Tom, Dick and Harry was into it. It didn't have a name then, though. She liked the pictures. They made her feel like a pop star. In fact, she still liked the pictures. They were the only photographs she had of herself as a kid, her skin smooth and supple, no need for no bastard collagen fillers or chemical peels. She chose two of the best, one of her kneeling in a pair of pink shorts, her T-shirt tied in a knot above her waist, and another where she was naked, leaning against the window, looking out at Pengoes Mountain. She put them into a new white envelope and slipped them into her handbag.

Cut a long story, Dai had never touched her. Once, when she was 13, he was tightening her loose bra strap and she felt the grey bristles of his chin against her cheek. She'd tried to kiss him because she thought he'd wanted her to. That's the way the boys from the estate tried to get their tongues into your mouth, pretended there was something in your eye or some shit. He'd pulled away from her. 'Get off gul,' he'd said. 'I'd rather eat my own sick than put my todger in a nigger's cunt.' Instead, he gave her cucumbers and dildos to play with, stood behind the camera saying, 'Kiss its Jap's eye,' or, 'Go on, gul, stroke your juicy peach for me.' It was around that time that she'd started to resent other children, because they were stupid and gullible and wanted to play netball. None of them knew what a vibrator was.

When she was sixteen she stole one of the photographs from where Dai kept them in his garden shed, and later, when Tommy Chippy came around the estate in his chip van, she showed it to him. She wasn't sure what she wanted him to do but he was a nice man, with sea-green eyes and a halo of tightly curled ginger hair, a body shaped like a teddy bear. He wore a black bobble hat and always gave her big helpings of scrimps and free sachets of vinegar.

'Bloody hell, love,' he said, picking it up from the counter.

He let her sit in the passenger seat in the van. She ate Everton mints while he drove around Ystradyfodwg and Penmaes, selling his out-of-date beef pies. When his round was over he parked up in the industrial estate. 'You know I've got this video-making business with my mucker in North Wales, then love?' he said. Rhiannon didn't know. She knew what a business was though. She had her eye on the hairdressing course at Ponty College, but to enrol she needed to provide her own kit. 'Yeah,' she said.

Tommy Chippy undid the fly of his Sta-Press trousers. 'The going rate's forty quid an hour. Won't get that stocking shelves in the Co-op, will you?' He squeezed the end of his pecker, its red head poking out of the sticky foreskin. It reminded Rhiannon of a nature programme Dai'd been watching on BBC2 the day before. 'Come on then, love,' he said. 'Let's see if you're any good. And don't forget to lick my balls.'

At first she'd worn a potato sack over her head. Lots of Tommy's customers were in the police; he didn't want them knowing how young she was. When his partner in North Wales realized that Rhiannon was black, Tommy started talking about something called a USP, said he needed her mouth in the shot. So he covered her eyes with a strip of black gaffer tape that took her eyebrows off when he peeled it back. She stopped doing the films when they asked her to fuck an Alsatian dog, the depraved cunts. They wanted her to smear a jar of Bovril over her fucking labia. By then she was a year into her college course, a hairdressing student with an addiction to white rum.

Meeting Bob Stone had been a bit of a godsend. At first he'd wanted her to give the hairdressing up. He offered to pay her a monthly wage just to stay indoors. But Rhiannon was hell-bent on being a successful businesswoman. Eventually he came around to the idea and started buying her handmade paddle brushes and razor stylers, the car so that she could get to her work placement in the Ogmore valley. Without him she'd never have been able to buy CF25. But the place was losing money hand over fist. Whatever she tried, three-page bloody adverts in the *South Wales Echo*, discounts for students, she couldn't get the kids from the city up to Aberalaw. And she was fucked if she was moving to Cardiff. Half of the fun was rubbing her success in Tommy and Dai's noses. Marc was a pain in the fuckin' arse, always asking her to marry him, taking her for meals with his hillbilly family, *as if* she was the kind of girl you took home. But he was as loyal as a dog with no legs; happy to pay the mortgage and keep his gob shut about it.

She locked the salon door and headed for the square. Johnny's BMW was parked in the drive. She knocked on the door of the YMCA and Louisa answered, the TV blaring in the passage behind her. 'This is for ewe,' Rhiannon said, pressing a gift box against Louisa's pancake chest. 'A load of top-notch 'air stuff.' It was cheap rubbish from the shampoo factory, but the packaging was the same turquoise colour as a bag from Tiffany's, embossed with *CF25* in fancy silver lettering.

'Why?' Louisa said.

'Ewer my friend, ain't ewe?' Rhiannon said. 'It's one of the perks of the job.'

Rhiannon followed Louisa into the kitchen and watched her

spoon coffee into mugs. 'I'll do those,' she said. 'Go and get ewer 'air washed. I've got an hour spare. I'll blow-dry an' straighten it for ewe.' She lifted her carry-case, showing it to Louisa. 'Go on, I got all my tools on me.'

Louisa took the goody-bag into the bathroom with her. Rhiannon took her photographs out of her handbag and wandered into the living room where Johnny was watching *Coronation Street*, a sausage-sized joint in his fingers. 'Hey mush,' she said, smiling at him. 'I din't make ewe late for the cop shop on purpose, ewe know. I din't know ewe 'ad to be there.'

Johnny squinted at her through a fog of cannabis smoke.

'I been thinking,' she said. She leaned against the doorjamb, the hiss of water sizzling out of the bathroom behind her. 'Iss not long till the trial now, is it? A week or somethin'. If ewe 'appen to go down, ewer likkle drug empire's going down with ewe, ain't it? It's a shame that is, cause 'airs still plenty of people round yere ooh need their uppers.' She stared at him. 'Ave ewe ever thought about my salon? I'm running an 'ighly successful business down there, I am. I could do some under-the-counter trade for ewe, couldn't I? I could wash all ewer dirty money clean.'

Johnny tickled his Doberman's ear, laughed, then turned back to the television.

'I'm serious,' Rhiannon said. She sat down in the armchair. 'I know this place. I know ewer target market. 'Ow much are ewe makin in a week, on average?'

Johnny grinned at her. 'In a bad one, a bag of sand.'

'Well,' Rhiannon said, surprised by his honesty, 'if ewe only go down for a year ewe've lost fifty-two grand already. I won't take much commission, mush: mate's rates and all that.'

Johnny looked thoughtful for a moment. 'But I'm not going down,' he said.

Rhiannon threw the envelope at him. He caught it between his knees. 'That's just something to remind ewe of me,' she said.

'In case ewe do, ewe can put 'em up on the wall of ewer cell.' Johnny quickly sneaked the envelope under the cushion on the settee. Louisa was coming in, a towel tied around her head. 'I'm ready now,' she said.

Rhiannon stood up. She went back to the kitchen and Louisa followed. 'I was just telling Johnny,' Rhiannon said, 'I could come back next week, on the day before his court case, cut his 'air for 'im. Those judges ain't too keen on men with long 'air, are they? Things like that, physical appearance, it counts for a lot.'

Louisa pulled a chair from the breakfast bar and took the towel from her head. 'That's a good idea, Rhi,' she said. 'It's on Wednesday. If you could come around on Tuesday night, we'd appreciate that. Thanks.'

44

Ellie woke at noon, her OED propped on Andy's pillow, her battered laptop and papers where his torso should have been. He'd been sleeping on the settee since she'd told him about the abortion. Last night she'd been awake until four, listening for the rattle of tablets, the snap of the cutlery drawer, worried that his death wish would return. The faintest creak in the joists and she imagined a length of rope fashioned into a slipknot, his bloated body swinging from the curtain rail. At half past three, when she'd heard him rummaging around in the kitchen like a rat, she ran downstairs, her legs leaden with dread. She'd found him watching *Tomb Raider*, eating vanilla ice cream straight from the tub. She'd stood in the doorway, unable to concoct an excuse for her sudden concern. 'When are we getting married?' she'd said, instead.

Andy stared past her shoulder, the ghost light from the TV flickering in the whites of his eyes. 'We're not,' he'd said, the table-spoon in his hand frozen in mid-air.

Now the quilt was folded on the arm of the chair, a cloud of synthetic filling leaking out of a hole at the bottom. Andy had gone to work, leaving her in a disorientating limbo. She wanted the comforting fact of Andy's existence. She wanted him to come back to bed and moan about money and snore. But she couldn't quite admit to wanting *him*.

He'd used the last of the milk so she counted the coins in her purse. She didn't have enough to buy it at the newsagent's so she headed for Spar. At the T-junction next to the Barry Cottages she saw the band's yellow Transit van struggling up the hill. Griff was driving. Ellie stood in the road and flagged him down. He pulled up next to her, the engine huffing. It had started to drizzle and there were a few droplets on the windscreen, a bag of Pembroke potatoes wedged between the glass and the top of the dash. Griff wound the window down, face red and clean-shaven.

'You still at your mother's, then?' Ellie said.

He looked at the petrol gauge, nodded.

'I sent her that text message, you know. I was only asking if she fancied meeting me for a drink.'

'What time did you send it?' Griff asked, quick as lightning.

'Half two.' Ellie shrugged. That was the time of the average Sunday lunch.

'No!' Griff said, grinning. 'Quarter to six. Nice try, El.' He stepped on the accelerator, the engine singing.

At the entrance to the square, two kids, less than ten years between them, were playing with a broken beer bottle, scraping names into a fence. As Ellie passed, one of them shouted at her. 'My brother wants to know if ewe'll suck him off,' he said. 'Fancies ewe he does.' Some people dropped sprogs as if it was a hobby, as easy to disregard as a half-knitted scarf or a part-solved jigsaw puzzle.

Ellie continued walking, the hanging baskets in America Place shivering in the wind. There was muffled barking coming from the YMCA, and when she looked up she saw Johnny standing in the window, knocking the glass and waving at her. Ellie blushed, remembering she wasn't wearing any eyeliner.

Johnny disappeared, and then reappeared, standing topless in the doorway, beckoning her with a curled finger. She followed him up the staircase, into the dim living room. 'Lousia's gone shopping,' he said, slumping on to the settee, his scrawny chest looking like a 15-year-old kid's, areolae the same size and colour as copper one-penny pieces.

Ellie straddled him. She pushed her face into his and then stopped, close enough for their breath to mingle. He smelled of marijuana. 'You're going to turn into a lump of pot,' she said, reaching underneath herself to unbutton his fly. She kicked and thrashed, throwing her jeans on to the floor while he calmly sat watching her. The stabbing pang was sharp and glorious as she descended down on him. She leaned backwards and gripped the edge of the coffee table, knocking an ashtray and a gift box from Rhiannon's salon off the surface. She knew now that he wasn't a solution to her problem. There was no reason to have sex with him other than wanting to. There was something remarkably liberating about this realization; knowing the experience was nothing more than a sweet, goodbye fuck.

'I only come when I'm on top,' she said afterwards, dried blood gummed to the insides of her thighs. 'Do you?' Johnny said. She was lying across his legs, the small of her back pressing on his bony knees.

'No.' She laughed. 'It's just a line from a song.' He hadn't mentioned the war in Iraq since that day on Penmaes Mountain. He hadn't talked about art. He'd stopped trying to impress her. His small pool of knowledge had run out. He was quite unintelligent, yet he'd managed to divide the village, and divided it had fallen. She lit one of his cigarettes, said, 'You don't like women, do you, Johnny?'

Johnny sniggered. 'Going to analyse me now are you?' he said.

'Tell me,' she said. She elbowed him in the gut.

'I was the oldest of ten,' he said. 'My mother walked out when I was fourteen. After a fortnight she came back, howling drunk, banging on the front door and screaming. She said she wanted me, but none of the others. She said she only loved me. My father opened the door, punched her in the nose and then slammed it closed again. But she stayed there all night, calling me. That pretty much made me public enemy number one in the Frick household.'

Ellie was frowning at him, waiting for the punchline, but it didn't come. 'I had an abortion a fortnight ago,' she said. 'In case you were wondering, about the blood.'

Johnny breathed heavily. 'Bummer,' he said. He pinched the cigarette from her hand and took a drag. 'You all right, like?'

'It was for the best I think,' Ellie said. 'It wouldn't have turned out much good: neurotic mother, drug-dealer father; one less fuck-up walking the streets.' She thought about the kids on the T-Junction. 'You wouldn't have wanted it, would you?'

'Oh . . .' Johnny said.

Ellie looked at her jeans lying limp on the carpet, the thrill of ripping them off conquered by the onset of stone-cold reality. She stood up and put them on. 'Andy's not talking to me. He found out about it a few days ago. I think he's going to throw me out. Don't fancy running away with me, do you?' She meant it to sound quippish, but there was a hint of longing in her voice.

Johnny shook his head. 'It wouldn't work, El. You know it wouldn't.'

Ellie smiled playfully. 'You don't seem the type to shy away from an adventure.'

Johnny laughed sourly. 'I'm not who you think I am,' he said. 'I'm no Ronnie Biggs, El. I'm a small-time drug dealer. You know, in the great scheme of things, I'm just the scum who feeds off the pond life.'

She did know this and she nodded in agreement.

'Aberalaw is the perfect place for me,' he said.

Suddenly the dogs ran out of the room, pounding down the stairs. Someone was coming in. 'Shit!' Johnny said. He jumped off the settee, passing the cigarette to Ellie. He did his fly up.

Ellie glanced out of the window and saw the BMW in the drive. Louisa was walking into the living room, dropping a heap of Kwik Save bags on the carpet next to the door.

'Just doing a bit of business,' Johnny said, scratching his neck. 'Ellie's after a bit of Coke.'

Louisa nodded. She looked fleetingly around the living room, noted the ashtray and the turquoise gift box on the floor. 'All right,' she said, face verging on a smile as she bent down and rummaged in one of the bags. She pulled a big carton of milk out, said, 'You want a coffee, El?'

'No thanks.' Ellie was standing next to the window, the cigarette clamped in her fingers. Johnny stood on the table and reached into the upside-down light-shade. He brought out two drugs wraps and passed them to her. As Louisa turned into the kitchen he plucked two twenty-pound notes from his own pocket. He was holding them up to the light when she came back in. She dropped to her knees and fiddled with the bags while Johnny opened the drawer in the TV cabinet. He put his money into the cassette bay of an old VHS video recorder. 'I'll see you out then,' he said, winking at Ellie. He kicked the drawer closed.

'Bye, El,' Louisa said.

'Nice doing business with you,' Johnny said when they'd reached the threshold, his face purple with trapped laughter. There was another plastic bag in the foyer, a frozen chicken jutting out of the top.

'Johnny?' Ellie said, remembering something. 'Did you send a text message to Siân, about a month ago?'

Johnny shook his head.

'You can tell me,' she said. 'I know she's your favourite.' She smiled, willing him to admit it. But Johnny only shrugged, his arms crossed over his chest, his hands balled in his armpits. 'I haven't got her number.'

45

Half past ten on a Wednesday morning, the middle of May. A hot sun was beating on a thin, oblong window at the front of Cardiff Crown Court. Johnny was trudging through the rows of wooden pews, flanked by his young solicitor, frame overwhelmed by a too-big black suit, broad navy tie draped around his neck, stiff white collar hiding his pronounced Adam's apple. Rhiannon had cut his hair. It was two inches long; a congress of black corkscrew curls, ruched back. He sat down at his table and quickly scanned the room, the bright ceiling lights reflecting in his ebony pupils. He bowed forward to listen to something his solicitor was whispering into his ear, had not noticed the girls sitting in the public gallery behind him. His erstwhile glamour had buckled under a rash of fear, Machiavellian wiles futile against the pompous onslaught of the British judicial system. Ellie felt silly for thinking her presence might bring him luck.

The jury filed in, a bout of noise as they eagerly took their seats and switched off their mobile phones. Finally the judge arrived, floating towards his bench in a distended black cloak, a cardboard box file propped under his elbow.

'He'll be orright,' Rhiannon said, grabbing Louisa's hand. She pulled it into her lap and rubbed at it like a worry bead. She was wearing a pink leather skirt, her eyebrows tweezed to nothing. She chomped loudly on a stick of chewing gum, baring her gold filling, nodding at the courtroom in front of her. She said, 'I know about these things, Lou, an' I know he'll be orright.' Louisa sat straight-backed, indifferent to the comment. She was wearing a grown-up-looking two-piece, beige with a row of mother-of-pearl buttons, her hair rolled into a sleek French twist. She crossed her legs and patiently waited for the proceedings, looking like she'd done it a hundred times before.

The Cornish detective who had been at the YMCA on New Year's Eve was the first on the stand. As he took the bulky courtroom Bible from the attendant, Siân leaned against Ellie's shoulder, her breath smelling overpoweringly sweet. She'd blown into the gallery at the last minute, like a human avalanche; powdery deodorant stains on the sleeves of her sweater, her hair piled into one of Angharad's bobbles, the ends full of thick snarls. The four of them sat together in the front row, like girlfriends at a pop concert, separated from the courtroom by a Perspex barrier. A journalist from the local paper sat behind them, the aroma of her takeaway coffee clashing with the waxy smell of furniture polish.

The prosecution lawyer asked for the background to the case.

The detective cleared his throat. 'Almost one year ago, my deputy and I received information about a drug-dealing operation at a farmhouse near Falmouth,' a quavering Cornish accent loping around the official words. 'The property belonged to the defendant, Jonathan Frick. I and my officers searched the property and found substantial quantities of cannabis at the address. A trial at Truro Crown Court followed, at which Mr Frick claimed the cannabis was for personal use. On that occasion he was fined for possession of illegal drugs. But shortly after, Mr Frick sold the property and bought a new property in south Wales. The family who purchased his former property reported a large cache of cannabis, cocaine and ecstasy tablets buried on the land they had recently acquired. In response, the Devon and Cornwall constabulary, together with the south Wales Police, immediately launched an operation monitoring Mr Frick's movements and behaviour at his new south Wales address. As a result we obtained evidence giving us reason to believe Mr Frick was again running, or was part of, a drug-dealing venture.'

Johnny-Come-Lately's chequered history unfolding like a butterflied steak. The journalist put her paper cup down on the floor and scribbled mad paragraphs of shorthand into her notebook. The detective glanced up from his papers, smiled, and then continued. 'On December the thirtieth last year, along with the south Wales Police, we obtained a warrant to search Mr Frick's new property, and we did so on the thirty-first of December last year. Again we found a substantial quantity of cannabis: two hundred and eighty pounds, to be precise,' he paused. 'That amount of the drug has an approximate street value of forty thousand pounds.'

'I wish,' Louisa said.

Suddenly the door of the gallery opened and the girls swung around to see who was coming in. Andy closed the door behind him and gingerly made his way to a seat in the back row, still wearing the torn overalls he'd put on for work that morning. Ellie felt the anguish in her face deflating like a punctured balloon. He'd come in search of closure. If Johnny went down, they could start anew, draw a line under the incident. There was a funereal atmosphere in the gallery, an uncanny blend of old endings and new beginnings. An attendant was passing evidence to the jury while the detective finished his testimony, sealed plastic bags containing drug specimens; half-smoked reefers with lipstick stains on the roaches, chunky cubes of brown resin packaged in greaseproof paper and bubble wrap.

When the detective was done, a short man who resembled a rodent was led into the dock.

'Who the hell is that?' Rhiannon said.

Louisa sighed. 'Mutton, a petty street dealer we know from

Wadebridge. He's going to stitch him up, I know it. Him and Johnny, they hate each other.'

He began to read from the oath that was Sellotaped to the lectern. He told a story about buying a stash of cocaine from Johnny in July 2002. 'It was a good summer,' he said, staring directly at Johnny. 'Plenty of emmets from up country, young 'uns, wanting C-dust and MDMA. Usually I don't bother with that stuff. But the grockles were paying big-time for the old gutter glitter.' He was there for twenty-five minutes, energetically chronicling his life as a small-time cannabis dealer. 'I bought five hundred quids' worth from him,' he said, 'and cut it again with glucose. In all I made a grand: like I said, a good summer.' It was obvious that the prosecution service had struck some sort of deal with him, enabling them to make an example of Johnny. The jury were enjoying his discourse. There were gentle rings of laughter when he told jokes about charging Londoners hundreds of pounds for herbal sleeping tablets and aspirin.

When the prosecution called Johnny, he limped to the stand, head hanging low, eyes focused on the Chiltern carpet. Ellie scrutinized him for a glint of the gall he'd displayed on the day she'd met him at the Pump House, some little part of her still holding out for him, but he looked like a child lost in the middle of a fairground, complexion like plastic.

'After you were charged you were released on bail, subject to conditions,' the barrister said. 'Do you remember that?'

Johnny nodded.

'A month later, your bail conditions were altered. You were subject to a curfew under which you were not permitted to leave your abode between the hours of nine p.m. and nine a.m. A somewhat draconian measure, don't you think? Would you care to tell us why?'

Johnny lifted his hand to his mouth to cough, but no sound came out. 'I was meant to report to the police station every day but one day I was late.' He pulled his arms in to his torso, his shoulders turning concave. It was as if he was trying to jump into himself, to dissolve into his own bones.

The barrister put a slip of paper in front of him. 'That's a contract you signed when you were released from Pontypridd Police Station. Will you read it please, Mr Frick?'

Johnny took a timid glance around the room, beginning uncertainly. 'I agree to attend Pontypridd Police Station every day at twelve o'clock, and sign the bail record in accordance with my bail conditions. I—'

'Thank you,' the barrister said, cutting him off. 'What time did you attend Pontypridd Police Station on Monday the twenty-third of February this year?'

'Twelve thirty,' Johnny said.

'That's all m'lord,' the lawyer said.

At lunchtime the jury was sent out, in a shuffle of footsteps and paper. The girls headed for the corridor, marching in single file. When they reached the concourse, Ellie spied Johnny sitting next to a rubber plant. His solicitor was standing next to him, fiddling with a ballpoint pen. Louisa and Rhiannon walked towards him, but Ellie made for the exit, Siân taking her arm. They sat on the concrete steps, Ellie shading her eyes from the searing sun.

'How do you think it's going?' Siân said. She was leaning against one of the great pillars.

Ellie lit a cigarette. 'It's not good.'

'Would you visit him in prison?' she said. Her pupils were dilated. She was on something for sure.

'Did you score pills from him?' Ellie said.

Siân shook her head. 'Valium. The doctor gave them to me, said my nerves are bad.' In the valleys, diazepam was the fix-it-all remedy, prescribed by incompetent doctors to treat any psychological disorders they were too busy to diagnose. 'How did you get here?' Ellie said.

Siân sniffed, took the cigarette from Ellie. 'Taxi,' she said. 'Why not? I can afford it, can't I? I closed the kids' savings account. They're still up Griff's mother's, eating Turkey flippin' Twizzlers every night, I bet.'

The girls were back in their seats at quarter to one, clammy skin sticking to the bright orange chairs. The journalist sat with her jacket pulled down around her shoulders, knees propped up on the seat in front. Andy was eating a sandwich from the vending machine, a streak of pickle across his lips. Ellie was looking at him when the gavel went down. 'On the charge of possession of illegal drugs with intent to supply, how do you find this suspect?' the judge said, Andy's eyes narrowing.

The jury foreman bent down in front of the microphone. 'Guilty,' he said.

Johnny hung his head, his shoulders slumped.

When the judge made his final deliberation, he called Johnny a scourge on a decent, law-abiding society. He said he had no choice but to sentence him to six years imprisonment, of which he'd serve a minimum of four. Louisa inhaled, her cheeks turning bulbous with air. She glanced around the gallery before letting it all out with a muted whistle. Rhiannon squinted hot-blooded at the judge, her cheeks crimson-red, as though freshly slapped. Siân looked mournful, scratching at her wrists with her blunt fingernails.

46

Ellie spotted the scratched roof of Collin's truck in a bay at the back of the car park, conspicuous against the sleek, gleaming contours of Range Rovers and Mercedes. She stood next to it, waiting for Andy to emerge from the court. 'What are you doing here?' she said when he approached. Andy leaned against the truck, his hand on his hip. 'I didn't have anything to do this morning,' he said. He shrugged. 'Old man's busy with paperwork. Thought I'd comedown for a run. Just out of interest. What about you?' He was looking at her the way his father did, eyes slyly skimming her frame.

'Oh, I'm just passing,' Ellie said. 'I'm on my way to the factory to pick the last of my wages up. Jane phoned yesterday. She said they'd been there for months.'

Andy nodded. 'You don't want a lift home, then?' He opened the door.

Ellie shook her head.

Andy jumped into the cab. He sat in the driver's seat, one leg dangling out over the step. 'Are you disappointed?' he said, a tinge of bitterness to his voice.

'You know what I think,' Ellie said. She threw her duffel bag over her shoulder. 'It isn't the street dealers who should be penalized, it's the Colombian cartels. Drugs should be legalized anyway. It'd cut the dealers right out of the equation. In the Netherlands only six people die from heroin overdoses in a year. In the UK it's about a thousand. What does that tell you?'

Andy looked at her, his blond eyebrows little circumflexes. 'Johnny,' he said, sighing. 'Are you disappointed by Johnny's sentence?' He picked his foot up and pulled it into the cab, drawing the door in, shielding himself from her answer.

Ellie stared at the gravel on the ground. 'No,' she said, 'I'm not. I couldn't care less about Johnny, And. I just want things back to how they were.'

Andy smiled, an ambiguous, Mona-Lisa smirk. He looked out over Cathays Park. 'It all comes out in the end, doesn't it?' he said. 'Like pus from an infected boil.'

Suddenly there was a fracas across the yard. A group of people were huddled on the steps of the court. Ellie turned to squint at the hubbub, her hand shielding her eyes from the sun. She could see Siân's red high-heel shoe lying sidelong at the bottom of the concrete steps. 'Siân,' she said, turning and running across the path. Behind her, she heard the door of the truck thud closed. Andy was following her and she slowed a little to let him catch her up. They pressed through the small crowd and saw Siân lying tits-up, her eyes closed, hip wedged against the lip of a step. Ellie dropped to her knees. 'Siân?' she said. She grabbed her floppy wrist, waving it in the air.

Siân opened her eyes, lazy pupils slowly scanning her audience. 'I'm OK,' she said. 'I just lost my balance there. I'm OK, I am. I promise.'

Andy slipped his hand under Siân's neck, gently cupping her head for a few seconds and then checking his fingers for blood. 'Can you sit up?' he said. He put his arm around her shoulder and slowly coaxed her upright. Her messy ponytail had moved to the side of her head, forced by the impact to behind her right ear. The group of onlookers began to disperse. Ellie watched as Andy supported the small of Siân's back and deftly lifted her on to her feet, unexpectedly moved by his dexterity and compassion. She looked at her watch, the rubies glowing in the sunshine. It was half past one; she was meeting Safia at two. She picked up Siân's shoe and handed it to her. Siân took it by the heel and held it motionless, her bare foot pressed on the concrete, eyes glazed and vacant.

'Will you take her home?' Ellie said.

Andy looked at Ellie, surprised by the question. 'Of course I will,' he said.

It was the end of the rush hour in the city. Students sat in front of the union building eating ice lollies. The cars on Cathedral Road emitted many different snippets of music, all merging to form a cacophonous cocktail of hip-hop, punk rock and bhangra. Ellie crossed the olive-coloured River Taff, thinking about the e-mail she'd received from her new editor that morning. 'Seems as though you know what you're doing,' it had said. 'I've got a feature on poetry by Iraqi asylum seekers and an interview with the curator of the Towner Gallery for you. And pitch me some of your own ideas.' She hadn't told anybody about it yet. Johnny was in custody and there was nobody else to impress. She imagined him in a cartoon, face trapped behind a grid of iron bars, long fingers clutching at them, like the In Jail square on the Monopoly board. There didn't seem to be any point in being ambitious now that he wasn't around.

As she turned on to Atlas Road, she saw Safia sitting on the bench in front of The Lansdowne, a compact mirror held up to her face. There was an open tube of mascara slotted between her knees. 'Hey, you,' Ellie shouted happily. She'd missed Safia. Over the past few months she'd realized that Safia was the only ally in her life. 'Are you ready for this?'

Safia threw her make-up into her oversized handbag. She jumped off the bench. 'As I'll ever be,' she said.

They walked into the dark mouth of the workshop together. Jane

278

was sitting under the stairs, the wage envelopes spread out in front of her. She glanced at her watch. 'I was just about to pack up,' she said.

Safia and Ellie were silent. They stood in front of the desk, faces sober. They waited for Jane to put the little brown dockets into their hands. They took it in turns to say thank you, both subtly curtseying, the way they'd agreed on the phone. They didn't laugh until they were out of the workshop, walking past the pebble-dashed sink estate behind the old city railway line. They were on their way to a beer garden, Safia beginning to count her money. 'It'd better not be short,' she said as they entered the pub. 'Four days and three hours they owes me. I've worked it all out.'

Ellie ordered lager and vodka and Bailey's and two slices of broccoli quiche, determined to squander the last of her mug-making income. She carried her stockpile to a table at the back of the makeshift garden and arranged it around herself in a semi-circle. Immediately it was bombarded by a cloud of black flies emerging from the open window of the butcher's shop next door. 'So what's you been up to?' Safia said, sitting down with her dainty glass of rosé.

'Nothing much,' Ellie said, voice full of the hauteur she'd reserved for Safia over the course of their last months at the factory. 'I cheated on Andy with a drug dealer from Cornwall. I had an abortion.' Without warning she found herself sobbing, tears pouring uncontrollably down her cheeks, as if her head was made of water. 'In fact I've screwed up really bad, Saf,' she said, pausing for a moment to catch her breath.

Safia reached across the table and caught Ellie's hand.

Ellie pulled her fingers away, planting them firmly around her glass. 'I know some women would kill for a guy like Andy, Saf, I do. But I don't want to live in Aberalaw and I fell in love with this other bloke – or the idea of him, anyway. I don't know. I thought he could take me away from it all, that we could go to

279

America, but he was fucking two other women as well. He got sent down this morning for intent to supply.' Ellie stopped suddenly, amazed that she'd managed to relate the story in such a short space of time. For months she'd been avoiding it because she'd thought the situation too convoluted to shape into words.

Safia was staring at her, a speck of pastry in the corner of her mouth. 'Go on,' she said, unperturbed.

'Well, I got pregnant,' Ellie said. 'I had an abortion and then Andy found out and now he doesn't want to marry me. So that's it.' Her mouth was so dry it felt like it was inside out. She downed her vodka chaser.

'I told you, didn't I?' Safia said. 'I told you you was pregnant.' She took a sip of her wine, said, 'I was pregnant once, El. I gave it up for adoption, at a pregnancy clinic in Manchester. Fourteen I was. Didn't knows it till I went into labour, gave birth in an allotment in Salford. I had to cut the cord with a pair of garden shears. Couldn't take it home, could I?' she said. 'My brother . . .' Her speech trailed off, a paper serviette balled up in her hand. 'I didn't tell you before 'cause you're adopted, ain't you? Thought it might upset you, like.'

In all the time she'd worked with Safia she'd thought her dippy and naive. She'd imagined her as an unwieldy, unworldly teenager, incapable of having sex, not someone cunning enough to conceal a pregnancy. She thought about the stories she'd fabricated for her in the factory: how Andy had known where her G-spot was, how his penis was nine inches long. Safia had never disputed any of Ellie's preposterous claims. Everyone loved a fantasy. That's why Mills & Boon's books did so well.

Safia laughed. 'I'm not gonna lie to you, El,' she said. 'For an intelligent girl you're quite thick. Nobody's gonna whisk yous off to no condo in Malibu, are they?' She smiled. 'It's no big deal, you know, an abortion. It's not *great*, but it's done. That guy going to prison is a good thing. You just haven't realized it yet.

280

Plus, the last time I saw you, you told me you didn't want to marry Andy.'

Ellie wiped her eyes with the back of her hand. 'Did your brother ever find you a husband?' she said. She set her vodka glass aside and started on the pint of lager.

'Twelve of the bastards,' Safia said. 'I rejected every one of them.' She reached into her colossal handbag and took out a packet of tissues. She handed one to Ellie. 'He hasn't stopped trying, though. Do you know I've got a new job? At the recycling plant in St Mellons. Honestly El, it's mad what some people chucks out.' She held a tube of mascara in the air. 'Urban Decay. It was still in the flippin' plastic.'

Andy'd been right about one thing. In the end it all came bleeding out.

47

'*Diolch yn fawr*,' Siân said as Andy pulled up against the Dynevor Street kerb. She struggled out of the cab, the graze on her right haunch beginning to throb. 'Are you all right?' Andy said. 'It was quite a bump you had.' He was bowed over the steering wheel watching her. '*Bendigedig*,' Siân said. 'Fantastic.' She slammed the heavy door.

'Are you sure?'

'Yes!' She fanned her hand in front of her face. 'Tell Griff that James is allergic to the PABA in some suntan lotions. He needs Coppertone. It's getting hot now. Also Niall's due for his MMR vaccine.' She gave him a big thumbs-up as she turned into the house.

There was a letter from Griff's mother on the coconut doormat. She recognized the handwriting immediately, big looping letters colliding with one another, a first-class stamp in the right-hand corner. She'd sent it by post, even though Siân's house was closer than Aberalaw's one-and-only postbox.

Siân sat down and opened it, her handbag still hooked over her shoulder, the house-keys still bunched in her hand.

'Dear Daughter—In—Law. I thought I would inform you that my son has spoken to our family solicitor with a view to applying for custody of the children. Since you haven't so much as bothered to enquire about

their wellbeing we all think he has a good chance.'
The nib of the blue fountain pen had pierced the gossamer
notepaper. The first time the children's names were mentioned,
their date of birth followed, placed between two clumsy brackets,
as if Siân could have forgotten the birthdays of her own kids.
She put it down on the table before she'd read the whole
thing. She flopped back on the settee.

What it was, she was exhausted. It was an incapacitating sort
of fatigue that couldn't be washed away with sleep. For most of
the past year she'd felt like her body was fastened to the national
grid and that there was pure electricity running through her veins
– a noxious, nervous energy that begged to be spent. But since
Griff had taken the children away, her muscles were as limp as
strings of tinned spaghetti. She absently prodded at the bruise on
her ankle, the pressure from her finger turning the mustardy colour
to a milky white. She'd been living on and around the settee for
the best part of a month. She hadn't been into the bedroom since
she'd stood in there dressing for Johnny in black stockings and
high heels, fuelled by her compulsion for the deadening effects
of MDMA. But she remembered how she'd left it, the underwear
drawers pulled open as if a burglar had ransacked them in search
of her jewellery and family heirlooms, bra straps and thongs
dangling over the sides like shorn umbilical cords.

The only other time she'd worn stockings had been when she'd
dressed as a St Trinian's schoolgirl for the August bank holiday
fancy-dress. She'd never had casual relationships or one-night
stands. Her life was a challenge and she'd wanted a bit of fun. But
it was too late for that now. She'd stood in St Illtyd's and made
her marriage vows. She wasn't *young*. She'd thrown the stockings
into the kitchen bin with the rotting chicken skin and pulled a
pair of jeans and a sweater from a pile of clothes folded on top
of the tumble-dryer. She'd been wearing them ever since.

She hadn't cleaned either. Cleanliness was next to godliness but Siân was a sinner. She remembered how her God-fearing nonconformist grandmother believed that people who were unfaithful were automatically sent to hell, strapped to boards and clobbered continually with the claw end of a hammer. She'd tried once to go to work in Hau Kung but she couldn't look at herself in the pasta-framed mirror without seeing her mischief written like a tattoo across her forehead. Gone was the doting, fretting image she'd seen in Niall's pupils. Now all she could envisage was her ghastly naked body, the bands of the stockings clenched around her thighs, her third rib poking out of her torso.

One time Ellie had come around, eyes wide with curiosity, asking questions about the kids. She thought Griff had sent her until she remembered that Ellie despised Griff, thought he was a sexist imbecile. Siân told her about the stockings fiasco in an attempt to mend the puncture in her conscience, but Ellie had left quickly, envy wrinkling her forehead. Siân knew that Ellie wanted Johnny for herself, but for the life of her she couldn't work out why. Andy was everything that Griff wasn't. He'd cook seafood pasta as good as look at an empty saucepan. He'd vacuum the house from top to bottom if Ellie had a hangover. Some people weren't happy unless they had something to be miserable about.

Another time, Beryl from number twelve came knocking on the patio door, concerned about the mess in the garden. 'It's not like you, love, to leave rubbish outside. Is everything OK? Because it'll attract rats if it's left any longer and the last thing I want is rats all over my new conservatory. Are you sure everything is all right, because I haven't seen the kids for a couple of weeks.'

Siân had invented a story on the spot, something about them being on an adventure holiday in Llangrannog.

The only two times she'd left the house was to go to the court case this morning, and to Dr Qureshi's surgery early last Monday. She'd wanted a pick-me-up, one of those orange-flavoured bottles of tonic she'd seen in the chemist. But she needed it on prescription because they cost about seven pounds. He'd prescribed her 10 mg of diazepam without even opening her file.

Now, for some reason, she was thinking about a picture of Marilyn Monroe that had been taped to the wall of the YMCA when Ribs and Griff had lived there. In it she'd been standing on a beach, wearing a Fifties-style swimming cossie, platinum hair billowing in the wind. Ribs had drawn a beauty mark on her face with red biro. Rhiannon always said that Marilyn Monroe was big-boned, a size sixteen, the way women were meant to be built. Ellie used to go on about her being an orphan; reckoned she'd spent most of her childhood in and out of Los Angeles foster homes. Siân didn't rate her as an actress. In the shop she'd watched *The Misfits* and *Some Like It Hot*, but Monroe was brazen and flirty; she lacked the grace of Audrey Hepburn (Siân's favourite). People were only besotted with Marilyn because her death was a mystery that could never be explained. Siân had loved that old ripped poster though. It was the only piece of decoration in the flat. She wondered what had happened to it. Johnny must have taken it down.

Desperate, Siân did a little tour of the house, gathering up all the medication and carrying it to the coffee table. She laid it out in front of herself: the bottles of Valium, two jars of ibuprofen, five strips of paracetamol, a bottle of Gaviscon and a bottle of Calpol. She began to take it all, a sample from each item in the row, the way she'd taught James to eat a bit of everything on his plate when he'd begun to develop a habit for only eating one kind of foodstuff at any given time. The only way to kill the madness was to kill herself, to nip it in the bud. The only way to protect her children was to wash herself out of their lives. She used to think she was in control, but now she didn't have a grip on much. When all of the containers were empty she lay horizontal on the settee, listening to her stomach rumble, her breath smelling of pharmaceuticals. After a while she began to daydream, about a time when people thought she was sensible. They used to go to her for advice. There was always somebody in the village who wanted to know how to cook perfectly poached eggs, or wash a window without leaving a smear. She started to dribble, the cushion wet under her chin. The sandman was coming and she gave herself to sleep.

She woke a little after seven, the sun falling out of a candy-striped sky. She saw herself sprawled on the settee and realized that she was looking down, from the air, a view similar to the one she'd once witnessed from a cable car in north Wales. She seemed to fly into the garden, energized by a light breeze, floating right through the glass of the patio doors. The peculiar sensation reminded her of a teenage experience with her mother's cough medicine: a woozy, nausea-induced hallucination. Outside, she saw Beryl sitting on a wicker chair in her conservatory, drinking coffee with her friends from the WI.

She was talking about Siân. 'She just sits on that settee day in, day out,' she said. 'She probably hasn't washed in a month, and no hide nor hair of the kids. Poor cow's so out of it she hasn't a care in the world.'

Siân stood amongst the women. She could smell their lavender perfumes and the papery, clinical stench of their panty-liners. But they continued to talk about her as if she wasn't there.

Eventually the conversation turned to the price of dried peas in the Kwik Save in Ystradyfodwg.

48

It was seven forty-five when Ellie stepped off the train in Aberalaw. The High Street was empty, the shutters pulled down for the night. The sky was an apocalyptic fuchsia pink, a swarm of birds swooping in graceful figures of eight. Ellie ducked into Hau Kung, and saw a new battery-operated ornament on the shelf behind the counter, a white china cat, its paw waving rhythmically at her. There were no humans in sight. 'Siân?' she said, shouting into the kitchen. Chan appeared, a soiled tea towel draped over his shoulder. He took a pen from behind his ear and waited for her order. 'Siân not in work?' Ellie said, disappointed. She knew Siân would have given her a discount.

Chan sucked his teeth. 'Bloody girl,' he said as he tested the biro on the edge of the notepad. 'She used to be good as gold. Now Zhan turns up when Zhan feel like it. One day here, next day gone.'

Ellie took the wage docket out of her duffel bag and pulled the last of the money out. 'Perhaps she's ill,' she said. She tried to focus on the menu, tipsy from an afternoon on the vodka. Chan laughed coldly. 'I know what kind of ill she is. Boozy-woozy ill. Too much firewater.'

Ellie ordered beef chow mein for Andy and a plain omelette for herself. She sat on the bench while she waited for it to cook.

During the hour-long train journey home she'd thought about

what Safia had said. The Johnny Ellie had known, when he'd turned up at the Pump House on a hot August in 2003, when he'd talked passionately to her in Ynysangharad Park about the Iraq war, was a sophisticated man, a bright, handsome man, but that's not who Johnny had turned out to be. And Ellie had known it, right from the start. She knew he was a chancer, out for anything he could get, and that he'd hypnotized her with a mixture of cliché and cheap flannel because she'd allowed herself to go under. She'd been about to marry Andy, to lawfully declare herself part of a happy family, but she didn't know what a happy family was, did not believe that she deserved to be in one. Why else would her own parents abandon her? Then she'd laid eyes on Johnny-Come-Lately, had spotted the self-destruct button furled in the crotch of his denim jeans, was immediately hell-bent on pressing it. She'd duped her own psyche, mashed him in with her long-standing fancies about the American dream, idealized him into some kind of answer. She'd been looking for a saviour on the dirty streets of Aberalaw, the very last place she'd find one. Now he'd served his purpose; shown her the error of her ways. Besides, love was something that needed to be learned, not something that flew in on the wind. That's the sort of thing couples who were celebrating their diamond-wedding anniversaries said on the TV. She could give it a go. If she didn't like it she could get divorced.

She walked to Gwendolyn Street, the bag of food clutched in her fist, a puff of steam oozing out of the plastic. When she reached the house she heard the faint clamour of music. Andy must have been in a good mood; even if he was the guitarist of The Boobs he only listened to music at Christmas and on weekends, the hum of the television audible at all other times. She opened the door and heard that it was coming from upstairs, a low warble gushing out with a hum of brass. There was an empty wine bottle propped presumptuously on the middle tread, a sticky film of beetroot-coloured liquid clotted at the base. She called him but there was no response, so she continued on up the stairs, the bag of food trussed around her wrist.

On the landing a ruby sunset flooded in through the bathroom window. She felt that same sense of foreboding she'd encountered on the High Street. She tried to listen beyond the music, standing frozen in front of her own bedroom door. All she heard was her own breath, the periodic suck of hot air. Then, after a moment, she realized it wasn't her breath. She'd stopped breathing. She pushed the door open. Andy was naked, lying on top of Louisa, her skinny white limbs spread across the mattress like the arms of a starfish.

Ellie remembered finding a nit in her hair, in a geography lesson in Form 3. She'd felt it move and she'd raised her hand, caught it, then crushed it on the desk with her thumbnail in the matter of a millisecond. When she'd looked up she'd expected to see the other kids staring at her, jeering, calling her a dirty orphan. But nobody had noticed. Andy and Louisa still hadn't realized that she was there.

She stood for what seemed like several minutes, fingers gripping the bag, a prickle of sweat on her top lip, feet glued to the carpet. She watched a pimple on Andy's buttock dance as his body moved. The music hit a crescendo and, because it was the sort of thing wronged women were expected to do, Ellie reached into the plastic bag and pulled out a food carton, hands shaking feverishly. She aimed the omelette clumsily at Andy's head. It landed on the mattress next to the couple, wobbling like a yellow brain as their bodies continued to thrash.

'Now I know why you don't want to marry me!' Ellie said, shouting, as she stepped into the room. 'You fancied a bit of blonde!' Louisa scuttled backwards, pinning herself to the headboard, her hands crossed over her breasts.

'Ellie,' Andy said, wrestling with the quilt.

Ellie took the second carton out of the bag and plucked at the cardboard lid. She threw the chow mein at them, bean sprouts and bamboo shoots showering over their shoulders like confetti. Andy used the corner of the quilt to wipe a splash of soy sauce from his chest. 'I didn't want you to find out like this,' he said, blue eyes a mixture of dread and relief.

Ellie realized that she had no edible ammunition left. She let the bag drop. She kicked the CD player over, the music stuttering and then stopping altogether. Andy and Louisa were staring at her resignedly, as though waiting for a storm to pass. 'Don't just look at me like that,' Ellie said. 'Tell me how long it's been going on. Give me some fucking explanation.'

'Oh, grow up, Ellie,' Louisa said. 'You're hardly innocent. You slept with Johnny, didn't you? I almost caught you that time at the flat.' She sidled closer to Andy. He put his arm around her, his fingers clutching at the curve of her shoulder.

'I never thought I'd catch you in bed with an Englishwoman,' Ellie said.

Andy's lips fluttered briefly. 'Never thought I'd . . .' He sighed, his sentence trailing off.

Ellie opened her half of the wardrobe. Her old student rucksack was in the corner, crumpled into a ball, bits of fluff clinging to the straps; the passport acquired for a cancelled field trip to Venice still poking out of the document pocket. She yanked dresses from coat hangers and shoved them into the bag, her eyes filling with tears. She didn't know where she was going so she didn't know what to pack. She grabbed what came to hand: a red silk scarf Jane had given to her on her twenty-first birthday, a pair of scuffed kitten heels with diamantés embedded in the strap, a pair of denim hot-pants she wore when she cleaned the house. As she moved towards her bedside table she caught a whiff of the pungent blend of food and sex that had permeated the room.

Louisa cowered.

'You make me sick!' Ellie said, snatching a handful of knickers and bras. She threw the rucksack on to her shoulder and scurried down the stairs, inadvertently kicking the empty wine bottle. The glass was still ringing against the floor of the hall when she slammed the front door closed.

She stood for a few minutes on the doorstep, spying around the village, her vision blurred by tears. In a beat she seemed to realize that Andy's consternation had been a symptom of their relationship, not an innate characteristic. He would be happy with Louisa, with someone who wasn't Ellie. She didn't know what she was going to do now. She was on her own. She was too old to go back to the children's home.

49

The sun set ten minutes later. The birds had vanished. The sky was the colour of oxblood, empty of starlight. Ellie was at the back of the YMCA, feeling her way along the path, her rucksack scraping against the jagged brickwork. She wasn't ready to face her mother and sisters in Ystradyfodwg and she knew there was nobody in the flat. She crouched in front of the plastic dog-flap and jabbed at it with her forefinger. It opened a little and then promptly clattered shut. Next, she put her hand in, stroking the cool floor tile on the other side. She dropped her bag on the floor and squirmed through the fissure, the frame grinding against her hips as if it was an old size eight dress. She was almost inside when one of the Dobermans appeared. It ran at her barking, but then seemed to recognize her and bowed to lick her face, warm tongue savouring the salt around her eyes. With a final shove she was in the kitchen, feeling her way along the grease-coated wall of cupboards. She found the light switch, the sudden luminosity making her wince.

She rummaged through the cutlery drawer in search of a pair of scissors, deciding that she was going to cut up Louisa's clothes. There were no scissors so she settled for a paring knife, holding it in front of her chest as she tiptoed on to the landing. She half expected to see Johnny standing in the darkness, a depraved smile on his face, the way she'd imagined encounters with convicted serial killers after watching sensationalist dramatizations of their crimes. What she saw was Johnny's mushroom painting, the light from the kitchen reflecting on it. She took it off the wall and reversed it, saw what she had always suspected was there: a white IKEA sticker with a striped barcode and the price.

In the bedroom there was one mahogany wardrobe, a blue Chinese-style dress hanging from the rail, yellow dragons embroidered on the puff sleeves. Ellie stabbed at its waist, the blade scoring easily through the skirt. She sat on the unmade bed and pulled three bras out of the side cabinet, hooking the straps around her knees, gouging at the tiny A-sized cups. Soon, she found Johnny's things, a pile of balled-up socks and elasticated boxer shorts. At the back of the drawer there was a packet of ribbed condoms still sealed in its cellophane cover; underneath it, a white, unmarked envelope.

Ellie carried it into the living room to have a look at what was inside. She put the uplighter on and sat in the middle of the floor. There were two photographs of Rhiannon, the first of her kneeling on a gaudy bedspread, a flimsy T-shirt tied in a knot at her waist. She was only about twelve years old, a brown mole on her jaw that had disappeared now, but her eyes the same glistening hazel. Ellie couldn't look away from it. She had never imagined Rhiannon being any younger than 30. She'd only ever thought of her as mutton dressed up as lamb. Even with the evidence set out in front of her, Ellie couldn't reconcile the Rhiannon she knew with the sweet-looking little black girl in the picture. In the second photograph she was naked, squatting on a windowsill, her crumpled pink undercarriage a shock against the rest of her smooth, bronze skin. Ellie gagged.

There was laughter in the square and she moved towards the window, saw two old men shuffling into the pub. She looked out over Aberalaw and tried to see it the way Johnny had: a classroom with no teacher. She had read somewhere once that it was easy to influence a populace. Apparently all you needed was a bit of grace, an air of mystery, a penchant for telling people exactly what they wanted to hear.

Ellie remembered the last time she'd been in this room, acting out a drug transaction. She looked up at the upside-down light-shade. She stepped on to the table and drove her hand in. With the tips of her fingers she felt the edge of something wrapped in polythene. She couldn't quite grasp it. She tried again with the knife, driving it into the hollow until she felt it stab into something. When she pulled the knife out there was a package stuck on its tip, a cube of white powder wrapped in polythene and brown tape, the size of a corned-beef tin. She turned to look at the video cabinet and jumped from the table, a sharp, brief pain in the soles of her feet as she landed. The recorder was still in the drawer, caked in a fine layer of dust. Ellie could see the wad of money inside, the Queen's eye staring up at her through the plastic window in the cassette bay. She pressed the chunky eject button but nothing happened: the cable at the back was frayed, the earth wire protruding. She was working on the screws with the tip of the knife when the doorbell rang.

'Louisa?' Rhiannon was shouting through the letterbox. 'Ewe there, Lou? I come to see if ewe're orright. Lou? Ewe there, babe? Lemmee in.'

Ellie froze, the knife in her hand shaking. After a while the shouting stopped and Ellie heard metal on metal, a mechanism twisting. Rhiannon had a key, and she was coming in. Ellie sat on top of the video, protecting it like a hen. The pictures were on the floor next to her. The coke was on the coffee table.

'What the fuck?' Rhiannon said. She was leaning against the doorframe, hand clawed around the handle.

'I broke in,' Ellie said proudly. 'I just caught Louisa in bed with Andy.'

'Well, well,' Rhiannon said. 'What a turn-up for—'

'How have you got a key?'

'Me 'n' Johnny were close, El,' Rhiannon said. She crossed her fore- and middle finger, 'like that we were. He asked me to look after the place, to look after Lou.' She was about to walk forward when Ellie pointed the knife at her.

Rhiannon laughed. 'What are ewe gonna do with that, El? Cut ewerself or somethin? Into self 'arm now, are ewe? Ewe're mad e-fuckin'-nough.'

'What are those?' Ellie said. She pointed at the photographs with the tip of the blade.

A light in Rhiannon's face went out, her mouth falling open.

'Who took them?' Ellie said. As she spoke, the answer came to her. 'No, don't tell me. It was Dai Davies, wasn't it? How did Johnny get them?'

'I gave 'em to 'im!' Rhiannon said, as if it was obvious. She stared at the floor for a few seconds, took a bottle of rum out of her pocket. She slugged at it. 'So fuckin' what?' she said. 'Iss not like 'e interfered with me. 'E paid me good money for 'em. Not like ewer likkle miss bloody perfect, is it El? Ewer a fuckin' orphan, for Christ's sake.'

Ellie shook her head. 'I'd feel sorry for you if you weren't so fucking vicious,' she said. She grabbed the pictures. Rhiannon attempted to move forward again and Ellie pointed the knife at her. 'Don't come near me,' she said. 'Go and sit on that chair.'

Rhiannon stared at her for a few seconds and then walked to the armchair. She sat down. Ellie, stunned that she'd listened, breathed a silent sigh of relief. One of the things she'd learned over the past six months was that Rhiannon was as scared of the world as it was of her. Reassured by this notion, she said, 'You think you're so clever, don't you? But you're as thick as ditchwater. And you look like a joke with your stupid comedy tits.'

Rhiannon crossed her legs. 'Oh El, ewe're awful jealous.'

'Listen,' Ellie said. 'You can have that lump of coke if you want it.' She eased up off the video recorder and slowly walked to the table. She put the photographs down on the surface, just out of Rhiannon's reach. She picked up the video recorder, surprised by how heavy it was. 'I'm going now,' she said, propping it awkwardly under her arm.

Rhiannon was weighing the polythene package in the palm of her hand. 'What, with that old thing?' she said.

'Yeah.' Ellie sidled towards the door, trying not to look too eager.

'Why?' Rhiannon said.

'Because I want it,' Ellie said. 'It's got sentimental value. You and Johnny weren't the only ones who were close. He fucked us all, didn't he? He slept with Siân as well. You know that, don't you?' She was inching out of the room. 'Come on, Rhi,' she said. 'You've got the coke.'

Rhiannon grinned as she sniffed at the tear in the polythene. She looked at Ellie. 'Wharever floats ewer boat,' she said.

'See you then,' Ellie said, turning into the kitchen.

'Not if I see ewe first, El,' Rhiannon said, voice echoing.

Ellie held the knife handle between her teeth while she turned the key in the deadlock. She picked her rucksack up off the garden path and headed for the railway station, cautiously tiptoeing into the night, the swag that Rhiannon knew nothing about clasped under her arm.

50

Early on a Friday morning, the salon was full of teenagers. Rhiannon sat behind the reception desk, the stationery drawer open. 'Studs is it, love?' she said, smiling at a girl with pillar-box-red dreadlocks, a bushy mono-brow.

The girl nodded hungrily. 'One pair please,' she said.

Rhiannon took a cardboard jewellery case out of the drawer, the size of a matchbox, and passed it to her. Next, a boy with a skinhead, a blurry blue tattoo on the back of his skull, then a woman with sun-damaged skin, small vacant eyes, freckles on her cleavage. It was the beginning of July and they were all on their way to a secret rave on Mynydd Fawr, wanted a little somethin' to keep them dancing till sunrise. Rhiannon's code word was 'studs'. She'd implemented a little under-the-counter system that worked like a charm. She'd sent Kelly on an ear-piercing course at the college and placed her framed certificate on the tiled wall. There was a notice in the window too that said, 'Ear Piercing Available Here'. That way, nobody thought anything about customers leaving the salon with jewellery boxes in their pockets. But there was no ear-piercing gun. If someone came in and asked for a piercing she told them the gun had been sent away for repair. She bought the empty packaging from the shampoo factory on the Industrial Estate, elegant plain white boxes, marked with one word – 'Hypoallergenic' – in fancy black lettering. She hid the contraband under the thin layer of cotton wool inside. When the teenagers had paid, she locked the drawer and walked them to the door, the heels of her new leopard-print Manolo Blahniks clapping on the new natural slate tiles.

She hadn't been able to visit Johnny until the second week of June, a month after he was sent down. First she had to find him. She assumed they'd taken him back to Cornwall. She had to fill a form in and then send it to the Prisoner Location Service, then wait for Johnny to send her a bloody visiting order. Cut a long story, it turned out he was only a few miles away, in Bridgend. She drove down there one Tuesday afternoon and parked the Alfa in the visitors' car park. Before they let her in she got searched by a female security guard who'd spent a little bit longer than necessary cupping her firm tits. Lesbian probably.

Johnny was sitting behind a pine table, arms folded. 'Ewe orright, tiger?' she'd said. She had happy memories of visiting her father in Wormwood and Swansea, but Johnny wasn't her father. The smell of disinfectant was overpowering.

He shrugged and laughed through his nose. 'It's like being on holiday here,' he said. 'They've got TVs, PlayStations, and every now and again some other con gets his girlfriend to throw an eighth over the railings.' He smiled but it wasn't his proper smile.

'I found the coke,' Rhiannon said.

Johnny snickered, unsurprised. 'Did you find the money?' he said.

'What money?'

'The two grand. It was stuffed in the old VHS.'

'Oh yeah, that,' Rhiannon said. She coughed. 'I gave most of it to Louisa to buy new clothes. Ellie broke in the flat and ruined everything she owned.'

What a fucking sly cunt! Rhiannon should have known she was up to something the way she was slinking out of the living room, that bloody old video recorder squeezed under her arm. The clever bitch! Sentimental value. *As fucking if!* Rhiannon sighed. 'Anyway, I'm almost out of the marching powder now. I was wondering if ewe planned on giving me ewer contact. That way I can build ewe a nice likkle nest egg, keep putting a bit aside.' If you didn't ask, you didn't get. 'What d'ewe reckon, mush?'

Johnny nodded. 'I'll send you a letter,' he said, mumbling, glancing around at the guards. 'His name is Mr Smith. That's how you address him, Mr Smith. But in the letter I'll write Mr Jones. There'll be a phone number. Not a real number, obviously. Just add two to every digit and that's the real number. So if it says three, it's five. If it says five, it's sev—'

'I got it!' Rhiannon yapped. He must have thought she was dull. She wasn't dull. Successful businesswoman, she was. She offered him a cigarette and he took it. A guard came over to light it with a disposable lighter. 'How's Louisa?' he said, blowing a puff of smoke into Rhiannon's face.

Rhiannon shook her head. 'Would ewe believe it?' she said. 'The silly bitch 'as only taken up with Andy. Honest, Johnny, ewe picked a right dead leg there. Moved in with 'im as well she 'as.'

Ellie had only been gone for a month, but it was as if she'd never been there. Over the dinner table on a Sunday, Andy and Louisa sat staring at each other like a pair of crossed eyes, the bunch of carnations Louisa always bought for Gwynnie in a vase in the middle of the table. Afterwards she helped out with the washing-up, talking about how many kids she wanted and what stupid Welsh-sounding names she was going to give them. Gwynnie thought she'd died and gone to fucking heaven. 'Ewe should 'ave left urgh years ago,' Rhiannon said.

Johnny looked confused. 'What about Ellie?' he said.

Rhiannon pursed her lips. 'Gone,' she said. 'Nobody's seen urgh arse for dust since the day ewe got convicted. That's why she did the flat over, love. She caught Louisa in bed with urgh fiancé. And then she disappeared without no trace.'

The YMCA had been empty for a fortnight when Rhiannon decided it was time to put it up for rent. She found three single men from the Dinham Estate, all unemployed. Two of them were registered alcoholics. The alkies agreed to share the bedroom. The other one accepted the settee. She put them all on sub-let contracts, acting as Johnny's agent, forging his signature. That way she was able to collect eight hundred pounds per calendar month. With her head for business it seemed like the obvious thing to do. They weren't the kind of people who'd look after the place, but she didn't have to worry about cleaning it up for four years. 'I decided to put the flat up for lease,' she said. 'I had to forge ewer signature but I guessed ewe'd rather that than let the place go to rack an' ruin. Iss a nice professional couple. E's a tree surgeon, the 'usband.'

Johnny nodded reluctantly, powerless to stop it. 'Where are the dogs?' he said, voice choked. He stubbed the cigarette out in the foil ashtray.

Rhiannon smiled. 'Louisa's got them. Andy loves it. He couldn't have dogs before, see. Ellie was allergic. He takes them for a walk up Pengoes Mountain every night.' She hooked her Burberry handbag over her shoulder. 'Lissen, I've opened an account for ewe. That's where all ewer rent money goes, and the profit as well when it starts coming in. Trust me, tiger, it'll be waiting for ewe when ewe get out. I'll be waiting for ewe.' She blew him a kiss and stood up. As she was about to walk away, she said, 'D'ewe get any pocket money in here? For cooking or doing laundry?'

'I do woodwork. I make magazine racks for hospitals and schools.'

She smiled. 'Buy some shampoo then, mush, 'cause ewer 'air's a bit greasy.' She walked over to the guard and asked to be dismissed.

Now she waved at the teenagers as they dawdled down the High Street. Griff's mother was on the opposite side of the road, wearing a horrible yellow twinset, the sun reflecting blood-red in her bright ginger hair. 'Excuse me, Rhiannon?' she said, approaching. 'You haven't got time to do my hair now, have you, before the party tonight?' There was a party at the Labour Club for The Boobs. They'd signed a record deal or some shit. That's all Marc went on about, day and night, a measly five-figure contract for two albums. The way the whole village was talking about it, you'd think they'd won a fucking Grammy. It kept Marc out of Rhiannon's business though.

'No problem,' she said, holding the door open.

'Just a shampoo and set,' Griff's mother said.

Rhiannon sat her down in front of the washbasin and tested the temperature of the water on her wrist. 'How are the kids?' she asked cautiously. The last time Rhiannon had seen any of Griff's family was at Siân's funeral two months ago. Dippy mare had only done herself in. Apparently Griff found her on the settee when he went looking for his birth certificate, a heap of empty tablet bottles on the coffee table. They had the funeral at St Illtyd's. The vicar called Siân an angel and read some sermon about the Virgin Mary. One of her cousins from west Wales came and read a poem in Welsh. The English translation was printed on the Order of Service, but Rhiannon didn't get that neither: some complicated nonsense about a woman made out of flowers. There was a spray of massed chrysanthemums on the coffin that spelled 'Mammy', but the best bouquet by far was the one Rhiannon had sent, shaped like a can of Red Bull.

They played the theme from *Dirty Dancing*, which Siân loved. When the undertakers picked the coffin up, James started screaming blue murder, a deafening, blood-curdling screech. Griff had to hold him grasped against his chest, his hand pressed over his mouth. Rhiannon had thought about her own father and fought off a couple of tears.

In a way she regretted sending that text message to Siân, the one where she'd pretended to be Johnny, inviting her around for a bit of fun. She'd used Kelly's mobile so that Siân wouldn't recognize the number. But in any case she knew Siân wouldn't have gone. She wasn't that kind of girl. With hindsight it was easy to see that Siân was no sort of competition. She was a sandwich short of a picnic, that one. She suffered from anxiety and OCD or whatever the fuck it was called. That's why she'd topped herself. It was all about the survival of the fittest around here and Siân didn't have what it took. Rhiannon wouldn't mind betting that that's what happened to Ellie as well. She was probably floating around in an estuary somewhere, bloated and rotten. There were a lot of people in Aberalaw who just weren't the full shilling. Luckily, Rhiannon wasn't one of them. Bloody successful businesswoman she was.

'It's going to take a bit of time,' Griff's mother said, leaning backwards into the basin. 'But what can you do? Life has to go on.'

Rhiannon massaged the shampoo into her hair, scratching at her scalp. 'Yep,' she said, emphatically. 'The show has to go on.'

51

Ellie was working her twilight shift in a bar called The Pink Diamond. It was a block away from Washington Square on MacDougal and 3rd. She'd taken the number 6 train, alighting at Astor Place. Above ground, the sun was still searing. The park was full of Italian tourists studying street maps and black boys from the projects wearing ridiculously wide-legged gangster-rapper jeans. West 4th Street was full of tobacconists' and body-piercing studios, thrift shops, sex shops and book stores. There was a car half parked on the sidewalk in front of a university building; the driver slumped asleep over the wheel, a cop tapping on the windshield. When she reached the bar there was a blank-faced thirteen-year-old girl with a nose stud, trying to fool the doorman with a fake ID. Nowhere was there a sense of peace, merely chaos. Ellie loved chaos.

It was the second time she'd been downtown that day. Earlier she'd pitched for freelance work at a meeting at the *Village Voice*. She'd arrived an hour early at the offices on Cooper Square in the East Village. 'Way too early,' the receptionist said. Ellie took a seat and watched as the employees straggled in wearing combat pants and leggings, trailing the odour of stale cigarette smoke. Eventually a woman in skinny jeans opened the door and called her in. 'Relax,' she'd said, sensing Ellie's anxiety. 'I just have a few general questions about what you like to do. It's better than talking about your grade-point average, right?'

'Travel,' Ellie said.

'Oh,' the woman said. 'Where've you been lately?'

'London.' New Yorkers loved London.

'What did you do?'

'Clubs,' Ellie said. 'The Electric Ballroom. Dublin Castle. Stuff like that.'

'What did you do this weekend?' the woman said.

Ellie laughed. She'd served eggs over easy all day Saturday, slept through most of Sunday. But she'd seen the flyers on the subway. 'I saw The Lychees at the Knitting Factory,' she said.

The woman's face brightened. 'Of course. The show. I was there too. One last question, Ellie. Why d'you wanna write for the *Village Voice*?'

'Look at me,' Ellie said. 'I've been dreaming about this job since I was a kid. Don't worry about me being British either. My Speak & Spell taught me to write in American English when I was three.'

'OK,' the woman smiled. 'I'm gonna be in touch.'

It was happy hour now but the bar was almost empty, a group of five men in suits, sitting on the leather couch at the back, four of them singing 'Happy Birthday' at the top of their drunken voices. A woman at the Internet point was checking her e-mails, a glass of Chardonnay balanced on the shelf. The room smelled of fried garlic and spilled beer. Ellie wrapped her apron around her waist and wiped the surface of the bar. She could see the date on the tickertape running across the bottom of the silent television screen. It was a year since Johnny-Come-Lately had tumbled into her life.

She still thought about him sometimes. For the most part she was grateful. As a feminist she'd always understood that happy endings were bullshit. There was no knight in shining armour waiting in the wings. But in an ironic way that's exactly what Johnny had been. In the end he chose the woman who wanted him most. Rhiannon would wait for his sentence to end because that's what Rhiannon was: a natural-born gangster's moll.

A whole four months had passed since Ellie had left the YMCA with the corner of his clunky VHS tucked into her sodden armpit. The worms of time had already begun to chew at Ellie's memory of that night, devouring bits of colour, snippets of dialogue, big portions of her fear. She'd sat under a streetlight on Aberalaw Station and worked on the fiddly screws, the blade of the paring knife wobbling with her effort. There was two thousand pounds, or thereabouts. Twenty-pound notes; every fifth one folded in a dog-ear at the right-hand corner. The first time she'd used one was at a coffee booth on Cardiff Central the next morning. She hadn't eaten for hours and she ordered a bacon baguette. She teased a single note out of her pocket while the attendant wrapped the bread in a paper serviette. Even after the woman had taken the money and then handed her her change, Ellie stood in front of the counter, waiting for the woman to realize that the note was somehow marked.

'Anything else, lovely?' she'd said, voice impatient. There was a queue.

Ellie shook her head, smiling guiltily. She was at Heathrow Airport six hours later.

When she arrived at the immigration desk at JFK, the man behind the partition asked her her reason for visiting the States. 'I'm on holiday,' Ellie said, lying. She was an illegal alien destined for low-paid part-time jobs, changing sheets in hotel rooms, mixing Long Island Iced Teas in crummy East Village bars. That's what immigrants did in the name of self-improvement, and Ellie was pleased to be no different. But in the hospital she'd promised herself that she'd make something of herself. She'd get her new life. She'd get a job at *The New York Times*. She'd get her Sunday picnics in Central Park.

He glanced at her creased passport. He waved her through.

She took a yellow-cab ride into Manhattan, telling the driver that she wanted to go to the Chelsea Hotel. It was the only hotel in New York City she knew the name of. But neither of them knew the cross street and they settled on the Waldorf. It cost two hundred quid a night but she was too tired to complain. She holed up for three days, ordering room service, listening to the wail of police cars on Park Avenue, her ear cocked to the window, as if hearing a new language for the first time. 'Goodbye cruel circus,' she'd said, pushing the voile curtain aside. She looked down at the weather-beaten awnings below. 'I'm off to see the world.'

Eventually she found a one-room apartment, the size of a large shoebox, on the third floor of a tenement on the Upper East Side. A cockroach ran over her foot while the realtor was still showing it to her, and since then she'd seen a few rats. She loved the rats. They made her feel like a real New Yorker. In the valleys, everyone complained about the rain. In Manhattan, it was the rats. It's funny; the only thing she missed about south Wales was the mining statue on Aberalaw Square. If she had time on a Saturday, before her lunch shift at the diner, she took a walk around Battery Park, looking out at Liberty Island. From there the two figures were not completely dissimilar, the gold-leaf flame in the torch of enlightenment a little grander than the bronze candle in the old man's Davy lamp. Of course, in essence they were poles apart. The mining family represented oppression, and Liberty – well, it was in the name.

Now, one of the men from the birthday party had crept up on her. He was holding a fifty-dollar bill in her face. 'Yep,' she said, registering it. Like all good émigrés, she'd learned to value the power of the God in which America trusts. 'What can I get you?'

'Five Coronas,' he said. He watched as Ellie popped the tops from the bottles in quick succession, pushing quarters of lime into the rims. 'You're a Brit, ain't you?' he said, pleased with his presupposition.

'Shush,' Ellie said, handing him one of the bottles with a lukewarm smile. 'I'm trying really hard not to show it.'

He grinned as he gave her a ten-dollar tip.

She stepped back a little, dazzled by the full onslaught of his big, bleached American teeth. She lowered her voice an octave, so that she was almost talking under her breath. 'Have a nice day now, y'all,' she said.

What's next?

Tell us the name of an author you love

| Rachel Trezise | Go ▶ |

and we'll find your next great book.

book army

www.bookarmy.com